T0062955

LOVE, WAR, *and* BETRAYAL

Margaret McCulloch

Abbott Press books may be ordered through booksellers or by contacting:

Abbott Press
1663 Liberty Drive
Bloomington, IN 47403
www.abbottpress.com
Phone: 1-866-697-5310

ISBN: 978-1-4582-1603-8 (sc)
ISBN: 978-1-4582-1604-5 (e)

Library of Congress Control Number: 2014909089

Printed in the United States of America.

Abbott Press rev. date: 6/30/2014

CHAPTER ONE

Uncle Sam drafted Ernie Tennyson in August 1967; he didn't want to leave home, but he had to be his own man now. His mama didn't want him to leave home, either; but she said foolishness consumed a man who stood idle; time passed him by, and he died in poverty with no credit to his name. She wanted him to meet his obligation, come back home in one piece, and take over the farm. In the meantime, she leased the farm to a good man and was not worried about her livelihood.

Ernie Visited his daddy's grave before he left. Ghostly green trees surrounded the cemetery and cast dark shadows around the tombs. As he walked toward his daddy's grave, he stepped carefully upon the dead. Some of the graves looked dangerous to put a foot. Green moss grew in wads like green frogs scattered about the cracked cement slabs, and the head stones leaned to one side as if they had been pushed from beneath by a powerful hand. He hesitated before his daddy's grave as if waiting for him to mention the beauty and the sweet smell of the bouquet of flowers he held before him. He placed them in the cement vase at the end of the grave, brushed his hands, got down on his knees, and said, "Daddy, Uncle Sam called me to the army; I'm going to serve my country like you did many years ago. Tracy got married and has a baby girl; and Mama is doing fine." Familiar words his daddy often told him came to mind: "Work hard, learn to be patient, and enjoy life. Remember Son, patience is not a gift we're born with. Patience is a virtue we die with, if we're lucky."

As he walked back toward the church, he remembered the day his daddy died. He had stood tall that day; yet he had never felt so small; he was a young boy, who had just been told that he would have to face the world alone, and he didn't know about life. Today he felt the same way about leaving home.

After Ernie left, Mrs. Tennyson got down on her knees and prayed for God to bring him safely back home. She got up, cleaned the supper dishes, read her bible, and went to bed, but she could not sleep. She stared through the darkness with thoughts of her husband, Mitchell. After he died, Ernie had problems getting adjusted to living without him. Now she had to get adjusted to living without Ernie.

Ernie wasn't excited about six weeks of basic training at Fort Benning Army Base in Columbus, Georgia. On the bus ride to the base, Ernie met Harold Hatcher, a likeable fellow with a slender build, long legs, sandy hair, fair skin, and bright blue eyes. His common sense impressed Ernie more than a man with a big brain filled with uncommon things. Hatcher came from Alabama, and they spoke the same southern language; they became friends right away.

When they got to Fort Benning, they got their ID cards and took a crazy test. Then the nurse drained blood from their arms and replaced it with nasty vaccines. After this, the barber cut their hair. Hatcher sat down in the chair, moved his hand over his sandy hair, and kissed it good bye. Ernie took Hatcher's seat and watched the clippers take all of his black hair down to the hide on his head. As he brushed his fatigues, he stretched his eyes at the man in the mirror; he looked an inch shorter than his true six feet and two inches, but he looked more mature than the farm boy who left South Georgia.

After they left the barber shop, they went to the mess hall to eat lunch. He and Hatcher followed the other GI's down the line to get their tray. Back at home, his mama gave him two choices before she put the ham in the frying pan. The army gave no choices and no menu. All of the GI's got the same thing, a peanut butter and jelly sandwich, vegetable soup, a brownie, and a choice of tea or milk. Ernie discovered right away that the mess hall was a mess; the cooks had never boiled eggs for the hunt. They used no salt or seasoning in the vegetable soup. On the other hand, the sandwich tasted good, and they allowed them to go back for another helping. He and Hatcher along with most of the other GI's went back for another sandwich and milk. At least, the food satisfied Ernie's growling guts.

After lunch, they went to the barracks. They assigned Hatcher and him the same quarters. Having a friend from the South made Ernie more comfortable. They unpacked their suitcases, and put their underwear and clothes in the proper places provided. Ernie smiled when he saw the New Testament his mama had stashed there.

After they finished unpacking, he and Hatcher spent the afternoon talking about their families, home towns, friends, girl friends, and sports. They both liked to hunt and fish; they both liked sports, especially baseball.

They called the evening meal dinner; he and Hatcher called it supper. They served dinner at six o'clock; Ernie was used to eating at seven-thirty. For dinner, they served baked chicken, carrots, creamed potatoes, rolls, and apple cobbler for dessert with a choice of tea or milk. They used no salt or seasoning in the vegetables, and they used biscuit dough in the apple cobbler. Ernie hated to complain, but a boy raised on a farm found it difficult to eat without salt and butter.

When they went back to the barracks, he got the New Testament his mama had put in his suitcase and lay down on his bunk. He felt a need for God more than ever. He opened the Bible, flipped through the chapters, read a few passages from Luke, and placed it back in his suitcase. After a hot shower, his tired bones made him forget the hard, uncomfortable bunk, and he slept.

The next morning after breakfast, Sergeant Fitzwater started maneuvers in basic military skills. Muscle strength and guts seemed to be more important than brains in the Army. From day one, the top dogs drilled them from sun rise till sunset. Sergeant Fitzwater told them what, when, where, and how. They had to figure out why. At seven-thirty every morning they lined up and learned how to salute. Then they went to the gym for exercises. They lifted weights, did pushups, jumping Jacks, and climbed nets on the wall. After they left the gym, they ran one mile, crawled under fences, climbed barriers, and jumped into deep holes. Fitzwater put them through drills worse than putting up fence posts in July. Basic training wore him to a frazzle. He hated exercises; he hated orders: fall in line, march, and crawl; he hated the food; most of all, he hated the automatic darkness that took over before he got ready to go to bed. The Army gave a good man a bad attitude.

In addition to training in military skills, stink duty and potato duty took the top of the list. His thumb lost its skin in the potatoes. If the Irish had kept their potatoes a secret, they would have given GI's a blessing in disguise. He hated the smell of the slop cans more than the potato peelings.

At night, they shined their boots, talked about women, read, or played games: checkers, poker, and other card games.

In spite of their dreaded duties, they had freedom on the weekend to go to their choice entertainment spot in Columbus, Georgia; but they had to come back to the base at a set time, and they had to have a good head when they got there.

The next weekend, Hatcher suggested they go to the movie theatre in Columbus, Georgia, to see "I Want to Live" starring Rita Hayward.

As they left the crowded theatre, they spotted two girls, a blond and a brunette. Ernie liked the looks of the blond and her eyes caught his like a flame in the wind when she accidently bumped into him. Ernie watched her as he and Hatcher edged their way toward the exit doors.

When they got outside, they waited for the girls, but the girls walked past them toward the city. Hatcher whistled and the sound carried right to their ears. The girls stopped in front of Belk's Department Store, and waited for them.

Ernie sidled close to the blond, leaving Private Hatcher no choice. Ernie introduced himself to the blond; then he introduced Hatcher to the brunette.

The girls claimed they had started home; the blond, Helen Parsons, lived in an apartment in the city, and the brunette, Erma Tyson, her friend, had come from Brunswick, Georgia, to visit her. The blond worked as a waitress at McDonald's, and the brunette had looked for a job, but she had found no work, yet. They had graduated from high school; Ernie decided that they had reached the legal age to date without their parent's permission.

Erma paid little attention to their conversation; she glued her eyes to the dresses displayed in Belk's store window. She took a seat on the store window ledge. Private Hatcher walked over and took a seat next to her and started a conversation.

Ernie asked Helen if they would like to go with them some place to have a beer, and Helen turned the question to Erma. She said she wanted to go home; her feet hurt. Helen called her a stick in the mud and a party spoiler. Erma finally agreed to go, but she was not excited.

Ernie told Helen that they knew very little about the city and asked about good night spots. Helen named over the different places to dine, dance, and drink.

Hatcher thought the Golden Gator Bar sounded like the perfect night spot, and they started walking. Erma balked, and refused to walk the three blocks to the bar. She complained about her feet again and kicked off her shoes. Hatcher sweet talked Erma and she agreed to go, but she wanted a cab.

Ernie flagged a cab, and they reached the bar in less than ten minutes. The Golden Gator sign flashed on a red brick building with two wide windows separated by double wooden doors. The street lights shimmered on large department stores and other businesses in the city. The night traffic slowed to a hum, and shoppers retired for the day.

Ernie pushed back the double door and waited for the ladies to enter the dimly lit bar. He and Private Hatcher followed the ladies and the waiter to a cozy table in the back corner. Ernie and Hatcher ordered draft beer and the women ordered salty dogs. The band played, while the singer imitated Elvis Presley's voice and sang his popular songs.

After several drinks and several swings, Ernie and Private Hatcher found themselves once again stuffed in the back seat of a smoky cab between Helen and Erma. The cab pulled up before Helen's apartment, and she invited them to come in for a snack. Ernie handed the cab driver five dollars, and the cab driver tipped his hat with a grateful smile and wink. Then he told Ernie if he should need a ride during the night, he could call the number on his card. He handed Ernie his card and left.

The ladies led the way up the steep steps and across the wooden porch to Helen's door. She unlocked the door and invited them inside. They followed the girls down a long hall and entered a neat little kitchen, where Helen invited them to have a seat at the small table. She pulled a variety of cold cuts from the refrigerator with all of the trimmings for a delicious sandwich; they ate with hearty appetites and drank all of her beer.

After they ate, the two girls invited them to spend the night. After the girls fell asleep, Ernie sneaked into the other bedroom and got Hatcher.

Ernie called the same cab; he worried all the way back to the base about the time. They were supposed to report back to the base before twelve o'clock, and it was after three o'clock in the morning. Hatcher told him not to worry, but Ernie had reason to worry. The next morning, Sergeant Fitzwater gave them KP and latrine duty for the entire week, because they disobeyed the rules.

When the girls awoke, the two soldiers had disappeared, and Helen was angry. She searched the base for Private Ernie Tennyson. She called numbers she had gotten from other GI's and pretended to be Ernie Tennyson's sister with urgent news from home, but the GI's pretended they didn't know anyone by the name of Tennyson.

Erma told Helen she got what she deserved; the guys wanted to have a good time, and moved on to another dumb blond. Worst of all, they used fake names.

Helen got fighting mad with Erma and told her to get out of her apartment. Their night on the town with Ernie and Hatcher ended their friendship.

Erma had been right about Ernie Tennyson; he gave not one thought to Helen Parson; he didn't even remember her last name. Besides, his thumb ached from peeling potatoes, and latrine duty was no Sunday picnic. He swept that night under the rug and stuck Helen Parson under the rug, too. When he closed his eyes at night, he saw home sweet home. He could see the fields covered with green sprigs; he could see the beauty of the peach orchard blooms; and he could smell the sweetness of spring on the farm.

Military officers scheduled his company's flight to South East Asia in two weeks; he wanted a weekend pass before they got shipped to Vietnam, but the sergeant told them that the government cancelled all furloughs for men with less than six months service.

The week before they finished basic training, all of the GI's in Ernie's company went from a Private One to a Private Two, and got a yellow insignia, trimmed in navy blue, on their shirt sleeve that looked like an up-side-down arrow head. At least they got a little credit for basic training in military skills.

CHAPTER TWO

In October 1967, all of the GI's loaded up on a plane and headed for Vietnam. They landed at Tan Son Nhut International Airport, but the name was not pronounced like peanut. A tall barb wire fence and watch stations surrounded the Airport near Saigon. The mountains toward the north reached the clouds. Stone Mountain in North Georgia was as high as Ernie wanted to climb.

The GI's rode to their bases on the back of big trucks; the higher ranking officers took the lead in jeeps. Ernie sat at the front of the truck and peeped through wooden rails as the trucks moved along the narrow road that dipped and rose to hills with streams and beaches on the side. They passed villages, hamlets, made of bamboo, and fine mansions surrounded by trees, and rice fields standing in water. In the distance, the terraces of rice looked like steps of green carpet across ancient tombs. Near the jungles, elephant grass and vines tangled with trees painted a picture of jungle fever.

Suddenly, a loud explosion brought the soldiers down on top of each other. Ernie huddled in the corner of the truck as it jerked and roared in high gear. A Viet Cong sniper threw a grenade at the convoy and hit one of the trucks ahead of them. The entire truck went up in flames.

Ernie and Private Hatcher felt lucky; they got assigned to Dalat, the capital of Lam Dong Province. Dalat was located in the southern part of the Central Highlands and had spring-like weather all year; that was a good thing. Some of the GI's got assigned to places well known for monsoons, typhoons, and hot weather.

A tall fence, with three strings of barb wire across the top, surrounded the base. Long rows of cement barracks with shiny tin roofs covered the area within the fence. The Army stored their military supplies in block storage buildings behind the barracks. Guards in three different watch towers protected them around the clock. Ernie felt good about their protection.

They got their assignments and went to the barrack to unpack. The floors shined, and they had clean toilets with Charmin. The menu and the mess hall interested Ernie more than their living quarters. To his surprise, the food was good; and long steam tables kept the food warm. They had southern fried chicken, green beans, and mashed potatoes. Best of all, they had apple cobbler for dessert. Hatcher said the cooks wanted to impress the new boys.

After dinner, Private Hatcher suggested that they check out the area. They walked down a crooked path and came to Lat Village. Pine trees, flowers, and green hills, with mountains in the background, surrounded the village. They walked on and came to a cement statue of a large chicken; they understood why the village was called Chicken Village. Ernie told Hatcher the chicken looked like the biggest rooster on the farm. Near the huts, children played and women washed clothes in large tin tubs. The beautiful orchids, roses, and hydrangeas around the huts took their attention. They made a circle around the village and walked back toward the base.

Before they got back to the base, they discovered that Lat Village had more mosquitoes than chickens; and they definitely flew here from Texas. The soldiers called mosquitoes the beasts of burden, because they caused yellow fever. Ernie was glad that he got the shot. In addition to the mosquitoes, the yellow jackets, and the big buzzing gadflies made Hatcher and him swing hands.

That night Ernie listened to Private Hatcher talk about Vietnam. After all, he needed to know what he was up against, and Hatcher was a genius when it came to the geography of Vietnam. He showed Ernie a map of Southeast Asia, and Ernie found the exact location of South Vietnam. The Communist in the North had these southerners covered and pushed down in a long turkey's neck next to the South China Sea, where it soon joined up with the Gulf of Tonkin. The South Vietnamese called their neighbors, the Kingdoms of Laos and Cambodia, but they didn't have a king ruling over them. In fact, a Democrat named Nguyen Van Thieu ruled South Vietnam; and Ho Chi Minh, a Communist, ruled North Vietnam. A line called the DMZ, or Demilitarized Zone, separated the North and South; but the Communist paid no attention to lines. The Viet Cong sneaked down the Ho Chi Minh Trail into South Vietnam. They named the trail for the North Vietnam dictator. The trail bordered Laos to the north and reached to the edge of Cambodia on the southern border. To top it all, Thailand and Cambodia gave the Communist rice to eat. The folk in South Vietnam wanted to stop the Communist from carrying supplies down the Ho Chi Minh Trail to the Viet Cong.

Back in 1963, the Southern ruler, Ngo Dinh Diem, wanted the minorities in the South to unite with the rest of the southerners, but they didn't like Diem. He was a Catholic and killed folk who didn't agree with his religious and political beliefs, so these boys formed a group called the NLF, National Front for Liberation, and fought for their freedom. The NLF joined up with the Viet Cong Communist and started a war with the South Vietnamese Government. They killed Diem with plans to get them a new man.

Contrary to the NLF's wishes, they didn't get the man they wanted; Duong Van Minh became the military leader for a short while; then General Nguyen Khanh ousted him, but Khanh got what was coming to him; he was soon forced into exile. Finally, in 1965, Nguyen Van Thieu became the leader of South Vietnam. Then in September 1967, a national election was held, and the people elected Nguyen Van Thieu as President of South Vietnam and Nguyen Cao Ky as Vice President.

After Lee Harvey Oswald killed President John F. Kennedy, Lyndon B. Johnson became President of the United States; and the Vietnam War became his top priority. In 1964, Johnson claimed that the North attacked two American ships in the Gulf of Tonkin. In retaliation, Johnson dropped bombs on North Vietnam territory.

Most of the GI's agreed that the United States military had no business on North Vietnamese's fishing ground in the first place. Besides, the North wanted the South to join up with them; they wanted the United States to stay out of their argument and go back where they came from. Ernie agreed with the North about this point. He was ready to go home before he got here.

President Johnson put General William C. Westmoreland in charge of all the United States troops. He helped Johnson call the shots and supported the president in all of his decisions. As hard as he tried, Westmoreland failed to lead the soldiers to a victorious conclusion to the war. The soldiers liked Westmoreland; he spoke often about the Vietnam War and showed his appreciation for the American soldiers' efforts. Ernie decided that Westmoreland discovered where the shoe pinched and covered the ugly sore spots with band aids.

By 1967, many folk in the United States protested the war; their sons, husbands, brothers, kin folks, and friends went off to fight this losing battle and returned in a casket or returned with wounds that ruined them for life.

Articles in the news gave details about Americans killed and wounded in the Vietnam War. Congressmen and senators criticized American war policy in Vietnam and urged the South Vietnamese government officials to have direct peace talks with the Viet Cong.

On the other hand, Johnson claimed that diplomatic peace efforts on his part had failed; North Vietnam refused to talk peace and stop the war. Johnson believed he did the right thing to send American troops to Vietnam. The Viet Cong tried harder with each passing day to take South Vietnam, and Johnson wanted to stop the Communist take-over.

In spite of the protests, Johnson announced that the United States would remain firm in Vietnam, and military operations continued. He resumed full scale bombing of North Vietnam; American military hit Hanoi where it hurt, but they refused to give up the fight.

Ernie had nothing to say one way or the other, since his opinion was wasted breath and not worth a struck match that had lost its flame.

At least one night a week, Ernie wrote to his mama about how much he missed her, her cooking, his bed; and how much he hated the Army. Before he closed, he told her to send him some more cookies and to keep writing him with the news from home.

When Mrs. Tennyson got a letter from Ernie, she cried. His letters kept up her spirit and helped her face a new day. As she moved the dust cloth over the chest of drawers, her eyes fell on the toy soldier standing on his dresser. She picked it up and ran her hands over the green suit that had faded and flaked with age. As she did so, her thoughts went back to the time she had bought the little soldier. She had been shopping at the dime store, and the tug at her skirt made her scold Ernie. He had continued to tug at her skirt and beg for the toy soldier. She had finally given in to his begging, and his eyes brightened with his smile. He had been only five years old at the time. Now he was a real soldier in a real war. She set the little soldier back in its place and continued with her cleaning. As she backed out of his room, she took one last look and closed the door. She seldom went into his room, because she always left with tears in her eyes. She pushed her dust cloth in her apron pocket and walked to the kitchen.

That weekend, Ernie and Private Hatcher went to the beautiful city of Dalat. They didn't have time to visit all of the sites, but they had heard some interesting stories about the Hang Nga Guesthouse that got their attention. The guest house was known as the "Crazy House" and "Fairy Tale House".

Ernie and Hatcher stretched their eyes at the sight of the unusual guesthouse. From a distance, the outside looked like a huge, ancient oak tree that had shed its leaves, leaving large, deformed limbs wrapped around its trunk in various places. The flat roof had poles reaching toward the sky at each corner, and ridges on the back edge dipped to a solid center. Windows of all shapes and sizes stamped its trunk from the bottom to the top of the tree. The house had five levels.

When they got a close up view of the guest house, it looked like an ancient, haunted castle, built of rough stone with rough structures of stone wrapped around it in various places. The flat roof seemed to be melted to the house, but the ridges on the back edge and the poles on each corner, as well as the windows looked the same.

When they went inside the guest house, they got another surprise. The ten guest rooms represented ten animals: the eagle, ant, kangaroo, tiger, bear, giraffe, frog, and spider. Each room's theme matched the animal represented with stone decorations and hand-made furniture. The stairs and halls resembled tunnels and caves.

When they told the other GI's about the unusual guesthouse, they all wanted to go see it the next weekend.

After six more weeks of training, all of the GI's in Ernie's company went from a Private Two to a Private First Class and got a more sophisticated insignia on their shirts.

CHAPTER THREE

Ernie Tennyson, a Private First Class in the United States Army, knew absolutely nothing about South East Asia; he knew nothing about military tactics. What did he know about colonels, generals, and majors? He did know that privates took the bottom lines on the list and followed orders of the higher ranking officers. He did know that he had a duty to serve his country in this war for the next nine months.

Sergeant Fitzwater moved his long legs across the front of the room, played with his dark mustache, and widened his bright blue eyes as searched the faces of the soldiers before him. He seemed to know the thoughts of every soldier in the room. His education and military training helped him move up the ladder, but he got on the same boat with the lower ranking soldiers when they headed for the jungle. He learned right away that he needed to know more about South Vietnam.

The sergeant moved his pointer over the map and pronounced the names of places that sounded like foreign countries to Ernie. Then the sergeant came to Dalat and showed them a picture of Lat Village, which was made up of a cluster of huts and fine houses on a hill near their base. Next, he showed them pictures of the jungle that surrounded the village and warned them about the Viet Cong that hid there and sneaked into the villages after dark to steal, kill, and destroy. He explained that the Viet Cong often lied to the people in the village with promises of good fortune to join their army. Afterwards, they destroyed the villages and killed the chiefs. The village people took turns and stood guard over their villages at night. On the other hand, many Viet Cong lived among the villagers in disguise.

When the Sergeant told them about the Viet Cong's tactics, Ernie wondered how he could stand up to the tough guys. He had not joined this band wagon in the first place, and he was not anxious to become a war hero, especially not a dead hero. Most folk believed the war was useless, since they could not win the fight. What would the United States accomplish from this war? The death and injuries of the soldiers didn't seem worth the effort. The North and South started this fight before he got here; and the fight would continue after he got home, if he ever made it home alive. They needed the powerful hand of God to save the foot soldiers and carry them back home alive. He would give a field of gold to be at home. The thing that irritated Ernie most of all was the fact that Americans came to Vietnam to help these southerners, and many of them fought against Americans. This made no sense at all, but common sense was not on the Vietnam War agenda.

Sergeant Fitzwater interrupted Ernie's thoughts when he raised his voice, "We will attack the Viet Cong Guerrillas and drive them into the arms of our blocking force on the opposite side of this hill. These Viet Cong Guerrillas plan their attacks well, and they have a variety of weapons: M1 Carbines, M2 Carbines, M14 rifles, M16 rifles, knives, home-made bombs, traps, and a few AK-47 they have captured or purchased illegally." The sergeant paused for questions.

Ernie wanted to ask the sergeant why he added the word Guerrilla to Viet Cong. His imagination put a big black bear right before his eyes. The bear stood on his hind feet, roared, gnashed his teeth, and slashed huge paws toward him. Ernie looked around the room at his buddies; they didn't seem to mind the term Guerrilla; he kept silent.

When no questions came forth, the sergeant said, "Men, the Viet Cong Guerrillas see with hawk eyes; hear with big ears; and smell with a nose like a hound's. You must never walk your dog in the jungle; that is a chance you don't want to take." He paused and continued, "Of course, most of us do not have a dog to walk," and the room filled with laughter.

The sergeant had delightful sense of humor under the circumstances. He told jokes to help them forget their fear; he reassured them with kindness and understanding; yet, he was courageous and decided.

Then Sergeant Fitzwater told them to never rush into an area before they checked out its dangers. In Ernie's way of thinking, checking out the area before an attack was similar to checking a snake hole for a rattler when one knew darn well the rattler was in the hole.

After the lights went out, Ernie lay on his bunk and worried about the war. He was as scared as a rabbit ahead of a shot gun. He didn't want to think about fighting, killing, and dying. He was afraid he would freeze in the face of the enemy and get his darn head blown to kingdom come. He wished he could live through this time with a blank mind. Being away from home was not so bad, but the thought of never making it back home alive was frightening. He covered his head with his pillow, so the soldiers would not hear him cry. He had not cried since his daddy died. Hatcher interrupted his crying spell by his loud snoring. The Soldiers called Private Hatcher the Z-Man and teased him about his enlarged adenoids that disturbed their sleep. Ernie turned on his pillow, looked to the man in the clouds, and prayed, "God, keep me safe through this horrible war; help me to be brave; and give me courage to face the enemy." He fell asleep and did not wake up until the horn sounded.

The next morning on the way to the mess hall, Private Hatcher pointed out the sun rise peeping over the mountain. The rays of the sun painted the horizon with streaks of red and gold that glowed like crystal under a colored light, but he was not going to an art exhibit. The day had come for their first mission. Like all American Soldiers, they thought about peace and freedom, while they prepared for the battle. This was a time in their lives they should be excited about life; yet, they feared death.

After breakfast, Colonel Switzer met them in the conference room and made a beneficial speech for the new boys, "Men, good days for war are not on the calendar; predictions about war are not in the tea leaves. However, we do know that war causes death, lost limbs, stress, mental disabilities, wounds, financial problems at home, and broken hearts that will never heal. Go to the battle for the victory. Good luck to each and every one of my men. "God bless America."

Ernie hated the colonel's reminder of all the tragedies caused by war. He didn't know how to fight; he never got into fights at school, and the military expected him to fight wild animals in the ditches and jungle. The military officers expected him to face the enemy with bravery and courage, while they sat behind a desk and drank coffee. The only thing he expected of himself was trying to find a way to save his hide. He wanted to return home and see his mama and friends. He wanted to watch the peaceful sunsets in South Georgia.

They threw on their gear and back packs, picked up their M16 rifles, fell in line, and marched toward the jungle. Each of them was weighted down with canteen, rations, and grenades that looked like avocadoes. The matted undergrowth of bamboo and foliage tangle their feet, but the wild flowers scattered around the pine trees painted a picture in a magazine.

They climbed the crest of a hill and looked down at the thick growth of trees they had to walk through. They came up on giant evergreens that he had never seen around home, but he recognized the palm, bamboo, coconut, pineapple, and banana trees. He wanted to stop and grab a banana, but he stayed with the group.

They walked for more than a mile through the thick jungle before they came to a clearing, where they stopped for dinner. He and private Hatcher sat on stumps and talked while the cooks prepared food.

About an hour later, Ernie followed Private Hatcher to the tables to dip from the big pots of food. They filled their plates with green beans, beef stew, potatoes, and a corn muffin. At the end of the table, they got a glass of tea and walked back to their stump to eat.

One of the soldiers yelled, "Weevils in the bread!"

Ernie broke his hunk of bread open and stared at the tiny black dots with distaste. They had clustered together as if bedded up for the winter. He had never entertained the idea of eating bugs. Hatcher told him the cooks spilled black pepper in the corn meal and took a big bite of his muffin. Then Hatcher said he could eat chocolate covered grasshoppers if he got hungry.

Ernie put his corn muffin on Hatcher's plate and ate everything else.

Before they had finished eating, gun fire and loud voices echoed through the trees. They threw down their plates and grabbed their rifles. A large number of Viet Cong surrounded them; they screamed strange sounds and struck like lightening with fist, feet, and weapons. The Americans returned rapid fire that carried the ear splitting sound of a thousand tambourines. The Viet Cong, who survived the battle, kept coming at them and yelped like a pact of dogs.

Ernie fell back and darted behind a tree; then he moved to another tree; he finally crawled behind a mass of vines and his heart beat in his ears. He slowly got up and turned in a circle with his rifle aimed at any moving target; he had seen the cops on television do the same thing. Two black boots moved in his direction and he set his aim dead on the Viet Cong; but he had never killed a man, and his finger froze on the trigger. "Think squirrel," he said to himself. Then the beast jumped him and yelped loud enough to make his ears ring. Ernie closed his eyes tight and pulled the trigger right on the Viet Cong's belly, bursting his guts. He got sick on his stomach and crawled as fast as he could away from the sight. He crouched behind another tree and prayed for an ambulance to come get the Viet Cong he had just shot. Then he saw a helicopter fall behind the trees to pick up the wounded, but it was an American pick-up.

Suddenly, he heard a loud noise coming from the nearby bushes, but he couldn't see what was making the noise. He jumped up and took off through the woods as fast as his feet would carry him. He tangled in vines and stumbled over roots, stumps, and snags in search of a safe place to hide. He turned down a narrow road surrounded on both sides by more jungle. He was out of breath, but he kept running. He darted behind another tree and remained still. For minutes, he thought the Viet Cong lost his trail. Then the vines and bushes stirred a short distance from his tree, and he crawled to another tree. Heavy steps drew closer as he quietly moved through the trees. He reached a dirty stream and waded to get to the other side. His boots squeaked with every step; he could feel dirty water squirting around his socks and soaking his fatigues. Suddenly a root caught his foot, and he fell into the puddle with a loud splash. He looked around at the trees and bushes surrounding him before he eased up the bank to solid ground. He spotted a stout limb hanging low from a giant tree and climbed the tree. Seated on a limb close to the trunk, he listened and watched the path below him. The devils still followed his trail. Minutes later, he saw tiger stripes moving through the bushes. Then he heard snarling and yelping, the sound a hound makes on a raccoon's trail. Low and behold, a dozen Viet Cong surrounded the tree. They paused a few minutes, mumbled words he didn't understand, and moved on; they never looked up. He climbed down from the tree and turned in a circle with his gun aimed to shoot. The leaves crunched beneath his feet and the wind whispered its warm breath around his ears; the Viet Cong disappeared.

Ernie looked at the tree and said, "What should I do? Should I climb another tree?" He had never confided in a tree before, but he had never been more scared in his entire life. He closed his eyes and tried to see God in the clouds. His mama had told him that a man was either a lost sinner or a born again Christian; he had to get right with God in a hurry. He was no saint, but he was not exactly a sinner, either. He may sin a little, but not enough to notice. Besides, he fully believed that all human beings, including Christians, sinned every day. Everybody had selfish thoughts, and in his way of thinking, one sin was as bad as another, except killing another human being, and he had just killed a man. The Lord knew he had no choice; he had to kill or be killed. He had broken one of God's Ten Commandments; one at the top of the list. Would God forgive him?

He had started to pray when he heard a strange noise coming from the tree. He thought a Viet Cong was perched in the tree. He slowly turned his head upward and saw a monkey staring him in the face. The monkey made a terrible racket. Ernie put a finger to his lips, and the monkey mocked him by covering his mouth with his paw; then the monkey jumped down from the tree and pointed toward another tree nearby.

"This tree is as safe as that tree," Ernie said to the monkey. I have to get out of this jungle."

The monkey jumped up and down and began chattering like crazy. Then he climbed the tree and hid behind the trunk. The monkey must have smelled the Guerrillas and was trying to warn him.

Ernie perked his ears to that horrible swishing sound of fatigues brushing against bushes. The jungle grass moved a short distance away. Terrified, he crouched behind a thick cluster of bushes. Just as he squatted, a Viet Cong sniper leaped from the bushes and forced him down. Ernie wrapped his legs around the Viet Cong in a tight vice, and the Viet Cong bit him. Ernie balled up his fist and came down on the Viet Cong's head with the force of a steel ball. The Viet Cong slumped forward and fell face down. Ernie held his M16 rifle close to the Viet Cong's head and dared him to move. He didn't want to kill him; he backed up with his gun still aimed at the Viet Cong. Then Ernie heard feet moving behind him; Viet Cong surrounded him with M14 rifles pointed close to his head as they spoke in a foreign language. The man on the ground jumped up, got his gun, and joined his comrades.

Ernie still had his rifle, but his gun felt like it was glued to his hands; he wiggled his finger over the trigger, but he changed his mind. If he pulled the trigger, he would never see day again. He thought about putting the gun to his temple and ending his life the simple way, but he didn't have the courage. He gripped the gun with both hands and shook with a seizure.

The Viet Cong bellowed a wolf call, knocked him off his feet, and stood over him; one came forward and took his gun; another robbed his pockets and took his grenades, while the other Viet Cong held his gun on him and stared at him with the eyes of a mad dog about to devour a shriveled, wounded animal. Then the bully Viet Cong, who had robbed his pockets, grabbed a wad of his hair and yanked him up. He screamed with pain and attempted to sit up. He finally let go of his hair and kicked him as they all spoke at once. Ernie assumed they used curse words, and they cursed him. The Viet Cong had trapped him. He clenched his teeth and prayed that they would not use the daggers they had in the wide belts at their sides. Goose bumps jumped about his arms and shivers went up his spine. He was a goner either way he turned.

Without warning, a sharp pain hit his leg just above the knee. The Viet Cong he had held his gun on had stabbed him to the bone with a long dagger. He laughed as he pulled the long knife out of his leg, and Ernie screamed with the pain that went all over him. Blood gushed from the wound and soaked his pants. He was bleeding to death, and he could not move his leg. He lay in a daze and held his wounded leg, while dark, dirty faces with brown, beady eyes stared down at him. Their language got faster and stranger; then their voices faded like a dying echo. A buzzing sound, like that of mosquitoes, roared in Ernie's ears; he pretended to be dead. They took turns picking up his limber arms and letting them fall. Thinking he was dead, they jabbered quick sounds, laughed, and walked away.

Ernie opened his eyes to a peep when he heard the monkey chattering. He seemed to be trying to tell him to get up and run, but Ernie couldn't move. He prayed that his platoon would find him. He worried about going to hell, since he had killed a man. The world turned in a fast circle and he saw stars. Then everything was dark and he passed out.

CHAPTER FOUR

Anna Ming, a Vietnamese teacher was walking home from school when she saw Chipper swing from a nearby tree. He often greeted her on the trail and followed her home to play with the village children. Today Chipper seemed upset. He jumped all around her and chattered with excitement.

She picked him up, hugged him, and said, "Chipper, I do not have a banana today. Come along with me, and I will get you a treat."

Chipper reached for her hand and practically pulled her through the vines into the jungle.

"Chipper, where are you taking me?"

Chipper continued his chatter and kept pulling her through the thick brush.

When she saw the green fatigues, she knew he was an American. With caution, she drew nearer. His wet clothes hung limber around him. A green helmet shaded a handsome face with broad jaws, thick, black eye brows, and a slender nose. His rucksack lay next to him. He was either dead or unconscious. She squatted next to him and checked his pulse. His heart thumped as strong as a jumping frog's, but he was still and did not move. Blood soaked the right leg of his fatigues. He had a serious leg wound that she could not see. She looked around and wondered where his comrades had gone. She could not leave him there to die. She quickly got to her feet, moved behind him, and put her hands under his arms. With all of her strength, she pulled him with backward steps toward their rice hut. Before pulling him inside, she peeped around the hut. Neither her grandmother nor her father liked Americans. If her father found him in the rice hut, he would have him killed. With her arms under his arm pits and locked around his chest, she pulled him to the back side of the rice hut and laid him on a bed of straw. She removed his hard hat, and sweat from his dark, short hair ran down his face.

His face wrinkled with pain and he said, "Water."

If she went home to get water from the tap, her grandmother would demand an explanation. She quietly made her way to the village well. As she leaned over the rim of the cylindrical hole, she moved her eyes around the hamlet. Children played behind the huts in the distance, but they paid no attention to her. She held to the rope, dropped the bucket with a splash and pulled it up. After filling the canteen, she poured the water left in the bucket back into the well, because clean water was scarce since the war began.

Back at his side, she lifted his head and put the canteen to his lips. He drank the water in urgent gulps and streams ran down his neck.

The pain in his leg was bad. He was barely aware of what was going on. She kept first aid supplies with her to doctor the children's skinned knees and scrapes. She opened her black bag and got a bottle of pills. Then she pulled his head up, pushed two big pills into his mouth, and gave him another drink of water to wash the pills down.

He heard a clicking sound; she had a pair of scissors and was cutting his pants. He could feel the cold metal crawling up his leg. He knew he had a stab wound in the fleshy part of his leg, just above the knee.

She cleaned his wound, covered it with an antibiotic cream, and wrapped a bandage tightly around the wound.

Then he felt soft hands caressing his face with a cool cloth. For a spell, he thought he was at home in his own bed recovering from a terrible illness, and his mama was by his side. Then he smelled a sweetness that was not the same as the smell of his mother. He stretched his eyes with surprise. A beautiful tanned face was looking down at him. She had the most beautiful brown eyes he had ever seen. Her dark hair was bowed with a purple orchid on one side. As she checked the bandage, her soft tan hands moved gently over his skin and gave him chill bumps. She had long slender fingers and pink nails. She pulled her hands to her lap and pressed them together in a prayer position as she looked at her accomplishment. Then she gave his arm a gentle pat and said, "I must go, but I will be back soon."

He watched the tall, slender figure disappear through the front door to the hut, and he called after her, "Wait! Come back!" But she did not return. She had taken his full attention. God had answered his prayer and sent an angel to save his life.

He wanted to go out and take in some fresh air, but he couldn't move. He tried to sit up, but the pain in his leg brought him down. He lay back with a good breath and grabbed his leg. He could feel the thick band of gauze. Then he saw the bruises on his arms, and he realized he had been stripped of his clothing and tended. The spirits of turpentine settled around him, and the pain pill the angel woman had given him worked a miracle. As he drifted to the twilight zone, he thought about getting back to his base.

Hours must have passed before she returned. Her beauty was breath taking and her presence heavenly. Most of the women he had seen wore a dress called ai-dai, but she was different, more beautiful. She set the tray on the floor next to his straw bed, and her hair fell forward with shimmering black glints seen in precious jewels. She was wearing a tight silk sheath becoming to her good figure. He tried to sit up, but the pain sent him back with a hard jolt on the straw. He grabbed his leg, and said, "My leg is killing me. I must be pretty banged up."

"You have a bad stab wound," she said. "You need stitches and medicine for the infection, but I do not give stitches."

"What is your name?"

"My name is Anna Ming, and I am Vietnamese from the village."

"Is this Communist territory?"

"This is not a Communist village. This is Lat Village near Dalat Province."

"My army base is at Dalat," Ernie said. "How did I get here?"

"I was on my way home from school, and Chipper, the monkey, led me to you. You lost much blood and were still bleeding. I knew you would soon die; I brought you here to the rice hut to tend your wound."

"I met that monkey before the Viet Cong stabbed me. He is the smartest monkey I have ever seen," he said.

"The village children have taught Chipper many tricks," she said.

"I need to get back to my base."

"As soon as you have strength to walk, you may leave."

"You saved my life! How can I ever repay you?"

"Chipper, the monkey, saved you."

"Where can I find this champion monkey?"

"He plays with the children around the village every day."

"Why did you bring me here?"

"I could not let you die and keep a good feeling in my heart," she said, and she paused as if gathering her thoughts. "I must tell you something. My father hates Americans. He says Americans are liars and dishonest frauds. You must not be seen in the village. Else, you will be tied to a bamboo post and skinned alive. My village enforces strict morality codes for women. The head of the house will kill a soldier who touches one of his women."

Ernie cringed and stretched his eyes. "Who is the head of the house?"

"My father is the head of the house. He is also village chief." Then she smiled, gave him a polite nod, and said, "I must go. Do not leave the hut for any reason. I will bring food and medicine." She looked at his tray. "Take your pills!"

As she walked away, he said to himself, "Wow! She is a bossy little Mama." His eyes caught her bare feet and he thought of twisting toes with her. She was very delicate and beautiful. Her beauty was natural, and he liked the way she moved. She looked better than Miss September hanging on his wall back at the barracks. He was in no hurry to get back to the business of war. He wanted to get to know this woman who had saved his life. Once again he tried to stand. The pain had eased, but he saw stars darting about the hut, and sat back down.

After taking the magic pills, Ernie fell asleep. When he awoke, he smelled food. Next to his bed, she had left a covered tray. He lifted the lid and a delicious smelling aroma filled his nostrils. He was starving, and his mouth was watering for the delicious food. He pushed his behind to a sitting position and screamed with the pain shooting up his leg. Finally, he got his stiff leg positioned on a clump of straw, and the pain eased. He picked up the glass of tea and two horse pills rolled to the corner of the tray. He washed them down and dug into the bowl of rice. A big egg lay next to the bowl of rice. He was used to chicken eggs back in Georgia. They had some over grown chickens in Vietnam. He wondered what they fed them. He bit into the big egg and chewed with a hearty appetite. Then he discovered the dark lumpy center. He punched the egg with his finger, and the half grown baby bird made him gag; he had already swallowed half of the critter. His mama always checked her eggs, especially if a rooster got in the pen with the hens. If she saw a round red spot in an egg, she didn't cook it, because that was a sure sign that she had ruined the little chicken's chance to hatch. He was too sick to finish his meal. He had heard that some Vietnamese served rats with rice. God how he wished he had a home cooked Georgia meal. The thoughts of eating rats, fermented fish, and half grown baby birds inside a boiled egg turned his stomach inside out. He finished off the bowl of rice and ate the hard roll to satisfy his growling guts.

He looked around the musty hut and thought about his neat room at home. The rice straw bed was nothing like the mattress on his bed at home, but it was better than no bed at all. The pill relaxed him and he fell asleep again.

The next day when he awoke, he saw that she had brought more horse pills and another tray of food with another bowl of rice. The Vietnamese ate rice three times a day. If they got hungry, they ate rice four times a day. Had they ever heard of rice pudding?

She brought food and pills two times each day. She also cleaned his wound and changed his bandage. Today, she had left a pan of warm water, soap, and a bath cloth. He had never been so happy to see that pan of water. He felt embarrassed about his rotten smell. He could smell his own stink that was an unpleasant mixture of sweat, tears, and blood. Whatever tears smelled like, he did not know. He just knew he smelled bad, and bad smells turned women off. He got busy with the cloth, soap, and water. He scrubbed his body from head to toe and washed his hair in the soapy water.

In the meantime, Anna was miserable at school. She wondered if the children had noticed her mind wandering away from their questions and her short replies. She could not wait to get back to the American. She was worried about his wound getting infection. He had made a strong impression on her at first glance, and her heart had softened for him with an unusual feeling. Her grandmother called her giddy feelings calf love. She had never heard of anything so ridiculous. Her grandmother had unusual beliefs and sayings. All that day, she walked on a cloud and thought about the American. She imagined his wide inquisitive eyes searching her mind. He must know that she had special feelings for him. Remembering the sensation of his touch when his hand accidentally touched hers made her think seriously about being in his arms. Contrary to her feelings for him, she was filled with self-doubt. On the other hand, she would never agree to the planned marriage that her father was set on. He wanted her to marry for wealth and convenience. She did not love the man her father chose, and he was not madly in love with her, either. He was wealthy, well educated, well mannered, and very courteous. He suited her father's image of a future son in law, but he did not suit Anna's taste at all. She did not care for his courteous sophistication. She liked a man with personality. The American's manners and life style differed from hers, but she liked everything about him. She was lost in thought and had no idea what she was thinking. She had not been able to pay attention to what was going on around her, and she found it almost impossible to concentrate on her duties. Foling interrupted her day dream when she asked if she could be excused. Anna grabbed her composure and told Foling that she may be excused. She must stop thinking about this American. She had a duty to the children; she must forget her silly dream.

Then she stood and faced the children. "Let us take a short break."

The children lined up quickly and marched to the play ground.

That evening when she arrived at the hut, she walked with poised straight shoulders and wore a long rose colored dress. Her headband matched her dress perfectly. She placed the tray of food next to his bed and the big pod of bananas took his attention.

"Bananas have potassium and they are good for a snack," she said.

He was drawn to her like smoke in the wind; he had never been more attracted to a woman. He wanted to make hay with her.

After she had finished her nursing duties, she surprised him by sitting down on the straw next to his bed.

"The food smells good," he said, taking a big bite of the meat.

"Bat is very good this time of year," she said.

He gagged and took a big swallow of tea.

"You do not like bat?"

How could he disappoint her? How could he eat another bite? He could feel the bat churning in his stomach. He cleared his throat, took a big spoon full of rice, and said, "The food is very good."

"Are you not going to try soup?"

He dipped a big spoon full of soup and swallowed it quickly. He was afraid to ask the name of the soup.

"Eel vermicelli is very tasty," she said. "Eat up. You will get strength back."

"I couldn't eat another bite," he said, slapping his belly.

"Tomorrow, I will fix you a special dish of cobra."

The thought of eating a snake made the bat churn to the tip of his throat. He had to tell her that he had to be excused. He had to tell her that he could not eat cobra. He swallowed several times, took a deep breath, and said, "I'm not used to eating such rich food."

"Do you not like my dishes?"

"You are a fine cook, but my stomach is bad. I have an ulcer."

"Bitter soup is good for ulcers."

"I think I should stick to vegetables."

"Buddhists eat only vegetables at special times of the year. Are you Buddhist?"

"No, I'm a Georgia Protestant."

"You must try green dragon."

"My God, where do they get the dragons?" He said to himself, and she must have seen the shock on his face.

"I am sorry that you do not like Vietnam food."

"We have some strange dishes in Georgia, too," he said. "We have alligator pears in Georgia. The pears come from a tree, and the peeling covering the pears is rough and brown spotted just like an alligator's hide."

"We eat real alligators and alligator snappers."

"What is an alligator snapper?" he said.

"An alligator snapper is a big turtle."

"Is the alligator snapper green?"

She laughed and said "He is not green. He is as brown as a mouse."

"I thought mice were gray," he said.

"Georgia must have different mice, too," she said.

"The gray mice are more sophisticated," he said.

"I must go now, but I will be back soon."

He lay back on the straw bed, and his shoulders ached about as much as his leg from lying in one position so long. The straw bed put pleasant thoughts about her in his head. As he dozed, he could feel her soft hands moving across his shoulders and back. A good massage would surely help his feelings. He got to a sitting position and moved his arms in a circular motion, forward and back. He could hear his bones cracking. After several turns, he lay back on the straw and slept.

The next day when he heard footsteps nearing the hut, he closed his eyes and pretended to be asleep. He could feel her presence nearing his bed. He opened his eyes wide with sleepy surprise and said, "I thought you would never come back to see me."

"I have told you that I will care for you through the bad days, and I am a woman of my words. Could you stand and move your feet this morning?"

"I tried to stand, but my legs put me down."

"You will get better as the days pass with rest and a good diet," she said.

He really didn't want to get much better just yet. She was immaculate, fresh from the tub, and the sweetness of her skin made him warm all over. He moved with a grunt and said, "My back and my shoulders ache worse than my leg today. I wonder if I could talk you into rubbing my back."

She gave him a questioning look and quickly held her head down. She blushed easily, and he liked her shyness.

She wondered if he really felt pain or just wanted to feel her touch. She ignored his request and set the tray of food next to the bed. As she started out, she looked back at him and said, "Sit up and eat your dinner."

"Please come back and talk to me while I eat. I promise to be a good soldier and keep my hands to myself."

"Very well," she said, and she came to the bedside and sat down on the floor next to his bed. A strange pulling force had taken her, and she wanted to be near him. She tried to ignore the feeling, but she could not deny her attraction for him. She liked his handsome face, his muscular body, and his courage. She felt his eyes upon her and she did not want to look at him.

"You are about the most beautiful woman I have ever seen in my life," he said.

"Your flattery does not go to my head. I always consider words carefully and weigh their worth."

"I am not trying to flatter you. I am simply telling the truth," he said.

The truth of the matter was that she had fallen for him, and her heart beat only for him. She lived from one meeting until the next to be near him. She sensed that he knew the feeling well, and he would not let go of the force. She could tell that he was very persistent and had strong ideas. She was very weak and submissive, so she must be on her guard and not let things go too far. She would not make after him. Besides, he could never be her lover, and she must not make his advances convenient.

"Your dinner will not be good after it chills."

He pushed himself up in bed and she removed the lids from the dishes of food. The delicious smell made his mouth water, but he did not want to be let down. He moved his eyes from the bowl of steaming soup to the healthy helping of rice that was decorated with chunks of red meat. "This smells good. What kind of famous soup do we have today?"

"Green Turtle soup is very special indeed," she said. "This soup is a rare treat that is only served on special occasions. The soup is good for healing."

Then he saw a large, brown, oblong creature covered with spines at the corner of his tray. Did the Vietnamese serve rare animals without cleaning or cooking them? He pushed back from his tray, pointed at the creature, and said, "What is that?"

She was hysterical with laughter. "The fruit is called durian, the "King of Fruits"; Durian has magical healing powers. When you remove the thorn covered husk and break the fruit open, do not be surprised."

"What will I find?" he said. "Does the fruit have an animal growing inside?"

She laughed and said, "The fruit had a very strong distinctive odor. Some say the fruit smells terrible, but you need to eat the fruit to get healing power."

"I thought I smelled something rotten when you placed the tray before me," he said. "I don't mean to sound ungrateful for all that you do for me, but I cannot eat that spiny fruit."

"You can taste the fruit; if you do not like the taste, do not eat it."

He ignored her suggestion and said, "This soup looks delicious." He picked up the spoon on his tray, dipped a small taste of the soup and put it to his tongue with caution. He hesitated with the thought of green turtles. He had never seen a green turtle. Neither had seen a green dragon. How did they make their turtles green? It seemed to him that everything he ate was green, red, or brown, and the rice came in all colors. His mama cooked collard greens, turnips, spinach, green beans, and garden peas. She never brought him any of the green foods he had heard of. To his surprise, the soup tasted delicious, and he wished he had more, instead of the rice.

"This soup hits the spot," he said. I was very hungry." But he was starving for some southern fried Chicken and gave her a hint. "The first day we arrived in Dalat, my buddy and I visited Lat Village. As we neared the village, we saw the statue of a large rooster. Why is the village called Chicken Village?"

"There is a legend behind the statue of the chicken," she said. "My grandmother says many years ago a boy and girl who lived in the village fell madly in love with each other, but their parents disapproved of their union. After their death, the statue was built in their memory."

"What does that have to do with a chicken?" he said.

"I do not know why they used a chicken to memorialize the couple," she said.

"Do the people in the village ever cook southern fried chicken?" He was hoping that she would take the hint and bring him something common, instead of green food.

"We seldom fry any kind of meat," she said. "Our dishes made from chicken are boiled, baked, or broiled."

"I guess I will have to get used to doing without southern fried chicken," he said.

"Your health will be much better if you do not eat fried food," she said. "In fact, you are looking much better already."

"My recovery was quick!" he said. Your soup worked miracles."

"I did not mean that you improved quickly like magic. I meant that you look better each day."

"I owe my life to you," he said.

"You owe me nothing. I will be rewarded for my good deeds. Now I must go back to the village. My grandmother has been asking many questions about where I have been spending my time."

After she had gone, he saw that she had left the brown, spiny fruit on the floor next to his straw bed. He picked the spiny fruit up, turned it about, and dug into its center; the worst odor he had ever smelled hit his nose. He threw the fruit to the far side of the hut and sat up on the bed. Then he pulled himself up, clutched the stick leaning against the straw wall, and hobbled to the entrance of the hut to take a look at the world. The sound of birds was music to his ears. Kilns filled the air with the smell of smoke mixed with boiled ham. She lived in a large stucco house surrounded by tall Tamarind trees. Tea bushes made a hedge across the front of the porch, and flower gardens with roses, hydrangeas, and orchids took most of the front yard. She had said her father was the chief, and he must have money. He had a gardener, and his house was elaborate in comparison to the huts with thatched roofs huddled in a circle nearby. They built sheds next to each hut for the farm buffalo. Next to the porch, they had stacks of ceramic crocks they used to store water, rice wine, and liquor. In the distance to his right, he could see children playing around the huts. A cloud of smoke streamed above a large black pot, where a woman stood and stirred its contents. He took a deep whiff. Thinking the pot was filled with monkey, he closed his mind and pretended chicken stew was boiling in the pot.

When he turned to go back to the rice hut, he saw a monkey playing with the children. Could that be the smart monkey, Chipper? He wanted to talk to the monkey, but he did not know how to make a monkey call. Perhaps he could draw his attention with a banana. He hopped back into the hut, pulled two prize bananas from the pod and went to find Chipper. At the back of the rice hut, he made his way through the bushes toward the cluster of huts.

Standing directly in front of the huts, Chipper held hands with two of the children as they sang and moved in a circle. The game looked similar to **Ring Around the Roses**. He stood his stick against a clump of bushes and leaned back against a pine tree to peel a banana. After several rounds, the children said farewell to Chipper, and he came toward the bushes.

When Ernie saw the monkey part the bushes, he smiled and held the banana out to him. Chipper made a grateful noise, took the banana, and sat down at Ernie's feet for the feast. Ernie let his buttocks slide down the side of the tree and sat next to Chipper.

"I wanted to thank you for saving my life," Ernie said as he rubbed the monkey's back. "I am sorry I have nothing more to offer."

Chipper looked up at him and held up one finger as he took another bite of his banana.

Ernie laughed and said, "Yes, I do have one more banana. Do you want another banana?"

Chipper moved his head up and down for yes and clapped his hands as Ernie peeled the banana. When Ernie handed it to Chipper, he spread his monkey paw, patted Ernie's cheek, and kissed him.

"You are a smart monkey," Ernie said. "Did you know that?"

Chipper shook his head up and down to say yes.

"I would like to take you home with me," Ernie said.

Chipper got up and reached for Ernie's hand.

Ernie held to his stick and made holes in the ground with his weight as he walked back to the rice hut with Chipper. Inside the hut, he showed the monkey his new home, and Chipper did cart wheels on the bed of straw.

"You would make a lonely man a good companion."

Chipper rolled out his lip and did a clown act for Ernie.

"Where do you stay at night?"

Chipper fell back on Ernie's bed and closed his eyes.

"If you want to stay the night, I will make another bed." Ernie began to pull straw from the large pile at the back of the hut, and Chipper helped him. Pretty soon, they had a nice bed next to Ernie's bed, and Chipper lay back on the straw and closed his eyes.

Ernie eased himself down on his own bed and watched the monkey. He couldn't believe the monkey was asleep. When Ernie finally closed his eyes, he could see Anna sitting next to the bed. Was he falling in love with this woman? He did not know if he loved her or not, but he wanted to make love to her. On the other hand, being skinned alive by her father would be a horrible death. Then he thought about his buddies and his duty to his country. Private Hatcher had probably searched the entire jungle for him. Then he remembered he had not written to his mama since he left his base. He wanted to write to her, but he had no paper or pen.

The next morning when he awoke, Chipper had gone and taken the bananas with him.

Anna came in before noon with fish, sauce, steamed rice, and spring rolls.

"I met Chipper," he said. "I saw him playing with the children, so I hid in the bushes with bananas, and he came to me. Then he came back to the hut with me and spent the night. He is the smartest animal I have ever seen."

She laughed and said, "I see that you do not have any bananas left."

"A thief in the night took the bananas and got away."

"He will come back for more bananas," she said. Then she pointed to his tray and said, "Very tasty fish."

Before tasting the fish, he asked, "What kind of sauce is this?"

"Nuoc Mam sauce is very good. The sauce is made from fish."

"What is this?" he asked, pointing to a strange dish on the tray.

"Green dragon," she said.

"So this is green dragon," he said. He had a picture in his head of a green spiny animal, but the dragon looked like a pineapple.

"Only Pattaya Beach grows the dragon fruit. Dragon fruit tastes like kiwi fruit, and the juice makes a delicious drink."

Ernie picked up his cup and said, "Is this green dragon juice?"

"That is green tea. Green tea comes from China. It is good for many ailments."

"Green dragon and green tea," he said, and he held his cup up as if giving a toast before the drink. He wondered what they put in the tea to make it green. What had happened to plain old Georgia tea? The best thing to eat in Vietnam was the oysters, crabs, and clams.

"Do you not like the green tea?" she asked.

"I prefer red tea," he said. "Don't they brew red tea over here?"

"Artichoke tea is made and sold right here in Dalat," she said.

"What is artichoke Tea?" Ernie said.

"Artichoke tea is made from artichokes," she said. "The tea is delicious. I never drink red tea. Red tea is not healthy."

"That is what we drink in Georgia."

"You must drink only green tea. It is very delicious and healthy. Green tea cures your aches and pains."

"Would it cure the ache in my heart for you?"

"I do not know about your heart." She was floating on air. He had made her loose her good judgment. Her common sense had gone out the window. She could not give in to her passion. The time was too soon. She would help him get on his feet and send him on his way.

"Umm, the dragon is delicious," he said. "Does the dragon keep you from aging? I have heard that the Chinese never grow old."

"They never grow old, because they only have birthdays every twelve years," she said.

"Do they forget their birthday every year?" he said.

"Old people often lose track of their age, because they are seldom asked their current age. The counting of years is in a twelve years cycle. They may be twelve, twenty-four, thirty-six, forty-eight, sixty, seventy-two, eighty-four, or ninety-six."

"You don't have January through December like Americans do," he said.

"The Chinese Year is named for twelve different animals; these animals are recycled every twelve years and repeated every sixty years. After the twelfth year, they start over from year one. Neither does a young child have to learn a new answer for his age. He need only remember the animal for the year he is born."

"Who are the lucky animals?" he said.

"The year of the pig is followed by the year of the dog, rooster, ram, horse, snake, monkey, and so forth. The Chinese New Year comes on January twenty-ninth this year. The year at hand is the year of the dog."

"I am a lucky dog," he said and moved a little closer to her. She moved from his reach and he said, "Lucky dogs also bite."

"You are so funny. I am very pleased to see that my patient is feeling better. I need to change the cover on your bed before I go."

The medicine woman made quick light steps around his bed as she put clean sheets under him, and he watched every move she made. All she needed was wings; she had the face, body, and halo. He wanted to ask her to lie next to him. Instead, he said, "Would you please rub my shoulders? They hurt from lying in the same spot so long."

She looked at him with meek concern. He had asked her once before to rub his back. What would it hurt for her to ease his pain?

She hinted her feeling by her body language and her sweet voice. She would not look directly into his eyes.

He pulled off his shirt and the tremendous muscles in his arms caught her eye. He was good to look at. She touched his arm muscles and said, "plenty of exercise, I see."

"Plenty of hard work," he said. "I have never had much time to exercise. Besides, I got plenty of exercise while I worked on the farm."

She sat down on the floor next to his bed and asked him to turn over.

He wanted to scream with the pain that grabbed his leg when he turned, but he didn't make a sound. He did not want to spoil the treat he had coming.

She oiled her hands with the ointment she had been applying to his leg and began massaging his back and shoulders. She rolled her hands like a professional; he closed his eyes with the sensation of pleasure from her magic touch.

Minutes later, she picked up a cloth and wiped her hands. "Now that should make you feel better."

"Don't stop. God that felt good. Your hands feel better than a feather bed in December."

"What is a feather bed?" she asked.

"Why it's a bed made from feathers," he said.

"You joke too often. I do not have time to stay longer. I must get back home. Grandmother wants me to go to the garden markets in Dalat today and buy her some fresh fruits and vegetables. They grow their own produce to sell. We use their carrots and cauliflower in stir fry foods mostly, but the avocadoes are good for dips and spreads. When you get on your feet again, you should go to the Dalat Market. The market is fabulous; they have many things to choose from besides fruits and vegetables."

"Do they sell dragons?"

"You are very funny."

"Speaking of your duty to your grandmother, I wonder if you would buy me a note pad and a pen from the market. My mother must be worried sick about me. I have not written to her in several weeks."

"I have note paper and pen on hand. If I can slip away from Grandmother, I will bring it to you this evening."

"Are you going to mail the letter for me?" he said.

"What need is there to write a letter if the letter is not mailed?" she said.

"I had not thought of that," he said, and he wanted to pull her down next to him and cover her with kisses.

"I must go now. Grandmother will ask what kept me so long." She turned back before going out the door and said, "Did you eat the durian fruit?"

He hated to tell her; he hated to lie. "That spiny fruit smelled rotten. I sailed it through the trees behind the rice hut."

"Shame on you," she said and left.

After she left, he buried his head in his pillow with good dreams. She was a special woman. She was different from any woman he had ever known. She had set a fire in him that would never burn out. His passion was obvious. He wanted her to stay with him forever. His dream was interrupted by footsteps nearing the hut. At first, he thought his dream had come true. She was rushing back to him. Then he realized that the footsteps sounded different from her steps. He quickly pulled himself up, grabbed his stick, hobbled to the back corner of the hut, and crouched behind a ton of rice stacked in bags. He remained as still as a stone and listened to the movement of feet around the hut. A loud bang hit the floor and a dragging sound moved toward the entrance as the human form pulled on the bag of rice. Then the feet moved around his straw bed and back to the other side of the hut. Afterwards, he heard heavy footsteps move out the door; he listened for the footsteps to fade before moving back to the front of the hut. He could see that a bag of rice was missing from the level stack. He moved around the hut and peeped out the front door. All was clear. He felt a need to go to the bathroom, so he hobbled out the door to find his tree behind the rice hut.

Early the next morning, Anna brought the paper and pen he had requested with his breakfast, but she kept her distance from him and was gone in a flash. He had not had time to start a conversation. He wrote a letter to his mama explaining what had happened to him and to let her know that God sent a beautiful angel to save his life.

When Anna came back to the hut that evening, she was unusually nervous. When he asked her if she would mail the letter he had written to his mother, she snatched the letter from his hand, shoved it into her bosom, and said, "You must leave this rice hut right away!"

"I am not feeling well," he said. "Give me one more day." He looked at her with a longing and said, "I will miss you."

She had a splendid feeling with his words, but she would not show her feelings. "You must be on your way immediately."

"Did you have a bad day at school?"

She dismissed his question and said, "Grandmother knows someone slept here in the hut! She says she plans to catch the Viet Cong who slept on her bags of rice."

"I have not been sleeping on her bags of rice. My bed is made of straw."

"I have no time for jokes!" she said, "You must go before the sun gets low in the sky. That is when Grandmother will come to the hut."

"Does she own a gun?" he asked.

"You are a crazy American! She will kill you!"

"I will leave before she gets here. In case she comes early, I will hide under the straw." He sat on the edge of the bed and looked up at her. "I don't know how I can thank you enough and pay you for saving my life."

"You owe me nothing! I want you to leave!" she said.

"Can I come back and visit you tomorrow?" he said.

"You must never be seen in the village! My father is coming home at the end of this week. You must forget you ever saw me."

"I will never forget you," he said.

After she had gone, Ernie thought the situation over. The open wounds on his arms, back, and legs had almost healed. He wanted to scratch the scabs off, but he knew better. He had to get back to his base; he definitely didn't want Anna's father to find him in the rice hut. He grabbed his stick, hopped to the entrance of the hut, and peeped around the straw before making his way down the narrow dirt path toward the huts. He could see gongs of rice liquor hanging from the edge of the porch. He didn't care for rice liquor, but a cool drink of water was a nice thought. He leaned heavily on his stick and hobbled toward the pretty stucco house, where Anna lived.

As he neared the front steps, he saw an elderly lady sitting in the porch swing. She glided back and forth and twisted a floral fan with dainty Chinese ladies dancing from pleat to pleat. As he drew nearer he could hear her talking to herself. "My, my, these gnats are pests! They are worse than mosquitoes."

When she saw the American soldier hobbling up to the steps, she brought her fan to a stop and nervously twisted her fingers. She had waves of dark hair, streaked with gray, combed back from her face and tied in a sweeping cluster on top of her head. She lowered her glasses and her quick brown eyes gave him a devil look as she spoke, "What is your business here, Soldier?"

"I need to use your phone to call my base. I have been wounded, and I need someone to pick me up."

"Be on your way!" she said, and the lines that seamed her face got deeper with her anger. She darted her eyes quickly from him to the sky and threw out her hand as if preaching. "Look what you have done! Your injuries are well deserved!"

He had no idea what she was talking about.

"Miss, I am Ernie Tennyson, an American soldier stationed at Dalat. I mean you no harm. I just want to use your phone, and I will be on my way."

"Do not make another step," the old lady said, and she flared the Chinese ladies toward him.

Suddenly, the front door went back and Anna walked out on the porch. She stared at him with shock and pretended she had never seen him before in her life.

"Good afternoon, Miss," he said as he moved his eyes from her head to her toes. He had not seen her more beautiful. A conical hat shaded her face, but he was more interested in the tight jeans and the body shirt that fit snugly against her breast.

Anna turned to the old lady and spoke in Vietnamese. The old lady swung her fan real fast before her face as she spoke. Then she pulled herself up from the swing and pointed at him as she talked to Anna.

Ernie had no idea what they said, but he did know their conversation was about him, and the old lady was none too happy with his being there.

Anna made short, quick steps to where he stood and gave him a hard, long glance that said she did not want him around, either. In a low whisper, she said, "You must leave! I asked you not to come to the village! Why do you want to needle the rice sack?"

"I didn't mess with the bags of rice. I need to use your phone to call my base."

"My grandmother will not allow you to enter our home. I will make the call."

He pulled out his billfold and handed her his ID card. "Thank you, Miss. I do appreciate your doing me this favor."

She jerked the card from his hand, and her eyes stabbed him before she turned to go back into the house.

Minutes later, she bounced back down the steps and said, "Someone will be here soon to pick you up, but you must leave now."

"Before I go, will you be so kind as to write your phone number here on my card."

"I will do nothing of the kind," she said.

"My commanding officer will ask questions, and I will be in hot water if I do not have an alibi for being away from the base. He will mark me AWOL."

"What is AWOL?" she asked.

"A war out law," he said.

"I do not understand."

"Write your number here, and I will go."

She jotted down her number, handed him the card, and rushed up the steps.

The old lady stood up again and pointed her finger at him with her angry words, "Why are you standing there gaping at my granddaughter! You have had your say! Be on your way!"

"It was good to meet you, Maim. Thank you for your help. I'll be going now."

As he walked toward the road, she shouted words at him, "I can see that your eyes blink with wicked thoughts. Stay away from my granddaughter! You are up to no good, and I will not allow you to use my granddaughter for your own pleasure."

He wanted to please her granddaughter while he pleased himself, but he did not tell her his intentions. She would not understand.

When he got to the road, he looked back at the old lady still watching him. She was full of the devil with a belly full of wrath and a grudge to grind; she was bent out of shape and trying to find fault with a perfectly innocent soldier. He wondered if she was going through menopause, or whatever it is that makes women crazy. On second thought, she was probably too old for menopause; she was too old to cut the mustard, and she didn't want her granddaughter to know the pleasure she was missing. He wanted to give her a piece of his mind. He had not asked her advice about one single thing.

He watched the old lady sit back down in the swing and make the Chinese ladies dance on her fan. She was still talking to herself, but she was not talking about the gnats. He turned back to the road and started walking.

Anna went to her room to avoid her grandmother's questions. Alone in her room, she searched her mind. Why had she let her feelings show for this American? Her father hated Americans, and she did not want to fall in love with this man. Most women were sentimental, emotional, and gentle; her father was hard, reasonable, and hateful. Women always fell head over heels in love, while men stood firm with their head over their hearts and used women.

She heard her grandmother's slow steps nearing her door, and she expected her to rush into her room uninvited, but she stood outside her door to have her say.

"Granddaughter, you must be on your guard. That American was giving you the once over, and I expect him to come calling again. Are you ready to set dinner?"

"I am not hungry, Grandmother. I have much work to prepare for school tomorrow."

Her grandmother's footsteps faded and Anna drew a deep breath of relief.

CHAPTER FIVE

Before Ernie walked a mile, he saw a jeep coming. Private Hatcher brought the jeep to a halt and jumped out to help him get seated.

"God, I am glad to find you alive," Hatcher said. "We have searched the entire southern jungle for the past week. I was worried sick about you."

"Did you cry?"

"This is no time to be joking," Private Hatcher said. "What in the hell happened to you? What is wrong with your leg?"

"Those damn Viet Cong almost killed me. They stabbed me to the bone. If I had not played dead, I would be dead. I almost bled to death. I was too weak to chew grits for several days. I still have a good back but my mind is as hollow as a Halloween pumpkin."

Hatcher laughed and said, "Your mind was hollow from the beginning."

"You have not heard the best part of the story. I was rescued by an angel, and she saved my life. Her name is Anna Ming; she is the most beautiful woman in the world, and she is a school teacher. She hid me in a rice hut, and waited on me hand and foot until today."

"Is that why you didn't call the base sooner?"

"I didn't call until I was forced to call; I wanted to stay with her. Then I met her grandmother, and she didn't take a liking to me at all. Her father is even worse news; he hates Americans, so I didn't wait around to meet him. I sure would like to ask her to go out with me, but she says her father will kill me."

"Take my advice and forget that woman," Hatcher said.

Private Hatcher turned and drove down the dusty road toward the base. He stopped at the entrance to the base, and Ernie thought about the first day he passed through those gates. He turned to Hatcher and said, "Man, I made an oath to serve my country, but I am seriously thinking about going over the hill."

"Right now, you have to get that leg checked by the doctor."

"I could use a few days of rest and relaxation."

Private Hatcher pulled through the entrance and drove to the medical unit. He helped Ernie get out and offered to help him walk, but Ernie grabbed his stick and hobbled inside.

The soldiers nicknamed Doctor Allen, Old Saw Bones. He would move his long legs around his small office, turn to his patient with muddy eyes stretched above wire rims resting on the middle of his nose, and ask stupid questions unrelated to the injury or illness, but he doctored all ailments, and he was certainly better than no doctor at all.

"You have a bad infection in that leg; it needs stitches, but the wound is too old to stitch up now." The doctor gave him a shot, two bottles of pills, and ordered rest and easy duty for six weeks.

"You lucky devil," Private Hatcher said as he drove toward the barracks.

"I wonder what the Sergeant will call easy duty," Ernie said.

"KP duty would suit you to a tee."

"You know how I hate those damn potatoes," Ernie said with thoughts of basic training at Fort Benning.

Ernie talked constantly about Anna. "She makes me feel like smoke in the wind being pulled up in the clouds."

"Man, you are talking crazy."

"Have you ever seen a woman that drove you crazy?"

"Every woman I snuggle with makes me crazy for a little while. Just looking at some women makes the blood in my veins run hot."

When they got back to the base, Private Hatcher said, "It's chow time. Let's go get something to eat."

When they walked into the large mess hall, Ernie's eye stretched with surprise. Balloons, hanging from the ceiling on long strings, and streamers danced around the room. A large sign at the front of the cafeteria stood out with bold print: WELCOME BACK ERNIE; all of the GI's had signed their names around the message. He couldn't believe his eyes. The guys sang, "For He's a Jolly Good Fellow," and tears came to Ernie's eyes. He had thought nobody cared. Every man in his platoon was there to celebrate his home coming. Ernie was sure that Private Hatcher had planned the party. His colorful personality made him popular with all of the GI's and they had pitched in to help him. Ernie had never felt more honored.

Sergeant Fitzwater, the squad leader, was a heavyset man with dark hair and a broad face accented by dark eyes, thick brows, thick lips and a broad nose. He slapped Ernie on the back and said, "Good to have you back." This calls for a celebration," and he motioned for the boys to bring in the beer. They had twenty wash tubs filled with beer to celebrate his home coming.

With a beer in one hand and the other free, Ernie walked around the room and shook hands with his buddies.

Sergeant First Class Fish was first in line. He was a tall slender man a long, classic nose that turned down on the end. The GI's called Fish a Bluenose Yankee behind his back. He was a comedian and the GI's liked his jokes. Most of all, they liked to hear him brag about his women. He bragged about his affair with Natalie Woods. He claimed that he met Natalie while on vacation in Hollywood, California, and she asked him to move into her magnificent pent house. Then she started talking about marriage, and he had business in Virginia. Fish was usually under the influence when he bragged. His stories must have come from the bottle.

Ernie moved on down the line to the priest, Father Crandall. He shook Ernie's hand, asked about his wound, and told him he had prayed for him every day and night he had been gone, and God had certainly answered his prayer. Crandall was a harmless gnat who tried to lift the GI's spirits. He placed a gentle hand on each man's shoulder, while he prayed for his well being, and he made cheerful conversation to make him feel better. On the other hand, he worried the hell out of the GI's, because they usually had nothing to make them happy.

Hobbit moved his short legs across the room and met Ernie with a big grin. He turned with a jerk, widened his round eyes, and his bushy brows moved up as he spoke. He told Ernie that every man in the room had worried about him, especially him, and he was proud to have him back. The most noticeable thing about Hobbit was his big ears that had white hair on the tips; his ears did not match his short, thin statue. The GI's accused Hobbit of being ignorant and uncultured, but his good nature was an asset; he seldom got angry with them.

Then High Hat met Ernie and told him how much he had missed him. He asked the details of how the Viet Cong attacked him and his injury. Ernie had never liked High Hat. He was a snob. He wore his cap on the tip top of his head and his big ears stuck out just beneath the cap. The rumor was that High had money running out of his ears.

Next, Private Wingate hugged Ernie and told him how much he had been missed. Wingate was one of Ernie's best friends. He often tagged along with Ernie and Hatcher, but the other GI's did not like Wingate, because he was a red neck from Alabama who had been born with a sarcastic nature; he liked to put the men in their place when they disagreed with him.

After he finally got away from Wingate, Private Slater, a monstrous man with huge muscles, grabbed Ernie in a bear hug and said some kind words. Slater walked around the barracks without a shirt showing his muscles and hairy chest. He was a demolitions expert and the soldiers did not usually go up against Slater when he pulled his practical jokes. One night after the lights went out; he put a large rat in one of the commodes. In the middle of the night, Private Wingate got up to use the bathroom. He stumbled sleepily toward the bathroom and as he entered, he heard a flopping sound that was familiar to a fish jumping in a large pan of water. He went toward the sound and screamed so loud that the GI's thought there was an air raid. They jumped up and got dressed before they discovered the rat.

Next was Sergeant Purvis, a native of Florida. He looked like the heavyweight prizefighter of the 60's and a man of great strength; he could out run, out lift, and out shoot, any man in the regiment. The entire platoon stood to attention when he gave orders. If they didn't respect him, they pretended that they did. The other GI's did not seem to mind taking orders from Purvis. He told Ernie he was proud he lived through the ordeal and asked how he survived. Ernie told the same story over again and moved on.

Then he shook hands with Private Huddle. All of the GI's found Huddle amusing. His worried very little, and he didn't give a turkey's tail about the war. He joked and carried on about the battles like he did after a good fight in the boxing ring. He asked Ernie if the Viet Cong tied him to a tree before they left him to die, and that was no pleasant thought.

Last, but not least was Private Staker. He came up to Ernie and talked about how proud he was to see him. Staker was that rotten apple at the bottom of the barrel. He was forever laughing about nothing. If he had nothing to laugh about, he would punch you in the belly and make a bird call to get your attention. He liked to tell jokes, and nobody laughed. At the range, Staker seemed clumsy and ignorant about guns. Every shot was a wild miss. The soldiers feared he would go on a wild shooting spree and cut them down. The sergeant threatened to lock him in the brig for a week with bread and water, and he took his aim more seriously. When it came to brains, they left him short, but in order for the war to go around, the military needed the dumb men as well as the smart men. Ernie concluded that the dumb men in the time of war got along better than the intellectual nuts, because they didn't know enough about the war to worry about what tomorrow held.

When Ernie popped the cap on the fifth beer, Private Hatcher hit the table with both hands and said, "You do not need another beer, E.T."

Hatcher often called him E.T., especially when he got aggravated.

Then Private Hatcher announced that he wanted to play and sing a song before everybody turned in for the night. He pulled his guitar out from the corner and walked to the center of the room. All of the GI's gathered around to listen to Hatcher's low alto voice match the music of **"God Bless America."** Hatcher had changed the ending of the song to "God Bless Americans". He also sang country music, and even the Yankees liked his singing.

Back at the barracks, Ernie thought about how much trouble Hatcher must have gone to for the celebration. He didn't know what he would do without Hatcher. He was a good listener and a good speaker. With hands behind his belt and his fingers falling limber, he could talk about history, education, law, religion, and the weather.

Ernie had never been so tired and sleepy in his life. He lay back, closed his eyes, and delightful pictures of Anna flashed through his head. Hatcher had said that being love sick in a time of war was foolish, and Ernie should forget her. He added that a man could not deal with women who were easy on the eye and hard on the heart. Ernie told Hatcher that he wanted to go to bed with Anna; afterwards, he would forget her. He didn't intend for any woman to mess up his head.

The next morning, Lieutenant Colonel Switzer, the Company Commander, sent for Ernie to come to his office. The soldiers called the colonel the Ice Man, because he never smiled. He carried his tall, skinny frame with straight shoulders and sat with perfect posture and the dignity of a king. He had a long neck and a small head filled with more brains than his head could carry. The men seldom saw Colonel Switzer. He stayed in his quarters most of the time. On occasion, he did speak to the entire company, which consisted of 170 men. The five companies in the division all went separate ways.

The colonel looked up as Ernie entered his office. "Have a seat, Tennyson." He flipped through the pages of what Ernie assumed to be his medical report, and said, "For the next few weeks, you are assigned to Major Maxwell. He needs a driver."

As Ernie hobbled out of the colonel's office, he met Lieutenant Scott. He stopped to exchange a few words and hobbled on toward the jeep, where Private Hatcher waited to take Ernie back to the base. Lieutenant Scott was different to say the least. He was as serious as a judge, and he never touched the bottle. The GI's called him Einstein, because his brains would fill the Grand Canyon. His IQ was at least 160, but his stories never made any sense to the GI's with common sense and common things on their minds. He talked about generating electricity and inventing things run by atomic energy. He liked to talk about atoms. Ernie had grown to think of atoms as little particles in the air with ears, eyes, and a mouth waiting to devour him. Lieutenant Scott made him feel more paranoid than he was before he got to Vietnam. The war also added to Lieutenant Scott's state of mental incapacity. Each time he told one of his tales, he lowered his head with deep thought like a science professor. The GI's always paid close attention to his lessons, though.

"Was that Lieutenant Scott going into the colonel's office?" Private Hatcher said.

"That was Scott in the living flesh," Ernie said.

"Scott went into the colonel's office three times this week. I asked Scott to put in a good word for the rest of us privates. Scott moves up in rank, while we privates sit back and say nothing. We will carry the brand, private, until our boots turn toward heaven."

"From the looks of things, my boots will turn up sooner than I planned," Ernie said.

"If we stick together and help each other, we can beat this rap," Private Hatcher said.

That night alarms sounded for the air raid; they jumped into their fatigues and rushed to the waiting jeeps. Ernie hated the air raids, but the foot soldiers followed orders just like the pilots and bombers.

The next morning, after Ernie drove Major Maxwell into Dalat to meet one of the colonels for dinner, he came back to the barracks and checked the bulletin board in the lobby for activities posted for the week and the orders assigned to each regiment. His wounded leg put him on easy street. He liked driving the jeep; he hated the jungle.

Every night that week, Ernie talked about Anna Ming; every night that week Hatcher tried to make Ernie see the light, but nothing he said soaked into Ernie's thick skull.

"You've got a picture in your head of that woman, and you'll keep it there until your heels are cooled. If you've got to have her, go after her and get her out of your system. Then you can whistle Dixie."

"I will never get her out of my system," Ernie said and looked at Hatcher with question. "What are you really like behind that cover? Have you ever been in love?"

"I loved a girl once upon a time. I had the same problem you have. Her daddy didn't like me; in fact, he threatened to kill me if I got his little girl pregnant. I did not know who else she had fooled around with, so I told her good bye over the wire."

"Didn't you want to see her?"

"You are damn right, but life without her was better than no life at all. That man threatened to kill me. I soon forgot her and found another girl, and that is what you need to do."

On Saturday night, Private Hatcher was determined to make Ernie forget Anna Ming by introducing him to other beautiful women at the Dalat Bar. Besides, they had happy hour on Friday night; the bar also had rooms upstairs that the GI's could rent for an hour to socialize with a woman of their choice. The charge for the room took care of everything they wanted.

Ernie borrowed Major Maxwell's jeep and they drove toward Dalat. After they passed the beautiful waterfall near Dalat Province, the land rose to hills covered with green; the land fell to valleys and low land with lakes and streams. The Dalat Garden Park had the most beautiful hydrangeas, roses, chrysanthemums, and marigolds in the world. When they reached the city, the sweetness of flower blooms mixed with pipe tobacco filled the air. They passed the Province's State Bank, Provincial Post Office, open-air coffee shops, a movie theater, and the Dalat Market. Weird bronze and stone sculptors decorated the porches and entrances to businesses. Buddha was the most popular statue of all. Men, women, and children moved along the streets to shop or eat at the popular restaurants.

Ernie followed Private Hatcher into the bar, and they got a table near the back. Ernie was not surprised to see painted women moving from one table to another to entertain the soldiers and rich executives in Vietnam on business. Bar Maids offered their services willingly and they charged very little.

When Mr. Goodman came into the bar, all of the GI's cheered. He came to the bar on a regular basis, and the soldiers looked forward to his treat. Before going to a table, Goodman moved his tall stout figure to the bar, adjusted his dark silk tie, buttoned his white linen coat, and slapped the bar to get the bar tender's attention. "Fix drinks for all of the GI's. I will pay for everything they order."

The balloon woman came wobbling around the tables with a tray balanced on her wrist. Goodman held his hand up for service, and she slowly splashed her heavy hips toward his table.

Another well dressed man came in, sat down at the bar, and ordered a highball. The bar tender said to him, "Would you like to have whiskey or brandy?"

The man said, "Brandy will do," and he lit an expensive cigar. A high classed prostitute on the make for the man's pockets, sat down next to him at the bar.

A Geisha girl came on the stage to the left of the rounded counter and sang as the band played, "You Move Me".

Ernie wondered if a woman had ever moved a priest. Why a priest lived his whole life without the love of a woman, but he must keep up his good name as a priest and control his emotions at all times. The Priest never complained about the pleasures in life that he had never tasted. Ernie assumed that the priest kept his Bible handy in case he needed God's help to resist sinning.

As Ernie sat and watched the women flirt with the men, he remembered his daddy telling him about his father's drinking and running around with cheap women. His mother had found out about one particular woman his father went with; she had told her husband that a man who stooped to the favors of a whore woman had very low intelligence. Ernie wondered if he could forget how smart he was tonight and stoop to the favors of a prostitute. His I.Q. got lower with every beer he drank and the women tempting him got real pretty. Private Hatcher was one of the most intelligent men in the company and he had already disappeared up the stairs with a painted woman on his arm. The particular woman Ernie had his eyes on did not look at all like a whore.

The smell of sweet perfume turned his foggy head to the brunette who had taken a seat next to him. She put her hand on his shoulder and tempted him until he was flushed with excitement. Her figure and movements fascinated him much more than her face. She had nice hair streaming down her back, but her long nose had a hump that ruined her face. Most of the other prostitutes looked much better than this woman, but he had decided that her face made little difference, since he was after sex. She did have bright red sexy lips. Ernie ordered another beer and forgot his raising as he followed her up the stairs.

When Ernie got back down stairs, Hatcher was still upstairs with his woman. Ernie wanted to leave that bar and get back to the base. He walked back to their table at the back of the bar and waited.

Loud voices near the front of the bar took Ernie's attention. Two GI's argued about one of the bar maids. They had definitely had too much to drink, because not one of the women was worth fighting over. They continued arguing and the argument led to threats. Then they started punching each other and knocked over tables and chairs.

Pretty soon, two military policemen came in and hauled both of the men to the brig.

A few minutes later, Private Hatcher came downstairs and joined Ernie.

Ernie said, "Let's get out of this place. The military police are swarming. They have already hauled two guys off."

Hatcher followed Ernie to the jeep and he sped away.

Ernie was happy to see his bunk. He went to bed right away and slept until the wake up call.

CHAPTER SIX

Anna's father came home for the weekend, and her grandmother told him about the American soldier who had come to use the phone. She explained that she had been suspicious of the American's behavior and he must speak to his daughter about this American.

The next week, Ernie called Anna a dozen times, but grandmother always answered the phone. He wondered if all girls in Vietnam bent to their parent's wishes the way Anna did. Girls in Georgia acquired certain rights when they graduated from high school. The girls in Vietnam seemed to have no rights at all.

Saturday after chow time, Ernie walked to Lat Village. Private Wingate's friend lived in the village and had told him about a short-cut through the jungle.

He expected Anna's grandmother to be sitting in the front porch swing. When he neared the drive, he saw Anna. She sat on the front steps. Her fresh and beautiful presence told him she expected him to pay her a visit.

"Hello, Anna Ming."

"Mr. Tennyson," she stammered, and her eyes glittered like a cat's eyes in the dark. "How is your wounded leg?"

"My leg is much better," he said. "They put me on light duty until I completely heal, but I walked here from the base."

"I am happy to see you on your feet again," she said and hugged her knees. Her ruffled skirt fell around tan toes that wiggled for him to sit next to her.

He stood for minutes and looked at her tan skin and slender arms hugging her knees. He twisted in his boots and looked toward the house. "Where is your grandmother?"

"Grandmother went to the market in Dalat. She always goes shopping for groceries on Saturday."

"Where is your father?"

"Father went to China today," she said.

"What a lucky break!" he said, slapping his cap to his palm. He sat down next to her with a kiss in mind.

She hugged her knees tighter, and her breast swelled above the low cut sweater she wore. Her perfume smelled wonderful, a cloud of sweetness that he longed to taste. "I came because I wanted to see you, and I wanted to thank you again for saving my life."

"I never know when my father will come home. Believe me; you do not want to meet my father."

Anxious to tell her how he felt about her, he searched her face with questions. How should he begin? Was this the right time? "I have thought about you a lot," he said.

Her eyes grabbed him with a passionate look and he knew what she was thinking. She changed the subject quickly and said, "Would you like some tea to drink?"

"Tea sounds refreshing," he said, hoping she did not return with green tea.

He turned his head and watched her walk up the steps. She turned back at the door and said, "Would you like a snack with your tea?"

"I am not hungry," he said, thinking she might bring one of those gosh awful rice cakes.

Minutes later, she came back and handed him a cup of hot tea. He was thinking of sweet iced tea his mama made. He pretended to sip the strong brown liquid, and the steaming aroma opened his sinuses.

She took a seat on the step below him, sipped her tea, and looked out yonder in deep thought.

"Anna, sit up here next to me. What are you thinking about?"

"I am thinking of nothing," she said. Feeling her face grow warm, she held her cup with both hands and kept her thoughts. "Why did I allow this American to sit with me?"

She bent over and began drawing little circles on the dirt with her fingertip, and he noticed the part in her hair revealed a very white scalp next to her dark hair.

"Do you think about nothing often?"

"I wipe all thoughts from my mind very often," she said.

"I suppose you never dream either," he said.

She could feel the red spots that covered her neck, and she wanted to jump up and run into the house. Instead, she looked up at the sky and said, "Never have I seen a more beautiful day. Earlier, the clouds looked as if the rains would come again."

"When people in my country have nothing to talk about, they talk about the weather. I didn't know people all over the world talked about the weather like the folk back home."

"Had you rather discuss this useless war that you are taking part in?"

He moved down next to her and said, "I want to forget about the war and talk about you and me."

"I have nothing to say about us," she said. "You must not come here again. Your lustful feelings for me will fade quickly."

"Lust or no lust, I want to kiss you before I die," he said.

She was shocked by his words. "Are you afraid of dying?"

"When I first came here, I was afraid to close my eyes at night, but I have decided that what will be, will be."

His eyes looked honest, and he seemed nice enough, but she had learned from her father that she could not trust Americans.

"Things could be worse. I am sure you will not die in the war. I will say a prayer for you," she said and looked at him with a serious face. "Are you religious?"

"I am a hard shell Baptist," he said.

"Baptist and Methodist think their religion is the only religion in the world," she said. "I am a member of the Catholic church. We confess our sins to the priest."

"I think it's nice to get your sins washed away every week. You don't have any sins to worry about all of the next week."

He saw that she did not like what he had said and tried to smooth his blunder, "The Baptist and Methodist do not forgive one week at a time. You have to be loaded down with sins before they take you serious. All of the sinning you do afterwards is put behind one of the coats in the closet."

"Have you seen the Dalat Cathedral?" she said.

"I haven't seen the Cathedral."

"The Cathedral is beautiful. You must visit when you go back to the city."

"The Catholics might not like for the Baptist to go to their Cathedral."

"They will be happy to see you. My father never went to mass with Mother and me, but she wanted him to go. He is a strong believer in Buddhism," she said. "Have you ever seen a Pagoda?"

"I do not know what you are talking about," he said.

"A Pagoda is a temple made of wood with a slatted roof."

"I have seen pictures of those Chinese buildings with up-turned roofs. Are you Chinese?"

"I came from the Cham Tribe."

"You came from a tribe?" he said. "We used to have Indian Tribes in South Georgia, but most of them left on the Trail of Tears and went to North Georgia. Are you an Indian?"

"I am part Chinese and part Vietnamese," she said.

"What happened to your mother?"

"The Viet Cong burned the Catholic school, and Mother was killed while trying to save her students. They rebuilt the school, and I teach there now. Mother taught me how to teach from a young age. She carried me to school with her every day." She sat silently and twisted her hands with a faraway look in her eyes, and tears ran down her cheeks as she continued, "I remember so well the lessons my mother taught. She wore long dresses that touched the tops of her feet. I can see her slender figure move around the class. I can see the desks, chairs, and books properly placed around the small room."

He put his hand on her knee and said, "Your mother was a good woman, and she gave birth to a beautiful daughter." Then he tried to soften her mood. "I will never forget the first time I saw you. I opened my eyes and I thought an angel stood over me."

"Do you have a girl friend back in Georgia?"

"I have several girl friends, but I have never made a serious commitment to a girl."

She felt a tinge of jealousy hold her heart, but she was thinking that she was foolish to be jealous over a man who she knew nothing about.

"What about you? Do you have a boyfriend?"

"Loyalty to family comes before all things. My father's wishes come first. He never approves of any of the men I choose to date."

"How old are you?"

"I am twenty, and I have already graduated."

"You are old enough to do as you please. Why do you sacrifice your life for your father?"

She lowered her chin and did not speak for minutes.

"Is your father against the Southern cause?"

"He hates the Saigon government for the way they treat the village people. They have suffered since the war started, and they distrust the leaders in the South and the North, as well as the Americans."

"Why do the village people distrust Americans? He said. "We came here to save them from the Viet Cong and the Communist dictator."

"My father would call you a foolish man. He says that our allies are no better than our enemies."

"Is your father a Communist living on southern soil?"

"There are many Communist living in the south, but my father does not advertise his political beliefs. On the other hand, he does not find favor with the South Vietnamese leaders. They have been unfair to the people in the villages."

"Is your father good to you?"

"He gives me all things that I ask for, except love. Once a year, he allows me to go to his beautiful villa on the beach in Saigon. Father entertains friends frequently; full- time maids keep his house, and an excellent chef takes care of the cooking. His chef takes pride in his special dishes."

"What does your father do for a living?"

"He is a shipping magistrate and owns a store on the water front in Dalat. He handles shipments of rice, fertilizer, and tin from Saigon, the Philippines, Taiwan, Hon Kong, China, and other places. He speaks three languages, because he does business with many nationalities, including Americans. He works every day, and he often goes away from home on business."

"I speak English and pig Latin," he said. "I was raised on a farm in South Georgia, and I am a hard working, mannered young man."

She laughed and said, "I suppose you earned the reputation for being a good student, also."

"I made good grades in math, but history was another story."

She placed her hand on his arm and said, "Hard work shows."

He took her hand and said, "I want to kiss you."

"I cannot waste my time thinking about you," she said.

"Why not think about me? You won't find another fellow as nice and good looking as I am. I believe you have been thinking about me since the day you found me in the jungle."

She did not know what to say. Her cheeks flushed and burned her ears. "How do you know what I think? How do you know the feeling I have in my heart? Besides, you are a man, and a man knows nothing about a woman's feelings; a man has an animal nature; he gapes and drools over young, innocent girls as if they were animals going through their first estrus."

"I am not an animal. I am a human being, a red-blooded American male. There is not a man on this earth who would not look at you twice. When I look at you, I get a knot right here," he said, throwing his hand to his chest. "I want you so much that I cannot stand it. Don't you feel something when I touch your hand?" And he reached over and took her hand.

She jerked her hand back and said, "You are despicable."

"Is that a Chinese word? he said. "I do not speak a second language."

"You do not listen to plain English, either," she said. "You must go."

"The expression on your face and the look in your eyes tell me that you want me to stay."

He was right; she did not want him to walk away, but she could not tell him. Her heart thumped in her ears, and a warm feeling churned her stomach. Her eyes captivated him with fiery passion as his lips neared hers. Suddenly the sound of a rumbling motor turned their heads and interrupted their kiss. The driver honked the horn and threw up his hand. On the passenger side, Grandmother held to a bag of groceries that hid her face.

"You must go quickly," she said. "Grandmother returned. The man who drives for her is friendly, but he will not defend you when she gets her stick."

Ernie jumped up and looked for a place to hide; but Grandmother saw him before he could move. He turned to Anna and said, "I will call you later." He ran to the back side of the house and walked behind the huts until he found his trail. Before he got back to camp, the clouds gathered in dark bundles that looked like a huge monster with big ears and a deformed nose. He must find shelter from the threatening storm.

He ran as fast as he could until he reached his camp.

Private Hatcher slapped him on the back and said, "How did things go with the village woman?"

"I am slowly winning her heart; but her grandmother never fails to spoil everything."

"Did you tell her you loved her," Private Hatcher said, and he grinned like the love thing was a big joke.

"I didn't tell Grandmother I loved her?" Ernie said.

"You are totally insane," Private Hatcher said.

Ernie had good reason not to love Grandmother, because at this minute she was spilling the beans to Anna's Father.

Dong Lee called Anna into the living room and closed the door. "Sit down, I want to talk to you," he said.

Before she got seated, her grandmother walked into the room. She sat down and spoke to Dong Lee as if Anna had left the room. "Anna has become impudent and immoral. She has lost all feelings for her own family. She was sitting on the steps with that American soldier. How could she feel no shame for her sins? She no longer acts as a granddaughter of mine."

On the other side of the room, her father added his critical remarks. He had set down his iron clad orders and she had no intensions of obeying him. "Anna, your brain controls everything you achieve and everything you fail. You no longer use your brain, so you have no mind; therefore, you are an idiot."

"How can you call me an idiot; how can you say such cruel things to me?" Anna said.

"How can a daughter of mine lose control of her mind?"

"I have control of my faculties," she said.

"I can see further into the future than you can, and my vision is clearer than yours."

"Seeing things in a different light does not mean that I am crazy or wrong in my thinking."

"Your grandmother told me about the American snooping around here several weeks ago, but I thought he had only come to use the phone; I gave you credit for having a brain at the time. I did not believe that you had invited him here, but your grandmother tells me that he came again today. Did you invite this American to my home?"

"His name is Ernie Tennyson, and I did not invite him here to your home."

"How does this man know you? Where did you meet him? How does he know where you live?"

She could not tell him the truth; she could not tell him a lie. "I was never formally introduced to Mr. Tennyson. He was near the village one day and he saw me walking home from school. He is simply a lonely American soldier who wants and needs a friend."

"He must go elsewhere to find a friend and friendly conversation. Do you understand me?"

"I understand, Father." She walked away from them and went to her room. They wanted to drive her insane. Maybe she was insane, because she could not stop thinking about Ernie Tennyson.

CHAPTER SEVEN

November 1967 came and Doctor Saw Bones had not dismissed Ernie. He still took advantage of his easy duty, driving for Major Maxwell. On Monday, right after lunch, Major Maxwell told Ernie to enjoy the rest of the day, and he went to his quarters.

Ernie snapped his fingers with rhythm and whistled a tune as he walked to find the village school.

Ernie's mind raced with rehearsed lines of what he would say to her. He often thought of things he looked for in the woman he married. She was pretty, sexy, and smart. Although he did not like some of the food on her menu, she cooked some tasty dishes. Three out of four good qualities in a woman passed the test.

As he walked through the jungle alone, he continuously turned his head and watched for the enemy. A squirrel darted around the tree next to the path, and Ernie jumped. The squirrel disappeared, and he walked on.

He came to a footpath and followed it along the banks of the river, where fishing boats rested with nets cast. The soft muddy path bundled around his shoes. When he reached the grassy spots, he rubbed the mud in the grass.

He turned right and walked down a buffalo path lined on each side with pampas grass, bamboo, kudzu, and curlicue vines. Then he spotted hemp plants; he stayed away from drugs that made his head turn with weird thoughts. He needed all the brains he was born with to stay ahead of the game and stay alive.

Suddenly the rush of leaves turned his eyes to a spider monkey peering down at him with the saddest eyes he had ever seen. He had long skinny legs, and the thumb was missing from one of his feet; but his tail was as long as a snake's. Ernie whistled, and the monkey scooted across the limb. Ernie walked on and looked back; the monkey had moved to the top of the tree.

Pretty soon, a bad smell hit his nose. Looking back, he discovered that he had stepped in a clump of skunk weed. The odor smelled worse than a skunk.

At the bottom of the slope, he crossed a brook of water and washed his boots. As he climbed another hill, he saw two women gathering firewood. They filled their basket and walked toward a cluster of huts surrounded by barb wire loosely stretched from post to post. Enemies had clipped the wire in places for entrance, and the hanging wire was ready to grab his legs. He stepped around the wire and walked on. Then a piece of barb wire, hidden by tall grass, grabbed his leg just above his ankle. The sharp prongs felt like giant needles piercing his skin. He yelled some curse words and limped on. He could feel blood running down his leg, but he had nothing to soak up the blood, except his sock. Minutes later the stinging stopped and he forgot about the cut.

He came to a wooden shed where the village people kept their oxen at night and during the rainy season. He had seen oxen in every village, but he had seen no pigs, except wild pigs and boar hogs. He wondered where they got the pork for all of their sweet and sour dishes.

Banana trees with flowers beneath them grew around the yards before the huts. The air filled with smoke from the fire under the black wash pots that steamed with stew. Gongs of rice wine, suspended on nails, hung across the porches; and the bamboo floors shined through the doors of the huts.

Then he came to a hut with a beautiful bed of purple orchids that he could not resist; he picked a small bouquet for Anna. He wished his mother grew orchids like that. Back in Georgia, folk paid a big price for orchids. He knew of no one in Liberty Springs who grew orchids.

He had not gone far before he saw a playground and a long white stone building with high windows across the front. Mulberry trees along the sides of the building made a nice shade. At each end of the building, large banana palms and pineapple trees gave the place a tropical look. A tall pole held a red and yellow flag that waltzed with the breeze next to a narrow walk, edged by pampas grass. The long, wide porch had several wicker chairs on each side of the entrance doors. This school looked more modern than any of the schools he had seen. They built many schools from bamboo and covered them with thatched roofs.

He walked up the steps and moved across the narrow porch to the entrance doors. He entered a large room furnished with an office desk on the right wall and several leather couches with matching armchairs arranged in a circle in the center of the room. Double windows covered with bright green drapes touched green jungle plants at each end.

Ernie noticed that they had decorated the walls in the foyer with political figures. He walked across the cement floor and stood on the colorful Chinese rug to observe the pictures.

Nguyen Van Thieu, President of South Vietnam, was a tall, slender man with dark skin, quick brown eyes, a high forehead, and short, dark hair parted on the left and combed neatly down to the side.

Madam Nguyen Van Thieu hung next to her husband; she appeared to be tall, tan, and slender. Her dark eyes and beautiful face accented by dark hair, parted in the center and combed back in a thick bun, added sophistication to her appearance.

Nguyen Cao Ky, the former prime Minister, and recently elected Vice President of South Vietnam, also appeared to be tall and slender. His dark hair was combed neatly back to reveal a high forehead; He had an oval face with dark brown eyes and thick brows.

Madam Nguyen Cao Ky was framed in gold right next to her husband. She was a tall, slender lady with brown eyes, a full mouth, pretty teeth, and a perfect face framed by dark hair that hugged her shoulders. She had an impressive smile; her appearance made one decide that she was friendly and kind natured.

Dinh Diem, the former ruler of South Vietnam, who was murdered, appeared to be a stocky built man with broad shoulders and muscular arms. His dark, bushy brows shaded black eyes, and his thick hair, the color of coal, was combed back to reveal a distinguished face.

Ernie didn't know the other woman on the wall; he assumed she was Dinh Diem's wife.

He walked down the hall to his right and stopped at each door to read the strange print. At the third door on the left, he peeped through the small window and Anna Ming's beauty stood out in her dark print. After the third knock, the door went back; she looked at him with shock.

"Good morning, Miss Ming." My, you look nice today." He made a big ado over her dress and handed her a cluster of flowers that he had stopped and picked along the way.

She grabbed the orchids and said, "What are you doing here? Sister Theresa will have you arrested, and—"

Before she could finish her sentence, the good sister came walking down the hall, and Ernie offered her his hand as he spoke, "Good Morning, Sister. My name is Ernie Tennyson. I am an American soldier, and I came to speak to your students about the United States of America."

"What a delightful surprise," Sister Theresa said. "If Miss Ming had only told me she expected you, I would have prepared for your visit. You must excuse me. I have another visitor waiting."

"How could you!" Anna said.

"Since I am here, I must keep my promise. If you will kindly introduce me to your class, Miss Ming, I will get started."

He walked into the room behind Anna and giggles sounded around the room. Little round faces framed by dark silk around dark eyes of wonder stared at him.

The classroom was a small square room with white stucco walls decorated with colorful pictures of animals, flowers, trees, and banners stamped with religious statements. She had arranged the students' desks, carved from heavy wood, before the teacher's desk that had been carved from the same tree. A small black chalkboard took the wall behind the teacher's desk. At the back of the room, she had heavy wooden benches on either side of a long wooden table.

Anna walked to the front of the room and announced that a visitor had come to speak to them, and she pointed at Ernie as if he were a freak from the circus. Then she went to the chalkboard and wrote "Welcome Mr. Tennyson."

Ernie thought of a speech in a hurry, and Anna translated his words for those who could not understand English. The students sat with serious expressions and listened to Ernie's story about America. Ernie talked about the American government, the people, jobs, and religion in America. He ended his short speech with "America is a land of golden opportunities. We live in a paradise in comparison to your country. We have a Bill of Rights in America that gives us freedom to worship and speak our mind as long as we do no harm to others. We have excellent schools and good jobs. Almost every family in America owns a car, a television, a computer, and a telephone. Most of the children in America have all of the modern conveniences, but they watch television too much."

Ling Lee, a little girl sitting on the front row, threw up her hand and moved her skinny legs to side of her desk before coming to a stand. With wide eyes of mistrust on Ernie, she said, "Mr. American, I would like to ask you one question?"

"Shoot," Ernie said.

"I do not want to shoot you," she said, looking at him with concern.

"Ask anything you like," Ernie said, trying to hold back his laughter.

"Why did the mean Americans come here to kill us? You killed my family and burned down my hut. Most of the huts in my village burned."

Ernie walked over to her desk and put a hand on her shoulder. "Please believe me, I was not the one who killed your family. The United States sent us American soldiers to your country to help you. We are here to keep the South Vietnam Republic from falling to the Communist in the North. The (NLF) National Liberation Front is helping the Viet Cong destroy your villages in South Vietnam."

"My father does not believe the NLF is Communist," a little boy named Tinton said. "Father says the families, wives, and sons of the NLF are born and raised in our hamlets; they are our neighbors, but we do not know they are NLF members."

"Americans have been told that the NLF was once an ally, but they turned against the leader of South Vietnam. Whose side are they on?" Ernie said.

A little girl named Mien spoke up, "The NLF is on our side."

"The NLF killed your Roman Catholic leader, Diem," Ernie said.

"Diem would not let our family pray to our God," Mien said.

Another little girl said, "My father said that Diem murdered his own people."

Yuan said, "My father did not like Nguye Cao KY."

Kayo said, "My father saw the Americans kill a Buddhist priest, and he said little children got killed, too."

Anna turned to Ernie and said, "The children have heard their parents say bad things about the South Vietnamese rulers, because they would not allow the Buddhist to practice their religious beliefs, rituals, or the celebration of traditional holidays of their ancestors."

Quang threw up his hand and said, "If you Americans did not come to kill us, why did you start dropping bombs?"

"The Communist attacked two of our ships in the Gulf of Tonkin back in 1964; the United States dropped bombs to stop their attacks."

Anna turned to him and spoke with anger, "American ships had no business in North Vietnamese territory."

"I agree with you," Ernie said. "I also believe that bombing North Vietnam afterwards was the wrong thing to do."

Hue, a little boy in the back, stood up and said, "The rice harvest was due when the Americans sprayed the orange poison. We lost our crop and everything we owned. My big brother joined the guerrilla forces after this happened."

Anna gave Hue a stern look, and he sat back down.

"The spray was not poisonous to your crops; the spray killed thick shrubs and vines in the jungle and on the road side, where the Viet Cong hid," Ernie said.

Hun Chu said, "I do not believe you! The spray was poison! We had to burn our rice fields."

Anna said to Ernie, "When the children see an American Soldier, they see orange; Agent Orange destroyed crops and trees; killed livestock, chickens, and pigs; farmers had no money to feed their families through the winter. In addition, the chemicals caused sickness and scars that marked many children for life. Worst yet, the chemical caused pregnant women to have children with deformed limbs, cleft palates, and mental disabilities. Your country's good intentions turned into a terrible disaster."

"I had nothing to do with Agent Orange. I only know what I have been told."

"The children believe what they have been told, also; do not blame them for their bad attitude toward you."

"The Americans threatened my family, and Father had to give them food to leave our village unharmed," Kahn said.

"My father says that the Laos leaders are giving the Viet Cong rice and supplies," Loire said.

Anna spoke up; "Laos is caught up in the middle of the two forces, and their close neighbors, Thailand and Cambodia will not lend a hand to help the Southern cause. In fact, they are giving the Viet Cong rice."

"I am happy that Laos is giving the hungry soldiers rice," Foling said.

A little boy sitting on the front, who had sat quietly through the discussion, came to his feet and said, "My family hides Viet Cong Soldiers from the Demist Police. They have set traps for all of you Americans. We want you Americans to get out of our villages and go to your own land."

The students laughed, and Anna spoke sternly to them in Vietnamese. The room got very quiet. Then she turned to Ernie and said, "These children will say and do anything. They feel as if they have no freedom. For this reason, many of their families work for the Viet Cong and the NLF."

Feeling more unwelcome than when he first arrived, Ernie said, "I have enjoyed being at your school. I wish each and every one of you a brighter future with peace and happiness. Believe me, I want to go home and tend to my own business."

The Children's reaction convinced Ernie that the Vietnamese opposed to all things Americans stood for, and their children believed their parents. Ernie had not been raised in Camelot, but he felt like his culture was of a much higher standard than the culture these children came from.

"Students, let us say our creed for Mr. Tennyson."

The students chanted with the rhythm of a song, "If we cannot live after our own fashion, make our own decision, claim what is rightfully ours, and worship as we please, then we are not living, but merely breathing the air God gives us. We had rather die for freedom than to live in fear."

As the children sang, he was thinking of what they had said. Why did the Americans come to kill their people? He wanted to tell them that the United States provided surplus foods to save the children from starvation, but they did not mention the good that his country did. The government sent them to Vietnam to fight a war and save South Vietnam, but they believed their people died from starvation, because the United States had wiped out the crops on their land.

A bell sounded and Ernie said to himself, "Saved by the bell."

"Students, we will have our break. You know the rules; get into line and march to the playground."

As Anna and Ernie followed the students outside, he said, "You have a much nicer school than schools I have seen in other villages."

"We are lucky to have a nice school. Many of the teachers at the other schools do not have supplies to teach with. Education in Vietnam is not free. Most of the rural villages have private schools; citizens in the villages support our school. Otherwise, these children would get no education."

They followed the children to the playground, and Anna offered Ernie a seat on the green lawn under a pine tree.

The children's laughter sounded around the playground. They moved up and down, back and forth, and around on the see saw, swings, and merry go round.

"The children are having a good time. They seem to have forgotten their worries," he said.

"They are occupied with their play, but they never forget. I never let them out of my sight."

"Why does the North Vietnamese government want to force the South Vietnamese to turn to communism? They should back off and let the south live as they please."

"The North Vietnamese government wants power and control," she said. "Power and control mean money. Over the years, the North grew and flourished, while the South became weaker. The South Vietnamese keeps a leader only a short period of time, because their government has no organization. Many people in the south are against communism; they are also against the anti-Communist beliefs of the French."

He did not give a donut about the French. He knew very little about the Vietnam government. He was interested in getting close to her and he was insane with desire. Just looking at her got him excited in a manly way. She looked incredible sitting there next to him.

She seemed to sense his passion, and she quickly changed his thinking with her words, "I apologize for my students' rude remarks. They have lived in terrible conditions since the war started, and they look for someone to blame. Besides, they hear their parents talk about the weak conditions of the South, and they want to be on the winning side. Since the Americans have not managed to stop the Communist, the students see no need for the war to go on. I agree with my students. Our leaders have failed us, and many of our people are ready to surrender."

"Are you ready to surrender to me?" he said.

"What do you mean by that bold statement?"

"I want you to go out with me. I am asking you for a date."

His nearness lifted her spirit like magic. She would not make after him like a lewd woman, but she wanted to make after him like a lewd woman.

"Since the war started, I seldom go out."

"Can I kiss you?"

She moved over and looked at him with surprise. "Children are all around us and you ask to kiss me. What is wrong with you?"

"Adam's desires are coming out in me," he said.

"Adam was the first man in your Bible," she said.

"How did you know about Adam?" he said.

"I am educated, and I have read extensively."

"I guess you know about Eve, too," he said.

"I vaguely remember reading something about Eve," she said.

"Let me refresh your memory. Eve was the one who made Adam sin in the first place."

"I will not lead you into sin," she said.

Suddenly a loud voice rang across the playground, "American likes Miss Ming," the student said and Anna came to her feet. She walked out to the playground and told them to get quiet. Their laughter ceased and she went back to the shade and sat down.

"The students know the real reason I'm here."

"My students know that I am not allowed to date American men."

"I will buy a black silk suit and wear a Panama hat. Your father would never guess that I am an American soldier."

"I must see about the children," she said, and she quickly walked toward the playground without answering him.

He decided that Anna Ming was a social worker, a counselor, a nurse, and a recreation director all in one. At first sight of her, he knew she was an unusual woman. Then he found out that she had intuitive powers that scared him senseless. This was one of the times.

A sudden outburst of gunfire popped around them, and the children panicked. Anna was near the playground, and Ernie was running toward her to help the frightened children. He shouted for them to get down, and he fell down with them. They crawled for cover behind the school.

Anna shouted, "Go to the tunnel!"

They crowded into the tunnel, and Anna counted heads as she called names, "Quant, Kayo, Kahn, Hue, Mien, Van, Luc, Hun, Ton, Lam, Key, Loire, and Yuan. Where is Zang?"

"I'll go look for him," Ernie said. He turned in a circle with his pistol aimed to fire at the Viet Cong. He side stepped around the building and ran to the playground. He saw Zang's legs sticking out from under the merry go round. Ernie ran to him and swept him into his arms. Back in the tunnel, he examined him from head to toe. He had cut the palm of his right hand and his little finger on the right hand.

The children got hysterical and Anna tried to calm them. "Zang is not hurt. He is just fine."

After Anna got all of the children back into the building, she turned to Ernie and said. "Parents who come here to get their children will inquire about your business at their school. You must leave at once."

Ernie put on his extra set of eyes and set out on the trail through the jungle to his camp. He was afraid to walk the beaten path from the village to his base; he stuck to the jungle trail.

As Ernie walked, he thought about the children. He was thankful the Viet Cong missed their target, and the children got into the tunnel safely. He also thought about Agent Orange and the harm it caused to more than three million Vietnamese people; tens of thousands of acres had been defoliated, including forest and rice fields, but he did not remind Anna of the facts.

He finally reached a familiar sight and walked on toward his base.

The GI's got two free days for Thanksgiving. They had the traditional Thanksgiving dinner: turkey, dressing, cranberry sauce, green garden peas, sweet potatoes, and congealed salad. Ernie did not like sage in dressing, but he covered each bite with a large chunk of cranberry sauce and cleaned his plate.

After dinner, the soldiers relaxed in the barracks, and they had plenty to talk about.

They discussed the Battle of DAK To in the Kontum Province that started in November 1967 and lasted almost three weeks. They bragged about South Vietnam's victory; they complained about the loss of all the American soldiers. They decided that the victory was not worth the death the battle caused. President Johnson tried once again to get North Vietnam to talk peace; however, the North refused his offer.

Another fierce battle they talked about was the Hill Battle 875 between the North Vietnamese and Americans, which involved Charlie and Delta Companies as well as Alpha Company. The Americans finally gained the crest of the hill, but the North Vietnamese had abandoned their position, leaving their dead and their weapons. More than 100 Americans got killed, more than 250 got wounded, and seven went missing.

All of the GI's got tears in their eyes when they heard about the Marine Corp fighter-bomber that dropped two 500-pound bombs on friendly territory. One of the bombs exploded in the exact location where the combined command groups, the wounded, and the medics were located. The explosion killed forty-two Americans and wounded forty-five including a company commander, on-scene commander, captain, and lieutenant. This was one of the worst incidents of the war that had happened since they came to Vietnam.

The soldiers joked and bugged each other about reenlisting when their time was up.

"I can't wait to reenlist," Ernie said with noted sarcasm. "I am so proud to be here fighting for this worthless cause."

Private Wingate said, "I had rather live on the streets or under a bridge in America than fight in this war."

The GI's had heard that Eugene McCarthy was running against Johnson for President of the United States, and their hopes soared. McCarthy wanted to end the Vietnam War and send all American soldiers home. Ernie was already thinking about throwing his hat to the wind and packing his bags.

CHAPTER EIGHT

Doctor Allen, or Old Saw Bones, dismissed Ernie, and he reported for duty. He dreaded the day ahead. In spite of his M16 and grenades, he was scared. He saw no way for the United States to out-smart the Viet Cong. He was more afraid of the Viet Cong than a man-eating wild beast in the jungle. The wild beast usually got out of the way, unless you got in his way first. The Viet Cong jumped from the trees, rushed from the bushes, and fought like wild animals.

They came to a small canal that joined a larger canal. They gathered bamboo poles and tied them together to make a bridge across the canal. Ernie said a prayer before crossing to the other side. He hated the thought of missing a step; if he fell into that canal, he was as good as dead. The Viet Cong hid under the water and stayed under the water for hours; they breathed through reeds they held between their teeth.

When they reached the other side of the canal, they walked more than a mile through the jungle before they came to a clearing and stopped to rest.

Suddenly, a whizzing sound flew over their heads and bullets hit the trees beyond the clearing. The Viet Cong had watched them cross the canal. In a stooped position, they dodged bullets, and moved through the bushes to a thick line of trees. Then they aimed in the direction the bullets came from and fired at back the Viet Cong. The battle went back and forth for several minutes before Sergeant Fitzwater called for backup.

A few minutes later, a United States helicopter with a machine gun on board circled the tops of the trees beyond their station and fired down on the Viet Cong. The Viet Cong quickly backed off and the firing ceased.

Less than an hour had passed before wailing sounds of terror came through the trees. The Viet Cong ran deeper into the jungle. The Americans moved quickly to close in on them, but they disappeared and carried their wounded and dead with them.

After Ernie got back to the base, he took a bath and went to the mess hall with Hatcher to eat supper. While they ate, Ernie told him he was not having much luck with Anna, because her father and grandmother kept close tabs on her.

Once again, Hatcher advised him to find him another girl friend and leave the Vietnamese girl alone, before he got his head blown off.

In spite of Hatcher's warning, Ernie called Anna every night; she always seemed anxious to talk, but her grandmother watched her like a hawk. She told Ernie that her grandmother always asked who was calling, gave her a lecture, and reported every call to her father. She was deathly afraid of him and feared that he would harm Ernie if she continued talking to him. Tonight, her father was in China on business, but she never knew when he would return. Ernie was not anxious to meet Dong Lee; but he was bound to run into the old chap sooner or later, since he planned to go back to Chicken Village very soon.

After Ernie hung up the phone, he went to the recreation center to socialize with his buddies. They all agreed that South Vietnam with their help fought a losing battle; they all agreed that the war got worse with each passing day. The United States sent additional troops to take the place of those killed; Americans dropped more bombs; and more Americans got killed.

Many people in South Vietnam treated Americans as their enemies. They blamed Americans for Agent Orange that killed their crops and their people; yet, the United States provided refugee camps to shelter and feed the homeless.

In Ernie's opinion, the United States fought to liberate the South from the Viet Cong; the Vietcong fought to liberate the south from Americans.

Ernie believed that a person should never interfere with a man's money; a man's woman; a man's religious beliefs; or a man's political beliefs. The United States interfered with at least three of the four, but they thought their interference was for a good cause - to prevent South Vietnam from turning to communism. They poured hard-earned American dollars into Vietnam to save them.

Ernie believed the United States wasted money for the cause. They would never convince the Vietnamese that Democracy was better than Communism; they would never convince the Vietnamese that Christianity was better than Buddhism. If the table turned, the Vietnamese would never convince Americans that their beliefs were better. This war could go on until the end of time; the Vietnamese would never change their beliefs; and Americans would never change their beliefs.

The South Vietnamese realized they fought a losing battle; the North Vietnamese outnumbered them. The North had cornered them and forced them to kill or be killed. Ernie wanted to live and let live; he wanted to go home.

Ernie lay down on his bunk and closed his weary eyes. He knew very little about war and politics. He knew that politics played an important role in war; he knew that war caused death, wounds, sweat, and tears.

The next evening, Ernie told Private Hatcher he was going to see Anna Ming. Hatcher told him once again that he needed to find another girl friend and stay away from Anna Ming, but Ernie paid Hatcher no mind and went to Lat Village.

Anna heard footsteps coming to her door and her heart pounded. She pushed the door back and said, "Hello, I was not expecting your visit."

"Could I come inside and talk to you?"

"We must sit out under the trees. I am watching the village children. Their mothers are cooking a feast for a wedding, and Grandmother went to the market.

The children met him with open arms. He was now a hero in their eyes. They gathered around him with dark brown eyes staring up at him with wonder; they needed love and attention.

Chipper, the monkey, hopped toward them, and Ernie reached out to him with a gentle hand. He remembered Ernie and acted proud to see him. He had never seen a monkey that was as intelligent as Chipper. His actions convinced Ernie that he was part human; he saved Ernie's life, and he would forever be grateful to the monkey.

All of the children in the village liked Chipper and his clown acts. The children made up their own games and songs. With this game, Chipper attracted everyone's attention. The star of the show climbed up on the barrel the children placed in the center of their circle. They slapped sticks together and sang made tunes while Chipper danced on the barrel, clapped his hands, stomped his feet, and made monkey noises. When the children repeated rhymes, Chipper rubbed his eyes and pretended to cry until one of the children petted him.

After Chipper's performance, he got down from the barrel and disappeared. Ernie gathered the children in a circle and told them stories about living in Georgia, and the games he had played as a youngster. Then, he showed them how to play baseball; they loaded the bases and he went to the bench under the shade of the pines to join Anna.

Ernie rested his hands behind his head, and she noticed his muscles swelling around the knit shirt; his good physique impressed her, but she said nothing.

"Anna, tell me how you feel about me. Do you like my company? Do you not want me coming around?"

"I like your company, but you know how my grandmother and father feel about you. If I should start seeing you, they will make my life miserable."

Their eyes met for a second, and she turned away from him. "The children are playing games, but they are also watching us."

"I don't care about the children watching us! If the children were not watching, Grandmother would be watching. I want you to go out with me."

She held her head down, and said, "My father will not allow me to go out with American men."

"He thinks I want you for only my side kick. Do you think I could visit him when he gets home from China and ask his permission to take you on a date?"

"I do not think you want to come to my home and visit. My father would get very angry and he would not listen to anything you have to say."

"What are we going to do about getting together?" he said.

Her lips quivered with her words, "I have thought of you since the day we met; I think about you when I should be teaching the lesson; I think about you as I walk back and forth from the village to the school; I think about you all day long; I am happy that I found you and saved your life, but we can never be together. I am Vietnamese woman; you are an American man."

"I would have never noticed that you are a woman had you not told me," he said. Then he yelled, "You are a woman and I am a man, and we are attracted to each other. You should listen to your heart and not your grandmother or your father. You are making excuses. You could go out with me if you wanted to."

"You must face reality," she said. "You and I come from a different race and different environment. Most important of all, we have differing religious beliefs. Plainly spoken, we come from two different worlds."

"I think you would like my world," he said taking her hand and squeezing it. "If you will promise to go out with me, you will never be sorry."

She jerked her hand from his hold, stood up, and fixed her eyes angrily on his as she spoke, "You must not think of me in that way ever again! We are not right for each other. We can only be friends. You should leave now. Grandmother will be home at any time."

"Do you really want me to go?" he said getting to his feet with a mocking laugh.

"You must not stay," she said.

"What kind of an answer is that?" he said, knowing that he could not walk away without kissing her.

"What I want makes no difference," she said. "I did not mean to lead you on. My grandmother's tongue is very harsh, and my father's temper scares me. I am afraid for you; he is mean when he is angry."

He stepped toward her and she fell into his arms. He held her close and words were not necessary. She wanted him more than anything; she drifted there in a dream for minutes before turning her head to him for a kiss that covered her lips with wonderful warmth that seeped through her and made her knees weak. She clung to him with a feeling she had never experienced.

She finally pulled away from him and stepped back. "The eyes of the entire village are upon us, and they are friendly with my Grandmother."

He let his hands fall to his side and said, "Love is a magical feeling sent down from heaven to worry the hell out of you."

"I have never heard the definition of love before."

"I will be going now."

She did not want him to go. She did not care about her grandmother and her father. She wanted to tell him, but he was already walking away.

"I Guess I will go find Private Hatcher for our daily exercise. Exercise is the only thing I have found that helps me stop thinking. If you ever change your mind and want to see me, here is the number for my barrack." He handed her the piece of paper with his phone number and walked away.

She had never seen a man like Ernie Tennyson. She wondered if he was married. He seemed to know all about love, and that meant that he had been with many women. The thought of his women made her jealous. This American had left her confused and feeling uneasy. Was this the feelings of love?

Her father had chosen a man for her to marry; she was sure she did not love him. On the other hand, she could never love this American, because he was a stranger from a strange land. Her grandmother had told her many stories about how men use and abuse women. She must be on her guard the next time he came around.

On her way to the house, Anna stopped at the rose garden near the porch and picked a rose. She twirled the rose on its stem and slowly plucked one petal at a time as she spoke, "He loves me. He loves me not." She floated on air for moments. Then she quickly threw the rose to the wind and said, "What am I saying? What have I done?"

As soon as Anna came into the house that evening, her grandmother started nagging.

"I saw you sitting on the bench with that American. Do not let this man wheedle you. Use your head and ignore his advances. He tells you things that make you think you are the queen of the village. My, oh me, if you whet his appetite once, he will come back for more. Let the stray go hungry, and be done with him. He probably thinks you are a cheap wench."

"I do not care what you say or what you think, Grandmother. He treats me like a lady should be treated and he is my friend."

"What do you know? One never really knows who their friends are. Your so called friendly feelings are calf's love."

"Grandmother, you often speak of calf love. Can you tell me what you mean by calf love?"

"Calf love is an immature love young children feel for the other before they reach their prime."

"I am not a child, and my prime is well underway."

"I can see that I am wasting my breath."

When Ernie got back to the barracks, he had a letter from his mama. She told him the folk at home were disgusted with the war. She added that her friends and neighbors formed a support group; they met every week to pray for families who had lost loved ones. They also prayed for God to watch over the soldiers still fighting the war and bring them back home in one piece. Last of all, she told him how much she missed him; she was marking days off the calendar for his homecoming.

CHAPTER NINE

Three days passed, and Ernie had not called Anna. She was restless with worry. She was afraid he had found someone else and had given up on her. She had to see him. To avoid her grandmother's questions, she slipped out of the house. The sun shined brightly in the western sky as she walked through the village. The village was quiet after the children and Chipper went to bed. In her fantasy, Ernie walked by her side. Why should her grandmother and father control her life? She wondered what would happen if she flatly refused to obey them. She wanted to see Ernie more than anything. She was tired of dreaming about their being together. She made a circle around the village and came back. She hoped her grandmother had retired for the night, but the minute she walked into the house, she began her questions.

"Where have you been?"

"I went for a walk through the village," she said.

"You have time to piddle around in the village when your old grandmother needs you. I think I caught a spot of cold, and I need medicine."

Anna felt the phone in her hand and her fingers moved like magic as she dialed Ernie's number. The ringing phone was a sound coming from another space in time. When she heard his voice, she was speechless.

Private Hatcher called Ernie to come to the phone, and he must have said hello a dozen times before Anna spoke.

"Ernie, this is Anna. I want to talk."

"I cannot believe you called me," he said.

"I came into town to get Grandmother Medicine; I do not have much time. I am near the post office at a pay phone. Meet me at the Dalat Park in fifteen minutes," she whispered as if someone may hear her speaking to him.

Anna hung up and leaned her head back on the glass. A knock on the phone booth door turned her eyes. A gawky man folded his arms and yelled, "I need to use the phone."

Ernie felt like shouting the good news to Hatcher, but he gave him a lecture each time he mentioned Anna's name. Instead, he found Major Maxwell in the mess hall and asked to borrow his jeep to go to Dalat.

"How long will you be gone?" Major Maxwell said.

"I will be gone no more than two hours, sir."

"This must me an important date," Major Maxwell said as he handed the keys to Ernie.

"Yes sir. Thank you, sir."

Ernie slowed down at the post office, and Anna pulled out behind him. The huge trees shaded a narrow paved road that led to a beautiful blue lake; the lake stretched as far as the eyes would carry. In the background, mountains stood like giants hovering over the lake.

Anna stopped before the lake, and Ernie quickly opened her door. She fell into his arms, and he held her close for minutes before kissing her. "I am so happy to see you." Their faces touched, and he kissed her over and over again.

"I did not want to call you," she said between kisses.

"You don't tell lies either, do you?" he said and pulled her closer.

"It seems cheap for me to have called you."

"You are not cheap," he said. "You are the best thing that ever happened to me." He kissed the tip of her nose. "Let's go to a motel."

"I cannot go to a motel with you!"

Ernie stepped back, walked around in a circle, and pounded his fist to his palm. "Why did you call me? I know you want me!"

"I called you, because I wanted to talk," she said, and she jumped back into her car. She was angry for giving in to her feelings, calling him, and meeting him like this.

He caught the door before it slammed and leaned his head close to hers, which was resting on the steering wheel. "Baby, I'm sorry. I didn't mean to yell, but I've waited so long to see you."

"I am ashamed that I called you," she said.

"I am happy that you called, and I am sorry I pushed you. I want our time together to be good, and I don't want you worrying about what you did afterwards."

"How can I stop the worry?" she said.

"The feelings we have for each other do not come often in a life time," he said.

She lifted her face, looked at him, and said, "What good is the feeling without the wings?"

He kissed her again, and she wanted him more than anything, but she was afraid to give in to her feelings.

"You can take your car back to town, and I'll pick you up." He cupped her face in his hands and kissed her with gentleness that was splendid.

"If you do not want to meet me, I can wait. Tell me what you want to do."

"I want you more than anything," she said.

"Park at the post office, and I will pick you up," he said.

Anna was scared. If she met him in a motel room, shame would gnaw at her worse than her grandmother's nagging; her guilt would make her miserable. On the other hand, if she did not go to him; she would be miserable. Either way, she lost.

When Ernie got to the post office, he pulled over and waited for her, but she kept driving.

Ernie pulled out behind her and watched her turn and go toward Lat Village. He was not at all surprised. She had changed her mind again, but he was convinced that she loved him and would call him again in a few days.

Ernie lay on his bunk and thought about his relationship with Anna. He loved a woman whose beliefs differed from his, and he could never change her. Her father and grandmother worshiped their dead ancestors; gave sacrifices to their spirits; and practiced rituals to protect their newborn children. Worst of all, they believed that heaven and hell were on earth. Ernie thought their beliefs were ridiculous.

On the other hand, his mama was set in her beliefs, and no one could ever change her. She was a hard shell Baptist and she believed a person must be baptized and saved by the grace of God before entering the gates of heaven.

Regardless of his and Anna's relationship, he could never go along with Dong Lee and Lena Ming's beliefs; he could get used to Catholic beliefs. Catholics taught practically the same things that Protestants taught. Both called their beliefs Christianity. He wondered if she could accept his beliefs. The parents taught their children the same morals and religious beliefs that their parents taught them; what parents bred, they fed.

Ernie put his useless thoughts about Anna aside, got his stationary, and wrote his mama. He told her about his activities since he had last written, expressed his concern for her health and welfare, and told her how much he loved and missed her.

CHAPTER TEN

The December wind blew frost on the window panes and roared through the naked limbs on the trees. Mrs. Tennyson stood at the window and looked across the lawn at the bare trees and the tan sod beneath them. She was usually happy at Christmas, but she missed Ernie and had no Christmas spirit. He was somewhere in Vietnam, a country torn apart by war. She worried about Ernie's health; she worried about his being hungry and cold. She turned from the window and the flickering lights on the Christmas tree took her attention. Her daughter, Tracy, would be home for Christmas, and she wanted to see her and her grandchild, but Christmas without Ernie would not be the same. He had always been the life of the party at Christmas. She looked at his picture on the mantle and said to him, "How I wish you could come home where you belong." His blue eyes seemed to brighten with her words. Her imagination had improved since Ernie went away. She turned from his picture and walked to the kitchen.

Ernie longed to be home for Christmas. Being away from home was the worst part of his duty to his country. He stashed his Christmas cards under his bunk mattress and lay back with visions of home. He could see the Christmas tree twinkle shadows on boxes wrapped in pretty paper. He could hear the fire crackle as it blazed with warmth. He remembered church on Christmas Day and the feeling of peace and good will toward men. Most of all, he remembered the family gatherings and good food they always had to eat: the smell of turkey rising from the oven and pecan pie with ice cream for dessert.

His sister, Tracy had sent cookies several times and he was waiting for some in the mail. Tracy encouraged him to be brave, but words on paper did not give him any courage. His mama sent some delicious tea cakes; the cards and letters he got were better than Christmas presents. He looked at the picture of himself before slipping it into the envelope. His face had the look of steel. His dark hair had grown to long stubs on the top and his eyes stood out like bright blue marbles. At least, he had hair on his head in this picture.

Ernie wanted to take Anna out on a date during the Christmas holidays. His time with her had been spent mostly on the phone, and he seldom got to speak to her when he called.

Anna had waited seven days for Ernie's call. When the phone rang, she rushed to answer it, but her grandmother beat her to the pickup. Ernie hung up on Grandmother and waited a few minutes before dialing again.

"Is Miss Ming there?" Ernie asked, trying to sound like a Southern gentleman.

"This is Anna Ming speaking."

"Hello, beautiful, I love that name," he said, "and your voice is sweetest thing I've ever heard."

When she did not reply to his remark, he said, "Anna, are you still there?"

"I am here, and so is Grandmother," she whispered.

"How would you like to go to a movie?"

She wanted to see him more than anything, but fear held her back. In spite of her fear, she said, "Yes."

"I will borrow the lieutenant's jeep. Be ready at 6:30."

"You cannot come to the village. Grandmother asks more questions lately. I will meet you at the rice hut," she whispered.

Her grandmother eyed her like a sly fox. "Who was that?"

"A friend of mine," she said.

He could hear organ music before he got to the porch. He had heard Anna speak about how much her grandmother loved to play the organ and sing. Maybe she was in a good mood. Nonetheless, he was about to enter her territory. He hesitated before knocking on the door. Then he hit the door three times with his fist very hard and very quickly.

Anna came to the door and the look on her face was a mixture of both shock and happiness. She stepped out on the porch and said, "You are insane!"

"I have come to face the music. I am going to talk to Grandmother and tell her that you are going out with me on a date."

"Grandmother will have a nervous monkey."

"If she doesn't agree for you to go out on a date with me, meet me at the bridge beyond the village in fifteen minutes."

Suddenly the organ stopped and he heard her quick, mean steps coming to the door.

"Who is there?" Lena Ming said.

"The American is here, Grandmother."

She poked her gray streaked head out the door and said, "You may come inside to have your say. I do not want the neighbors to hear this."

"Thank you, Mrs. Ming," he said and he walked past Anna to follow the old woman to the living room. She jerked at the sash on her apron and threw the apron on the end table. The anger in her eyes had already told him all he needed to hear. She sat down in her arm chair and rested her hands in her lap. He had his eyes dead on her; she glanced at him and quickly jerked her head back. Her ill will toward him had begun to get on his nerves. She was a cold hearted woman.

"What do you have to say to me," Lena Ming said.

Ernie took a breath and spit out his words." I would like to take your granddaughter to the movie in Dalat. I promise to be a gentleman and have her home by eleven."

"You are an impudent man! I do not like your monkey shine," she said. The brown spots on her hands flashed at him like ugly rocks, and her words bit him like a cold wind. He had no idea what monkey shine meant. He had heard of Georgia Moon Shine, and it did not come from the sky on a dark night. In fact, Moon Shine made everything dark, but he had not touched a drop of whiskey.

"I will not give you permission to take my granddaughter any place. I object to your being in my home."

"I have tried to be a gentleman and do the right thing, but you had rather hear lies." He got up and rushed out without looking back. He drove directly to the bridge to wait for her.

When he saw her walking toward the jeep, he waved to her. White lace fell around her wrist, and a full skirt of bright prints flared over her feet.

He opened the door for her and said, "You are about the prettiest girl in this country, Anna Ming. Did you go to the beauty parlor to get that hair done?"

"I fixed my hair," she said, touching the cascade of dark curls at the nape of her neck. He wanted to take her into his arms and make love to her on the spot. Likewise, the sight of Ernie made a good feeling flood her head and heart.

"I am thrilled to see you, but I am terrified. Grandmother went to bed and I slipped out. If she awakes and finds me gone, she will tell Father, and he will lock me away in my room."

"Forget about Granny Grump and Father tonight. This time belongs to us. If Granny Grump discovers you have sneaked out, she can swing on my words until you get back home."

His sense of humor was simply delightful. He took her hand as he drove, and she wanted him to kiss her again. Ernie parked in an empty business parking lot on Khu Hoa Binh street and they walked down the street toward the theatre. They could hear the Cam Ly Water Fall near the bus station. The Dalat Market stalls spread the smell of pineapples and bananas to the street. As they passed the market, she examined the strawberries, bananas, and apples. She got some apples to take with her, and Ernie thought about his mother's fresh apple tarts. How he missed home and his mama. At the end of the bins, he saw the flowers and bought an orchid. He stuck it in her hair and they walked on to the theatre.

After he bought tickets, popcorn, and cokes, he found seats near the back and they settled for the movie. A romantic scene flashed on the screen and she felt his hand gently moving above her knee. A thrill flashed through her and she felt warm all over. She politely removed his hand to his lap. She was glad there was an armrest between them.

After the movie, they went to the Restaurant at Villa Nine to eat dinner. The restaurant had two levels with long glass windows and a low ceiling. Painted scenes in bright pastel colors stamped the walls, and wooden tables and benches took the floor space. Ernie ordered a bottle of wine before ordering dinner. She quickly ordered sweet and sour chicken, a green salad, and spring rolls. He ordered fried chicken, a baked potato, and a tossed salad with French dressing.

While they waited for dinner, they talked and sipped wine; the waiter brought their food and it was the best thing Ernie had eaten since he came to Vietnam.

"What are you thinking about, Anna Ming?"

"I am thinking of the plans I must make for school next week."

"I do not believe you, Anna Ming. Are you thinking about me?"

"You are really stuck on yourself," she said.

On the way home, he hit the brakes, pulled to the side of the road, and pulled her close. She had no time to protest. She froze in her seat and melted to his embrace. She was crazy for a spell. Then she felt his hand under her blouse, and she said, "We must stop right now," and she moved over to the window.

He pulled away and the drive was quiet. He stopped in front of the house, switched off the jeep and pulled her close. His kiss good night was one to dream on the next week.

"Let me make love to you," he said.

"Two people should love each other before having sex," she said. "Besides, I do not want to have sex in the front seat of this vehicle."

"We could get in the back seat," he said.

"You have some very good jokes under your cap, but I believe a woman and man should make plans to get married before having sex," she said.

"A time of war is no time to talk about marriage," he said. "How in the hell do you think we could get married. Your father would kill me and you would not have a husband. Besides, life is too short to plan for tomorrow and forever. Taking chances is a way of life. Everybody sins and takes chances. You have to gamble to win, and I am playing this game to win."

"You make life sound as if it was a game," she said. "I do not want to play your game."

"You will never win if you don't play the game," he said.

"I have to go inside. Grandmother may be watching."

He walked her to the door and she paused. She wanted him to tell her that he loved her, but he kissed her on the cheek and lifted her chin and said, "I had a wonderful time tonight. I will call you when I get a chance. Good night, Anna Ming. Have a merry Christmas."

He was gone in a flash. She stood and watched the tail lights on the jeep disappear over the hill. Her head was still in a magnificent spin from his kiss.

As Ernie drove back to the base, he discovered Anna had left her apples in the seat. He turned around, went back to Lat Village and put the apples in her mail box; he added a sweet note.

The next morning when Anna went out to get the mail, she found the apples and her note. "Thank you for a wonderful evening. I will think of you until I see you again. You forgot your apples. Ernie Tennyson."

Anna grabbed the bag of apples and walked back up the drive with angry thoughts. "Does he not know how to spell the word love?"

The GI's had the traditional Christmas dinner at the mess and it was nothing to brag about; the Army cooks seemed to get no better with practice. Ernie piled a thick slice of rolled turkey on his plate and topped it with a splash of giblet gravy. He wondered how they made the gravy. The dressing was not so bad when covered thoroughly with gravy and cranberry sauce.

CHAPTER ELEVEN

After Christmas, the soldiers expected to get back on the jungle trail, but they got a nice surprise, a three days pass. Sergeant Fitzwater pulled some strings to get tickets to the Bob Hope Christmas show in Saigon and chartered a bus for the trip. Bob Hope was the best comedian in the world, and one of the most admired men in America. Before President Kennedy died, he had presented the Congressional Metal of Honor to Bob Hope for his good will tours over the world to entertain soldiers.

The soldiers got excited about seeing Bob Hope. They heard that Elvis Presley, Dolly Pardon, the Platters, the Beatles, Helen Redi, Kenny Rogers, Tom Jones, Johnny Mathis, and Elton John would perform in Bob's show. Seeing these stars in the living flesh was a chance of a lifetime.

The soldiers also got excited about going on a tour of Saigon with its fabulous bars, beautiful women, and exotic hotels.

The trip from their base to Tan Son Nhut Air Base, where Bob Hope was to perform, tired them out, but they soon forgot their tiredness and their excitement mounted. After they cleared checkpoint, they passed several bunkers, airfield sheds, and block buildings before reaching the stadium set up for the show.

The men came off the bus, stretched their limbs, and walked to the stadium. The space was longer and wider than a football field and bleachers surrounded the wooden platform where the stars would perform. Straggly trees in the distance offered no shade, and the weather was warm. An hour later, the stadium was packed, and many of the soldiers had to sit on the ground around the entire space.

When Bob Hope came out on stage, the soldiers gave him a standing ovation.

Bob said, "I wish you boys would sit down. I am tired of all of this clapping. Let's get this show on the road."

Everything he said was funny and jokes rolled off his tongue like butter on top of a hot roll.

One of the soldiers shouted, "How do you remember all of those lines?"

"I've been shooting the same lines to women for fifty years. One of my favorite is: I am tired, honey, I have to get some sleep."

Before calling out the stars, Bob told the soldiers how proud America was to have them serving in the military, and thanked them for their service. Then he asked which star they wanted first.

"We want Elvis!" the soldiers shouted, and Bob granted their wish.

Elvis came on stage and the audience went crazy. He shifted the dark hair falling over his brow, pulled the microphone close to his mouth, and spoke in a low, sexy voice, "Thank you, ladies and gentlemen." Then he wiggled his legs, and his black satin coat danced over his tee shirt and shimmered under the lights with diamonds as the most beautiful voice in the world sounded across the stadium with "Heartbreak Hotel."

The audience begged for more; Elvis came back and sang, "Love Me Tender." Afterwards, he got an ovation that the City of Saigon heard, but he left the stage quickly.

When Dolly Pardon came out, the soldiers forgot about Elvis. The whistles, shouts, yells, and fainting acts made Dolly twist in her shoes and laugh. Then Dolly introduced Kenny Rogers and they sang "Islands in the Stream".

Helen Redi sang "Could I have this Dance," and soldiers jumped up on the stage and danced with her.

Tom Jones sang, "Say You'll Stay until Tomorrow," and the audience begged for more.

The Platters got a standing ovation with "Twilight Time."

Johnny Mathis was next with two of America's favorites: "Chances Are and It's not for me to say."

One of the best performances of the night was "A Hard Day's Night," by the Beatles, and they got a standing ovation.

Last, but not least, Elton John and Kinki Dee sang, "Don't go Breaking my Heart."

The show lasted more than two hours and the performers came back on stage two or three times.

When Bob said good-bye, his laughter and funny jokes turned to tears and compassion. He bragged about the bravery of the men for their patriotic duty to the United States of America. He also told the soldiers that they had been the best audience he had ever performed for on tour.

The show ended and the soldiers got on the bus. Less than a half an hour later, lights glittered on Saigon. Traffic in the city was bumper jam with cars, buses, trucks, motorbikes, and bicycles. The crowded sidewalks bustled with people moving in two different directions around stalls, vendors, and stands on wheels that advertised goods for sale. Every now and then, the motor bikes and bicycles left the street and took to the sidewalk to get around the stalled traffic. Small coffee houses with tables near the sidewalk looked inviting, and the garden cafes busily served a line of customers.

Near the center of Saigon, the Rex Hotel, where they would be staying, flashed with colorful light like a circus in the sky. They finally reached the parking lot, reserved for the hotel guest, and walked to the Rex Hotel. They darted traffic when they crossed the street, since some of the cycles moved in different directions, and the other vehicles could make a right turn on the red light.

They checked in and went to their rooms to unpack and take a quick shower before going out to eat. The Rex Hotel rooftop served some of the best food in Saigon. A host met them and directed them to elevators. On the fifth floor, they walked on a carpet of grass across the Rooftop Bar and Restaurant for dinner. Small lights shined on water fountains, huge green bonsai trees, and replicas of pagodas, temples, and sculptures of famous people. Last, but not least, the Rex

Elephant and rotating golden crown took special places on the roof. After they all got seated, a waiter came and took their orders. Most of the soldiers ordered the sea food platter, with all the trimmings, and tea to drink. The view of the city was spectacular with every street and building in the spotlight under the stars.

After dinner, they visited the Roof top Beer Garden. The huge circular bar had a large round table in the center of its circle. They displayed drinks of every kind, color, and description around the entire circle. A man at the circular bar took orders for drinks. The soldiers all ordered a drink, and a Vietnamese singer entertained them. They relaxed and enjoyed the view of the city before returning to their rooms. On the way back to the elevator, they spotted the swimming pool on the roof, but their tired bodies needed rest, and they went to bed as soon as they got back to their rooms.

The next morning, they went to the Rex Hotel breakfast bar on the roof top. First of all, they ordered coffee, and went back for a second cup. Vietnam lived up to its reputation for having the best coffee in Asia. Next, they filled their plates with eggs, bacon, rice, and toast, a variety of fruit, yogurt, and country bread.

After breakfast, they went on a sight-seeing tour of the city to get a taste of Vietnam's history and culture. First, they visited the beautiful French designed Notre Dame Cathedral in the center of Saigon, which was built of stone and overlaid with bricks. The beautiful stained glass windows, framed in an arch, added to the beauty of the Cathedral, and the magnificent bell towers standing 190 feet on top of the Cathedral took their attention. The inside of the Cathedral was extravagant with its arched ceiling, padded pews, and altar. Before moving on, they got a close up view of the white granite statue of the Virgin Mary in front of the Cathedral.

Next, they went to the Museum of Vietnamese History with its collection of antiques and historical material. After they left the museum, they visited Vietnam's Reunification Palace or Presidential Palace; the Memorial Temple for Heroes; and several pagodas, where the Buddhist worshiped.

Last, but not least, they visited the Saigon Opera House. The Opera House was one of the most beautiful French Colonial architectural designed buildings in Saigon. The Angel on each side of the sculptured work of art gave a feeling of holiness. Huge columns of etched stone supported the roof, and wide cement steps led to an entrance that was like an exotic tunnel in the open. The golden gates before the entrance made Ernie think of heaven and the saints. Dismissing the fantasy and facing the facts: during the Vietnam War, the Opera House seated 800 South Vietnamese politicians in the Lower House assembly.

Afterward, the tour driver took them to Cholon, or Big Market, located on the banks of the Saigon River. As they rode, the soldiers talked about the rumors that had spread about American soldiers, who had deserted the army. Many believed these deserters went to Cholon and ran a black market trade with stolen goods taken from the United States Military.

They got off the bus and went on a walking tour of Cholon. The influence of Chinese culture and history was evident at the sight of the Quant Am Pagoda with its wedge roof pointing upward and its colorful columns engraved with Chinese enigma. They passed several other Pagodas and colorful buildings with arched doors; they had very few windows.

They moved on through the Chinese section to the Ben Thanh Market and on to Minh Mang in Cholon. An old man was sitting on the street with a dirty blanket wrapped around him, and the weather was warm. He did not move, blink, or make a sound as they passed. Just ahead, they saw another man with a long gray beard; he leaned heavily on his cane as he moved slowly down the street. He looked as if he needed a good meal and a good bath. A dog got off his honkers and licked the old man's feet; he lashed out at the dog.

After a tour of Minh Mang, they got back on the bus and the driver carried them back to the Rex Hotel. They passed the Continental Palace, a large, square, three stories hotel with a flat roof overhanging the ground floor. Arched windows, for each room, and a patio, protected by iron rails, stretched across the entire length of the hotel.

The sergeant carried them to the Saigon Club for lunch. Trees surrounded a large brick courtyard and sidewalks led to three entrances. Green ferns draped cement vases sitting next to white columns on each side of steps. On each side of the entrance, palm plants brushed a stone floor. As they entered the reception area, statues of animals greeted them, and jungle plants waved in the breeze of a stirring ceiling fan. The large dining room had only a few tables that had not been taken. Each table was covered with white linen and centered with a candle. Men dressed in white suits and straw hats, sat next to their women, dressed in bright colors.

The GI's ordered the Chinese special; they had a choice of meat served with vegetables, vermicelli soup, and spring rolls. They also had a choice of different kinds of wine to drink. The club was almost like a restaurant at home, except they served white and red wine, rice wine, and vodka.

Back at the Rex Hotel, they showered, got dressed, and left the hotel in groups for a night on the town. Ernie's group wanted to rent bicycles, but bicycles left unattended quickly disappeared. Horse carts, cycles, and three wheeled taxis crowded the streets. Peddlers tried to make a sale, and beggars rattled a tin can for a dime. The sergeant ordered them to stay clear of the pushers with monkey powder and other drugs.

They also avoided eating joints called holes in the walls. These places had a reputation for placing containers of food, cooking utensils, and eating utensils on the floor, where they washed dishes. On the other hand, these eating joints had the reputation for serving good, nutritious food.

They checked out the garden cafes and moved on past the dark alleys, and discos. The Ho Chi Minh City nightclub had disco dancing, and the music was loud enough for a street audience.

In front of the Hard Rock Cafe, the GI's whistled at a pretty Vietnamese girl. She was wearing a bright skirt and a low cut halter top. As she crossed the street, the wind whipped her long, dark hair, and her skirt flew up revealing her skinny legs. She caught her skirt, looked back to see if the soldiers had seen her legs, and quickly moved on across the street.

They went into the Hard Rock Café to order an American burger and fries. The friendly waitresses made them feel welcome, and the live band was worth listening to. After eating, they checked out the Rock Shop to get a souvenir to take back with them.

Then one group of soldiers went to the Go2 Bar, famous for drinks, music, and dancing. Ernie and six other friends went to check out the Apocalypse on Thi Sach Street. They had heard that the Apocalypse had exotic dancers and stayed open later. The bar was packed with people, but they finally got a table. They had already eaten, but the food smelled delicious. The music and beautiful dancers told them right away that they chose the right spot for entertainment.

Before Ernie finished his first beer, one of the dancers came over to the table to flirt. Private Hatcher teased the jeweled gold bands on her arms that sparkled under the colored lights. Her jet black hair fell around a pretty face with smooth dark skin, accented by dark eyes. She wore a bright green gown that revealed every curve of her body. She stood before them and smiled as she pulled a string on the gown. Ernie and Private Hatcher watched with fascination as the gown dropped around her feet, revealing a body suit that left very little to the imagination. She began moving her hips and hands to the music; the soldiers asked for more.

Five drinks later, the dancer invited Ernie and his friends to a party at her home. Like most drunk fools will do, six soldiers took her up on the invitation. Ernie stuck close by Private Hatcher as they followed her inside her front door. When they all got inside, they saw more women than men. Ernie didn't come for an orgy; he wanted a place to sleep. He sat down on a soft couch and paid little mind to the strip tease performance of the dancer standing before him. He drifted in the twilight zone; Hatcher and Wingate's laughter floated around his ear. A light from the television outlined a provocative, nude body making sexy movements. She pulled at his arm, and he struggled to stand before staggering behind her down a narrow hallway. A bright light hit his eyes, and he fell on the bed next to her. She immediately cuddled close to him; he could feel her nakedness. He squirmed from her side and got up to make his way back down the narrow hall. Back in the room with the couch, he fell back down for a good night's rest. His head turned and he could not focus. She had put drugs in his drink. He heard the flip of a switch, and a dim light threw shadows around the room and outlined her nakedness. He sat and watched her with blurred vision in his drunken stupor. He lay back and closed his eyes to rest, but she sat down on his lap; her fingers teased his ears, neck, and face before she plastered him with a kiss. Then he felt her hands move to private places, and he wanted to scream, "Stop!" He was too horny to resist the pleasure. She was a prostitute and he had no money to waste, but he had lost control of his good mind. He had not intended to go to bed with this whore; but she had pushed the goods his way, and he had taken her up on her offer. Some pimp was probably getting rich by sending her customers every night. He had nothing against prostitutes, but he had no respect for them. Worst of all, he was afraid of getting a disease. What could he do? She was a wild tiger; she had met her mate for the orgy; she was a fire cracker with a short fuse about to explode, and she took him down in the explosion.

After all was said and done, he wanted to sleep, and he did not remember the rest of the night.

The next morning, Ernie opened his eyes and there next to the couch stood a beautiful woman with a figure like Miss World. She had her hair covered with a black silk scarf studded with sparking stones. The scarf fell around her shoulders and shined with glints of red. She raised her brow with concern and said, "Did you sleep well?"

"Hell, I don't know if I slept or passed out. Who are you?" he said.

"Do not tell me that you do not remember last night," she said.

"You must be the dancer," he said with flashes of her image coming back to him.

"I am Laquan Chan," she said.

"That is an unusual name, Miss. I am glad to know you," he said.

She shifted her eyes with curiosity and walked with straight shoulders to the chair across the room. Sitting with poise, she moved her hands as she spoke. Her voice had the rhythm of a song, but she was not singing. She was quoting lines of poetry that he did not understand. Then she stood with a sexy pose and stared at him. She could not believe how handsome this man was. The dark hair covering his chest and arms turned her on.

"Ernie returned her stare with a confused look."

"Did you say your name is Laquan?"

"Laquan," she said with a big smile. "I am looking forward to going to America with you."

Ernie jumped up, pulled up his pants, and looked around the room for his shoes. "I have to go," he said. "I have to find my platoon. They are in Saigon some place."

"Are you not going to take me with you?"

"Hell no, you can't go with me. I am in the United States Army. There is a war going on out there," he said, wondering what she had on her stupid mind. He found his shoes, rammed his feet in and did not bother tying the laces. At the door, he said, "I had a good time, Miss. I hate to rush off, but we are due back at our base this afternoon before five," and he looked at his watch.

She ran across the room and grabbed him in a tight hug. "I want to go with you. Please take me with you," and she kissed him again in the mouth.

Ernie squirmed from her embrace; he wanted to wipe his mouth. He was forever getting himself into cracks; this time, the crack had swallowed him. What was going on in this woman's head? She was a loony tune if she thought she was going with him. He had to run to get away from her; he had his hand on the door knob, but she was still talking about last night.

Looking down with embarrassment, he said, "I was drunk last night. I do not remember coming here." He wondered if she wanted money. Turning back to her, he said, "I am sorry I got drunk last night. We probably had a night to remember."

She walked over to the door, put her arms around his waist, pressed her body close, and whispered,"If you will take me with you, you will enjoy my company."

Considering her proposal with disgust, Ernie said, "You do not seem to understand, Miss Laquan. I am in the United States Army, and I have to get back to my base right away."

"Wait! I am going with you," she said "We can live on your base."

Ernie put up his hand and said, "No, you are not allowed to go on my base."

"You used me and threw me to the dogs," she said and tears rolled down her face.

"Listen, Miss Laquan, I met you at a bar; I got drunk; I wanted to have fun; I thought you wanted to have fun, too. Besides, I have a girl friend in Dalat."

She clasped her hands to her chin, and said, "You told me you loved me last night." Then she grabbed him in a tight hug. "I want to go with you. Please take me with you."

"Hell, I can't take you with me," he said, pulling away from her embrace. "Listen, I am walking out that door, and I am not turning back. You need to get your head straight."

"You cannot leave me! You and I got married last night," she said.

"Lady, you have lost your mind. I was drunk, but not that drunk!" He ran out the door with his shirt swinging in his hand. He looked north and south. He was on the outskirts of Saigon, but he didn't know where his hotel was located.

As he searched for the Rex Hotel, his mind was on that crazy girl who claimed he had married her. He wanted to get out of Saigon as quickly as possible; he prayed that he never laid eyes on that woman again. He took notice of every street, building, stop sign, and red light. Then he saw a large sign in the clouds and walked toward the Rex Hotel.

When he walked into the room, he shouted at Hatcher, "Why in the hell did you leave me?"

"That dancer had your undivided attention, so I got lost with a woman of my own," Private Hatcher said.

"You should have never left me alone with that woman," Ernie said.

"What happened?"

"That crazy woman said I married her last night. She wanted to go back to the base with me!" Can you believe that bull? I didn't tell her my name or the name of my base. What will I do if she follows us? Should I tell the sergeant?"

"Keep your mouth shut! What went on in Saigon stays in Saigon."

"I hope to hell Laquan Chan stays in Saigon," Ernie said. "If Anna ever finds out that I slept with a prostitute, she will never look at me again."

"Anna will never know about last night, unless you are crazy enough to tell her."

"I wouldn't tell my dog about last night," Ernie said.

Hatcher laughed and said, "All of us had whore women last night, so we can't say anything bad about you."

Ernie got busy packing his bag and was ready to go back to Dalat. They all left their rooms and met in the lobby at the same time to walk to the bus.

CHAPTER TWELVE

On the last day of January, the people in Vietnam celebrated TET, a religious, cultural, and national celebration that was the most important event of the year to welcome the arrival of spring with hopes for a better year.

The American generals were not worried about an attack during the celebration, since the North and South had agreed to cease fighting during the TET holiday.

The people in Vietnam went all out for TET. They decorated the cities, villages, and homes with bright colors; they wrote slogans that told different things about the celebration; they sent out greeting cards to their friends and families; last, but not least, they celebrated with their friends and families with games, music, dancing, and a big feast cooked and eaten outdoors.

The city of Dalat flamed with decorations, blossoms, kumquat trees, and flags. A huge banner stretched across the street with large print: "WELCOME TO THE NEW YEAR OF THE DRAGON LUNAR YEAR." People crowded the streets in Dalat. They had decorated the floats with thousands of colorful flowers that looked like the scene on the cover of a magazine as the floats moved slowly down the street. The people on the floats wore masks; the dancers wore suits that disguised them as part lion and part dragon, the symbols of strength to scare away evil spirits. They also shot firecrackers, beat drums, struck bells and gongs to ward off evil spirits. The noise could be heard a mile away. The Lion Dancers rushed out with graceful movements. Then they stomped their feet, leapt, bent their bodies, jumped and whooped.

Ernie said, "I have never seen anyone dance like that."

"They are dancing to ward off evil spirits," Private Wingate said.

"Where are all of these evil spirits coming from?" Private Hatcher asked.

"Don't ask me?" Private Wingate said.

Ernie, Hatcher, and Wingate walked by the crafts and arts display booths and stopped before a tall bamboo pole. Clay gongs decorated with gold paper ingots swung around the top of the pole. They had drawn a bow and arrow with white powder on the ground. Private Wingate explained that the bow and arrow drove away evil spirits, also.

Private Hatcher said, "Thank God for the pole. The Viet Cong are sure to stay away today."

After the parade was over, families and friends from Lat Village had a feast to celebrate the New Year. The sun sparkled with warm rays from a deep blue sky making it a glorious day for a feast. By noon, the village people from the surrounding hamlets began gathering for the feast.

Ernie and his buddies had heard about the big celebration taking place near Chicken Village. They did not have an invitation, but Anna Ming was sure to be there and this was Ernie's chance to see her. Private Hatcher and Private Wingate got excited about the celebration, also. They told Ernie that they did not need an invitation, since many soldiers attended parties held for high-ranking officers without an invitation.

Tables, covered with red linen cloths, sat on a hill of green carpet with paths leading to a pine forest. The women busily stirred big pots steaming with banh Chung, banh day, bamboo soup, and sticky rice. The food spread a delicious smell around the area. After they finished cooking and serving, they joined their men to celebrate. A group of older men reserved a quiet corner behind the tables, where they sat and played a game of elephant chess. The children on the grounds played games, danced, and shot firecrackers. The elderly handed out money to the younger children.

"Looks like everybody from Chicken Village is here," Private Hatcher said.

"I wonder why Anna is not here," Ernie said.

"Look at that," Private Wingate said, pointing out a man dressed in a black silk shirts and black pants with a wide belt and a silver buckle. "He is a bandit."

"Whose side is he on?" Ernie asked.

"He does not have a side; he is on his own side. He is a member of the KKK, a group of thieves who are marked by their black dress."

"Why don't the village people run him off?" Private Hatcher asked.

"He befriends his foes to their faces, and the village people trust him."

The sound of guitars blended with sweet voices and sang popular Vietnamese songs; spectators snapped their fingers and tapped their toes to the sound. Men, dressed in bright ao ba ba, tipped their felt hats to women and asked them to dance. The women dressed in the traditional Ago Dai, but the young girls wore bright new dresses, and the boys wore new, black pants, and colorful shirts, a custom of the occasion.

The women crowded the tables with foods that Americans had never heard of. Wingate, Hatcher, and Ernie fell in line behind the older men and children to fill their plates. Ernie watched Hatcher and Wingate dip food without hesitation; but Ernie got a good look at every pot before dipping. He had learned his lesson in the rice hut, and he had no desire to taste skunk, cobra, bat, steamed armadillo, or duck eggs that the Vietnamese enjoyed.

Private Wingate said, "Look! Roasted frog in gravy," and he dipped a big helping.

Ernie wanted to croak. He liked deer meat, chicken, pork, and beef. He passed up the Chao, and rice porridge, but Private Wingate and Private Hatcher tried all of the strange dishes. Ernie studied the platter of Banh, which looked like an American omelet. He took a small helping and moved on to the rice, pork, and bean sprouts, which always burst with a delicious flavor. Then he spotted the pickled onions and took several rings. He topped his plate with a Cha Gio, Viet spring roll, and walked to the end table that was set with plastic jugs of tea, Bi Hoi (beer) and

Ruou Gao (rice whiskey). They set a tub of ice and mugs next to the other drinks. Beer on ice was not one of his favorite drinks, but he filled his mug to the brim and walked to a distant table where Wingate and Hatcher sat.

Private Hatcher said, "The polka passed and the square dance is on, where oh where has your lover gone?"

Private Wingate joined him in laughter. Ernie ignored them and began tasting the variety of foods on his plate. The food was spicy and made his tongue draw up in a curl. They used something stronger than lemon juice to season the food. As he ate, he eyed the shoofly pie, which was not his favorite dessert. Every time he cut into the brown sugar and molasses, he looked for a fly.

"Did you get a helping of that fat scut?" Private Wingate said.

"Don't care for scut," Private Hatcher said.

Some of the GI's called the rabbit a scut. What a funny name for a rabbit.

Minutes later, Ernie saw her walking toward the tables. He set his plate down and said, "There she is. I will see you boys later." He got up and walked to the end of the table where she stood.

She walked toward him with the grace of a ballerina, and she looked like a bride on the cover of a magazine. Her hair was a cape of rich mink falling down her back. She had hats of many colors, and the hat she wore always matched her dress. Her dress was made of pink silk roses embossed on white satin under a long flowing smock that flared around her ankles with the rhythm of music.

"Hello, Anna Ming," Ernie said as he took a bow.

She widened her eyes with surprise and said, "What are you doing here! Are you crazy! My grandmother is here, and she tells my father everything."

"Please forget Granny Grump and Father today. We are here to have a good time."

"Get lost Ernie Tennyson!"

"Let's get lost together," he said.

"I will not!" she said and turned to walk away.

He grabbed her arm and said, "Come with me. I have some friends I want you to meet."

He practically dragged her to the table where Private Wingate and Private Hatcher sat. As he introduced her to his comrades, he could tell that her beauty impressed them.

"I am very pleased to meet you," she said, and she looked back to search for her grandmother. "Grandmother sees me. She is coming this way."

"Let her come," Ernie said, and he met the old woman with open arms. Mrs. Ming was so embarrassed that she forgot what she was about to say. She tugged on Anna's sleeve and whispered something into her ear.

"What did she say?" Ernie asked.

"She wants to know what you are doing here."

"Tell her I came to see you, and I am not going away."

Anna looked from the old woman to him and moved her mouth without the sound, "Are you crazy?"

"I never could read lips," he said, and Private Hatcher and Private Wingate held their laughter.

The old woman stood back and spoke in Vietnamese.

"If she is inviting us to dinner, tell her that we already have our plate, thank you."

"She told me to ask you to leave."

"She is always asking me to leave, and I will not leave today. Do you understand?"

The old woman threw up her hands and started to walk back to the crowd.

"See, Granny is not a big green monster like all of you thought she was."

Mrs. Ming turned on her heels and pointed her finger at Ernie as she spoke, "I am not a big green monster; you are the big green monster!"

Hatcher and Wingate held their sides with laughter.

Ernie said, "You told me your grandmother could not hear well. She hears as good as I do."

"She is wearing her hearing aid," Anna said. "When I get home, she will have more to say than I wish to hear."

"If you don't come to our table to eat, I will make a big scene," Ernie said.

"Get your plate and come sit with us, "Private Wingate said.

In spite of her grandmother's anger, Anna fixed her plate and went back to their table to enjoy her dinner.

Private Wingate and Private Hatcher kept her busy answering questions about the food.

"You should try Nuoc Mam," she said.

"No thank you," Private Hatcher said. I do not like the smell of fermented fish."

"Fermented fish?" Ernie said. He had eaten Nuoc Mam sauce in the rice hut, but he didn't know it was made from rotten fish.

Ernie finally convinced Anna to dance and pulled her away from his friends. She took his hand and moved her feet with his in perfect time to the music. He had not stepped on her toes a time. She was accustomed to the jumping, skipping, and twisting dance steps, but she had never done the square dance before. After the first swing your partner, she was lost. Then the band played a slow Vietnamese love song, and he pulled her close. Their bodies swayed to the music and that wonderful romantic feeling set them apart from the world. Her heart quickened and the feeling of love made her dizzy. She completely forgot about her grandmother and the other peering eyes around them. A decade must have passed since she had felt so near heaven. She closed her eyes, rested her head on his shoulder, and hummed with the music.

The good feeling hit Ernie, too. Holding her close helped the dream he had of being in bed with her. He could feel her body pulsing with desire, and he was so aroused and so crazy that he thought he would seduce her right there.

"Let's go some place where we can talk," he said. She turned her face, and the feel of her lips brushing his cheek drove him mad. He took her hand and led her to the old wooden bench hidden behind a pine tree.

Just as they got to the tree, he pulled her to him and kissed her. A delightful weakness dazzled her; she returned his kiss with an eager longing that promised him the world and gave away all feelings she had denied.

He was feeling a little crazy himself. He held her tighter, and his lips became frantic for hers again. Because he wanted her so much, he could not pull away.

She finally pushed him back and sat down on the bench. He waited for her eyes to meet his with favor, but she turned away from him as if she felt ashamed.

"Ummm that sugar was good," he said and pulled her close again. "Let's sneak away from this place," he said. "We could walk down in the forest."

"I cannot sneak away with you," she said. "Besides, the Viet Cong hiding in the jungle might blow our heads off." She buried her face in her hands.

"Are you crying?" he said and put his arm around her.

"Why did you kiss me?" she said. She must explain to him the customs of her country; she must tell him that men and women should never hold hands in public. He had broken all the rules by kissing her in public.

"If these folk have never kissed before, they don't know what they are missing," he said, "Like I said, that kiss was umm, umm good."

She blushed, but she was thinking about what it would be like to be in bed with him. She wanted to feel his hands moving over her nakedness; she wanted to stay with him forever. Contrary to her wishes, she jumped up and said, "I must go back and show my face in the crowd. I have earned a bad reputation. You have not asked my father's permission to go out on a date with me. The entire village is staring at this tree that hides us. They will brand me as easy."

He laughed and pulled out a Johnny Walker 555 cigarette. "Care for a smoke?"

"No, thank you."

He rested his hands above her head against the tree and said, "Do you mean to tell me that your father must give me permission to kiss you?" He quickly bent over and covered her mouth with another delightful kiss. Then he cupped her chin in his hands and said, "I want to be alone with you. Will you meet me tonight at the bridge beyond the village?"

"I must be with my family the next three days. We will leave tonight and return to my grandfather's home in China. We will go to the Pagoda, pray, and worship at the family altar; My father will light incense on the altar in memory of my mother and my ancestors before her. Afterward, we shall eat the food previously offered to the spirits of the dead. Then we will visit the graves of our ancestors and clean their graves. Afterward, we will exchange gifts and visit other relatives and friends. Last, but not least, we will pay kowtow to Grandpa; kneel down to him, the highest honor of respect one can show to his elders."

"You tell the grand old chump that you have met this handsome American, and I want him to give us his blessings. If I have a good week, I will give all the credit to Grandpa's spirit."

"My grandfather is not dead. He lives in China," she said. "You must never make fun of the spirits."

"I don't believe in dead spirits," he said. "What can a spirit do? A spirit is like a ghost. Have any of your dead ancestors ever moved their lips or lifted a finger to help you? Have any of those spirits ever grabbed the food you offer them; do they gobble the food down as a living human being?"

"I still live under my father's roof; I must take part in his rituals."

"Is your grandmother divorced from your grandfather?"

"They are not divorced; they do not believe in divorce. However, they are much happier when they do not see each other often."

"I can understand your grandfather's thinking," he said. "When will you return from China?"

"We will have our last meal on the third day of TET and stay up for the arrival of the New Year. After we say farewell to the spirits of our ancestors and burn paper offerings, we shall do good deeds for others and come back home."

"This TET celebration is unbelievable," he said. "Why is New Years Day in Vietnam so important?"

"We celebrate the coming of a new year, which some call a spring festival. Sometimes, such as today, uninvited soldiers come to our celebration."

"Are you saying that we are not wanted here at your celebration?"

"You came without an invitation," she said.

"You did not answer my question."

She ignored his question and said, "I must go now."

"Wait, do you have leap year on your calendar?"

"One whole month is added to the Chinese calendar for Leap Year. Why do you ask simple questions?"

"In America, the woman can rightfully propose marriage to a man on Leap Year."

She blushed and said, "I would never ask a man to marry me. My ancestors would curse the vows I made."

"I do not believe your ancestors' curse could bring you bad luck," he said and kissed her hand.

The warmth of his lips on her hand made her head spin with excitement. Then he kissed her neck, pulled her close, and said, "Let's go to a motel."

"Have you lost your mind?" she said and quickly walked away from him. As she walked toward the village, her anger gave her nervous energy, and her heart hammered like a drum in her ears.

Anna got back to the village before her grandmother, and she was thankful for that. She wanted to be alone and prayed that her grandmother would stay at the celebration the rest of the day.

When she got to her bedroom, she locked the door and kicked off her shoes. Then she lay down, covered her face with her pillow, and cried. She was in love with this American and she could not see him; she could never be with him; she could do nothing about her feelings. She felt happiness; yet, fear took her.

When Anna's grandmother came home, she was huffy. She pulled off her conical hat, threw it on the hall tree, and called out to Anna, "Granddaughter, come here this minute! I have some words to say to you!"

Anna came and stood before her. "What did you wish to say to me, Grandmother?"

Before settling in her rocker, she picked up her snuff stick and stuck it in her mouth to wet it properly before dipping the stick in the snuff to coat the ragged end.

Then she sat down with a heavy body and took a deep breath of disgust as she picked up a piece of printed cloth and her small sewing kit. "I am tired of wasting my breath. You are too stubborn to listen to words of wisdom. Why did you invite that American to the TET Celebration?"

"Grandmother, I did not invite Ernie to celebrate TET. He and the other soldiers came on their own free will."

"They had no business being there! I saw you dancing with Mr. Tennyson, and I saw you saunter down the path with him." As Lena Ming spoke, she jerked the bright silk print around in her lap and positioned her scissors with anger. "Who does this American think he is? He ruined your reputation!"

"Grandmother, I have done no wrong."

"You have done much that is wrong. The entire village saw you disappear into the woods with him."

"We did not disappear! We merely walked a few yards away."

Lena Ming held the bright print up and said, "This cloth is one yard!" She snatched the cloth to her lap, grabbed up her scissors and began slicing the edges of the cloth.

"I saw no harm in having friendly conversation with Mr. Tennyson or the other soldiers, for that matter."

"I know about that American."

"You know very little about Ernie," Anna said. "You jump to conclusions."

"My conclusion was easily reached; this American probably has a wife in America."

Anna felt a painful lump in her throat, and her heart beat in her ears.

"You cannot see at all! You are blind! I do not believe you had only a friendly conversation, either. My eyes still see very well. You are drawn to this young man like a plant to the sun's rays, and you had best turn yourself around in the opposite direction before he bends you to his liking."

"Grandmother, why do you nag about the men I choose to keep company with? I am old enough to make my own decisions."

"You have listened to his soft soap until you have gone soft in your head," she said. "How could you believe his lies? Would you entertain a man for a song and dance?"

"Grandmother, how could you say such a thing?"

"You are no school girl. You must know that you are making a fool of yourself. We will be the laughing stock of the village. Gossip spreads quickly throughout the village; Whispers fly about Anna Ming and the American she entertains. The village women saw the American kissing my granddaughter, and gossip turns to big lies. I am outraged! I am ashamed to walk through the village and visit my neighbors. If you do not know any better than to keep company with an American soldier, then you must have help with making your decisions. I will speak to your father when he comes home. He will put a stop to your foolishness!"

As she folded the edges of the printed cloth and began hemming, she continued flapping her tongue. She raved about Anna's improper conduct and her morals. One would think that the dreadful war would put a damper on gossip, but one would be wrong to think so.

Disgusted with her lecture, Anna said, "I think I shall go to my room, Grandmother. I will speak to you when you lose your anger."

"I will never lose my anger."

"Then I will never speak to you again," Anna said, and she turned quickly and walked toward her bedroom.

Anna had tried to hide her feeling for Ernie, but she could not forget him. She had never felt the love in her heart for another man that she felt for Ernie. She also liked Ernie's bold and brave nature; but he was kind with his boldness, and he did not easily lose his temper. She had never seen him angry, and he was a natural comedian at times. More than likely, he told white lies, but his lies made her happy. She was afraid her weak submissive nature would soon give way to his desire to have sex; she must not let things go too far before he promised marriage.

Ernie's religious beliefs differed from hers, and his culture differed from hers; he knew very little about her country, but many people, who differed in their beliefs and came from different cultures, loved each other. Her mother believed in the Catholic teachings; her father believed in the Buddhist teachings.

She walked to the window and looked out on the night sky dancing with glittering stars. Everything she looked upon was beautiful. Tonight she could probably see the man in the moon. She prayed many times to meet a man such as Ernie, and her dream came true. She loved Ernie; he had taken her head and heart. All of her father's money meant nothing to her without Ernie.

She walked back across the room with thoughts of another face-to-face confrontation with her father. His anger boiled each time her grandmother told him about Ernie. She feared for Ernie's life; her father's brutal words scared her senseless.

An hour must have passed before her Grandmother came to her door and knocked. She told her to get her things packed. An hour later, her father came home and they went to China to celebrate TET.

While the Vietnamese celebrated TET, the Viet Cong began the TET Offensive, a series of surprise attacks against the South Vietnamese that destroyed lives and cities all over the south.

During the TET offensive, Tra Van Tra, a Communist, was one of the main instigators in the attack on Saigon; he wanted to start an uprising to overthrow the government of South Vietnam in hopes that he could return to Saigon, the city where he had spent his youth as a liberator. Tra Van was a short man with dark skin and a happy face, who wore a dark-green uniform that was not decorated with metals or ribbons; yet he was the highest ranking member of the revolutionary army. His plan to overthrow Nguyen Van Thieu failed.

On the other hand, Tra Van was no worse than many of the other South Vietnamese troops, who pretended to support the South Vietnam government. They knew before hand that the Viet Cong prepared for an offensive, but they did not tell the South Vietnamese government or the American officers.

Another main target of the TET Offensive was Tan Son Nhut Air Base. The Viet Cong outnumbered the Marines, and several security police lost their lives.

The turning point of the war came with the TET Offensive and added fuel to the flames of anger in the United States. Television stations reported the details of the brutal offensive and showed bloody scenes that resembled horror movies of American soldiers who fought and died in battles; they also showed villages burned to the ground. The United States sent more troops to Vietnam, dropped more bombs, and fought more battles, resulting in the death of more Americans.

CHAPTER THIRTEEN

Three days later, Anna returned from China; she expected Ernie to call her, but she had not heard from him since she saw him at the TET Celebration. She had fallen in love with him, head over heels, and had thought constantly of ways to get in touch with him. She was thinking seriously about calling him again.

As luck would have it, Lena Ming announced that she was returning to China that weekend to visit her mother. Her mother had called and told her she had not been feeling well and wanted her to come and stay with her a few days. She asked Anna to go with her, but Anna told her she had work she must finish at school.

Anna saw her chance to finally be with Ernie without her grandmother's hawk eyes watching her; however, her grandmother insisted that she meet her in China on Friday, and she would not stop nagging. Anna finally promised that she would meet her in China on Friday of that week, but she had no intentions of doing so.

On Friday, Anna did not show up in China, and Lena Ming went crazy with worry. When Anna returned home from the Dalat Market, the phone jarred the wall with its ringing. She set the bags of groceries on the counter and picked up the phone. "Hello, Ming residence."

"Anna, is that you?" Her grandmother said and caught her breath.

"Grandmother, you called our home. Who did you think would answer the phone?"

"I have been worried to death about you. Why did you not come to Mother's like you promised?"

"I was exhausted after I returned from school. I have decided not to come."

"Did your father come home for the weekend?"

"He called and said he would be out of town on business."

"Are you there all alone?" Lena said.

"You worry too much, Grandmother. I can take care of myself. Try to relax and enjoy yourself."

"You know I cannot relax. I am worried sick."

"I do not have time to talk right now." She hung up the phone and said to herself, "If Grandmother comes home early, she will spoil everything."

Mrs. Ming turned to her mother and said, "Anna was contrary and would not come with me. She is wild and completely out of control. She sneaks around with an American soldier each time my back is turned. Her father and I told her what we thought about her lewd behavior, but she pays us no mind; she is very stubborn."

"Dong Lee needed to help you discipline Anna after her mother died. If you ask me, Anna was a problem child from a very young age. Her mother spoiled her. If she lived under my roof, she would do as I said, or she would get out on her own. Send her to me and I will straighten her out."

"Mother, you are not able to help yourself," Lena said. "Hold up your head, so I can fluff your pillow."

Her mother rested her head wearily on the pillow and said, "You did not help matters by moving to Dalat."

"Dong Lee graciously gave me a home, Mother. He still gives me money every month."

"Anna needs a firm hand on her behind," her mother said.

"She is more than twenty," Lena said. "She is too old to spank."

"I could spank her! I could give her a licking she would never forget."

In the meantime, Anna anxiously waited for Ernie to call. At six o'clock, the phone rang and Anna whispered into the receiver, "Grandmother went to see her mother. I will fix dinner for you."

"Are you sure the neighbors will not mind?"

"Do not make me laugh," she said. "Can you be here around seven?"

"I will be there anytime you say."

When Anna met Ernie at the door, her heart skipped a beat and her skin grew warm. "Come in," she said.

He followed her to the living room, where she offered him a chair, and she disappeared behind a door of beads.

Ernie sat down on the couch and looked around at the white room that breathed with Chinese culture. He paid no attention to the beauty of the room the last time he visited Anna. Grandmother riled his feathers. The slick hardwood floors shined around the Chinese rugs like cane syrup in the evening sun. Wine silk drapes, embossed with gold flowers, hung from bamboo rods and covered the double windows. Moving his eyes around the room, he noticed that the silk drapes had the identical designs as the couch and rug. He ran his hand over the wine and white silk flowers, and moved the tip of his boots around the designs on the Oriental rug. Sculptured animals decorated the end table next to the couch. Then he studied the silk paintings on the walls and tried to put meaning to the strange forms. Huge Chinese vases filled with red roses sprayed the room with the sweet smell of spring, and incense burned in a small copper urn sitting on the organ. The chalk white walls contrasted with the bright paintings framed in gold on the walls. He thought about the painting on his wall at home. That Georgia artist named Butler Brown drew circles around Vietnamese artist. They couldn't hold a candle to his work. The Vietnamese art showed strange qualities that he could not explain. To say the least, their art said nothing that he understood.

The sacred, sculptured animals on the end table seemed to leap at him. They gave him the creeps. He thought about all of the spirits of the dead she had visited and wondered if they represented Great Grandpa. He got up, walked around the room, and checked out the other pieces of sculpture.

He had never seen sculptured forms like these, and he had seen many sculptured works of art in magazines. His eyes fell on the statue of a beautiful oriental woman. Her face looked peaceful, and that was good news. As he turned to go back to the couch, his eyes caught a small sculpture of Buddha standing on a shiny cabinet in the corner of the room. He had never met Buddha, so he walked over to introduce himself to the man. "I am pleased to meet you, Buddha?" My name is Ernie and I am a proud American from the United States." He walked closer and Buddha's eyes seemed to glare at him. He saw no need for all of these sculptures and pieces of bronze. He walked back to the couch and sat down. He knew very little about art and sculpture. He knew that some of the sculpture he had seen was scary. The temples had sculptured figures of famous men and popular animals. They must have worshiped the elephant, because he saw sculptures of elephants everywhere he went. The Vietnamese carved elephants on the walls of buildings next to their gods. Anna took pride in Vietnamese Art. She bragged about their theaters, too. She thought theaters in Vietnam out shined every nation. The actors stood on a stage, in the living flesh, and pantomimed stories that he did not understand at all.

He wondered what was taking her so long. At the same time, Anna stood before her mirror, checked her face, straightened her hair, and sprayed another dab of perfume around her neck. She wanted her night to be perfect.

As he waited, the crazy thought of stories his mama told him came to mind. The holy men built Noah's Ark from gopher wood. He told his mama that he had never seen a gopher tree. He wanted to know where gopher wood came from.

Suddenly she appeared behind the beads and they clanked with her entrance. "I heard you talking to Buddha," she said.

"I was beginning to think that Buddha would be my sole companion for the night."

"I am sorry I took so long." She walked over to Buddha and ran her hand over the piece of art. Buddha is a special work of art. Do you see that his right hand is pointing toward the earth?"

"I thought he just got tired of holding his arm up."

"Seriously, he is asking the earth to bear witness to his virtue. He seeks justice for all people."

"Maybe we should ask him to seek justice for us, since Granny Grump and Father Ming do not want us seeing each other."

"Buddha would not bless our union, since you are not my father's choice for a mate."

He was in no mood to listen to a lecture on Buddhism. "If I am your choice, then that is all that matters to me. By the way, you look beautiful tonight."

"Thank you. Come with me to the kitchen while I finish preparing dinner."

The kitchen was small, neat, and decorated with oriental trinkets. Fresh flowers and incense spread a sweet smell around the room. She had everything perfectly placed and polished. The large urn of rice liquor on the counter looked tasty. He opened the cabinet to get a glass and his eyes caught the usual dishes, the most colorful dishes he had ever seen. He poured himself a drink and sat down at the table. Directly to his right, a serving table covered with floral linen had fancy teacups, candles, and a large bowl of fruit. He had eaten enough bananas since he came to Vietnam to last him a lifetime. His potassium level must be perfect by now.

The basket of cookies at the end of table looked better than the fruit. He could not resist the temptation. The cookies tasted like the teacakes his mama used to bake. The food smelled spicy and delicious. He wanted to ask what she was cooking, but he hated to sound rude. He prayed that she was not roasting bat, skunk, armadillo, or cobra.

As if she had read his mind, she said, "I am cooking something that you will like."

"What's that?" he asked.

"Chinese stir fry."

"What is stirred in the fry?" he asked.

"Chinese vegetables with fried pork covered with sweet and sour sauce. I made the sauce from green pepper, pineapple, soy sauce, and tomato sauce. This is served with brown rice."

"That's some kind of stir," he said. "Umm, the sauce smells delicious."

"Come; sit here at the head of the table."

"Is this your father's chair?"

"How did you guess?"

"The chair is special, different from the others."

"You are a special guest," she said. "What would you like to drink?"

"What do you have to drink?" he said.

"Rice wine, red wine, coffee, or green tea," she said.

"I don't want anything green to drink or eat," he said.

She pulled out a chair and sat down across the table from him. "I must bless the food."

As she prayed, candles in pewter holders threw a dim light on her face, and he wanted to kiss her, but he had to eat this special dinner that she had cooked especially for him.

She opened her eyes, lifted her head, and said, "The pleasure of your company is all mine. I hope you enjoy your dinner."

"Thank you, beautiful lady. I am happy to be here." He picked up his bright red napkin, smoothed it across his lap, and searched for his silver. How could he eat with these two long sticks? How primitive could they get? He did not know how to eat with sticks. He was too embarrassed to ask for a fork. He picked up the sticks and studied them. Then he pushed them together with his thumb and forefinger to begin the big task. The first dip was a hit and a miss. Then he had a hunk of pineapple on the stick. "Got you," he said to himself. Just as the sweet smell hit his nose, the pineapple rocked and came to a tumbling mess in his lap.

He contemplated what he should do. He twisted the ivory sticks, but nothing happened.

She watched him struggle with the sticks and tried to hide her laughter, but he sensed her eyes on him and became even more fumble fingers.

"Place both of the chops in one hand," she said as she walked around the table. She stood behind him and placed the sticks in his hands as if he was a young child taking his first lesson in learning how to hold its spoon. The warmth of her bosom behind his head sent a good feeling through him that told him he was no longer a child, but a grown man in heat.

"Cross the sticks at the base as you lightly pick up your food," she said. "There! That was very good. Now, let us try once again."

"What is the name of the fragrance you are wearing?" he said.

"Do you wish to know the name of my perfume?"

"I want to know the name of that special scent, because you smell scrumptious. You smell um, um, um, good!"

"What does this word scrumptious mean?"

"The word scrumptious means delightful or heavenly. I want to buy a bottle of your perfume and spray my bunk with it. Then I can imagine you lying next to me with your head right here," and he pulled her head down to his shoulder. "I could also imagine your legs wrapped around me like an octopus."

She let go of the chopsticks and became hysterical with laughter. "I have never seen one as funny as you are." She walked back to her place and sat down. "My Aunt Sean, who lives in China, gave me the perfume that I am wearing. The name of the perfume is Chloe, and it is very expensive, too expensive to spray on your bunk."

"Do you think I might find a cheap substitute for the fragrance?"

"I do not think so."

"Then you must give me your blouse to tuck under my pillow."

"You are a crazy American if ever I have seen one."

"I am crazy about you."

"Stop this foolishness and let us enjoy our dinner. I took many pains to prepare the food."

He held the sticks precisely as she directed and made a dash for the stir-fry once again. With his mouth opened and waiting, he brought the sticks to his mouth and the clump landed in a wad next to his plate. "They got overbalanced," he said.

He fumbled with the sticks until she got up to pour warm tea from the pot. He grabbed a handful of food and crammed his mouth full.

She came back with the tea and warmed up his cup. When she started to sit back down at the table, he spoke up, "I cannot eat with these sticks. If you don't mind, I would like to have a good old-fashioned spoon or fork. I am tired of opening my mouth and catching nothing, and I am starving. Do you folks have forks in Vietnam?"

He had never heard her laugh so loud. "Very well, I will get you a spoon and fork."

She came back with a large spoon and a fork with three prongs and his eyes grew to them as he spoke, "Three prongs are better than one, but I sure would like to have one of those soup spoons you gave me in the rice hut. Are you familiar with regular forks and spoons used in America?"

She laughed, but she did not answer his question. Instead, she said, "Food good?"

"This is the best Chinese food I have ever tasted."

Have a shrimp roll," she said and passed the plate of rolls to him.

"They smell good," he said and bit into the roll. "Umm they are delicious."

"Thank you. I have cooked shrimp rolls only three times. I will get better with practice."

"You do not need any more practice," he said and looked at her as if to say he had another meaning for his words.

The meal was delicious and Ernie was impressed.

After dinner, Ernie opened the bottle of wine he had brought and poured her glass to the rim. "I bought you something." He closed her hand around the small box, and said, "Happy Valentine's Day."

"You are my kind of man," she said. "This can be my birthday present."

"When is your birthday?"

"My birthday was last week on February Eighth."

"Did you turn twelve, twenty-four, or thirty-six on your birthday?" he said.

"I am more than twenty, but I am not twenty-four. I will have a real birthday when I am twenty-four."

"I only remembered the month and day of your birthday. I keep up with age from one year to the next."

She carefully pulled the tape from the gold paper, folded the paper to keep, and lifted the lid with wide eyes of excitement. A smile covered her face and she said, "Gosh, you have very good taste; the ring is beautiful." The diamond chips shimmered with different colors around the black onyx ring.

"I hope the next gift I buy for you pleases you as well," he said and he kissed her again.

"You are making my head swim with dreams that will never come true," she said.

"This is no dream. When the war is over, I will ask you to marry me."

She handed the ring to Ernie and said, "I want you to put the ring on my finger. I will call the ring my engagement ring until you can give me a real engagement ring."

He pulled her close and said, "When you get to America, I will make you the happiest woman in the world."

Ernie took the ring, lifted her left hand, and said, "Anna Ming, will you be engaged to me?"

She giggled and said, "Ernie Tennyson, I will be the happiest girl in the world to be engaged to you."

After he had slipped the ring on her finger, he swept her off her feet with a wonderful kiss. The wine put her in the mood for romance. She could not wait to be in his arms. She wanted him to hold her and never let her go.

"I feel like dancing. I have some tapes in the jeep," he said as he pushed his chair back. "I'll be back in a minute."

He came back and she met him in the living room. He had a stack of tapes by American artist. He said, "I could not go a week without Willie Nelson, and Merle Haggard."

He pulled her close, and they danced through Willie, "You Were Always on my Mind," and Merle Haggard came up with "If We Make it Through December."

She was not familiar with American Country, but she liked "Against the Wind," by Bob Seger.

"As you know already, I am not the best dancer on the block," he said. He pressed his body close to her and she made no fuss. She had never danced on air before, but she felt as if they danced in outer space against the wind. Then he kissed her on the neck and her heart went to the races. When the song ended, he cupped his hands around her face and covered her lips with a kiss that overwhelmed her with passion. She had lost control of what she might do next and prayed that he did not take advantage of her mood. When they parted lips, he talked about how much he liked the song, and told her she was a great dancer. She knew the song had ended when he pushed her back toward the couch. He sat there holding her hand and wanting to carry her through the bead door to the unknown. He got up and put on another record. "Have I Told You Lately," by Rod Steward was absolutely delightful, but he had never told her that he loved her. She rested her head on his shoulder and the stars in the sky seem to move around them.

Then Ben E. King sang "Stand by me" and Ernie softly sang with the music. The song put him in her confidence. She trusted him completely.

"Wow, you are the most unusual woman I have ever met. I sure do like you."

She wanted to slap him; he liked her, but he did not love her. None the less, she clung to him and they sailed around the world on the peaceful waves of the blue sea. Cupid's bow pierced her heart, and she was under the spell of love. She put her hand to her head, and said, "I think I've had too much to drink. I feel a little dizzy."

He cupped her face in his hands and whispered, "I want to make love to you." Then he touched her lips with his fingertip before covering her lips with a wild hungry kiss.

She pulled away and walked to the window. She did not want to be just another woman on his string. She looked at the moon and the streaks of light coming through the trees as she spoke, "I think you should go now."

"I can't go just yet," he said. He walked up behind her and put his arms around her. Then he turned her to face him and looked deep into her eyes as he softly spoke her name and said, "I want you."

"As I have said before, I think two people should be in love before they make love."

"I love you," he said.

She could not believe he had finally said the three magic words. Her head was spinning and her feet walked on a cloud as he guided her through the bead door to her bedroom. She sat down on the bed and watched him unbutton his shirt. She worried about her grandmother coming back and catching her in the bedroom with him. She had dreamed about going to bed with him. Now, the time had come, and she did not know if she could go through with her dream. He pulled her down on the bed and the minute his lips touched hers, she lost all control. He pulled her closer and kissed her neck as he unbuttoned her dress. She stood next to the bed and pulled her dress from her shoulders. It slipped down her figure and fell around her feet. She sat back down on the bed and he unhooked her bra. He pulled at the straps on her bra and she let it slide over her hand. She realized she was about to open Pandora's Box.

Her nakedness sent a surge of delight through him, and he kissed her all over, making marvelous shivers cover her. Lying naked next to him, he came down her body with warm kisses. He was kissing her where no other man had touched, and she was wild with passion. The nervous and shy girl who entered the bedroom turned into a sexy, seductive woman, who was begging for an orgy.

"God, I want you," he said, and she was a slave to his wishes. She responded like a panting slut. Her response urged him to please her. Her breasts felt warm and firm against his chest, and her words sounded crazy. His warmth inside her made her frantic for more. She clung to him with a desire like she never experienced, screamed his name, and turned her head with madness. They moved to the rhythm of an imaginary love song and melted as one as they drifted over gentle waves of the sea that flooded their minds with pleasure and made their hearts gallop as a flurry of euphoria flooded them. The passion that had burned within him for months was satisfied. Her pleasure filled him with masculine pride and gave him an ego like that of a wild stallion that had conquered the rage of a virgin mare.

During those blind, blissful minutes, she had lost her virginity. He had been more wonderful in the flesh than in her dreams. She would follow him to the end of the earth. She cuddled against him and said, "I love you."

"Do you love only me?" he said.

"I love only you," she said. His questions had set her to thinking. He probably thought she was a loose woman. She lay quietly by his side and continued, "My father chooses all of the men I go out with. I have not seen the man my father chose for me in several months. If I was still seeing him, I would not be with you. I can only love one man at the time."

"I am happy to hear that you love only me," he said.

"My father will never approve of our relationship. I have told you already how he feels about Americans."

"You can trust me," he said.

"My father warns me often and she repeated his words, "Daughter, you must keep your distance from American men. They are out to get what they want; then they will cast you aside."

"I will never cast you aside," he said. "I love you Anna Ming."

"Since I was a very small child, I have trusted people too much. When I was a little girl, there was an old man in the village that all of us children loved. We would gather around him, and he would tell us stories that would make us stretch our eyes with wonder about what would happen next. When my mother learned that I was among the village children who listened to the old man's stories, she scolded me. She said that she did not trust this old man, but I did not understand why she distrusted him. She punished me by making me stay in my room for one week. My mother would not allow me to go outside and play with the village children. At that time, I thought my mother was mean to deny me my privileges. Years later, I learned that my mother had good reason not to trust the old man. He had raped her when she was a small child, and she had never told her parents. She would not have told me, but I would not let the issue of her punishment sleep. Today, I feel the same pain that I felt the day my mother told me about the old man."

Ernie sprang up from the bed and looked at her with disbelief. "I didn't rape you! I cannot believe you said that."

"I do not believe your promises. You may have taken a wife for all I know. Why should I believe you?"

"I am not married. I love you, silly."

"You think I am silly?"

"I do not think you are silly, but your thinking is all messed up. Believe me; I love you more than anything. I would marry you tomorrow if I could."

She smiled and he kissed her.

"We must get dressed and go back to the living room,"

He had not felt so relaxed and happy since he came to Vietnam. "Why do we have to go back to the living room?"

"I am afraid Grandmother will come home early, since I did not go to China as I had promised."

They got dressed and went to the living room. She invited him to get comfortable on the couch while she went to the kitchen to fix drinks.

Ernie went to the stereo and put on an album by Willie Nelson, lay his head back on the couch, and hummed along, "Good Times."

Suddenly bright lights lit the room and hit Ernie in his eyes. He jumped up from the couch when he saw the tall man with broad shoulders dressed in black. Ernie thought he might be a bandit and he was speechless.

He glared at Ernie, shrugged his broad shoulders, and pressed his lips tightly together before speaking. "Where is my daughter?"

"Are you Anna's Father?" Ernie said. Dong Lee probably weighed more than two hundred pounds, and he was anxious for Anna to come from the kitchen and defend him.

"I am Dong Lee, Anna's father in the living flesh." His sharp brown eyes shined with mistrust and cut Ernie's heart out.

"Ernie jumped up and offered his hand. "I am glad to meet you, Mr. Ming."

"I am not pleased to meet you!" He said and ruffled the dark beard that edged high cheeks. Then he pushed a hand through his dark hair as he searched Ernie's face with contempt. "Where is my daughter?"

"She is in the kitchen," Ernie stammered.

When Anna came in, Ernie could hear the ice hitting the sides of the glasses with nervous jitters.

Her father turned to her with angry eyes. "What is this American doing in my home?"

"He is my friend. I invited him to have dinner with me."

"You must ask him to go out the same way he came in," Mr. Ming said. "He brought bad luck to my business for many days past. I lost money on my shipments."

Ernie had no idea what the crazy man was talking about. He knew nothing about his shipments.

"I will not ask Ernie to leave!" Anna said, surprised at her own words. She never talked back to her father.

"If you do not ask him to leave, I will throw him out!" He gave Ernie a mean look and turned back to Anna. "Go to your room, Daughter."

Anna ran to her bedroom and threw herself across her bed. She fisted the mattress and cried. Her father's angry voice coming through the wall filled her with fear. She was afraid her father would kill Ernie.

Dong Lee went to his liquor cabinet and poured a glass full of liquor. He turned back and stared at Ernie before turning the glass up. He gulped all of the liquor down at once. Then he slammed the glass down on the table next to the stone Buddha.

"Sir, I would like to ask your permission to see your daughter again."

"I am surprised that you have not asked to move into her bedroom."

"I only want to visit her now and then. I cannot change the way I feel about her. I cannot stay away from her."

"I can change the way you feel! I have said what I meant to say. If you value your life, you will go away and never lay eyes upon my daughter again. Do you not realize that you are ruining her life? I want you to leave my home this instance! Do not come around her again."

Ernie moved his eyes toward the door to see how far he had to leap. Dong Lee stepped forward and looked at him as if he would literally choke him to death. His face was like wax, and his eyes shined with madness. The only thing moving was his mouth. Angry words flew from his mouth and hit Ernie right in the face like a hailstorm.

"You sucked my daughter up with your lies and charm, no doubt."

Ernie tried to remain calm. He respected his elders, but he had lost all respect for Dong Lee Ming. "I wish you nor your family ill will or harm, sir. Your daughter is a friend of mine."

Dong Lee turned red and his voice got louder "Americans are murderers! They have caused me much harm and destruction! I would like to do away with Americans!"

"Sir, I would thank you not to include me in your plan of destruction. I have not harmed you or your family. You have marked my comrades as criminals, and this is not true. Do not take your spite out on me."

"As I have said, Americans are no friend of mine or my family. Get out of my home!"

Ernie put up his hand. "Wait! I will go peacefully. I do not want to cause trouble."

"You have caused trouble already. I did not give my daughter permission to keep company with the likes of you. Do you see the door! Get out of my house and leave my daughter alone!"

Ernie moved toward the door and stopped at the stereo to get his tapes. He had to get Willie out of the tape recorder and his hands fumbled. He dropped the tapes he was holding, but he quickly gathered them and grabbed Willie before backing to the door. "Good evening, Mr. Ming." He quickly opened the door, ran across the porch, and jumped the steps hitting the good earth with both feet.

As Ernie drove back toward his base his mind raced with thoughts of his predicament. Why had he fallen in love with a woman with such a strange family? Her father was a weird odd ball, a Marblehead, an animal from another planet who had singled him out to hate. Dong Lee was definitely the devil offspring of Anna's Grandmother, a chip off the old block, a worthless man, a big bag of blubber. He was also a selfish man who never thought of others feelings or needs. He had forbidden Anna to see him again. Her grandmother was as strange as her son. She changed with the moon and her temper grew worse with every quarter. She knew absolutely nothing about men and was more superstitious than his mama. Why could she not see that he was a good, honest man without a mean bone in his body? How could spirits of the ancestors hold influence over their lives? Anna had spoken of unfavorable spirits, but she had not told him that her father was a fool. Now he understood why her obligation to her father was the most important thing in her life. Her father had brain washed her. He could understand the importance of a family, and he could see gathering for funerals, marriages, and celebrations, but he did not go along with their worship and rituals for the dead spirits. Their beliefs had clashed with his. He was tempted to give Mr. Ming a Holy Bible, so he could read up on Jesus Christ.

Anna was nothing like her father or grandmother. He wondered how she had grown up to be so beautiful and kind. He concluded that she had inherited her mother's genes. Her mother must have been a hell of a woman.

He wanted to go back to the village, knock on her window, and ask her to come out and meet him behind the house. He wanted to kiss her good night; he wanted to plan another secret meeting. Thinking better of the idea, he kept driving toward his base.

In the meantime, Anna was still in her room. The house was quiet and she thought her father had retired for the night. She eased down the hall and went to the kitchen for a drink of water. To her surprise, her father was sitting at the kitchen table.

She turned to go back to her bedroom and her father shouted, "Come in here! I want to talk to you."

"Why did you go behind my back and invite an American to my home!"

"I was going to tell you, but you are never around when I need to talk with you. Besides, you have never approved of anyone that I chose to go out with."

"I will do the choosing, and I will certainly not choose an American! You know what the Americans have done to our village. How could you think of going out with that man?"

"Ernie is a nice man, Father. He had nothing to do with the destruction in our village."

"Have you lost your mind?" He paused as he searched her face." You must be in love with this beast! Your brain stopped working." He pushed his hands in his pockets and walked across the room. Turning abruptly, he said, "If you have fallen for this American, you are a fool! He is probably a married man with children!"

"At times, you speak so foolish, Father."

"My words are not foolish; you are foolish! Mr. Tennyson is very brave with his dirty tricks. He sneaks here to see you while I am away from home."

She suddenly turned into a small child; her father punished her for bringing a friend home from school. She lowered her head to avoid her father's eyes upon her.

"You are blinded by love! You believe anything this man tells you! Your mother had a strong will, also. I wish you could see the mistake you are making. I cannot convince you that I am right and you are wrong. You must find out for yourself, and you will see clearly with time. I hope you come to your senses before it is too late."

She sat with a stubborn chin and said, "You have painted Ernie as evil and corrupt. He is a decent man, and he loves me."

"You are headless, my dear. You listen to your heart. When your heart rules your head, you cannot reason. This crazy American probably tucks dozens of women in his closet."

"I know he loves me!"

"You know nothing! It is obvious that you have abetted this American in his wrong doing. You have made plans for the future, no doubt."

"I am a fully grown woman in my prime, Father. I am entitled to certain rights set by the laws of the state."

"I am the law," Dong Lee said. "No man can come in a snatch you away from me! You will do as I say!"

"I will do as I please, Father. You must loosen the shoestrings. You cannot control my life as you controlled my mother's life. I will not make the same mistakes that Mother made."

"If this American tries to carry you off against my will, he will pay for his mistake. He will pay with his life. I forbid you to see Mr. Tennyson again! You must stay away from him! Have I made myself clear?"

"I understand what you have said, Father, but I am a fully grown woman, and I have my rights."

"You will do as I say, Anna Ming."

She got her glass of water and rushed back to her room. She looked at the picture he had given her, held it to her heart, and kissed it before placing it back in the gold box under her silk scarves. If her grandmother found the picture, her father would soon know and punish her. Anna quietly closed the drawer and she felt eyes upon her.

The next morning, Anna left for school and skipped breakfast to avoid her grandmother's questions.

When she came home from school that evening, her grandmother had gone shopping for groceries in Dalat, and Anna thanked God for that. She went to the kitchen, fixed a glass of hot lemon tea, and filled a bowl of rice. After she ate, she went to her room and locked the door

CHAPTER FOURTEEN

The TET offensive continued through February 1968. The night before their next assignment, Sergeant Purvis met with the platoon in the conference room. He talked more than an hour about the TET Offensive.

"When the TET Offensive began on January 30, 1968, the South Vietnamese and U.S. forces found themselves unprepared for battle. The North Vietnamese attacked cities throughout South Vietnam. One of these cities was Hue. The city was poorly defended, and the North Vietnamese forces soon occupied the city. Highway One, an important supply line for the United States, runs from Da Nang to the DMZ and passes through Hue, which allows access to the Perfume River and divides the northern and southern parts of the country. In addition, Hue is one of our bases for the United States Navy." Purvis paused for a drink of water and continued.

"Then this month, the United States and South Vietnam forces gradually drove the North Vietnam forces out of Hue, but they destroyed the city; 5,000 civilians killed; 668 American and South Vietnam forces killed; and another 3,707 wounded. As a result of these battles, political support for the war dropped even more in the United States."

Hobbit raised his hand and said, "Many of the boys, who got a draft notice, burned their draft cards, and they say anti-war demonstrations have increased everywhere."

Purvis said, "I have heard the same thing." Then he got back to his lecture about the TET Offensive. "Another attack I want to mention is the one that took place right here in Dalat Province. This battle between the North Vietnamese forces and South Vietnamese Military Police and American Military Police caused much bloodshed. The bloody battles started the last day of January and lasted through February 9, just last week. The Americans suffered several casualties during a rocket attack on their compound at Dalat. The intense fighting went back and forth. The South Vietnam Military Police won one and lost one. However, the South Vietnamese held strong defensive positions throughout Dalat from the beginning till the end of the battles; they regained control of Dalat. Around 200 Viet Cong got killed. The South Vietnam forces had fewer casualties, but they had many injured, since they didn't have enough supplies or support." Purvis stopped again for a drink of water.

"I have explained these battles to all of you to show you why our support and protection of the hamlets and villages is so important." He paused and pulled down a hand drawn map to describe the jungle around Dalat, where the Viet Cong had set up camp. "Our job is to drive the Viet Cong from these camps to prevent them from destroying the nearby villages."

Then Sergeant Purvis explained the situation. "The Viet Cong controlled more than half of the rural villages in South Vietnam the first part of this year. With the help of American soldiers like our company, we have slowed their progress. We must stop them from taking control of additional villages in the South." He paused for questions.

Next, Sergeant Purvis talked about all the good things the United States had done to help the Vietnamese. All of the GI's looked at each other with disgust, but they listened. "President Johnson started a program called CORDS which provided food and medical supplies, machinery, and household items to the village population to regain their loyalty. The United States government also provided training programs for local Vietnamese in the military to protect their villages from the Viet Cong; as you know, the South Vietnamese military needs our support to get the job done. We Americans must do more to save the villages."

Before turning in for the night, Sergeant Purvis showed them a bridge they had to cross that was located less than a mile from the village they had to check the next day. He explained that they must travel over this bridge in order to carry out a surprise attack and come up on the back side of the Viet Cong camps.

The next morning, Ernie followed the other soldiers to the dining room for breakfast. After they ate, they checked their ammunition, and supplies. With their M16 rifles in place and belts hanging with grenades, they threw on their backpacks and set out on the long walk through the jungle. The foot soldiers got the short end of the stick. They did not slow down for the rain, and it had rained all morning.

Today was another day and another fight; Ernie dreaded the fight. The Viet Cong hid in the shadows of the still bushes, the tall grasses, and the mud at the edge of still waters.

They walked for more than a mile and reached the bamboo bridge. As Ernie walked across the mesh of swinging bamboo, he thought of that log in the creek back home. The bridge swayed and brought him back to Vietnam. He wanted to grab the side ropes, but his buddies walked with brave straight shoulders and hands to their sides. He would not be a coward in the face of his comrades.

After they crossed the bridge, they bogged the swamp and canals. Ernie squashed the mud and listened to his feet squeak at his boots. Thoughts of moccasins in the mud scared his toes to a curl; lying face down in that rotten muck made him nervous; his fear of leeches sucking the blood from his feet was even worse; most of all, he feared an alligator snapping off his leg with one bite.

They finally reached the other side of the swamp and walked on dry land. Next to the trail, a suspicious looking man swung a scythe over the tall grass. He wore a shabby coat that looked two sizes too large. The Americans recognized disguises and bombs. Ernie refused to shoot a man down in cold blood, but Sergeant Fitzwater killed him on the spot.

After a short rest, they started toward the Viet Cong camp. Their path grew narrow and a thick growth of trees shaded their steps.

Pretty soon, they met a woman who was heavy with child. She moved around in a heavy-footed fashion and gathered wood in a basket to carry back to the village. Like all women here, this woman worked hard. Ernie never wanted his pregnant wife to load wood. He wanted to lend the woman a hand, but the sergeant trusted no one. Ernie joined his comrades and walked on.

They crossed a shallow stream and came to an open wasteland that was dense with woody plants and wild berries. He wondered where all the elephants stayed. He seldom saw an elephant. On the other hand, he seldom saw a bird; he missed the birds singing.

They reached a rice field; women in the field gathered rice. They wore conical hats that dipped and rose like slow butterflies. Their bent backs straightened and their hostile brown faces turned angry eyes toward the soldiers for stomping down their rice. They walked on across the field.

Suddenly a loud scream came through the woods and the sergeant held up his hand. Thinking Viet Cong surrounded them; the sergeant gave them the signal to move back. Then he gave orders to go in parties of two and surround the Viet Cong camp. The first rounds of fire brought the brave Viet Cong from their straw huts in a rage. When the Viet Cong saw that Americans surrounded them, they ran at the Americans and yelled words that made no sense.

An hour later, the Americans had wiped out the Viet Cong camp. Then they took the weapons they left behind and set fire to the straw huts, where they had been staying.

On the way back to their base, Ernie thought about how easy this mission had been; however, he hated to think about the poor man the sergeant killed. The clothes he wore marked him; and Ernie wondered if the sergeant killed an innocent man.

Sergeant Purvis told them to think of all the death and destruction the Viet Cong caused. He added that the shoe on the other foot took the exact steps. Death bothered Ernie, regardless of who got killed.

Ernie loosened his load, sat down on his bunk, and stretched his neck. He tried to straighten his back, but he couldn't move for a spell. He wanted to take a shower right away. He had heard men tell that they took a bath on Saturday; that statement turned true in Vietnam. He stunk like a dog that caught the skunk.

He finally straightened his back and started to the bathroom to get a shower. Suddenly, a hard sting hit his hip; he yelled a curse word with the pain that shot through his hip and moved down his leg. He dropped his pants and found the devil bug, scorpion, in the center of his crotch; its long jointed tail whipped, and its nipping claws hit at him. He slowly slid his shorts down his legs, eased them to the floor, grabbed one of his army boots, and slammed the devil bug scorpion until its guts oozed out on the floor. He carried his pain to the shower to wash away the sting. Then he soaked the red welt with alcohol and checked his clean clothes inside out before putting them against his fresh skin.

The Vietnamese soldiers believed the scorpion was a sign of the devil and evil spirits. These scorpions would edge their way into the barracks and settle in wet places. Their sting was sharp and worse than any bug bite Ernie had ever experienced. The first time a devil bug bit him, he thought a Viet Cong had slipped by the window and shot him. He had been stung more than a dozen times, while his friends had not been touched. Was the devil after only him?

Ernie lay on his bunk and stared at the darkness with thoughts of his school days. He had paid little attention to Old Malloy, his history teacher. Ernie had been a carefree teenager and did not see the importance of history. Malloy assigned a report on Paul Revere, and Ernie had made up a story to go with what Malloy had told them in class. Ernie imagined how Paul Revere must have felt, except he did not have a horse. If he did have a galloping friend, he would climb upon his back and ride off into the sunset. This was not Lexington, concord, nor Boston, but he felt like a true Patriot. He wished with all his heart that Thomas Paine would come to life again and read his famous speech to the North Vietnamese officials. In his opinion, they needed to use A bit of Paine's Common Sense and famous words: "Tis time to part." Ernie believed it was time for the North and South to go their separate ways so he could go home.

Before going to bed, he got his note paper and wrote his mama. He told her the usual about how much he missed her; what he had done that week - the trip to Saigon to see Bob Hope; and gave her a brief description of the area around Dalat.

Mama, pretend you are standing on a mountain looking down at South Vietnam. You see a forest of thick green with narrow, crooked trails banked by ridges of stone that dip and rise till you reach the end of the trail. Open stretches in the jungle let you view the rice fields. Then you see another trail connected to the one you just left. In the distance, you see a bridge suspended from long ropes of bamboo with handrails made from fishing poles clinging to each side of the bridge. Below the bridge, you see a stream rolling over sharp rocks that gives you goose bumps. On the other side of the bridge, you see still another trail. Moving your eyes down the trail you see a canal with children wading in the mud, and you cringe with fear of leeches and snakes. The sound of a Vietnam boat puttering downstream quickly sends the children to the shore. They disappear behind a line of trees to their village. The village is made up of a cluster of huts with pigs and chickens running freely. Papaya, banana palm, and coconut palm trees surround the huts. Behind the huts, you see women tending a vegetable garden. Other women are cooking rice, in a large pot, over an open fire. Near the village, a river flows with fresh water. You see the women go there and fill large vats with water and bring them back to the huts for drinking and cooking. The roar of an airplane or helicopter circles over your head and carries you back to the jungle trail. Then an explosion in the distance makes you fear for your life. Suddenly artillery fire takes you to a battle close by in the jungle. The loud firing stops, and the enemy disappears; you suspect he has a secret tunnel nearby. After the sun sets, figures with dark hair, dark skin, and dark feet move back across the bridge with small kerosene lamps flickering to light their way. You long to go home and taste the American way of life.

CHAPTER FIFTEEN

The weekend came and Ernie looked forward to spending some time with Anna. She promised to meet him at the bridge at six o'clock. Ernie borrowed Major Maxwell's jeep and went to the bridge near Lat Village to meet her.

Ernie paced back and forth across the bridge and checked his watch. She was fifteen minutes late. He worried that her grandmother or her father had hog tied her to the bed post. He walked down the path leading from the main road to wait for her at the tree line. He looked up at the tree above him, and he saw two eyes peep from the hollow. Up came a flat face and a hooked beak. The owl pushed himself out of the hole and rested his sharp claws on the rim. His Mama had said an owl was a bad omen. Should he turn tail and run? Should he forget Anna Ming? Since he came to Vietnam, he talked to himself, and that was a bad thing. He sat down with his thoughts and ran his hands across the grass that bearded the hill before a lake that flowed under the bridge. Anna's father was a beast. He could not believe he risked his life in this war for the likes of a man like Dong Lee.

He came clear across the country and fell in love with a girl he had nothing in common with. She wrapped him around her little finger and tied him in a knot; he couldn't forget her. He told himself that a woman would never get the best of him or tie him down. He thought about the girls he dated in high school; he slept with them and forgot them. He never fell for a girl before Anna; he questioned his sanity. Private Hatcher told him to find another girl friend. Perhaps Hatcher had been right; maybe he should break it off with Anna.

He looked at his watch and threw a rock across the lake. The sun turned to an orange ball and slowly rolled behind the mountain. Streams of light pushed around its peak and threw amber streaks of light through the trees that etched the shore with shadows that looked like deformed monsters.

As Anna walked across the narrow bridge over the lake, she looked back every few steps to see if her grandmother's spy followed her. She prayed that no one noticed her leaving the village. Minutes later, she reached the end of the bridge, where they usually met. She watched the stream as it flowed under the bridge and reached the beautiful lake that was bedded by white rocks. Beyond its banks, wild flowers splattered the slope.

Ernie saw her standing on the bridge and walked back up the slope toward the bridge.

She saw him at the same time and ran to meet him. "I am sorry that I am late. Grandmother watched me all evening; after she went to bed, I slipped out."

He fingered the white lace handkerchief pinned over her hair and said, "Why are you dressed in your Sunday best, and I am dressed in drab fatigues."

"Your attire is fine," she said. "I wanted to go to the Cathedral in Dalat. I thought you might like to see the Cathedral, and I need to pray about some things."

"Why are you wearing a handkerchief on your head?" he asked.

"I must wear a head covering to enter the Abby. Do you not like my dress?"

"You look beautiful," he said as he touched the sleeves of the blue cotton trimmed in lace. "You look like Cinderella going to the Ball."

"You are my handsome prince," she said. "I have to be home before the clock strikes twelve; else, I will turn into a pumpkin."

"Your father will carve me into a pumpkin," he said. "Where is he tonight?"

"He comes home this weekend. He goes to China almost every week."

She smiled and her radiance shined more beautiful than the stars. Her attraction for him shone in her eyes and gave him a feeling of pride.

She took his hand to walk down the slope to the jeep, and he felt the glove covering her hand. "Why are you wearing gloves?" he said.

"I always wear gloves when I go to the church," she said.

"You must direct me," he said as he opened the door to the jeep.

"We can drive to Dalat, park in one of the business lots, and walk to the chapel."

They passed a garden of sweet smelling blooms bordered by shade trees, shrubs, and vines that led to a covered passageway with an entrance to a large stone building. They walked through its arched doorway and entered a foyer that led to three sections. The pool table, chairs, and card tables told them that the first room was a game room. They walked on and entered a large dining room. The long mahogany table was covered with a brown silk table cloth that blended with the wood on the ladder back chairs. The table was set with silver, china, and crystal perfectly placed. They walked on to the next section, where the nuns lived in nice furnished apartments.

The thought of being a priest entered Ernie's mind. The priest lived like a king in comparison to privates in the army. This place looked like a utopia beside his army tent in the jungle. They had a headwaiter who waited on them hand and foot; they had a cook who cooked their food and served their meals. They had a housekeeper who cleaned their rooms and washed their clothes. On the other hand, a priest couldn't have sex with a woman. All the luxuries in the world would not make up for a woman's company.

Anna interrupted his fantasy by the pull on his arm. She led him through the foyer, and they entered a chapel that was surrounded by stained glass windows. The carpet felt like a soft cloud under their feet, and the cushioned benches, with their fancy curved backs, made Ernie want to take a nap. Several hundred candles burned in a row across the pulpit. He followed her down the slopping isle to the altar; she took his hand and motioned for him kneel with her as she prayed. As he watched her kneeling there, he felt closeness to her that he had not felt before. There was something special about her that he could not explain. A halo sprinkled with a splendor of glory shined about her.

"Holy Mother, we thank you for the blessings you give us each day. We honor your place and your name. We praise you for giving us life and keeping us. Forgive us for our sins and evil thoughts. Forgive us for all that is immoral and wrong in your eyes. We praise your sacred name. Amen" She made the sign of the cross, and Ernie tried to follow her lead, but he crossed his hands up; he did not touch his heart two times like he was supposed to do.

Ernie felt as if she had prayed for God to forgive her for having sex with him, but she would soon sin again. In fact, he had a sinful plan in mind after they left the Abby, and their lovemaking was not a sin in his eyes.

When she got through praying, he got up; but she stayed on her knees; she motioned for him to kneel again. Then she passed a silver tray with unleavened bread. He took a small piece of the bread and chewed, but he tasted nothing at all. They could have added a little sugar or salt to the dough. She placed the little plate back on the small table in its proper place, and began chewing the bread. Last of all, she passed him a small glass a little bigger than a thimble and told him to drink. The grape juice was supposed to represent the blood of Christ.

They left the church and walked the same path back to the jeep. He opened the door for her to get into the jeep, but she fell into his arms instead. He held her close for a long time before either of them spoke. She felt a wonderful wave sweep through her as he touched her lips with his fingertip. Then he brushed his lips to her forehead and her nose.

Back at the lake, the moon cast light through the trees surrounding the lake, and the stars twinkled on their shadows as they walked to the edge of the water. A cool breeze whispered through the trees; the frogs croaked; the night creepers chirped; the water rippled with rhythm over the fish.

"The moon is beautiful tonight," she said.

He stopped and pulled her close. "You are the most beautiful thing I've ever seen. His lips covered hers with a warm sweetness that made her crazy with desire. Her heart rushed to her knees, and her head was dizzy. Breathless and unable to speak, she rested her head on his shoulder. Anxious for him to kiss her again, she moved her face to his. His kiss was gentle; then his kiss was hungry and wild.

He went to the jeep and came back with a quilt. As he spread the quilt next to the tree, she said, "We cannot! Not here!"

"Are you ashamed to say what we are going to do?"

She turned her head, and he said, "We will make love right here under God's heaven."

The faint sound of Elvis Presley sounded from the jeep's radio with "Can't Help Falling in Love" and she felt giddy, wonderful, and marvelous. They melted together; and the clouds of heaven seemed to lift them and carry them away to some place in paradise.

They listened to music, laughed, and talked for hours. She promised to meet him again that weekend. He gave her a quick kiss, and she ran toward the village. Her heart tried to trip her feet in a run back to him; but her head turned her feet toward home with a rapid pace.

She hated to meet him in secret. At times, she felt as if she was going insane, but their stolen time together made her forget her grandmother's tongue-lashing. Ernie's laughter, conversation, touches, and lovemaking made her forget all things, except the feelings she had for him. The next week she would have wild dreams about him that would linger until she heard his voice again. Then their stolen moments with a few stolen kisses drove her wild. She ached to be with him at all times. When she went to bed at night, she dreamed about his love and his caresses. In her fantasies, she lay in his arm all night every night.

In the meantime, Lena Ming missed Anna and began a search for her. She aroused the entire village. They searched the village and asked about her at every hamlet. She disappeared without a trace. Her grandmother imagined the Viet Cong carrying her away. She saw her granddaughter locked away in their secret shack. She saw her murdered and thrown into the river. Who seriously questioned the public about a missing woman in times of war? She suspected foul play right away.

When Anna got home, she went to bed and did not bother checking on her grandmother.

Ernie lay in bed and thought about Anna. She certainly believed in the Catholic teachings. He had not expected a trip to the church. She believed in heaven and mentioned that heaven was where all the Gods lived. Both of them believed in heaven. On the other hand, Dong Lee Ming drilled the teachings of Buddhism into Anna's head. This confused the most devout Christian, but she leaned more to Catholic teachings, and that was a good thing. Dong Lee believed a man could create his own heaven or hell on earth, by either becoming an ideal man, or by becoming a man who practiced evil. Dong Lee thought the spirits of the dead controlled his precious life and possessions.

His mama often spoke of spirits. When she talked about spirits, he thought about ghost in the corners of the room, above the ceiling, outside the windows. Now the woman he loved talked about spirits; these spirits took the guest bedroom in the house. If these spirits came from a feeling in the heart, he understood, but these spirits of the dead that Buddhist believed in gave him the creeps. She told him that spirits surrounded them at all times, but their body disappeared. The idea of a spirit watching him at all times, especially when he needed his privacy made him paranoid. He already felt as if monkeys, Viet Cong, grandmother, and Dong Lee watched him. He wanted to meet up with Gabriel; he needed some good news, and Gabriel always brought good news.

He never argued about things he knew nothing about; but he spoke his mind about his Christians beliefs. Protestants believed in heaven; they believed God held their lives in his hands; they believed in one God in three persons - God the Father; God the Son; and God the Holy Spirit.

He wanted to tell Mr. and Mrs. Ming about the church called "Faith Healers". His mama carried him to that church when he was a young boy. The folk danced, shouted, and laid hands on the sick to heal them. Then one night the preacher's faith got out of hand. He took a rattlesnake out of its cage to prove to the congregation that God would protect him. The snake bit the preacher right away; he let go of the snake right away; the congregation ran from the church right away; and the preacher died right away. His mama never attended the healing service at that church again. If anyone mentioned the service, she told them to stay away from the faith healers.

Still another ceremony his mama talked about was the foot washing at the church. A good foot washing soothed tired feet at the end of a long day.

His tired brain closed his eyes and he forgot about religion; he fell asleep.

The next morning, Anna's grandmother found her fast asleep in her bed. She roared out at her, "Where did you go last night?"

"What are you saying, Grandmother?" Anna said and yawned sleepily.

"You went missing last night, and the entire village searched for you at midnight."

"I have been right here, Grandmother."

"You do not lie with a good face," her grandmother said, and she slammed the door with anger.

CHAPTER SIXTEEN

The Vietnam War continued in March 1968. North Vietnam refused to talk peace; South Vietnam refused to surrender to the Communist; and Americans' efforts failed to stop the Viet Cong from taking the Southern villages and cities. Most of the soldiers believed that the Communist would soon take over South Vietnam. The war twisted, dipped, and turned like a fierce tornado and destroyed everything in its path.

As Ernie listened to Master Sergeant Spencer's lesson, he thought about the next fight in the jungle. Spencer talked about the traitors in the South and added that one must choose his Vietnamese comrades carefully, since friends turned to foes in the blink of an eye.

The weather near Dalat stayed warm most days; today the weather turned hot with sun rise. The rays of the sun streamed through the trees and warmed their hard hats as they walked. The thick bushes and trees blocked their view of what was ahead, but they kept their eyes wide open. The sight of the jungle frightened him. Snakes and tigers lived in the jungle; they had killed several cobras, but had not met a tiger face to face.

Before sunset, they reached the designated spot for their camp. After they set up their tents, they gathered firewood for the cooks.

As darkness fell, mosquitoes swarmed, lit and stung. They slapped mosquitoes and watched the drop zone. A helicopter flew low over their camp and Ernie ran behind six other privates to pick up their food and supplies. They dropped large coolers with vegetables, meats, and everything the cooks needed to stir up a good meal. The cooks didn't announce what they had on the menu. The GI's always got a big surprise; sometimes they liked the surprise; sometimes they lost their appetite.

Pretty soon, the smell of strong coffee drifted in the air and Ernie wished with all his might that he had one of his mama's biscuits. He watched her pull out that big tin bowl she kept in the cupboard. She always used that same bowl, and the bowl always held a small amount of flour left over from the last batch of biscuits. She gathered all of her ingredients and placed them next to her bowl. Then she sifted the flour into a high heap. After bumping the flour from the sifter, she set it behind the bowl. With that done, she gathered her fingers close together and dipped a wad of grease from the big tin can next to the cabinet. She almost never measured anything; she knew the exact amount of all things she used. After she buried the hunk of grease in the middle of the heap of flour, she used the other hand to pour the milk. Then she squeezed the grease into the flour, added the milk, and squeezed the mixture until the mixture made a big mess on her hand. She used the fingers on her left hand to rake the mess off her hand. Then she took that big mess and kneaded it. She turned the dough over and over; she punched it with her fist each time she turned it over. Next, she turned, punched, and mashed the dough into a big ball. She said kneading was the secret to a good biscuit; sometimes she kneaded the biscuits sixty times. After she finished kneading the dough, she pinched off pieces of the dough and rolled each one between her two hands until she formed perfect little balls that stood up like store bought rolls. She put each one on a flat pan with plenty of grease on the pan. Before sticking them into the oven, she slapped the pretty rolls as flat as the pan itself. He wondered why she mashed the biscuits flat; Of course, he never questioned her reason, he just ate the biscuits. Sometimes he ate four biscuits.

They called chow time before his daydream ended, and he never ate his mama's imaginary biscuits. He pulled himself up and fell in line with his tin plate. As they neared the smoking pots, he saw grits bubbling. They seldom got grits in Vietnam, and hot grits with eggs hit the spot. The Yankees passed up the grits and took extra eggs.

After two cups of coffee to wash it all down, Ernie and Private Hatcher went back to their tent. They sat down and talked while they shinned their boots. The Viet Cong usually hit after dark like a thief in the night, and Ernie hated sleeping in the tent; when he got good and tired, he could sleep on the limb of a tree. Thunder cracked the clouds with a loud boom; the downpour of rain hitting the tents cooled the night and calmed the mosquitoes. Ernie finally fell asleep and Hatcher awoke him the next morning trying to find his cigarettes.

After breakfast, they went back to their tents and waited for the march. Before they started out, they heard a noise behind their tents. Sergeant Fitzwater peeped out the flap and saw a Viet Cong. He sneaked through the bushes and disappeared. He ordered them to grab their M16 and go quietly around the side of his tent. The area got as quiet as a mouse.

Less than an hour later, the Viet Cong neared Sergeant Purvis' tent and whooped a war cry. Sergeant Purvis turned his machine gun in a circle; he expected them to perform a war dance before they fell to their death. Three Viet Cong lay dead. Sergeant Purvis approached them with caution; Hatcher and Ernie stepped up to help Purvis. He placed his foot on the first Viet Cong's belly before moving on to the next.

Minutes later, the sound of gun fire followed by a loud explosion rocked their camp. Wood, limbs, and dirt rained down on them and smoke stifled them. With M16 rifles thrown across their shoulders, they ran toward the sound.

Master Sergeant Kipper shouted orders for them to get down. Ernie and his buddies fell on their bellies before the thunder of explosives surrounded them. A sniper hit Private Bentley in his shoulder.

Ernie eased across the trail and pulled Bentley behind a log. Then he saw Sergeant Fitzwater lying face down on the bamboo. He eased his rifle to the ground and checked Bentley and the sergeant's wounds. Blood had soaked the sergeant's shirt. Ernie grabbed the sergeant's radio and called for help. A few minutes later, a medical man came in on the radio. Private Hatcher came to Ernie's aid, and they drug Fitzwater and Bentley to the pick-up zone.

Ernie felt relieved when he heard the helicopter whipping the air. It moved straight down to the pick-up zone and paramedics rushed from the helicopter with stretchers. The Viet Cong started firing at the helicopter as it lifted, but they didn't get a hit before the helicopter disappeared.

Ernie went back to his position and picked up his M16. After a short time, firing guns sounded again and bullets hit a pile of dirt in front of him. Suddenly, a bullet grazed Ernie's shoulder and numbed his senses. He turned and ran through the trees. Sweat dripped from his face and his hands shook worse than a junkie's. He searched for a safe place to hide. Blood had soaked his shoulder and he felt faint. He fell to the ground and called Hatcher.

When Hatcher found Ernie, he fell on his knees beside him and Ernie reached out to him. Hatcher helped him stand and Ernie leaned heavily on Hatcher's shoulder as they moved through the brush back toward the clearing. After Ernie cooled his face and drank some water, he felt better.

The battles always ended with fatalities, bloodshed, and wounded soldiers. They found several dead Viet Cong. Two of their men had been wounded and carried to the hospital. Ernie had lost a lot of blood, but he walked back to camp with his comrades. When they reached the base, Hatcher insisted that he let Old Saw Bones take a look at his wound.

Doctor Allen cleaned the wound, bandaged it, and gave Ernie two bottles of pills, one for infection and another for pain.

After a bath and chow time, Ernie went to the recreation room to socialize with his buddies. The men smoked, drank hard liquor, and voiced concern about Private Bentley and Sergeant Fitzwater. They sent them to the base hospital in Dalat; Colonel Switzer had talked with them; they told him they felt fine.

Then the GI's argued about who was right and who was wrong about the recent My Lai Massacre. Americans went into a South Vietnam village and killed women, children, and old men in their own homes. The massacre outraged people all over the world and they got angrier about the war.

Hatcher said the Americans thought the village had been abandoned; they shot at Viet Cong; they killed the people who lived there.

Staker said the Soldiers' ignorance was no excuse; they should have checked the huts in the village before they started shooting. He added that the Americans committed a terrible war crime.

Private Slater said that the government officials often voiced their concerns about the Vietnam War, the corruption, and the number of Americans dying; but they closed their minds to the facts and did nothing to help the situation in Vietnam.

Private Wingate said Americans destroyed Vietnam, while they saved it from a Communist take-over. Then he criticized Johnson for drafting more Americans to protect Saigon.

All of the GI's spoke up for Robert F. Kennedy; they believed he would beat Johnson if he ran against him for President of the United States.

They got off the subject of politics and started talking about women. Sergeant Fish, a clown from Virginia, told funny jokes and very tall tales about his women.

Ernie had little to say about Anna. Hatcher often told Ernie that Anna's crazy father and grandmother would never agree for him to have a relationship with her, and he should forget her. Ernie loved Anna, and she loved him. His mama had once told him that love endures all things.

The next morning, before they hit the trail, Colonel Switzer sent for Private Tennyson and Private Hatcher. On the way to the colonel's office, Hatcher bet Ernie that the colonel wanted to commend them for their bravery the day before.

Colonel Switzer not only wanted to commend them for saving Private Bentley and Sergeant Fitzwater, he told them he had recommended they receive a medal for their bravery. In addition, he promoted them to corporals.

When they told the other GI's the colonel promoted them to corporals, they gave a loud cheer. Ernie couldn't wait to write and tell his mama about his promotion. She would be proud.

CHAPTER SEVENTEEN

On Sunday, Anna called Ernie and asked him to come to the village. The children wanted to see him. She explained that her grandmother had gone grocery shopping in Dalat, and her father was not expected home until later that evening.

As usual, Ernie borrowed Major Maxwell's jeep and took off toward Lat Village. The children ran to him with open arms; then they sat in a circle and listened to stories about his country. Afterward, he and Anna sat on the wooden bench under the trees beyond their play area and talked.

When Dong lee saw them walk up the steps, his teeth drew blood from his bottom lip. He opened the door, pulled Anna into the house and took a stand in the door to block Ernie's entrance.

"You are not welcome here. I have told you once before to leave my daughter alone."

"I am in love with your daughter," Ernie said.

Anna stood silent and listened to her father rake Ernie over the coals and make threatening remarks. Her father's anger filled her with fear. She ran past him to her bedroom, threw herself across her bed, and cried.

"I want to marry Anna as soon as I get out of the Army," Ernie said.

"Why pay the fiddler who plays for free?" Dong lee said. "I have not called you a liar, but I do not believe you speak the truth. My daughter is beautiful, but she is young and foolish."

"I never lied to Anna about anything," Ernie said.

Looking toward the sky, Dong Lee said, "You promised Anna the moon to have your way with her, and she believed you; Anna expected a big orange ball to fall into her lap. You promised her diamonds and gave her cut glass. How cheap can a man get? She is a fool to believe anything that you say; she is a fool to wait for you when she could have her choice of men. None of these gentlemen suit her; she prefers to waste her youth on the likes of you."

Ernie bravely stood up to the devil. "Anna and I fell in love, and we can't change what we feel," Ernie said.

Dong Lee swung his heels against the porch post and looked up with a squint against the evening sun as he spoke, "I will waste no more breath on you. Get out of my sight!"

"You think I am sorry, trashy, and just plain worthless; but you are wrong," Ernie said.

"Trash is exactly what I was thinking, but I did not say the words that suit my tongue at this moment," Dong Lee said, and he kicked at the porch post again.

"I have asked your permission to date your daughter, and I have tried to do the right thing," Ernie said.

"I have tried to hold my temper, but you have stretched my patience to the point of no return. I will never give you permission to go out with Anna. Do not think me foolish enough to change my mind, either. Be gone! Get off my porch!"

Ernie tried to see through the opening in the door. He wondered where Anna had gone. She was probably locked in her room and afraid to come out. He wanted to force his way into the house and talk to her. Instead, he looked at Dong Lee and said, "Good evening, Mr. Ming. Have a nice day."

As he drove back toward his base, he thought about his predicament. Ernie feared that crazy Dong Lee might shoot him if he visited Anna again.

In the meantime, she sat in her room with the door locked and wrung her hands with worry. When she heard the roar of the jeep, she ran to the window and watched Ernie drive away. She thanked God that her father had not harmed him.

She walked across the room and sat down on the bed. She hated facing her father. If he caught her with Ernie again, she was afraid of the consequences. She took a bath and went to bed without supper.

The next morning she was hungry. She went to the kitchen to eat breakfast, and her grandmother started nagging. "Your father told me what happened yesterday while I was in Dalat."

"Please leave me be alone, Grandmother."

"Let this American go his way! He is a no good scoundrel. He flees to fling with every pretty woman he meets. He is making his way from your bed to a bed he thinks more exciting. Afterward, he finds a new partner to swing. Do You think your old grandmother knows nothing about life? Why would I lie to you? My blood runs in your veins. You are my granddaughter and I want what is best for you." She saw tears slowly running down Anna's face, so she quieted for a moment.

"I know what is best for me, but you and Father refuse to let me have a happy life. You have arranged my future. Why must you make decisions for me? I have a mind of my own and a good mind at that."

"You know well that arrangement of marriage is a custom in our country. Your duty is to your family and the man chosen for you to marry."

"My duty is to myself! I will do my own choosing. I no longer believe in the customs of my people. I am in love with Ernie." With her final words to her grandmother, she rushed from the kitchen and went to her room.

She got so sick of her grandmother and father tending to her business and chewing Ernie to threads. She got her purse and scarf, closed the door and walk down the hall. On the way out, she got a hat from the hall tree and closed the door behind her. The sun shined brightly in the eastern sky. Today was a perfect day to walk to school. While she walked, dreams of Ernie filled her head. She was sure he loved her as much as she loved him.

At the same time, Ernie worried about Anna. Between Dong Lee and the Viet Cong, Ernie found himself wedged between the beast and the devil. Dong Lee forbid him to date Anna and threatened to kill him; the Viet Cong threatened to slaughter Vietnamese women caught with Americans at dance halls, clubs, bars, restaurants, and theaters.

In spite of his fear, he continued seeing Anna when she could sneak away from her grandmother's watchful eyes. He carried her to nice restaurants such as Ngoc Hai, Café 100 Mai Roofs, or Restaurant at Villa Nine at the Continental Palace and enjoyed traditional cuisine or seafood. Anna liked one particular restaurant, because it had a verandah, where they danced and looked down on the city of Dalat. She also liked the romantic atmosphere of the cave restaurant. It reminded Ernie of underground Atlanta. Couples wrote love notes in different languages that they posted on the walls of the restaurant.

Ernie counted his money before entering these restaurants. A meal with three vegetables and a meat cost about five dollars and that was expensive on a GI's salary. Most of the time, they went to cheaper restaurants to enjoy a sandwich and a drink.

Ernie was careful when he chose drinks from the menu. Their coffee made from vomited up beans made Ernie sick; and Ca Phe Trung, coffee topped with egg and sugar, disgusted him. He enjoyed rice mash, mandarin juice, and Coq au Vin, but he usually settled for a coke, since he disliked green tea. He wondered why they did not let the tea ripen before they harvested it.

Ernie had never eaten noodle soup for breakfast, but noodle soup was one of Anna's favorite breakfast foods. Ernie certainly didn't want eggs with a chicken or duck growing inside, which was a specialty dish in Vietnam. Neither did he have intentions of ordering cobra, turtle, armadillo, or monkey for dinner. When he saw monkey on the menu, he thought about Chipper, the monkey that saved his life. Ernie usually settled for rice to be on the safe side. Anna never tired of eating rice. She explained the ancient myth behind rice that she called a legend.

"Rice is "God's gemstone" and the symbol of life with magical powers. God dropped a bag of rice and a bag of grass from heaven to a spirit. He told the spirit to sew the grass and plant the rice, but the spirit got the bags mix up; he planted the grass, and sewed rice. The grass thrived without tending, but the rice did not grow. Afterwards, farmers realized that rice must be planted, transplanted, and cultivated."

Sometimes they went to clubs that had a band or a piano player where they drank wine, and danced, but Ernie always kept his eye on the door and searched for an exit before they got a table.

When Ernie didn't have much money, they went to the Valley of love for a ride on the lake in a paddleboat. They also enjoyed walking around the Dalat Flower Park with its beautiful scenery and colorful flowers. Anna liked the Dalat Market best of all. She liked to look at the pottery, fine China, trinkets and jewelry; she liked to taste the vegetables and fruits; she liked to show Ernie the different kinds of tea, especially the Artichoke tea, a product of Dalat.

CHAPTER EIGHTEEN

April 1968 in Vietnam was another month of bombing and killing. Ernie and his platoon still played hide and seek with the Viet Cong. The Viet Cong did the hiding and the Americans did the seeking.

Sergeant Fitzwater came back from sick leave, and the GI's welcomed him back to lead the way. They came to a hilly region made of rock ridges that looked like the faces of monsters lurking at them. Ernie had looked in the face of the enemy so many times that all things turned to monsters.

Sergeant Purvis took out his compass and announced that they had gone over the line into enemy territory. Ernie thought he was telling a joke, since the entire country was enemy territory.

Suddenly, the sound of artillery fire surrounded them, and a loud explosion made their ears ring. The sky turned orange with flares. Continuous explosions hurled sparks and rocks around them. Bullets hit the slope and dirt exploded falling in wads around them. Ernie fell on his belly and crawled for cover behind his comrades.

Hatcher said, "That fire is getting closer. We have to do something in a hurry or burn in hell."

Then another round of grenades whirled violently through the air and fell with a screeching roar next to Ernie and Hatcher. The smell of dynamite and smoke stifled them as they groped through the thick fog. They struggled to breathe; they fought the smoke with their hands and tried to see what was ahead of them.

They held the Viet Cong down for more than an hour in the heavy smoke. The roar of a fighter plane was music to their ears. The plane circled the sky and Sergeant Fitzwater directed them to the right location to drop the bomb. After the first bomb, the plane circled the sky with threats to drop more bombs.

Then the roar of a helicopter sliced the air just above the trees and swung to the ground close to their station. The medical rescue unit jumped out and picked up the wounded.

The Viet Cong backed down and moved out, but the fire forced them to take a different route back to their base camp. As they walked toward their base, the sun painted the horizon with the blade of a gold sword that shimmered with horizontal rays of light. The wind roared through the trees and they groped for their hats.

Finally they spotted dim lights in the distance that sparkled like suspended stars. God watched over them and led them back to camp.

When they got back to the barrack, they went to the showers. Smut disguised their faces, and they couldn't identify their comrades.

After they went to the mess hall to eat, they came back to the recreation center to talk. Their conversation was interrupted by a special news broadcast.

"An unidentified man assassinated Doctor Martin Luther King today at the Lorraine Motel in Memphis, Tennessee; April 4, 1968 is a day for mourning a great leader. King lived on 39 years. He advocated peaceful means to settle disagreements; yet he died from violence. People loved the American Clergyman, activist, and leader of the American civil rights movement. He also earned the Nobel Peace Prize for laureate."

Martin Luther King's death resulted in racial tension and unrest all over the United States. Reporters mentioned that Dr. King disliked war and violence. He had stated in one of his speeches, "The Vietnam War is hindering society's social reform programs."

Later, the GI's learned that James Earl Ray, a fugitive from Missouri, killed King; after they arrested and convicted Ray for King's murder, the jury sentenced him to serve 99 years in the Tennessee State Penitentiary.

The next day, the GI's walked in search of Viet Cong in the villages several miles from Dalat. Near one of the villages, they saw a little Vietnamese woman digging potatoes in a small garden. When the sergeant questioned her about Viet Cong, she dropped her basket of potatoes and stared at him with vicious eyes of hatred. He decided that she could not speak English. The pain and despair of her people was evident in her eyes.

They saw smoke rising in the distance and walked on. Near the village, children gathered near the path and watched them with curiosity. They threw up hands and smiled at them to let them know they meant them no harm.

One little boy ran up to them and spoke in short sentences, "You Americans?" Then the boy turned to the other children and spoke in his local dialect.

They soon came to a cluster of huts surrounded by coconut, pineapple, sugar cane, and orange groves. Ducks and chickens ran freely around the huts. The family dog lay under the shade of the tree and took a nap. In the distance, children sat on the grassy slope before a pond and held their poles with dreams of catching the biggest fish in the pond.

After asking a dozen useless questions, Sergeant Fitzwater said, "How far is it to the next village?"

"I cannot guess miles, but the distance is very long walk," the woman said.

Before they got to the next village, they decided that the woman had been right about the distance being a long walk. They finally saw a man leading his buffalo, and they stopped for the sergeant to inquire about the nearby village.

"Sir, could you tell me how far it is to the next village?"

The man stopped and looked at him, but he did not speak.

When they finally got to the next village, they understood why the woman stared at them with anger and the man leading his buffalo would not speak to them. Bandits had almost destroyed the entire village. The vandals left only one shabby hut without damage. Many of the villagers ran into the woods and hid for fear of being captured.

The GI's neared the hut that was still standing with caution. Inside, they found a woman hiding in the back behind cardboard boxes. She was pale with fright and her hands shook with nervousness. Her dark, shaggy hair covered her eyes and matted her face. She was too scared to speak. Sergeant Fitzwater told her they came to help her.

She still hovered in the corner and refused to speak. She finally pushed her hair back and told them her name was Furze. The bandits kidnapped her family and killed her husband, the village chief.

She asked if they would stay and protect her through the night; she expected the bandits to return.

Sergeant Fitzwater explained that she must go with them and he would provide transportation for her to travel to a refugee camp, where she would have food, clothing, shelter, and protection.

She ran to the back of the room and grabbed a box to take with her.

The people in the villages had a belly full of the Viet Cong burning their villages and destroying their homes. The people had to leave their hamlet and rebuild their village in the jungle. Many of the people surrounded their village with spikes, poisoned arrows, and traps to stop the Viet Cong.

On the last day of April 1968, the soldiers bragged about Americans winning the Battle of Dai Do along the Demilitarized Zone, where the Communist brought supplies to the Viet Cong. On the other hand, the soldiers got depressed about the number of United States Marine who sacrificed their lives to win the battle.

April 1968 came to an end, but the war continued. The North had no intentions of settling differences with the South by peace talks.

CHAPTER NINETEEN

In May 1968, the Viet Cong started a Mini TET and attacked Saigon and many other cities in South Vietnam. They also hit American Special Forces at Kham Duc along the Laos border, and their attack rubbed President Johnson the wrong way. He ordered additional American troops to protect Saigon, the capital city, and the American bases; but the Viet Cong got ahead of the game and the American forces couldn't stop them. The GI's were afraid their base was the next target.

The United States supported South Vietnam with men and military supplies; therefore, the South outnumbered the North with artillery, war tanks, and aircraft; but they mastered war tactics which surpassed their weapons and helped them win the fight.

The Viet Cong used homemade bombs made from empty shell cases left by the Americans; they made booby traps from boards, sharp nails, and cement blocks; they made axes and hatchets from sugar cane stalks, and they usually stole the sugar cane; they had more tricks up their sleeves than a magician pulling rabbits out of a hat. They didn't drop many bombs, but they planted millions. Troops could be walking down a path or along a canal that appeared safe, and suddenly fall into a pit of bamboo with hidden poison spikes.

The next morning, Ernie and his buddies loaded up on jeeps and drove toward a village, about twenty miles from Dalat, where they suspected a Viet Cong camp. They jogged up and down with the bumps as the jeep slowly moved across the rough terrain with its crooked trails and steep ridges. Behind them, they could see a beaten path of through the thick elephant grass. Looking below, they could see farmland stretched across the hills to the base of the mountain. They traveled for several hours and halted before a thick growth of pine trees. The soldiers jumped to the ground and stretched their limbs before beginning their journey through the jungle.

They came to a river and set up tents behind the slope of a hill with a deep valley below. After they set up their tents, they began digging a trench around their camp. When they finished, their trench was fifty feet long and three feet deep. With the trench finished, they carried stones and boulders, from the foot of the mountain, stacked them before their trench to protect them from the mortar fire. All that day they toiled like prisoners under heavy guard. Their finished bunkers stood tall and strong; the Gorillas could not easily win the fight.

Ernie looked at the ditch and pile of stones and thought about a steel bunker. Before the sun fell below the tip of the mountain, the cooks called chow time. After they ate, they went to their tents and sacked out.

The Viet Cong attacked when least expected, and Ernie feared their attack more than a pack of hungry wolves. They possessed night vision.

During the night, the sound of artillery fire surrounded them, and a loud explosion rocked the earth. Ernie and his buddies jumped into their fatigues, grabbed their M16's and dashed out of their tent. An enormous fire behind their tents sent them for cover in the trenches.

Sergeant Kipper whistled his signal for them to find a position next to him. They crawled along the ditch until they reached Kipper. Ernie got a place next to Hatcher, who was lying on his belly with his head stretched to the side.

Then several grenades exploded all at once about twenty feet from their ditch. A dozen or more soldiers jumped into the ditch next to them, and Sergeant Kipper ordered Slater, weapons specialists, to man the machine gun they had set up in the center of the ditch line behind a barricade of rocks. The first round of fire Slater sent tore through the dark and struck the Viet Cong like a bolt of lightning. If the Big Bang Theory turned out to be true, the next round would result in the creation of another planet. Machine gun fire sounded continuously and cut down every Viet Cong around their camp. Ernie and the other soldiers in the ditch lowered their rifles and waited. Sergeant Kipper told them the Viet Cong had backed up, but they would probably be back.

Ernie climbed out of the ditch behind Hatcher, but a cramp grabbed his leg, and he fell back into the ditch. They had no room to turn or stoop. The fire quickly spread and the soldiers got nervous.

Ernie looked up through the fog of smoke and whispered, "God, save us."

Minutes later, God answered his prayer; spears of lightening slashed the sky, and the earth rumbled with rolling clouds that sent a downpour of rain.

Sergeant Kipper gave orders for the men to follow him. They crawled in the mud behind Kipper a safe distance from the fire that was quickly taking the forest.

The Viet Cong failed to trap them in the fire, and they all survived the attack; they marched in the rain back to their jeeps. The rain soaked them, and Ernie wondered how the Israelites survived forty days and nights trying to reach the Promised Land.

After they got back to the barracks, Ernie felt the heavy load on his back after he removed it. Before going to the mess hall, they took a shower.

Later that night, they gathered in the recreation room to socialize. Tonight, Hobbit was the star of the show. He got up from his chair, and his bushy eyebrows moved up as he stretched his eyes and grinned to get everyone's attention. "I don't know about you boys, but I am glad to be alive after that round with the Viet Cong today. They are the wildest bunch I have ever met up with. If the Lord had not sent the rain, we would still be fighting the animals. That fire probably got out of hand and burned the villages we tried to save."

The next morning, they loaded up in jeeps and went to a village near the area they had been the day before. The busy sea front near the village appeared peaceful. Women walked along the shore in strapped feet; others carried large vats of water toward the village. These tough little women carried the large vats of water with ease. Still others walked toward the village with baskets, filled with market goods, balanced on their heads. A young Vietnamese boy walked near the water with bent head searching for turtle eggs.

As they neared the huts, shabby surroundings made the village look dirty and unhealthy; the smell of fish was unpleasant. A shaggy dog sniffed around the garbage cans that needed to be emptied.

They followed a cloud of smoke to the back side of the huts and found women cooking large pots of food over an open fire, while others sat on wooden benches before a black wash pot, filled with boiling water, and dipped white chickens into the water to pluck. Judging from the number of pots on the coals, they planned a big feast for the entire village.

The women did not seem surprised when Sergeant Fitzwater began his questions. The woman who spoke for the group told him there had seen no Viet Cong in their village. Fitzwater did not believe her. He suspected her husband was a Viet Cong. Before they left the group, a young girl came from one of the huts and offered them tea, but they never took food or drink offered to them by the people in the villages.

Ernie followed the other soldiers as they moved around the huts. Old men sat on their porches with watchful eyes on children who played games. Sometimes the old men would disappear in the woods to keep from answering questions. The first man they questioned denied having seen any Viet Cong in the area. They went to the next hut where an old man with a long chin beard sat in his rocker and smoked his pipe. He told them a regiment of Viet Cong camped near their village two days before; and the younger men ran into the jungle to hide from the Viet Cong. They often captured young boys and forced them to join their forces.

They moved on down the line of huts and asked questions. A woman, who had remained in her hut, came out and volunteered information: the Viet Cong came two days before; the women gave them food, and they left. She also told them that Americans gave guns to bad people, and the Viet Cong used these guns to kill Americans.

The people in the village trusted neither Americans nor the Viet Cong. Both forces had killed their people and Americans also destroyed their crops with spray.

Ernie followed the other soldiers from the village across a rice field. The farmer behind his plow kept his eyes on the rice and continued bogging the furrows behind his water buffalo. The sergeant stopped and watched the farmer a few minutes and walked on across the field. The farmer's dress did not mark him as a Viet Cong.

Before turning in for the night, Ernie pulled his writing pad and pen from beneath his mattress and settled on his bunk to write to his mama. He told her how homesick he was and how stressed out he was over the war; He told her about camping in the jungle; he told her about the villages he had visited, and the poverty he had seen; he told her that he believed it was a sin to kill another human being, regardless of the cause; and he told her how lucky he felt to live in America.

CHAPTER TWENTY

During the first part of June 1968, Ernie and his platoon got orders to report to Lane Army Post in Nha Trang the following Monday. Ernie had decided that they would be no better at the fight in another place.

Americans would die trying to stop the Viet Cong; the North would finally take over the South. Ernie had faced reality; he would be fighting until his time was up. The soldiers had said that Westmoreland held the forces together; but the Company Commander changed about every three months, and they kept moving the soldiers around.

The night of June 5, 1968, was one of the saddest nights Ernie and his buddies had spent at Dalat Army Base. Their conversation about their transfer stopped abruptly when the television flashed Walter Cronkite on the screen with a special report from CBS:

"A sniper killed Senator Robert F. Kennedy only hours after he won the California and Dakota primary elections for the Democratic nomination for President of the United States. The sniper set his aim on Senator Kennedy when he saw him walking through the kitchen of the Ambassador Hotel; Kennedy died twenty-six hours later."

Kennedy's death shocked the GI's. Silence and sadness fell over the room. The soldiers had pulled for Robert Kennedy; he had promised to end the Vietnam War. They concluded that the mad lunatic needed help for a sickness that the best doctors in the world could not cure.

Later they learned that a man named Sirhan Sirhan, a twenty-four year old Palestinian/ Jordanian immigrant, was convicted for Robert Kennedy's murder and sentenced to life in prison. Sirhan claimed he was framed.

Then they heard more bad news: General Creighton W. Abrams replaced General Westmoreland, the Commander of United States troops in Vietnam. Worst of all, President Johnson defeated Eugene McCarthy in the primary election; the soldiers lost all hopes of seeing an end to the Vietnam War.

Two weeks had passed since Ernie had seen Anna. He wanted to spend some time with her before he left Dalat. On Sunday, she finally sneaked away from her grandmother and met Ernie at the Restaurant. He waited until they finished dinner before breaking the bad news. She broke down in tears and they left the restaurant. They sat in the jeep and talked.

"I want to spend the night with you," he said.

"How can I spend the night with you?" she said. "Grandmother would have her search party looking for me; she would report my absence to the police and make a big scene."

"Go back home and I will be at your door in a few minutes. If Granny Grump does not want me to stay there with you, then you can go with me."

"Are you crazy? You have certainly lost your good mind!" she said.

"I am crazy about you, and I am leaving tomorrow."

"Grandmother goes to bed with the chickens," Anna said.

What time do the chickens roost in your neck of the woods?"

"Just to be on the safe side, come a little after eight."

"How will I know when to walk up to your door?"

"I will turn on the porch light after Grandmother goes to bed."

"I will see you at five minutes after eight. Synchronize your watch. I have exactly 7:20 at this minute."

When Ernie got to the Ming residence, the porch light was on and Anna was waiting. Just inside her bedroom, he grabbed her, swung her around, and kissed her. She pulled away and ran around the room with laughter as he chased her. He cornered her near the bed, and their laughter ceased with a wild passionate kiss.

He touched her lips with his fingertip, covered her lips with a kiss, and unbuttoned her dress. She lay naked by his side, cuddled against him and said, "I love you, and I would like to spend the night with you, but Grandmother may get up during the night and check on me. If she discovers that my door is locked, she will not stop knocking until I open the door and let her inspect my room."

"I am not worried about Granny Grump, and I am in no hurry to get back to my base," he said and moved his eyes around the bedroom. She had a closet full of clothes, and she had stacks of books on her desk that reminded him of his own room at home. After he made love to her the second time, she lay in his arms and dozed. He had fallen asleep when a loud pounding at the door startled him. He tugged at her shoulder and she sat upright in the bed before coming to her senses. "Grandmother is at the door! Get up and hide in the bathroom."

Ernie grabbed his clothes and ran through an open door to the adjoining bathroom. He looked around the bathroom for a closet. The bathtub with its four curved legs was his only choice. He stepped into the bathtub, quietly pulled the curtain, sat down, and waited. He peeped around the wine curtain and moved his eyes over the dishes of carved soap and colorful towels with pictures of oriental trinkets that decorated a dressing table next to a sink. The sound of dripping water turned his attention to the commode, which needed a new float.

Anna opened the door and yawned as Mrs. Ming's eyes meddled past her and searched her bedroom. "I thought I heard voices," she said."

"The voices you heard came from the music on the stereo, Grandmother."

"Turn that thing off," she said and walked back down the hall toward her room.

Anna slammed the door with anger. Then she pressed her ear to the door and listened to her grandmother's steps fade down the hall. She stepped away from the door and waited a few minutes before going to find Ernie. She went to the bathroom, jerked the shower curtain back, and laughed at the sight. Ernie was crouched in the corner of the tub.

"You do not choose good hiding places. The bathtub is the best place to look first."

"Do you see another place in here to hide?" he said as he got out of the tub. He looked in the mirror above the sink as he ran fingers through his hair. "Where is Granny Grump?"

"She went back to bed," she said.

"Good, I hope she stays in bed and minds her own business." He pulled her to him and kissed her as she made backward steps back to the bedroom. She lay in his arms and he did most of the talking. He tried to convince her to get an apartment in town and start living her own life. He told her he could come back and visit her when he got a pass.

She explained that her father would kill her before he allowed her to move out on her own. Her father's fits and terrible temper frightened her. He had threatened her many times before when he got angry.

"Why do you have to answer to your father, explain every detail of your life? Is he a perfect saint?"

"On the contrary, he lives in sin. He ran around on my mother. He still slips around with women, but he never brought a woman home to meet the family."

Two hours later, he kissed her good night. He promised to meet her at the Villa Nine Restaurant the next morning at eight o'clock to say good-bye. He quietly closed the door and had started down the hall when Lena Ming in her fleecy gown blocked his way.

"What do you think you are doing here?"

Ernie stood to attention and said, "I was just paying your granddaughter a friendly visit, Mrs. Ming."

By this time Anna had heard her grandmother; she came out into the hallway, and her grandmother looked at her as if she would literally choke her to death as she spoke, "You invited this American to your bed! My eyes deceived me! You have lost your good mind! Your father will kill him, and his death is well deserved!" Then she said, "Put on your clothes!"

Ernie dashed out the front door and jumped in the jeep.

"Why are you looking at me with evil eyes, Grandmother? You cannot keep me tied to your apron strings forever. I am a grown woman with the needs and feelings of a grown woman. Do you not remember your younger days?"

Her grandmother stood and stared at Anna with shock and did not speak. Lena Ming wished she could make Anna see her mistakes. She hated to see her granddaughter throw her life away. If Anna got pregnant, that American would run the other way. He came to Anna for only one thing. If Anna earned a bad reputation, men would use her rest of her life. She would never find a husband. No man proposed to a lewd woman.

"You should feel shame for what you did," her grandmother said. "You should act your age and keep your head. A decent woman would not stoop to lust as you have done. You act as if you are a sixteen year old street girl."

"I do not know how a sixteen year old street girl acts; I never lived through that time, and I do not act my age, because I never had a chance to do the things that teens do. Think back to the time when I was a teenager. While girls my age went out on dates with boys of their choice, I sat here with you and Mother to rock your memories. You have not allowed me to have a life.

You have never allowed me to make my own choices, and I cannot enjoy life. You scared me with your bad mouth about men and sex, but I will no longer listen to your foolishness. I will be out of my prime before you give your approval for me to love a man."

"Your speech must have been practiced for days. You must save your words for your own daughter. What will you tell her about your lover?"

"If you do not stop interfering in my life, I will never have a daughter, a son, or a husband."

"If you continue the chase, you will never catch a man."

"That will be my heart ache and your celebration, Grandmother. Please go away and leave me alone." Anna slammed her bedroom door and stood at the window to look out at the village. She could imagine herself in America, the land of the free. How she yearned to be with him forever.

The next day, Anna's grandmother and her father put their heads together; they cornered her in the living room and raised hell for more than an hour about Ernie Tennyson.

Anna finally walked out of the room and got away from their judgmental remarks. Her father called her back; he called her three times before she went back and listened to his hateful remarks.

Dong Lee looked at her as if she had committed murder and said, "You have gone against my wishes and the wishes of your old grandmother once over. Worst of all, you have gone against the wishes of your mother in her grave. You are a grown woman and I do not know what to do about your defiance."

"You are right, Father. I am a grown woman and I have the needs of a woman. I want my freedom." Her eyes pleaded for his understanding, but he said nothing and she continued, "Father, I do not mean to go against your wishes, but you have no right to control my life. Please, stop fussing at me; let me have my freedom!"

He spoke with anger in his voice, "Have you had sex with that American?"

She considered his question with distain; his dirty mind disgusted her. She had rather he punished her by beating her with a cane. She finally said, "Father, I am in love with Ernie." She ran to her room and slammed the door.

She leaned against the door and listened to his footsteps move toward the kitchen. She sat down on her bed and the memories of her childhood clouded her brain. She saw her family gathered around the sacred altar. She watched them cry with sadness and rejoice with happiness. That time had passed; her beliefs had changed. She disagreed with her father's beliefs and ideals. She hated his religion; she hated his Gods; she hated his evil spirits. She wanted to tell him that she did not believe that life ended with death for Christians who believed in God the Father. Most of all, she wanted to tell him that she would never marry the man he chose for her. She loved Ernie Tennyson, and her father's wishes meant nothing to her. She would go to the end of the earth with Ernie. She would abandon her family for him.

She believed her father's religion was only a cover for his sins. He craved worldly things: power, money, liquor, and women. Whispering feet slid on the wooden floor and she sat upright in bed with wide eyes of curiosity. Her grandmother peeped into the door and said, "Dinner is set."

"I am not hungry, Grandmother." She could not face them both at one time. She got up, cleaned her room, took a warm bath, and settled back with a book. She read until she fell asleep.

When Anna got up the next morning, she heard her grandmother talking to her father. A few minutes later, she heard the front door slam and the roar of her father's motor as he pulled away.

Anna called the school to tell Sister Theresa that she would not be at school until around lunch time. Then she called a cab to take her to Dalat to meet Ernie. She was at the Villa Nine Restaurant waiting for Ernie before he got there.

Ernie asked her to eat breakfast, but she felt sick and depressed; she had no appetite.

"I'm going to miss you more than a cool drink when I am thirsty," Ernie said.

She forced a smile, but she found no words to say. After they left the restaurant, they stood on the street corner to say good bye; he held her in his arms and whispered sweet words that she needed to hear. "I am coming back one day and steal you away from your father and grandmother. You are going to America with me." Then he kissed her long and passionately. "Be good, and write to me every day."

She promised to write, and kissed him good bye. Tears streamed down her face as she stood on the corner and watched him walk away. She waved until he was out of sight. She could not bear to see him get on the bus and drive away.

That night, her grandmother was her usual critical self. She was ready to judge the jury. She came into Anna's room, uninvited, and sat down on the edge of the bed to begin her questions: "Did the American get what he wanted before he went away?"

"Grandmother, please do not ask me vulgar questions?"

"That American is no good for you. He is the devil over all of our enemies. You cannot breed character in a man who has no character."

"Why are you so harsh in your judgment? You know nothing about Ernie!"

"I am an old woman. I have lived in the age of reason. That American dangles many women on his string. Women greet him at every corner."

"I do not believe you speak the truth. You do not understand the feelings of love, because you have never loved."

"Is there need to understand a fool?"

"Do you call Ernie a fool, because he makes his own decisions? Do you call me a fool, because I refuse to listen and obey your wishes?"

"The answer to both questions is yes," she said.

"Grandmother, please go away and leave me in peace and quiet. I hate your opinions and I am so tired."

"You must heed my words, Granddaughter. A man keeps a clean reputation, while his bad seed sprouts in the woman and marks her as a whore. A man can enjoy sex with a string of lovers, and he never gives the number of lovers a second thought, but a woman who sleeps with a man out of wedlock is a whoremonger and makes an unfit wife. This is the accepted rule over the world, even in societies that claim to believe in a heavenly father and freedom for all. Remember my words, Granddaughter. A woman is a prisoner to the man she loves."

"Your words are old fashioned and made in your head. Ernie loves me, Grandmother."

"Love comes in time to those brought together by the Gods."

"Ernie does not have the same God; his God is the heavenly father; his God is the same God that my mother believed in, and I think their God looks on our relationship with favor. I am sure that I love Ernie, and I will never love another!"

"Arranged marriages endure. The husband respects his wife and he will be a good father, but a man does not respect a woman who gives her body to him before marriage."

"Ernie respects me, and he will be a good father to our children. He never did anything disrespectful."

"Your marriage must be arranged, and you must not stray from the flock."

"My father was betrothed to my mother. I have heard her complain about her father having arranged her marriage. My father was not a good husband, and he is a terrible father."

"Hold your tongue, Granddaughter!"

"I will not hold my tongue, Grandmother. Why does Father shame me for the same sins he practices?" Anna said. "What will he do about his mistress? He slips to her bed at night. My mother knew he had flings with other women, but she allowed him to crawl back to her bed and never complained."

Her grandmother walked to the window and looked out. "Your father sinned, but his sins are easier to bear. He never made promises to other women. He loved your mother. Some men make promises that they do not intend to keep. This American's promises are like the melting snow; they quickly disappear and are forgotten."

"You know nothing about this American, Grandmother. How can you judge his character and intentions?"

"I am an old woman, and I know about love and lies."

"My father wants to control me and watch me bow down to his wishes. My mother always obeyed him, but I will no longer bend to his wishes."

"Disrespectful words about your father are not a good thing for the Gods and your spirituals ancestors to hear."

Anna looked to the ceiling and shouted, "Hear me Gods of my ancestors! I love Ernie and not one of you will stop me!"

She turned back at the door and said, "The words I have spoken are facts, my dear," and she went back to the kitchen.

Anna sat before the mirror and answered the questions on her mind. Why should I have to sneak behind my father and grandmother to see Ernie? I am a grown woman. I am free; yet, I am my father's prisoner. I have been a prisoner of his religious beliefs and his family's traditions from the day I was born. My grandfather denied my mother a happy life by his control over her decisions. He never let her realize her dreams. Like my Grandfather, my father is a liar and a cheat. His God is a God to suit his purpose. My father treated my mother like a slave, and he never considered her needs. While my father enjoyed the riches and pleasures of his prime, my mother slept at the other end of the house with desires that my father never satisfied. My father must have known why my mother turned a cold shoulder to his affections. I now understand my mother's secret longings and dreams. My mother hated being a slave to my father's wishes.

CHAPTER TWENTY-ONE

In June 1968, Ernie and his platoon reported to Lane Army Post in Nha Trang. After Ernie and Private got unpacked, they went to the mess hall and ate dinner.

After dinner, they walked around the base and got acquainted with some of the soldiers from another company.

Later that evening they walked down town. Palm trees shaded Tran Phu Street in the day and street lamps lit the streets at night. Beyond the trees, they could see a long stretch of beach, and the roar of the ebb tide grew louder with time. A section of earth and rocks piled along the shore caught the high tide and trapped seaweed. An orange sunset fell on a lonely angler rowing his small boat toward the shore with his catch for that day.

They moved down the slope and got a better view of the ocean. They watched a fisherman move a wide rake back and forth across a huge pile of oysters for the market.

Moving on along the shore, they stopped and watched three young boys fight the strong waves to get their boat to shore. After they pulled the long wooden boat to shore, they jumped into the boat and used five gallon buckets to gather the shrimp and lobster from the bottom of the boat.

Ernie and Hatcher left the fishermen with their catch and walked back to their base. Ernie said, "I wish I was sitting on the bank of the creek with a pole in my hand."

"I like to fish, too," Hatcher said. "The last time I went fishing, I went with my brother to the river. We have a place in Alabama that is famous for white perch."

After they ate supper, they got ready for bed and slept on dread of the next day. Ernie wished he could curl up in a cave and sleep until the war ended. He had conditioned himself to the most horrible things imaginable, because he knew nothing about tunnels and bunkers, except what he had been told.

Their first mission at Lane was to investigate suspicious Viet Cong bunkers and tunnels. Highly skilled in guerrilla warfare, the Viet Cong dug tunnels under the earth that stretched up to twenty miles long. Some Viet Cong stayed underground for weeks or months at a time. They set up firing positions at the ends of tunnels near their villages for protection; they controlled more than one half of the villages in South Vietnam. They moved from one place to another through these tunnels and sneaked into the southern camps, assassinated the chief, tortured the South Vietnam soldiers, burned villages, and took hostages. They caged human beings like farmers caged their chickens.

Ernie walked behind his platoon with Master Sergeant Kipper in the lead. The thorn bushes grabbed their fatigues; small trees flaunted their limbs and slapped their hard hats. They moved up the slope with caution. The platoon leader stopped and pulled out a map. He squatted and concentrated with his hands moving toward the East. The men concentrated on what lay ahead. The thicket of pine trees, elephant grass, tree trunks, and bamboo vines looked like the jungle in Dalat. Crocodiles and snakes lay quietly waiting in the streams for a bite.

They walked more than six miles from their base in unbearable heat. The GI's had grown used to the pleasant spring-like climate in Dalat, and the hot weather in Nha Trang took them by surprise. Getting used to hot weather would take some time. If the temperature kept rising, the men would die from heat strokes rather than gunfire. Sweat drenched their uniforms; the hot wind parched their lips; and sweat sketched their faces with dirty lines. They rubbed their eyes and wished for a refreshing shower.

The sergeant threw up his hand when he spotted the Viet Cong tunnel. He walked over to a pile of logs on the slope of a hill and ordered the GI's to start moving the logs.

Poisonous snakes, rats, spiders, scorpions, and ants living in the tunnels made them dangerous to put a foot. The Viet Cong sometimes planted dangerous creatures in the tunnels for booby traps, and built the tunnels with sections that trapped poison gas. They carved holes on the sides of the tunnel for throwing poison spears. Although harmless, bats also roosted in the tunnels.

Master Sergeant Kipper sent the three American tunnel experts, who came with them, to investigate the bunker; the GI's called these experts tunnel rats. They carried a .45 caliber pistol, a bayonet, a flashlight, and explosives to plant and destroy the tunnel. They eased down into the small entrance, with their flashlights aimed at dark walls, and crawled a few feet to plant the explosives.

Just as they got the explosives in place, they saw two Viet Cong crawling toward them. They backed up, quickly, climbed back to solid ground, and signaled the demolition expert to trigger the explosives. All of the other GI's moved back with the explosion that threw dirt to the sky, leaving a long, wide hole in the earth with two dead Viet Cong.

After the dirt settled, the GI's moved closer to the site, and Master Sergeant Kipper ordered Ernie and Hatcher to pull the buried Viet Cong from the dirt. They pulled the burned Viet Cong soldiers out of the dirt and laid them on the grass; a medical technician checked their vital signs; both men still breathed, and they begged for help, but war spares no enemy pain or death; they left them there to die.

Then the tunnel rats went back into the tunnel and brought out fifty M16 rifles, ten machine guns, 50 rounds of ammunition, and a M79 grenade launcher.

Afterwards, they followed Master Sergeant Kipper to a river and set up camp behind the slope of a hill. As they gathered wood for a campfire, the sun sank behind the mountain and carried the heat into the earth. A cool breeze blew in a cool night.

Private Quant boiled a huge pot of rice and roasted squirrels and rabbits for supper, while the other soldiers sat around the campfire and drank beer.

Father Crandall, the priest, blessed the food and said a prayer for God to be with them through the days to come. He usually worried them with his prayers, but today they felt a need for his prayers.

After they ate, they sat beneath the full moon and watched their shadows sway to the sound of rhythmic voices blending with the sounds of whippoorwills, crickets, frogs, and owls. The sound of a wolf howling at the moon interrupted their singing. Ernie wondered what a wolf and the moon had in common. The moon controlled the tide. Was the wolf asking the moon about the tide and the weather?

Before turning in for the night, they went down the hill to the river to take a bath. They burned small lamps made from bottles filled with kerosene and settled under the mosquito netting. Ernie lay wide awake and worried about the Viet Cong attacking during the night. He was tired of the killing; he wanted to live and let live; he wanted to go home.

When men at home talked about war, they voiced their worry about the deaths and injuries, but they never felt the fear that soldiers feel. One never knew the footpath until he trampled the vines, bogged in the mud, dodged the bullets, and cringed with the blast. The folk at home had not seen men fall and die; they had not stumbled over dead bodies; they had not fought or run from the fight to save their lives. Ernie prayed that he made it back home alive. Getting killed in this war haunted his dreams. His daddy had told him that brave men do not have weak stomachs; and brave men do not cry, but he found it difficult to be a brave man, especially when he had to pick up a dying man who begged him for help. Pictures flashed on his brain of the two dying Viet Cong he and Hatcher pulled from the tunnel dirt. The fire from the explosion charred them as black as coal.

They camped out all that week, and the tunnel rats destroyed five tunnels. Ernie's height disqualified him as a tunnel rat. On the other hand, he and the other GI's supported the tunnel rats and fought off the enemy when they attacked. They expected the devils to hit at any time, day or night.

On Friday after dinner, they walked back toward their base. Ernie could feel the blisters on his feet sticking to his socks; but he nor the other GI's complained about the long walk.

As soon as they got to the barracks, they hit the showers. Ernie could smell his own bad odor. His hair also smelled like stinking sweat. After a bath and chow time, they met in the recreation room to socialize; they smoked, drank, and bragged about women they had slept with.

Ernie had never been happier to see an army bunk. Tonight, he could get a good night's rest. On the other hand, he wished he had not emptied that liquor bottle. Liquor impaired his ability to think and interrupted his sleep. When he had too much to drink, he thought about Anna. He missed her; he dreamed about being with her, but his dream ended too soon.

As usual, when he drank too much, he woke up with a headache. He took two pain pills and headed to the shower. Then he and Hatcher went to the mess hall. It took only a few days in the jungle to make him appreciate the mess hall. He learned that back at Dalat. He sat down at the table and noticed his nice surroundings, and the food was good. He was hungry, and he ate with a hearty appetite. They stayed on base three days and searched for Viet Cong the next four days.

In the meantime, Anna got ready to go to school. The students occupied her time during the day; but she missed Ernie, especially at night. She looked forward to his letters. She kept an eye on the mailbox to keep her grandmother from getting her mail. She spent many sleepless nights with a book in her hand.

When she got home from school that evening, she wrote to Ernie.

Dear Ernie,

You left me lonely and depressed. I miss you very much, and I hate the Army transferred you when our relationship had just begun. My mind is filled with memories of our time together. I need not close my eyes to see your face, hear your voice, and feel your touch. We come from two different worlds and you do not understand my beliefs and traditions, but our love for each other will make all other things small and keep us together.

The children asked many times what happened to the nice American. You won their hearts the day you saved Zang, and they want you to come back to visit our class.

My grandmother questioned me after you left. When she learned that you had been transferred, she said good spirits took you away to protect me, and she believes the spirits will drive you away from me. She preached a sermon about the right thing I should do in case you return. When the time comes for you to return to your homeland, I do not know what I will do.

The war brings even more sorrow with every sunrise, and the stress is hard to cope with. The enemy destroyed a small village north of us on Monday last, and many of my friends died. I try not to think about the war, but its destruction is all around me. Many of the farmers had no crop this year. The United States Government sends Uncle Ben's Rice from Louisiana. I am not familiar with Uncle Ben or Louisiana; but I am sure you know where Louisiana is located in your country. We are grateful to them; but I wish Americans had not destroyed our crops in the first place. Laos is also furnishing our families staple rice. I worry about the children who do not have enough to eat. If the war continues, they will have no rice or bread.

I look forward to visiting you as soon as you have a weekend free. I will love you as long as God gives me breath.

Love, Anna

Ernie sat on the edge of his bunk and pulled the small bedside table before him and answered Anna's letter.

Dear Anna,

I miss you as much as I miss home and Mama's cooking. The days are a month long without you. I have relived every minute of our times together, but dreams fade with the morning sun; I must face my duty. I never drank hard liquor before the war, but now I drink anything at hand to help me sleep and forget the day.

If possible, I will make arrangements to take the weekend off when you come to visit. If I had a car, I would come to see you. On the other hand, Grandmother would stand in our way.

I have another month and one half in this War and I cannot wait to get back home.

Love, Ernie.

CHAPTER TWENTY-TWO

Three weeks later, Anna Ming got on a bus and headed for Nha Trang, known for its beautiful beaches lined with white sand and clear ocean water. Ernie had reserved a room at the Ana Mandara Hotel and would meet her there at eleven for lunch.

The hotel on Tran Phu Street impressed Anna; the seashore and the ocean along the street made it the most beautiful street in Nha Trang. As she walked to the registration desk, she noticed the bar to her right. She took an elevator to the third floor and found their room. The room with its expensive furniture, television, telephone, and fireplace impressed her even more than the hotel. A canopy fell around the bed that resembled the crown of a king with a flowing robe of gold. A sweet smell filled the room from the vase of red roses on the Victorian table next to the bed.

A rush of excitement made her pulse pound as the time drew near for Ernie to meet her. She smoothed her make-up, fluffed her hair, and turned before the mirror. She wanted to look beautiful and she was. She wore a long, green silk dress stamped with bright green flowers. The jade beads shimmered and blended perfectly with the dress. Gold leaves swept her hair behind her ears and let it fall down her back. She kicked off her shoes and ran her toes around the oriental designs on the carpet.

When she heard Ernie knock, she rushed to the door and pulled it back. There he stood in the living flesh.

"Hello, beautiful, I've missed you," he said, and his eyes adored her. He pulled her into his arms and kissed her with a wildness that was wonderful. Then he pushed her back and said, "Where would you like to have dinner?"

"Let us walk and look for a nice place to eat."

She was pleased with the restaurant he chose. The Chef's Palace was a large Chinese restaurant with a floor of colorful stones and shiny mahogany tables for seating large families. Smaller tables along the windows seated a small family. Ernie noticed the decorations right away. Ancient Chinese figures danced on the ceiling; red tassels around the lights threw colored light around them; and Chinese chimes moved in the breeze and carried a soft rhythmic sound through the restaurant. Partitions of glass stained with flowers and birds of beauty separated the buffet of steaming food that smelled delicious. The chef came to the buffet and filled the steaming tubs with rice, chicken, beef, and oriental vegetables. He wore a tall top hat of white, and a red apron protected his clothes.

The waiter served them wine and caviar right away. Then he came back with his pad to take their order. As usual, her anxious and romantic mood made her lose her appetite. She looked up from the menu and said, "I think I will have the bird's nest soup."

Ernie wanted to chirp. Had he heard her say bird's nest soup? Did they have bird's nest on the menu with the food? He wondered if the bird's nest was green. He continued looking at his menu and pretended she had not said that. He ordered a seafood platter with the trimmings, a salad, and a potato. They both ordered tea to drink, but he especially asked for red tea with sugar and ice; she ordered hot, green tea.

After the waiter left, Ernie said, "Did I hear you correctly? Did you order bird's nest soup?"

"Bird's nest soup is delicious."

"Do they actually make soup from a bird's nest?"

"They certainly do make soup from a bird's nest," she said. "They collect bird's nest from the Swiftlet group of farm birds. They also search for Swiftlet's bird nests in the wood."

"I'm not going to ask what they put in the soup; I have no use for the recipe. I'm not going to waste precious time arguing about Vietnamese food." He took her hand and lifted his glass for a toast. "This night is dedicated to Anna and Ernie for their dreams and their future."

"That is the sweetest thing I have ever heard you say. This will be a perfect weekend," she said.

After dinner, they had Cognac and listened to music in the banquet room.

Back at the motel, He walked in behind her and immediately kissed her. The wine turned her head like a spinning top, and she wanted him to make love to her. Suddenly she remembered the beautiful gown her grandmother had made and given to her for her wedding night. She had kept it in her hope chest for almost a year. She walked over to her suitcase, got the gown, and went to the bathroom to dress. As she pulled the thin gown over her head, she had a warm urgency for him right then.

When she walked into the room, he said, "Wow, you are beautiful." The white, soft silk gown, embroidered with pink roses, made her look like an angel, the angel who saved his life that day at the rice hut. He held his arms out to her and she lay close by his side. He fingered the flowers on her bosom and said, "Your gown is beautiful."

She smiled and said, "My grandmother made my gown by hand. She asked me to save the gown for my wedding night, so we must pretend until that night comes."

"Grandmother is very talented if she can make a garment like that," he said. "How is Grandmother doing?"

"I think Grandmother has a split personality. Her mood swings, and she is hard to live with. Sometimes she is nice to me and cooks my favorite dishes to please me. At other times, she nags me about my staying in my room; she gripes about my coming home from school a few minutes late." She ran her hand over the gown and said, "If Grandmother knew I was lying in bed next to you with this gown covering my body, she would have a duck."

"Pull that damn gown off this minute; you are not wearing that precious gown in my bed," he said, and reached the bottom of the gown, pulled it over her head, and let it hit the floor. Then he pulled her close and said, "You are more beautiful without the gown." Their closeness burned with an erotic pleasure. His gentle touches and warm kisses sent a good feeling through her that took command of her whole being. He pulled her down on the bed and she closed her eyes and went to heaven as he explored her body with a tender love that made her feel special. The wine mixed with her feelings for him made her head spin with a wonderful dizziness. He was anxious for her to surrender to him and she did. He was warm inside her, and she was wild with passion. The good feeling took her too soon, engulfed her whole body. She was crazy with words. For minutes, she soared wildly; then she wiggled lightly against him and settled with a quiet bliss. She experienced a perfect, premature, orgasm.

Her pleasure filled him with a feeling that lingered long after her calm. He whispered sweet words that she needed to hear, and she wanted him to tell her again that he loved her, but he was quiet. They did not sleep; they shared their needs, their secrets, and their love. Tomorrow she would leave him again and live on dreams until she was with him again.

She played her fingers on his chest and recited poetry.

"My love for you is the spring time rain, the smell of sweet lavender, the fire that warms me on a cold winter night.

If you take my heart, I will weep no more, my anguish shall be yours, and the tears you shed shall be mine.

I will go with you over the mountains and down through the dark valleys.

Memories of you will live with me forever, and I will love you till death separates us."

After her love poem she closed her eyes and silence surrounded them.

"What are you thinking about?" he asked.

"I love you so much," she said and paused with thought. I dream about our wedding day. Weddings in Vietnam are great celebrations. You have never seen a more beautiful sight. The villages and the wedding site come to life with fireworks. The parents and ancestors of the bride welcome the groom and his family. After the bride and groom repeat their vows, they share a cup of tea and one betel nut to symbolize their union as one. Then they go to the groom's house to make offerings to his parents and grandparents. His parents often hang a picture of a male child in the room where the bride and groom will stay the first night they are married. This picture brings good luck to them to have a baby boy." She smiled at him and said, "I want to have a baby boy for you when we are married."

He remained silent. He did not want to build up her hopes of a wedding in the near future, especially not a wedding in Vietnam. He had always enjoyed fireworks on the Fourth of July, Christmas, and New Years in America, but he never wanted to hear or see another fireworks show; he didn't want to remember the sounds of war: guns spitting fire, bullets singing and zooming, and bombs exploding across the tangled jungles and the deep, dirty, ditches where he cowered to die.

She interrupted his thoughts with her apology, "I should not be talking about weddings and such with the war still going on, but I am a dreamer."

"Our time together is not a dream," he said. "We are really here in bed together."

"You are a level headed squire. You never worry about tomorrow."

He didn't know what a squire was, but he worried about tomorrow more than she knew.

A loud explosion interrupted his thoughts. He jumped up and rushed to the window. Air raids screamed around the city. He went to the phone and called the base. The enemy bombed the mess hall at Lane, but they gave no details about the damage or number of deaths.

They slept late the next morning and had breakfast at a small coffee shop. As they ate, he could see happiness and excitement shining in her face, and her eyes shone with love for him.

After they ate, they walked next to a long row of palms and moved down a grassy slope to the beach. The sun sprinkled the sea with silver sequins and its twinkling rays made the white sand sparkle. They admired the beauty of the beach and blue water that stretched further than the eye could see. Large, white birds dipped and gawked at the rippling waves. As they walked and looked for shells, the sand was warm and light under their feet. They stopped and tickled their toes in the water with a circular movement; then they walked on. Pretty soon, they tired of walking and sat down on the sand to admire their seashells. A soft breeze carried the smell of her sweetness and stirred his desire; he pulled her close and could not stop with one kiss.

She pulled away finally and looked toward the sky. "Look!" she said, pointing to a flock of White Sea gulls that gawked at the ocean's roar as they dipped and sailed across the waves. "They look so peaceful. They do not know about the war, I suppose."

"At times, I wish I had wings," he said.

"This is the most romantic place I have ever been," she said.

"Any beach would be romantic with you by my side," he said.

"Let's build a sand castle," she said.

"The tide would tear our castle down," he said.

She piled their shells in a heap and began writing in the sand.

A Day at the Beach
The salty sea breeze gently blows.
The sun dips seaward with red and gold.
A soft blue heaven floats above.
Bent waves whisper words of love.
Divers in wet suits dive to explore.
A beagle sniffs and roams the shore.
Children listen to the shells found.
Conch shells mimic the ocean's sound.
The sun hides behind the day.
Shrimp boats anchor and get their pay.
The flood tide rushes and fills the bays.
Lovers try to stall the hands of time.
Sea gulls fly and fall into rhyme.
The tide reaches the tall stone wall.
Castles of sand crumble and fall.
With balanced shadows, surfers glide.
White sands wash ashore with the tide.

"That was a darn good poem," he said.

"Poetry is the most powerful form of literature in Vietnam. I have been writing since I was a small child. My mother taught me many things about writing. She wrote iambic pentameter, mostly."

"I know very little about rhymes," he said.

The dampness from the ocean breeze fell on them and fringes of dark hair fell around her face as they walked. She was more beautiful than he had ever seen her.

"Walking on the beach with you is better than sitting by the fire on a cold winter night in Georgia."

"I have dreamed about going to Georgia with you."

"Maybe your dream will come true very soon," and he changed the subject. "Are you hungry?"

"I am starving," she said.

They walked back up the hill to the road that met a narrow bridge. They saw a cluster of beach side restaurants a short distance away. As they walked on the narrow walk-way next to the bridge, they met more pedestrians than vehicles. She stopped and looked down at the angry stream that rolled beneath the bridge and turned to him. "I have often wondered why the waves are so strong. Where does the water get such strength to roll like that?"

"There must be an angry God behind the water," he said. He had meant his remark to be a joke, but she did not take it as a joke.

"That makes sense," she said and they walked on.

They passed several restaurants overlooking the waves, but they walked on until they reached the Coconut Grove; the perfect place to eat. Round tree tables with wooden benches filled the large patio, and the cool breeze carried the smell of broiled lobster and Chinese sauce.

They waited for a table, and got a choice table with an ocean view. He saw that the Coconut Grove specialized in seafood, and he was pleased. She usually ordered Chinese food, and Chow Mien was her favorite. He had eaten Chow Mien in Georgia with a fork, but he didn't care for celery on the end of a chop stick that fell in his lap before it reached his mouth. He finally talked her into ordering broiled lobster.

The waves stirred a romantic mood that matched the music coming from the bar next-door. She had a faraway look in her eyes, and seemed preoccupied with unpleasant thoughts.

"Do you want to talk about what is bothering you?" he said, taking her hand in his.

"I have this feeling that bad omens surround us," she said. "At times, I am psychic."

He threw his palm before her and said, "Read my future, lady."

"If I could read your palm, I probably would not be here."

"Have I made an unfavorable impression to your dead ancestors' spirits?" He touched her face and looked deep into her eyes.

"I believe my mother would have approved of you," she said.

"The old man is a different story," he said. "Are you worried about his finding out about our secret meeting this weekend?"

"I worry about tomorrow. The war seems to be getting worse."

"Don't think about tomorrow; live for today," he said.

"We must never stop worrying about tomorrow," she said. "You are involved in this terrible war, and I have nothing to look forward to, except our stolen hours together."

"Think good thoughts; be optimistic. The war will end soon, and I am coming back to Lat Village and steal you away from Granny Grump and Father."

"What a delightful thought," she said and smiled.

The waiter brought their order and they laughed and talked about the future while they ate.

"Let's go to Cham Towers of Po Nagar."

"Are you going to ask Po Nagar to forgive you for having sex with me this weekend?"

"Po Nagar is a Buddhist temple, and I thought you might be interested in learning about the Buddhist religion as well as the monks' unusual life."

"I will never understand the Buddhist religion, but the Monks sound interesting."

"They believe that man must reach enlightenment; they also believe in reincarnation and ultimate Nirvana. They live in a monastery and arise very early to work in the field. They eat one meal each day, pray in the temple, and talk to the elders. Then they go to bed before ten o'clock."

"I don't see how they get anything done with that robe flouncing around their legs. Farmers back home wear work pants or overalls. They would die of a heat stroke wearing a long robe. Besides, farmers back home work from sunrise till sunset when the weather is good."

Cham Towers Pagoda with its slatted roof stood on a hill of rocks surrounded by trees and plants. The main attraction was the tall stone statue. When Anna told him the statue was Yan Po Nagar, he told her he thought he was King Buddha resting on his marble pedestal. Po Nagar was dressed in a skirt and sat with crossed legs next to curved steps with dragon rails. Ernie assumed that the dragon held the secrets of those who prayed to Buddha. Po Nagar held objects in each of his ten hands; these objects stood for particular religious beliefs. Anna told him that Po Nagar spoke to a Hindu Goddess, the slayer of the buffalo-demon. An ancient brass urn divided the width of the steps, and they got narrow near the stone entrance. Above the entrance to the temple, Ernie spotted a goddess with four arms; she stood on a buffalo and held to a hatchet, a lotus, and a club. God knows what that woman had in mind. He didn't ask Anna. Instead, he turned her attention to the clear view of the river and the city of Nha Trang. They stood and looked at the sight several minutes before entering the temple.

Ernie opened the double doors and they stepped into a large room that smelled like incense mixed with green pine straw. Dim lights fell on a Monk dressed in a brown robe. Soft brown eyes peered from thick glasses with dark rims. His hair had been cut around the bald spot on top of his head. He smiled, extended a warm hand of welcome, and invited them to sit on a bench near the front altar. Then a Buddhist priest draped in white came from a back door and entered the pulpit like an American trial judge, the symbol of purity, moderation, patience, kindness, and justice for all. The Buddhist worshipers sat in a circle and passed the sacred cord to unite them in worship.

As the priest blessed the sacred text, Anna whispered, "He reaches for the realm of Neiva."

"Is Neiva Heaven?" Ernie asked.

"Buddha believes that Heaven is here on earth."

"Are you kidding? Hell is here on earth."

"Never mind," she said and flipped her hand at him.

They walked across the tile floor and Ernie wanted to run back out the door. Buddha seemed to be inviting them to come closer. Anna told him that the people around the altar burned the paper and offered food and incense to the spirits on the anniversary of their death. When the ceremony ended, they ate something.

Ernie thought their ceremony was foolish, but he had found many foolish things about this country.

They finally left the Pagoda and walked around the city. The French colonial homes with their sculptured hedges added beauty to the landscape. They stopped to take pictures of a Catholic Church with twin towers centered by a huge clock. They passed magnificent shops, restaurants, and bars. Then they went to the Cho Dam Market to admire the arts and crafts and buy some fruit.

On the way back to the hotel, Anna stopped at every store window to admire the clothes and shoes.

"I cannot remember having had so much fun in my life time, but I must be at the bus station before six. Grandmother thinks I am spending the weekend in Saigon at Father's villa."

"I wish I could take you back to camp with me," he said. "I will try to get a weekend pass soon, so we can celebrate before I go back to Georgia."

"Until I am by your side again, I will think of you," she said.

"Give my regards to Granny Grump," he said, pulling her close for one last kiss.

"Be careful on your way back to camp. Good bye, my love."

After pulling away the third time, she quickly rushed away.

Anna slept on the bus ride back to Dalat. When she got home, her Grandmother asked a million questions about her weekend in Saigon. She wanted to tell her that she spent the weekend with Ernie and he was wonderful. Absence makes the heart grow warmer, and they had been starved for each other.

When Ernie got back to the barracks, he went to his bunk to take a nap. Before he got out of his uniform, Corporal Hatcher came in and handed him a letter. "I got your mail for you today."

Ernie looked at the envelope with surprise. "This is from Anna's grandmother," Ernie said tearing into the letter.

"She probably wants you to come have Sunday dinner with the family," Corporal Hatcher said and shook with laughter.

"I had soon have dinner with a den of wolves," Ernie said and read the letter aloud.

"Dear Mr. Tennyson,

Anna does not know that I am writing you, but I feel that it is my duty to write and tell you the truth about Anna, since she does not have the heart to tell you. Since you left, Anna is as wild as the young cats in the jungle. She goes out every night, and I believe she visits the Dalat bar, where she entertains American soldiers. Several of her suitors have picked her up at my doorsteps. The day after you left, she went out with another man. I followed them to the hotel in Dalat. She did not return home until the next morning at five o'clock, and she smelled like rice whiskey. The women in my family have never taken to strong drink. This caper is a disgrace to my family. When I confronted her about her suitor, she clamped her mouth and did not speak to me for days. Now she slips out often after I have gone to bed. She takes my advice as a grain of salt and quickly brushes it from her mind.

Before Anna met you, her father betrothed her to a nice Chinese man, and we looked forward to her marriage to Chang. He would give her a good life and make her a good husband. You live in a completely different world. Your customs and religious beliefs cannot be accepted by Anna's father and me. Besides, Anna will never get accustomed to your life style.

I am writing you to say that the change in Anna is your entire fault. You tore up our family, and I will never forgive you for this. I want you to leave her alone. When your time is up, and I do pray that the time is soon, I want you to quietly return to your country and forget about Anna. Please let my family return to normal and live in peace. Do not write or try to contact her again.

Lena Ming

"Can you believe this old biddy? She is a fool if she thinks I believe these lies."

Corporal Hatcher's eyes grew wide with disbelief. "I can understand your dislike for Grandmother. I cannot believe what she said in that letter. Why don't you call Anna and tell her about her Grandmother's letter."

"I don't want Anna to know that her own grandmother is her worst enemy. Anna loves me and would do anything I asked her to do. She would wait for me until the end of time."

"I wish I had a woman like that," Corporal Hatcher said. "But I am afraid her grandmother and father will make trouble for you the rest of your life."

At the same time Ernie and his platoon looked for tunnels and bunkers, the Marines at Khe Sanh still tried to save their base; they had battled with the Viet Cong and North Vietnamese since January 1968. The Marines turned their calendar to July, and the United States decided to withdraw all useful military material and destroyed everything else at Ke Sanh. In spite of the United States closing the base, the North Vietnamese continued their shelling. On July 9, 1968, the North Vietnamese attacked the base with a large force of infantry. They put up their National Liberation Front flag on July 13, 1968.

CHAPTER TWENTY-THREE

Before July 1968 ended, Ernie and his platoon got transferred to Da Nang without notice. Da Nang was one of the major port cities in Vietnam. Since the United States had taken the destroyed city of Hue back from the North Vietnam to secure Highway One, they had heavily guarded the highway, which was an important supply line from Da Nang to the DMZ. The air base at Da Nang was also important, because it was used by both the South Vietnamese and United States air forces.

In spite of the typhoons and hot weather in Da Nang, the GI's liked the change in duty. Guarding a supply route sounded much better than fighting the Viet Cong in the jungle. They got settled in their barracks and learned how to get around the area the first day. The next day, they stayed in class all day and took instructions for their military duties that would start on the following Monday.

Ernie wrote to Anna before he left Nha Trang, but he didn't tell her that he had been transferred, since they couldn't visit each other; her grandma would never allow her to fly to Da Nang, especially not to visit him. Besides, he had only three weeks before his time would be up, and he planned to visit her in Dalat before he went back to Georgia.

Ernie and the other soldiers looked forward to going to Da Nang on Saturday evening. They wanted to watch the trading vessels come in to port and have a good time at the river port bar.

Private Hobbit got too excited to be still. He moved his short legs around the room, widened his round brown eyes, and raised his bushy brows as he bragged about finding him a girl at the bar.

Sergeant First Class Fish never let Hobbit beat his time with the women. He told Hobbit that he had been with some of the most beautiful women in the world, and the bar maids in Dalat could not measure up to his women.

Hatcher told them they must not get serious with a bar maid; their duty to the United States Army and to their country came first.

On Saturday, Ernie, Corporal Hatcher and ten of their buddies got on the bus right after lunch and headed for the city of Da Nang. When they got off the bus, they all stuck close together and walked toward the River Port Bar. They always looked for Viet Cong. Sometimes they sneaked down from the mountains into Da Nang, attacked the citizens with machine guns, and planted poison spikes around their villages. They had killed many innocent women and children. For this reason, each of the soldiers carried his gun, one grenade, and a back pack with a few supplies and water.

As the group of soldiers walked down the street in Da Nang, the roaring sound of bomber planes stalled their feet and turned their eyes to the sky with worried frowns. The planes roared like a lion and smoked like a train fed with coal.

Corporal Hatcher turned to his buddies and said, "We need to go back to the bus station! Let's go!"

Before they had time to turn around, a pointed warhead tore through the clouds, dived for the city, and struck like lightening with a shrill shriek. The loud explosion pierced their eardrums. They fell to their knees and crawled through the black smoke in search of cover. This was not fireworks at Times Square on New Year's Eve. Flames from the explosion shot sky-high and fragments of bricks, glass, mud, debris, and rocks hurled through the air with the force of a hurricane that flooded the streets. Sparks of fire lit the rooftops, and the flames rapidly spread over the entire city. A blazing hell surrounded them.

Ernie got swept up with the screaming mob; He turned, twisted, and searched for Corporal Hatcher and his buddies in the crowd. He saw Privates Wingate, Staker, and Hobbit, but he didn't see Corporal Hatcher. He kept moving his eyes in search of Hatcher.

Traffic jammed the streets and a thousand horns honked continuously as another bomb whirled violently through the sky and fell with a screeching roar behind them on the city. Spouts of fire and debris fell on and around the screaming mob as they held arms above their heads and pushed through the crowd.

This brush with death sent Ernie to a nearby alley. With wild eyes of fear, his courage waned and his bones became brittle. Sweat dripped from his face, and he choked from the horrible smoke. He crouched on the hard surface between two buildings and covered his ears to drown the voices of terror on the street. Minutes later the bombing stopped. He slowly crawled down the alley toward the street, but he couldn't see any of his buddies. His hand touched a body, and he jerked his hand back at the sight of a young Vietnamese girl. At first sight of her dark head, he thought she was Anna. He felt sick on his stomach. He closed his eyes tight and held them for minutes before getting up the courage to check her pulse. She was dead! He jumped to his feet and steered his gun before him as he side-stepped and jumped over bloody bodies. When he saw a building with a clearing around it, he ran to the back side and moved on through the ruins of the city.

Looking back at the smoking city, worrying about what had happened to Corporal Hatcher and his buddies, and remembering the dead woman he left on the street, he felt like a coward who had broken the last vow against God. He had left his friends. Worst of all, he had left his best friend, Harold Hatcher. He worried that Hatcher might be dying and need him; but he could not go back to find him. He looked up to the heavens and prayed for God to look down on his buddies and Corporal Hatcher with favor and take them back to their Da Nang base. Then he said a quick prayer for God to help him get to a safe hiding place to spend the night.

Just outside the city, he came up on a gigantic ant bed that hid everything in view. He threw a grenade at the monsters and watched the dirt rain toward the sky. He pictured a Viet Cong with ants in his breeches running through the jungle in search of a water hole. Ernie left the ants and moved on with thoughts of going home. He had only ten days left in Vietnam, and he was lost with no way to get back to his base.

Pretty soon, he was so tired of walking that he thought he would drop, and his boots already had holes in the bottom that trapped dirt and mud. He heard a loud stir of sticks around the trees and gasped with shock when he saw the large black spotted cat staring at him. The black beast sat on his haunches, and his tail rested on the ground like a black snake. The cat had violence in its eyes and warned him with a loud roar followed by a flipping tongue. Ernie pointed his gun at the beast with one hand and held up the other hand in a submissive manner to apologize for meddling on his territory. The cat lunged toward Ernie, and he shot him. His aim had been good, but the cat was strong. He turned in a run and disappeared in the jungle. Ernie thanked God for sparing his life.

On the trail again, Ernie ran up on a wild hog. The critter stopped its rooting, and the quills on his back stood stiff like a hairbrush. He stared at Ernie as if weighing the danger. Then he took off in a run. Ernie's delightful thought of a piece of fried ham wilted. He had not eaten since dinner and he was hungry. He was also thirsty; he stopped and drank a few swallows of water from his canteen, and looked at his compass. From where he stood, his compass pointed southwest, but he didn't know south from north or how to get back to Da Nang. Besides, the North Vietnamese had probably taken the city.

After a short rest, he twisted his neck, stretched his tired limbs and walked on. He was sailing against the wind, but he was still sailing. He could not stop thinking about Corporal Hatcher. He depended on Hatcher to give him directions in Vietnam.

Before long, the smell of water hit his nose. He followed the smell and came to a narrow brook running with water as clear as spring water. The water trickled over a path of stepping stones that led to some secret place. He unloaded his pack, removed the strap from his shoulder, propped his gun on its stock, and leaned it against a nearby tree trunk. Then he got on his knees and slurped up the cool water in big gulps. When he had quenched his thirst, he filled his canteen and sat by the brook to do some serious thinking. He thought about going back to Da Nang to find Corporal Hatcher, but he was too scared to turn back. He was starving and had to find food. He had enough money in his pocket to buy a decent meal, clothes, and shoes, but his money was worthless.

After sitting a spell, he got up and began walking again. He spotted a patch of cane bamboo and thought of fish for supper. He cut a nice pole, stripped it, and made a fishing pole. He had no use for a pole without the line and hook. He thought about the twine in his backpack and quickly searched its contents. The twine and gem clip he found made him smile. His fishing gear was as good as gold. Now he had to find some bugs or worms. As he dug in the damp earth, he thought about home and his old fishing spot on the creek bank. He found a cricket and three earthworms.

With his fishing gear and bait, he moved on down the trail to search for a stream. Hours later, he reached a creek with a small stream that ran beneath a fallen tree. He walked to the bank, sat down, and cast his line. He had learned to be patient when fishing. He must have waited more than an hour before something hit his line. He pulled up a slimy eel, and the thought of his mother's eel with its crispy batter came to mind. He laid the flouncing eel on the bank, gutted it, cut it into small pieces, and washed it in the creek.

After he found wood to build a fire, he sharpened a long stick, threaded it through the eel, and roasted his catch. His mouth watered for the eel. He had never been hungrier, and the eel was delicious, even without the batter and salt.

After Ernie ate, he stretched out on a nice dry spot, closed his eyes, and thought about Corporal Hatcher. Then Anna came to mind. He longed to see her, to hear her voice, and feel her warm body against his. He soon fell asleep and slept through the night.

The next morning, he opened his eyes to bright sun rays hitting his face. He was thankful he was still alive. He pulled himself up, gathered his gear, and started out again on his journey. The heat was unbearable, but he kept walking in hopes of finding a United States base. He came to a small clearing and pulled out his compass. The needle pointed toward the west. He prayed that he was taking the right direction and kept walking.

Pretty soon, he moved through a cane patch. The blades slashed his face and hands, and gave him a mad itch, but this was no time to be thinking about a warm shower. He sat down at the edge of the cane patch, wiped his brow on his sleeve, and lay down on the grass to rest a few minutes.

Before sunset, he reached soft sand near the ocean. He stripped off his dirty clothes and waded in the water near the shore to scrub his filthy body. After he bathed, he sat on a ridge of rocks until the sun soaked up the water dripping from his body. He got up, dressed in his filthy clothes, and found a spot behind the rocks to sleep for the night. As he lay staring at the rocks, they turned to sculptures of weird animals with monster faces. He tried to see good in the creatures, but his mind's eye was set, and the images in his head did not turn into beautiful mermaids. He had heard that a sun stroke would make you have hallucinations. Did he have a sun stroke? He fell asleep. When he awoke, he felt better.

After miles of walking, clucking sounds of chickens hit his ears; with thoughts of a friendly village nearby, his hopes soared. He walked toward the sound and ran up against a tall fence topped with bob wire that was too tall to climb. He found a place where the fence did not meet the ground and lay flat on his belly with the wire pushed forward to squirm to the other side of the fence. He stood up, brushed the dirt from his pants, and looked around for the enemy. He prayed that he was not approaching a Viet Cong Village. The trees were sparsely settled, but vines covered the ground. He finally reached a run-down shack covered with bamboo vines. Chickens ran with fright under the shack and through the trees. The sight of the chickens put a smile on his face; he would have chicken to eat for several days. If he found eggs, he would have eggs for breakfast several days.

From the looks of the shack, years had passed since anyone had darted its doors. He needed to rest, and the vines covering the shack almost hid it from view; he felt safe to stay here for the night. Brown, pithy wood hung from the sides of the steps, and the rotten boards looked dangerous to put a foot. He pulled himself up on the porch and took light steps to the slab door. The mass of spider webs at the top of the door stretched and moved with the door as he pushed it back. He cautiously peeped into the room before making his entrance. The smell of rotten meat turned his stomach and told him something inside the shack was dead. Thoughts of one of the Chickens trapped in the shack came to mind. He stepped into the room and looked around. A dirty, yet colorful, couch and chair, stained from months of rain, sat against the right wall before a brick fireplace that was missing a dozen bricks. He looked above his head to see from whence the rain had fallen and saw large gaps in the roof. He walked past the couch and came to a narrow door that was standing open. He could smell rancid grease mixed with a rotten smell before stepping into the small kitchen. A wooden stove sat against the back wall. One section of the flue had come apart and black smut had fallen around the back side of the stove. Brightly painted dishes covered one section of the counter. The rest of the counter was crowded with black pots, an iron kettle, and an iron frying pan.

Looking to his right, he saw another door that led him to a small bedroom with a single bed, a lumpy mattress, and bed linens. Shabby clothes hung on a cord line across the end of the room. A beautiful mahogany dresser, etched with flowers around a mirror with three wings, stood next to the outside wall. He looked at the image staring back at him and could not believe how shabby and filthy he actually was. Moving his eyes from the mirror, he spotted a Chinese jewelry box. He opened the wooden box, and his eyes stretched with amazement at the rainbow of colorful jewels. He moved the jewelry around and admired the beauty of the shine. He closed the box and picked up a pouch of rappee lying next to the box. The Vietnamese soldiers traded rappee for things of value. The black coarse tobacco resembled snuff. He stuck the pouch in his shirt pocket.

Then he walked across the room to another door. He stuck his head in and stepped back at the horrible sight. There before the iron bed was a skeleton, a human skeleton! The skeleton sent a wave of shock from his head to his toes and paralyzed his feet. He stared down at the skeleton and hoped to God that the thing did not come to life. Careful not to touch the skeleton, he cautiously stepped around it and prayed that her bones did not have a haunting spirit. The skeleton had to be that of an elderly woman, since long, gray hair lay around the bones sticking out from her face. Her hair had not melted with her skin. He wondered if the old woman had a husband or lived all alone in the wood. She must have died from lonely cabin fever. She was miles from civilization and probably had no neighbors or family to visit. Old people like this slowly faded away in body and mind; their minds usually went first.

He stood dumbfound for minutes. He had three choices: he could sleep with the skeleton; he could sleep on the ragged couch; or he could sleep under a tree in the jungle with snakes crawling around him. He decided he would take his chances with the skeleton; she was a harmless bag of bones. Before he could think about sleeping, he had to find food.

He went outside to see what he could find. He needed water to scald, pick, and clean the chickens. He also needed wood for a fire to cook them. He found an old well curbed with rotten boards with a tickle attached to a wooden frame above the well. The ragged rope and rusty tin buck hung from the tickle, and the end of the rope lay over the top board around the well. He grabbed the end of the rope and let it ride on the tickle to lower the bucket into the well. When he heard the bucket hit the water with a splash, he looked up to heaven and said, "Thank you, God." After he drew up the bucket of water, he remembered that he had no container for the water. He set the bucket of water on the ground, went back into the shack, and came back with a large aluminum pot that he found under the kitchen sink. He poured the water into the pot, and drew up buckets of water until he had filled the pot.

After he carried the water into the shack, he set it on the stove, and went back outside to find wood. In no time, he had picked up enough limbs to build a bond fire.

Before going back outside to kill the chicken, he hooked the flue back together and started a fire in the old wood stove. Then he put part of the water in another pot to scald the chickens and saved the rest of the cool water to clean the chickens and to drink.

Back outside for the kill, the chickens saw him coming and shouted a loud clucking chorus as they ran under the shack. He hated to lie down in the tall grass next to the house. To be on the safe side, he stomped down the grass and weeds; he lay down on his belly and aimed his rifle at the brood of chickens huddled at the back corner of the shack. That's when he saw the chicken eggs scattered on the ground under the shack. He wanted eggs for breakfast, but he didn't want to crawl under that shack. Besides he couldn't separate the good eggs from the rotten eggs; he didn't want an egg with a baby chicken growing inside. He dismissed the thought of eggs for breakfast and set his aim on the chickens. He killed five chickens before he stopped firing. Then he walked around the shack to gather his prize.

Back in the kitchen, he saw that the old wood stove still worked like a charm and the water was already boiling. He dipped the chickens in the boiling water, plucked their feathers, and washed them. Then he poured out the used water, rinsed the pot, and refilled the pot about half full to gut the chickens. He was glad that his mama taught him how to clean chickens. Since that chicken lesson, he never ate another gizzard, because he learned that day what the gizzard held inside. After he gutted the chickens, he used the other pot to boil them.

Right away, the delicious smell of chicken overcame the rotten odor in the shack. He rested on the ragged couch about an hour before testing the chicken. He pulled one of the chickens and placed it on one of the colorful plates he found in the cabinet. The tender meat fell off the bone and he ate the entire chicken, except the part that went over the fence last.

After he filled his belly, he made himself a nice comfortable bed from the old covers on the bed and wished for an Aladdin's lamp to rub magic into the night.

The minute he got comfortable, the noise under the shack made him sit upright. He got up and quietly made his way through the front door to the edge of the rotten porch. He jumped to the ground, and the roosting chickens let him know he had up set their nap. He walked around the shack to check for enemies and returned to his bed. He covered his head with the dirty blanket and slept.

The next morning he opened his eyes, and the first thing he saw was the skeleton; she seemed to stare at him with anger. He thought about the dead spirits that talked to Anna's father. His own spirit had sunk to his belly and was begging with loud growls for food. He got up and went to the kitchen to eat another chicken.

After he finished eating, he filled his canteen with fresh water from the well, washed his face and hands, and went back to the kitchen to pack his chicken to carry with him. He found some white towels in the kitchen that looked clean; he wrapped the three chickens he had left in the towels, packed them into his backpack, and went back to the bedroom to get his jewelry. He ignored the skeleton's watchful eyes as he loaded his backpack.

He left the shack and found a footpath to follow toward the unknown. He had not walked far when the tops of the trees nodded to the wind, and the sun hid behind a nimbus cloud. The clouds twisted angrily beneath the other, and thunder drummed a threat of storm. They had arrived in Da Nang just in time for its tropical monsoon climate with typhoons. He dreaded the rain; especially with no shelter, but the rain fell in splattering rushes. Water soaked his clothes and settled around his toes inside of his boots like a stagnant pond. With each step he took, his boots bogged deeper into the mud; the gravity of the earth pulled him heavily to the ground, and drained his energy. He wished to run up on an abandoned tunnel to sleep the night away; but he had no tunnel, and he had not found a friendly camp or base. He could not survive like this forever. Near sundown, the rain finally ceased, and he reached a grove of banana palms to rest for the night.

By the next morning, his clothes had dried, but his stomach was empty. He pulled one of the chickens from the towel in his backpack and ate until he could eat no more.

He had walked only a short distance from the trees when he heard voices. His heart patted his back and beat in his ears. He feared Viet Cong in his path. He had experienced the same feeling many times before. He took off in a run down the footpath at the edge of the jungle. When he stopped to catch his breath, the pounding feet came nearer. The Viet Cong gained on him. He darted behind a pine tree to hide. The jungle grass waved, and the bushes moved only a few feet from where he was standing. He held his breath, and his brain was completely blank for minutes. Then the sound of heavy footsteps stumbling through the vines brought him to his senses. From the black clothes they wore, they looked like bandits rather than Viet Cong soldiers, but they had him trapped. He wanted to run, but his feet turned to lead. A tight vice squeezed his heart. He wiggled his toes and fingers as they grabbed his arms, yanked him to his feet, kicked him, and knocked him to the ground. His head collided with a rock, and pain stabbed his temple. His mind whirled with confusion, and he felt like he was on a roller coaster, and he saw only flashes of the world.

After they turned his pockets out and stole his jewelry, they grabbed his backpack and pulled out the chickens he had wrapped in the towel. He had never heard such laughter; they laughed, slapped hands, and spoke in a strange tongue for several minutes. Then they dangled a coarse cord before his eyes and tied his feet together. The thoughts of their stringing his head on a poll made him crazy; he begged them to spare his life. One of the devils held back a large knife, gripped the handle, and pulled it back in a death threat toward him. They liked knives.

Then they hoisted him onto a stretcher made from bamboo vines. As they walked through the jungle, his body bounced on the rough bamboo vines and his head felt as if it would explode. Where were they taking him? What would they do to him? The Viet Cong tortured prisoners until they stopped breathing. He had heard stories of how they tied American soldiers up and beat them to death. Some had been castrated, blinded, and drowned. Afterward, they cut off their heads and carried them on poles back to their post to brag about their feat. How does a man prepare to die? He thought about his mama and prayed for God to save his life.

They walked for miles and stopped before an old wooden shed that was leaning to one side. After removing the chain from the door, they kicked it back, and locked him up. The bamboo roof had spaces wide enough to see the sky, and the smell of old hay soaked in urine took his breath. He held his nose and sat down on what appeared to be a feed trough. As he hovered below the rotten rafters, gray manure immediately spattered his shoe. He looked up to see white birds, without tail feathers, roosting above his head. Chicken Village was a good thought; the Viet Cong would never imprison an American soldier in enemy territory. He leaned back on the rotten wall and cringed with the thoughts of the filth around him. He wiped his foot through the sod of hay to clean his shoes. As he did so, he felt a stiff, lifeless hump beneath his foot. Thinking it was a dead Viet Cong, he jerked his foot back. Looking closer, he saw that it was an animal. He quickly toed the sod to pry it from its grave. As he brushed the hay from its fur, he stared with shock at the sight. He could not believe the Viet Cong buried animals in the chicken house. Was his grave below the manure? He moved to the far corner of the shed, huddled in the corner away from the chickens, and fell asleep.

The next morning, the sun streaked through the cracks of the shed and the shrill sound of a rooster brought him to his feet. Strange little birds pecked all around him. He peeped through the rotten boards to see twilight falling on a village with stilt houses. Anna had told him the Highland group of people, who lived apart from other ethnic groups in Vietnam, lived in stilt houses to protect them from snakes, vermin and beast as well as the floods they feared. They kept their animals in the shelters beneath their houses. On the other hand, she had not mentioned their political beliefs. He wondered if the Viet Cong had taken their village. No life stirred around the huts. Thinking of escaping, he pushed frantically at the rotten boards. A large hunk of dry rot fell to the outside. He pounded harder and faster. Suddenly, the door went back with a bang! They had come back for him.

They walked along a beach for more than a mile with his sore body bouncing on the bamboo stretcher. Dragon boats packed with anglers made their way toward the shore

Beyond the beach, they climbed a grassy slope and came to a tall chain link fence with a chained gate that creaked when they opened it. They forced him to stand and pushed him forward into the pen; he fell on the ground and ran his tongue around his parched lips. He was starving and dying of thirst.

He sat up and looked around the pen. Wounded soldiers with open wounds and a heap of dead soldiers attracted blowflies that swarmed and lit on their sores. He moved his eyes around the pen in search of Corporal Hatcher; he thanked God that he was not here. Men with scraggly beards, and ponytails tied with bamboo vines stared at him with hollow eyes. They looked like foreign creatures, but their camouflage fatigues and insignia on their sleeves identified them as American soldiers, his brothers. He screamed to the top of his voice and an eternity of hell embraced him.

Hours later, the sound of shuffling feet neared the wire pen. The gate flew back and two Viet Cong Officers came toward him at the end of the pen, his station. They yanked him up and ordered him to march. He walked with short crippled steps, and pain shot from his ankles to his toes. He hobbled behind them and entered a narrow hall. On each side, cells housed prisoners dressed in purple and red stripped cotton. At least they had a cot to sleep on. He decided they must be officers or higher ranking military prisoners. Some of the men had bandages on various parts of their body. He wished they would speak to him, but their eyes never met his.

At the end of the long hallway, they entered a small office and quickly saluted the man sitting behind the desk. Their commander stood, returned the salute, and gave orders for them to beat the prisoner. He did not realize the commander was ordering them to beat him, but the varmints carried him to an open court and slashed him with a stick each time he refused to answer their question. They accused him of being a spy with a secret mission. His only mission was to get back to South Vietnam and go home. They finally gave up on his answering their questions; Ernie crawled to the corner of the room. He cringed with pain and begged for mercy, but his begging was useless.

The feel of cold steel to his raw feet was soothing. Chains clanked, and a door opened. They untied his hands and feet; Then they disappeared and locked the steel door. Their footsteps faded to silence and he stared at four gray walls without windows. He looked up and flicks of light came through small slits in the ceiling.

He crouched in the corner of the room and prayed. The brutal heathens had left him to perish and die. They had locked him away in a dungeon. They ripped his clothes and left cuts from the bamboo stick on his wrists and body. The deep slashes already looked infected.

After an eternity of feeling helpless, he jumped up and walked around the room in search of a way out. As he pushed frantically at the wall, one section separated and moved back. Had he found the path to freedom? He squeezed between the spaces and entered a dimly lit room tangled with cobwebs. With both hands swinging at the webs, he crept forward. Shadows darted around his feet! He looked down to see a hoard of black rats nibbling at his britches. He screamed, stomped, and shook his legs free. They squealed and scurried away. Afraid to move, he wiggled his toes and braced himself. His ankles ached from the cuts left by the cord.

Back in his cell, he thought about all the stories he had heard about prisoners of war. Did the Communist want an even exchange of prisoners? He had heard that the South Vietnamese had packed several thousand Viet Cong prisoners on ice and stored them at the rubber plantation. The red tape to get a prisoner out of a prison camp stretched from Saigon to Hanoi. Besides, he was not a high-ranking officer, so he was the bottom candidate on the list. He would die in this dungeon before they called his name.

Loneliness gnawed at his soul. He longed to touch another human being and hear the sound of a human voice. He missed the close ties with the men in his platoon. He had no friends; he had no place; he had no business being here. They shut him away from the world of civilized folk. His mind was crowded with the thoughts of their torture and his death. How could he escape this death trap? He was exhausted; his head was splitting with pain, but he would not admit defeat until his last breath. They rounded the prisoners of war up like a rancher heads up a herd of cattle to drive to the salt. The solitary confinement that followed was another hell. The torture was almost unbearable. They tied him up, beat him, stuck pins under his finger nails, and left him begging for his life. They gave him only bread to eat and water to drink. He welcomed death. Isolated from the world, he drifted in silence with a blank mind.

In the meantime, the commander of the Army had ordered a task force in the Navy to cross the China Sea into enemy territory and capture the prisoners that the North Vietnamese had captured.

Miles from the prison, the sailors docked their ship and tied it to a huge rock banking the shore. As they set out on their journey, the night was cool with moving shadows from the breeze, and the moon glittered and bounced on their steps. They crept along the edge of the water, passed a dock, and turned down a path that led to a Bamboo Bridge that swayed nervously in the breeze. They swallowed their fear and continued their journey toward the prison. After they crossed the bridge, they waded through a wooded area surrounding a Viet Cong Village, and reached a clearing around the foot of a mountain that rose above the prison like a giant. A valley gaped below the ridges of the stone mountain and stretched to the north. They moved around the mountain and came to a tall wire fence that surrounded seven buildings that were about eight feet high and twenty feet long. They smiled at each other and shook hands. They had found the prison.

The wire fence topped by sharp spikes made their entrance impossible; they had chained the prison entrance gates and locked them from the inside. They sneaked around the fence to check for guards and found two standing less than ten feet apart. The guards had guns resting on their shoulder as they paced back and forth across the grounds before the entrance gates.

They quickly closed in on the guards, gagged them, tied them up, and carried them to the small building near the entrance gates. With the guards locked behind the doors, they stole their keys, came back to the entrance, posted two of their own guards, and entered the prison grounds. In a hunched position, they trailed one behind the other toward the buildings.

When they reached the first building, they grabbed the two guards, gagged them and tied them up. They tried to get into the building through the entrance doors, but they had locked the doors. The building had no windows they could use to get into the building. In a hunched position, they trailed one behind the other to the end of the building, where they spotted a round metal pipe that ran from the ground to the roof. One soldier climbed up and motioned for the others to follow. They made their way to the round vent in the center of the building to get inside. In their excitement, they yanked up the round structure and set it down without thought. The vent rolled like a basketball to the edge of the roof and hit the ground with a loud crash. The soldiers immediately heard voices and rushing footsteps. They quickly lay on their bellies and cradled their heads in their arms.

"Here!" one of the guards said, standing over the globe vent. They expected the worst. The soldiers felt relieved when they heard the guards joking and laughing.

"This is the fierce mountain lion!" one guard said, and he kicked the globe vent to the side. Then they walked back to their post with silly giggles.

The Americans breathed a sigh of relief, stood, and stretched before sliding down the tin cranny. Each one hit the floor with a bang, driving his legs up a notch into his groin. They recovered in minutes and began exploration in the darkness. When they reached the door, they unlocked it and moved into the hall way. With their backs pushed against the cement wall, they side stepped through the hall to the front of the building. Two guards sat in a foyer. They slipped up behind them, grabbed them, gagged their mouths, and tied them up.

An iron grill and a thick steel door stood before ten steel steps that they had to get to before entering the prison cells to free the Americans. They struck a match, lit a stick of dynamite, and moved back; the explosion tore the door from its hinges.

The frightened guards on the other side of the door heard the explosion and saw guns pointed at them at the same time. They quickly dropped their drawn weapons and threw up their hands in humble surrender.

With the guards locked in cells, they opened all the other cells in the prison. More than fifty American soldiers and twenty South Vietnam soldiers walked out of the prison, including Ernie Tennyson.

Once on the prison grounds, they crept up behind the building in-groups of three, whirling grenades behind them to stop the Viet Cong on their tails. When they got safely on the other side of the fence, they wanted to shout with joy, but they remained silent. They quietly crept along the foot of the mountain and made their way back around the Viet Cong village to their ship.

The sun rose and threw shimmering rays in the path of white wings circling the sky. The breeze stirred the sail as the ship eased toward the friendly shore. Soldiers on shore stretched their eyes as they ran to the edge of the sea and shouted to their comrades.

Ernie awoke in a strange room. The medicinal smell was welcomed. Books, pictures, and messages decorated the room, but there was no laughter. Ernie looked around the room at the wounded men with mauled faces and bandaged bodies. Some of the men lay on their backs with elevated arms, feet, and legs swinging in straps. Others had casts covering their limbs and stared at the ceiling. Many of the wounded groaned, grunted, and cried out with desperate pleas for someone to help them.

Ernie didn't remember the war; he didn't remember anything or anybody. He was living and breathing, but his mind was blank; yet, he recognized the sounds of pain and suffering; but he did not remember the violence that brought their pain and suffering.

A nurse came in to attend the soldiers. When she reached Ernie's bed, she paused for minutes before speaking as if she knew his condition. She told him he was at the United States Army Field Hospital north of Saigon.

After she walked away, Ernie turned his face to the wall to avoid the sight of the wounded soldiers in the room. He did not know Saigon from hell.

The next day, a medical specialist came in to see Ernie. He examined him from head to toe. The specialist was followed by a head doctor who asked Ernie a thousand questions, none of which he could answer. The head doctor diagnosed him with Post Traumatic Stress and told him they would keep him in the hospital for six weeks to run test, evaluations, and start his therapy.

Ernie had no idea what the man talked about. He thought of everything; he thought of nothing. He didn't remember his name; he didn't know where he came from; he didn't know his people; he had a blank mind.

CHAPTER TWENTY-FOUR

Three weeks passed and Anna had not heard from Ernie, but she held to a thin thread of hope for God to save his life. She listened to the news every day, but there was no good news. American efforts had failed; the war got worse; and nobody won.

Anna thought of all the bad things that could have happened to Ernie. Had they captured him and locked him away? Had they sent him out of the country? She feared most of all that he was among the thousands killed that month. She unfolded the last letter he had written her and read it again. Then she folded it carefully and ran a finger over the Nha Trang postmark. Where had he gone from Nha Trang? She had called his home in Georgia a dozen times, and each time the woman who answered the phone told her Ernie was not at home; she had also called his base, but he had not returned her calls.

She heard her grandmother calling her to breakfast, and she held her mouth tightly with anger. Her grandmother guarded her as a prize jewel. Early every morning, Anna was faced with dreadful questions. Her grandmother questioned her lack of appetite, her depression, and her restlessness. Then she would remind her that she had warned her about getting involved with that American. If her grandmother read an allegory, she could figure out the meaning before the end of the story. Anna wanted to scream at her for her hasty conclusions.

She put on her housecoat, went to the kitchen, and sat down at the table.

"What is this secret you keep from your old grandmother?"

"I have no secrets, Grandmother."

"When you were a small child, you never lied to me, but you have a habit of lying to me lately. You had best listen to my advice. The American was no good. He did not love you; his feelings were that of a lustful, foolish man, and he made a fool of you, also."

"Ernie loves me," Anna said. "I am convinced that something terrible happened to him, or he would have been in touch with me."

"How could you love this American? Americans are to blame for the bombing that destroyed our people and caused long term illnesses; they are responsible for destroying our crops, our animals, and our trees."

"Grandmother, "Americans are not responsible for killing our people and destroying our villages. The Viet Cong are responsible for most of the deaths of our people. Americans cannot help the South Vietnamese people if the people are against them."

"Americans have no business here." She saw that Anna was crying and she raised her voice, "Stop that bawling! This American sucked you up. You were his little trinket on a string. He corrupted your mind and spoiled your life. Put his memory to bed."

"Grandmother, you should not judge Ernie and say hateful things about him. You really do not know him."

"Regardless of what I think of this American, you must face reality."

Anna rushed back to her room in tears. She wrung her hands, and cried as she lifted the silk scarves and took out Ernie's picture. He was such a handsome man. She had often dreamed of having a son with his dark, curly hair and wide blue eyes. "I love you," she whispered to his picture. "Why did you leave me? Why have you not written to me?" She feared the worst; she prayed for the best.

She closed the chest drawer and walked to the window to look at the day. She thought of a thousand reasons he had abandoned her. Was her father right about Ernie? Did he have a wife and family in Georgia? If so, his secret love affair with a Vietnamese woman would ruin him; his wife would divorce him and take everything he owned. Had he lied to her from the beginning? Did he have children? She had been blinded by love. She had been a stupid fool to think she could feel love flow from his being to her heart. Do fools ever change?

At times, she felt as if her father's prayers had cursed her. Her mother had always told her that no human being could put a curse on another; yet, she wore an amulet on a solid gold chain around her neck to protect her from evil spirits, harm, and injury that her father and grandmother spoke about.

She got up from the bed and dressed to go to the beach to get away from her grandmother's hawk eyes.

As she walked along the shore, she felt free. The ocean's eternity of blue water waved and rushed in covering her feet with foamy white bundles of bubbles. She watched the water swell to giant waves, rush in and crash against the rugged rocks. She marveled at the sight of the rocks withstanding the pressure of the tide. The sea breeze on her face; the sound of the ocean; and the sprinkling rays of the sun lifted her spirits with memories of their last hours together at Nha Trang. She had a pocket full of memories that would remain with her forever. He had captivated her from the beginning. She had nursed him back to health, and made the mistake of her life by falling in love with him. Their time together had been an imaginary adventure in a beautiful dreamland. The dream had ended.

Then a hard object caught her toe; a beautiful seashell was beneath her foot. Its shape was a perfect heart that curled on the edges to an inside of pink pearl that shined like a diamond. She turned the shell carefully in her palm with the feeling that the shell held good fortune. She stuck it in her pocket; she would buy a gold chain and wear the heart around her neck with her amulet.

She sat down on the sand and hugged her knees with the sight. The white birds dipped and sailed with the rhythm of a song, and she imagined sailing away with them to a far away land. Her imagination carried her to a waiting ship and she followed the sea to America, where he sat in the shade of a large sycamore at the edge of a green meadow. She could see him clearly there before her as she recited poetry.

Just this side of the ocean, where the road comes to an end; she walked the beach and search for his long lost ship to come in.

Her eyes grew tired and weary from the bright evening sun, but she walked and worried until the long day was done.

By chance she met another, where the road comes to an end. He was also searching for a long lost ship to come in.

She had no love in her heart for this lonely man; she kept walking and waiting for his lost ship to come in.

Tomorrow the sun rise will find her where the road comes to an end.

She walked up the sandy hill and sat down on a bench before a row of palm trees. The village children came running past her and ran toward the water. She watched them splash the waves and listened to their laughter. A young girl with long dark hair and a happy brown face clutched an orchid in her hand and smiled as she gave it to Anna. Her eyes sparkled with happiness as she spoke. "You are very beautiful. You must wear the orchid in your hair."

"Thank you," Anna said, and the girl dashed away to meet her friends, who waded near the water's edge. Anna remembered the orchid Ernie had bought at the market for her to wear in her hair. Anna sensed that the little girl had read her sadness and wanted to cheer her, but all of the orchids in the world could not cheer her. Remembering the happiness in the young girl's face for having done such a good deed, Anna stuck the orchid in her hair and waved to the girls. She had once been happy without a care in the world. Laughter and a spirit for life once filled her being. Then she saw life for what it really is. She discovered how cruel people are. Life had dealt her a dirty blow and her heart had no soft spot or compassion. She learned that she could trust no one. Now she seldom smiled or talked with her friends of old. The war had caused her mother's death and would haunt her memory the rest of her life. Now the only man she ever loved had either jilted her or was missing in action. What had the war accomplished? The North still ruled over most of the country, and the bloodshed had been useless. The Viet Cong still seemed eager for blood. She sat there and turned thoughts until the energy drained from her body and her mind was in turmoil.

Back at home, she moved around in another world and daydreamed. She was absent minded, and at times, she had no mind at all. She found herself doing things that had no beginning or end. She found herself in places and did not know how she got there. She could not concentrate or pay attention to one subject for a long time. Her grandmother's company got on her nerves, and her feelings showed. Worst of all, the neighbors asked questions that her grandmother answered frankly.

At night, when she closed her eyes and tried to sleep, visions of his face, his smile, his blue eyes, and that boyish grin flashed in her brain. She could hear his voice and feel his breath on her skin. When she finally fell asleep, she had nightmares about the war; and Ernie was the main character. She could see him running, sweating, hiding, and fighting hand to hand with the Viet Cong. She could see herself standing over him as he lay in a clump of vines without breath, without life. She had found him and had come to save him. She could see him looking up at her, begging for her help. That same horrible nightmare came back again.

Mrs. Ming was worried about Anna. She noticed that Anna had not eaten breakfast that morning.

"What is bothering you?"

"Nothing is bothering me. I am not hungry."

"I do not believe you. You have not been hungry for several mornings past, and you do not look well. Have you taken to strong drink?"

"No, I have not been drinking," she said. "I feel fine, Grandmother."

Lena Ming could not open her granddaughter's eyes. One could never make a stubborn ox change its course, but she must hold on to the reins with all of her strength.

"I beg you, Anna, to listen to words of wisdom. I am old, but I am wise. That American was out to get into your pants. He threw you to the tigers; the cats can tear you to shreds for all he cares."

"Grandmother, I cannot change what happened yesterday, and I cannot forget Ernie. I love him with all of my heart. I love him so much that I hurt all over. Your words are easy, since you have never felt pain in your heart for a lost love."

"You know nothing about pain, until he uses you up, and you realize that he made a fool of you."

Anna heard her father come in. She turned her face to the wall and closed her eyes. Minutes later, her father came into her room. She sat up, and he lashed out at her. "You have a comfortable home, food to eat, and clothes of your choice. Why are you fretting?"

"I am not fretting about anything, Father."

He threw up his hands and became hysterical. "You are brooding over that sorry American! How could you love a man who is helping to destroy our country?"

"Father, you should not blame Ernie for the Viet Cong's destruction. Ernie is an honest man; he loves me and he wants to marry me."

"You will not marry this fool!"

She lowered her chin and calmly said, "Father, I will marry him when he comes back."

"This American is not coming back for you."

"He will come back for me, unless he is dead."

"You are stubborn like your mother. She never listened to me."

"My mother was a good woman. She cooked your meals, washed and ironed your clothes, kept the house clean, and taught school. She worked like a servant for you, but you never gave her credit."

"I loved your mother, but she never seemed to have her head together. This American does not have a head to think with."

His words were a waste to his ears; his words were a foreign song that had no melody to match the words. "Father, you have never felt the love in your heart that I feel for Ernie. I cannot make my heart cold to the feelings of love. I cannot stop loving Ernie."

"You will stop loving this American! If he has been killed in battle, his death is well deserved!"

After her father left, she fell back on her pillow and thought about how cruel he had always been. Her father craved power and money. She could not believe he was an honest man. He made women feel inferior to him. He believed that women should be meek and serve their masters willingly. He had never really loved her mother. He used her for his pleasure, to bear his child, and keep the house. Neither had her father loved her, his only daughter. Her father never allowed her to have male friends of her own choosing. Other than his choice for her, Every other man she mentioned was unfit for her, especially this American. Her father treated her friends as if they had a disease that she might catch by merely being friendly with them. What would her father do if he knew she had given her heart, soul, and body to Ernie Tennyson?

CHAPTER TWENTY-FIVE

At the same time, Mrs. Tennyson wrung her hands with worry about her son. Ernie had stopped writing. She feared the worst; yet, she hoped for the best, and continued preparing for his homecoming. She invited all of his friends, their neighbors, and kin folks to the celebration. She hummed with excitement as she cleaned, cooked and decorated. The house sparkled with every piece of furniture in place. The dining room was the center of attention. She covered the long mahogany table with a white lace table cloth and centered the table with a large vase of red roses. On one end of the table, she set several silver trays filled with a variety of sandwiches, chips, nuts, and sweet treats. On the other end of the table, she set the three tiers chocolate cake she made; she decorated the cake with white frosting and swirled red roses over the top. Next to the cake, she set a large crystal bowl that bubbled with red fruit punch.

Ernie's friend, Nolan Copeland, made a large welcome home sign and strung it across the front porch above the steps.

Mrs. Tennyson stood at the door and greeted Ernie's friends as they arrived. Ernie's friend, Nolan, got there ahead of the other guest. He was excited about Ernie's home coming and couldn't wait to celebrate with him.

After the guest started socializing and eating, Mrs. Tennyson went back to the door; she watched and prayed for Ernie to pull into the drive, but the cars passed on by the house. She prayed to see a military vehicle, but Ernie never showed up. At six o'clock, the music stopped and the guest left. The room was empty and quiet. Ernie's celebration was over, and Mrs. Tennyson realized that he may never come home. After all the guest left, Nolan took down the sign, and Mrs. Copeland helped her clean the kitchen and dining room. After they left, she got ready for bed and read her bible. Her faith never waned; she believed that God would bring her son back to her.

The weeks turned to another month; Mrs. Tennyson had heard nothing from Ernie. She still searched the mail each day with high hopes, and she prayed every day for god to spare his life and send him home.

Tracy came home only at Christmas time. She had written to her mother and was aware that Ernie was missing in action. She had sent her mother information about the Red Cross and the Missing Person's Bureau, but the calls that Mrs. Tennyson had made did not turn up any important information.

Mrs. Tennyson's brother, Willie, and his wife, Mary, visited often and tried to lift her spirits. Mary helped her around the house and was a good listener.

Willie was old fashioned and plain spoken. He said, "I don't see why they don't let our boys come home. Vietnam is no business of ours. The next thing you know the government will drop one of those nuclear bombs and destroy the world. The cave man would come out to a barren, charred land. How would nature fill the gap? There would be no nature. Reconstruction would be left to a few. Where are the leaders? Where are the people? The earth would be hell."

Mrs. Tennyson agreed with Willie's conclusion. She thought of the days of their youth. Willie had always taken up her fights at school and put the bad mouth on her enemies. After their daddy died, Willie had been like a daddy to her. He quit school and took a job to support her family. Those years had been both happy and sad. She laughed to herself at the thoughts of their old times.

Willie's wife, Mary, handed him a list she had made of places to call for information on soldiers missing in action. Willie made the same calls that Mrs. Tennyson had already made, and got the same answers. Then Willie called Fort Benning Army post and told the woman at the other end that Ernie Tennyson had been in Vietnam over a year and was supposed to come home the first of August, but his mother had not heard from him in over two months. She told Willie that the location of the camps in the jungle made it difficult for the soldiers to send and receive mail. She added that the United States Army had searched the records for him and traced him from Dalat to Nha Trang, and on to Da Nang, where records showed Ernie Tennyson's last assignment on August 5, 1968. Shortly after his assignment, the city of Da Nang got hit by North Vietnamese bomber planes. The Army tried to locate all of their soldiers who had been reported as missing in action, and she would let Mrs. Tennyson know something as soon as possible.

Another month passed and the search party never called back. Soldiers missing in action seemed to have gotten lost in the shuffle. Mrs. Tennyson got on the phone and called again. She told them she was sure her son was alive, and she would never give up hopes of finding him.

Mrs. Tennyson paced the floor and worried. She got a glass of tea and went to the back porch to rock her worry. As she looked out across the back lawn, she noticed the ragged rope swing swaying in the old oak tree. She could see Ernie sitting there with his toes barely touching the ground as he tried to push off. My, how time flies. It seemed like only yesterday when he had run through the field with his dog at his heels. She looked at the sun and realized it was time to have lunch. She no longer cooked big meals, but she would have a big dinner for Ernie when he returned.

The next morning, Mrs. Tennyson didn't get excited when she heard a knock at the door. She expected to see Nolan or Mrs. Copeland when she opened the door, but she faced her brother Willie.

Mrs. Tennyson's face brightened. "Come in, Willie."

He followed her to the living room with slow, short steps, and slightly bent shoulders.

"Can I get you something to drink? I have coffee on the stove."

"No, I came to talk to you about Ernie. I wanted to tell you about his condition before you see him," he said, swinging his hat between his legs and looking down.

Mrs. Tennyson's heart took a dip. "Was he wounded?"

"That damn war messed him up," Willie said. "His leg got injured somehow, and he limps a little; I wish I didn't have to tell you the rest."

"What's wrong with Ernie?" Mrs. Tennyson asked.

"He lost his recollection of everything."

"Has Ernie lost his memory?" Mrs. Tennyson said with a puzzled look.

"He doesn't know anybody. He doesn't know his Aunt Mary or me. He stares at us as if we are from another planet."

The lump in Mrs. Tennyson's throat moved and she felt as if she would choke. She caught a deep breath of shock. Then her eyes widened with confidence. "I am sure Ernie will recognize me."

"I hope he does recognize you," Willie said. "You can ride with me, and I will bring you back."

"I'll drive my car," she said. "I wouldn't want you to have to bring me back."

As she followed Willie to Oakdale, her mind flashed memories of Ernie. She worried that he wouldn't recognize her, either. She must look after him and make him remember. If he didn't remember her, he would surely remember Nolan. Ernie and Nolan had been best friends since grade school. She did not want to bother Tracy if she could work things out on her own.

Two hours later, she walked into Willie's living room and stretched her eyes with disbelief. Ernie had a blank stare and sat with perfect posture as he moved the large wooden rocker back and forth. He looked as strong as a rugged mountain and was decorated with brightly colored pins near his shoulder. The yellow stripes shining on his sleeve added life to the drab khaki uniform. She squatted before him, placed her hands on his knees, and studied his face with concern. His wit had disappeared, and his laughter had quieted.

He stalled his rocker and gave her a puzzled look that said he wanted to ask her name. "Ernie, don't you remember me? I am your mama." She kept repeating the same words and hugged him with tears streaming down her cheeks. "I thought you got killed. I am so happy that you are back."

Ernie recognized her presence; but he didn't recognize her face.

"Ernie, try to remember," she said. "You went to Vietnam and fought in the Vietnam War."

He looked at her as if to say, "God! Don't remind me. Where am I?"

She squeezed his hand, stood up, and said, "You will be alright. You will soon remember me." She couldn't hold back her tears.

"Honey, come on to the kitchen. I got some pop," Mary said. "After you have something cold to drink, you'll feel better."

Mrs. Tennyson sat at the small metal table with her head buried in her hands and cried. She had thought of so many things to tell Ernie, and he didn't even know her, his own mother. She could in no way imagine what he had been through. His experiences had been so horrible that he had chosen to completely wipe them from his memory. "I can't believe he doesn't know me. I was sure he would recognize me, but he doesn't."

"Don't worry, honey," Mary said. "His mind is confused and it's going to take a spell for him to straighten things out. That war and all that killing he saw messed up his thinking. Willie says he never heard tell of a man losing his memory, but I knew a man once that forgot everything."

"Did this man ever get his memory back?"

"After about five years. They say that a sudden shock brought it back to him."

"What do you mean?"

"They say a sudden shock will bring memories back," Mary said.

"What did the doctors say about this man?" Mrs. Tennyson asked.

"He said that forgetting everything was a way for a person to get away from horrible situations he doesn't want to face."

"Do you suppose Ernie forgot everything on purpose?"

"The doctor says in the case of lost memory, the subconscious mind takes over," she said.

"The subconscious mind?" Mrs. Tennyson said.

"Yeah, he says the subconscious takes over because the mind can't take on any more stress and worry."

"I understand what you're saying," Mrs. Tennyson said. "I have to get Ernie to a doctor."

"Doctor Sampson is a good doctor," Mary said.

"Is he a head doctor?"

"He's a Yankee doctor, but he's a good doctor."

"Is he here in Oakdale?"

"His office is near the city. Willie and I both go to him when we get sick. He helped Willie's rheumatism."

"The government should send me a medical report," Mrs. Tennyson said. "Do you suppose I should take Ernie to a specialist?"

"I reckon Doctor Sampson is a specialist. He knew what was wrong with Willie and he always hits the ailment like a hammer to a nail- right on the head."

Mrs. Tennyson smiled, thinking how much she reminded her of her mother.

"When Ernie sees the familiar sights of his youth, he might snap back to himself."

"That's what the doctor told the other boy's family that I told you about," Mary said, and she rested her elbows on the table with a worried look. "Ernie's got to be looked about."

"I'll look after my boy," Mrs. Tennyson said. She felt sure that he would recover if she took him home.

Mary got up and walked to the sink. "Let me get my dinner started."

"Could I use your phone," Mrs. Tennyson said.

"Sure, the phone is on the end table in the living room."

Mrs. Tennyson called Nolan and told him the news.

"He will remember me," Nolan Said. "What time will you be home?"

"We should be home before three," Mrs. Tennyson said.

"I can't wait to see Ernie," Nolan said.

After lunch, Ernie made no move to get up from the table. He sat and stared around the kitchen until Mrs. Tennyson had the car loaded and ready to go. He didn't say good bye to his uncle Willie or his Aunt Mary, but they hugged him and told him to come to see them.

As Mrs. Tennyson drove back home, she talked constantly, but Ernie didn't say a word. She was happy that he was still alive. She observed his actions as she drove past the dirt lane leading to the house. But his face showed no indication that he recognized home. When she pulled up before the house, his expression still didn't change.

This stranger had told him this was his home, but he didn't know home from hell. He stood at the end of the drive and stared at the colonial home surrounded by peach trees in bloom. The evening breeze stirred a sweet smell of peach blooms mixed with honeysuckle. Crepe myrtle, shrubs, lilies, and azaleas set a perfect landscape across the neatly trimmed lawn, but he had never seen the beautiful house or the flowers in bloom. In fact, he had not seen, felt, or touched anything that gave him a feeling of belonging, affection or warmth. He stepped inside the front door and was taken by the wide staircase with a slick banister of oak wood. He set his bags on the floor and walked from one room to another. The rooms smelled musty from settled dust, but his room smelled clean and the bed looked comfortable.

He walked back to the living room, turned on the radio, and went to the front porch. He sat with perfect posture and moved his rocker back and forth to the music coming through the screen. "Like a Rock," he hummed, trying to put a name to the voice. Maybe he had once been like a rock, but he was no longer solid like a rock. The war had left its toll on his heart and had taken his mind. There was no link with his past in the things he saw and heard; yet, he knew about places and time: he knew the day and the dark; he knew the sky, stars, clouds, sun, rain, and the storms; he knew the smell of damp earth, dust, and flowers in bloom; he knew about people being born; he knew about people dying; and, somehow, he knew about God. He knew all these things; yet, he knew nothing. Where had he been all of these years? He was suddenly a grown man with a blank mind on a strange planet. There may be light at the end of the tunnel, but he was in a dark tunnel, and there seemed to be no end to the tunnel.

Ernie stalled his rocker at the sight of the red convertible pulling into the drive. A tall skinny man with sandy hair rushed up the porch steps. "God, it is good to have you back home," he said, and he grabbed Ernie in a bear hug.

Ernie did not know this man and felt uneasy about his crowding his space. Ernie watched the man's brown eyes danced with excitement as he fisted him on his shoulder. Ernie stood up and searched the stranger's face as he shook his hand. He tried to fit a name to the long, bony face, but nothing came to mind. He didn't know this man from Adam. He didn't know what to say, so he sat back down in his rocker.

If Ernie forgot everybody else in the world, Nolan thought he would still remember him. Nolan's smile faded and his large teeth clamped down on his pouting lip. He felt his heart draw up in a hard knot and he quickly turned his face away from Ernie. Mrs. Tennyson had told him how it would be, but he had not given it much worry, because he didn't believe Ernie had lost his memory. He thought it would be like old times. He couldn't believe Ernie sat there before him in silence and stared off in space. What could he do? The Ernie Tennyson he knew no longer existed.

Feeling stupid and embarrassed, he took a chair next to Ernie and thought of the strange encounter he once had with a man on the street. He had run up to a man and hugged him, thinking it was his Uncle Chadwick Copeland, and the man gave him a fool look and walked away. Now, he felt just like he did that day.

"I see you've still got good taste in music," Nolan said. "That song must have been written for you."

Ernie stared at him with confusion.

"Hey, Old Buddy, let's go for a ride," Nolan said. He got up and urged Ernie, "Come on. We might run up on some new girls in town." Nolan had felt like celebrating the minute he had heard Ernie was home and had built his hopes to the sky. He had already planned a night on the town.

Ernie just sat there pondering for some time before he got up and followed Nolan to the car.

Nolan pointed out his 1970, red, Corvette convertible with a proud grin. "How do you like my car?"

Ernie didn't seem excited at all. He climbed in, sat back, and stared straight ahead.

Nolan drove through Liberty Springs and pointed out familiar sites of their youth. Ernie took notice of every street, building, stop sign, and red light. In front of the post office, the flag waved lightly in the breeze, and he felt a light tug at his heart. He turned around and watched the flag until it faded in the distance.

The small town of his youth that had once held a special place in his memory was now a blank spot in his mind without affection, warmth, or attachment. Like the people he met, this town stirred no memories, and his life had no particular meaning.

Nolan drove on to Tadem County High School and talked about things they had done and the squabbles they had been in. He got on the subject of baseball and drove to the baseball field. They got out and walked around, but Ernie showed no signs of remembrance.

Nolan drove back to Liberty Springs and said, "I took over the Dingus' Bar and Grill when Pa died. How would you like to have a cold beer?"

Ernie shook his head and Nolan could have sworn he saw some happiness in Ernie's face.

Nolan told Ernie that he had remodeled the Dingus' Bar and added an elegant restaurant and lounge. He bragged about the live band and the crowd he had on Saturday night; they came to his bar to dance, dine, drink, and listen to music until the early morning hours.

Ernie followed Nolan into the crowded bar and a loud roar hit him in the face. He didn't know where he was or how he got there. If you are someplace you have never been before, you are lost. People gathered around him, tugged, touched, and watched him with admiration and curiosity. They laughed, joked, and told stories of old. Ernie listened to the strangers with interest, but he knew nothing about what they said. His friends stood around him, and he didn't see a face in the crowd he knew. He felt like a stranger in a foreign land. He had tried like hell to remember, but he could not bring a single incident to his mind. These mechanical forms with strange faces and strange voices dazzled his brain. He tried to remember names with familiar rings and faces to fit names, but neither came to mind.

Nolan called out to the crowd, "Drinks are on the house!"

Bob Owens slapped him on the back and said, "You used to come with your daddy to the shop when you were a child. Your daddy was a fine man and one of my best friends. I sure do miss him."

"When Ernie made no reply, Nolan quickly said, "He got tangled up with those Vietnamese vines."

"That war was a terrible waste. I'm glad you got home in one piece." He got up and walked to the jukebox. "Let's play a song for the war hero!"

The voices of Alabama made Ernie's feet move with a familiar rhythm. Alabama must have been one of his favorite bands, but he could not remember their faces.

On the way back to Mrs. Tennyson's, Nolan had little to say. He had about decided that Ernie would always be a stranger, and he was just wasting his time and breath. Then the cleaver thought of a new friend was a good thought. Ernie may never remember his old friend, Nolan Copeland, but he would remember his new friend. He wouldn't let him sit back and watch life pass him by. Regardless of his state of mind, Ernie would always be his best friend.

Back at home, Mrs. Tennyson showed Ernie to his old bedroom with its adjoining bath, helped him unpack, and laid out clean towels. Ernie looked around the large room with wonder. The four poster rosewood bed looked inviting. He went to the double windows, pushed the white chintz curtains back, and raised the windows. For a spell, he stood and looked at the moon and the shadows around the house. He didn't even know his family and friends. Unable to make sense of it all, he went to the bathroom and took a bath. As he slid under the cool, clean smelling sheets, he had a feeling like he had experience before. Somehow, he felt at home, but he still did not remember home. As he closed his eyes to sleep, he told himself that what he had forgotten was not nearly as important as what he must remember. He always had nightmares. He wondered why he could hear guns fire and see men dying.

After Mrs. Tennyson went to bed, she worried about Ernie. She had already made an appointment with a psychiatrist.

The next morning, Nolan came in just as they sat down to eat breakfast.

"Come have breakfast with us," Mrs. Tennyson said.

"That bacon smells delicious," Nolan said, and he took a seat at the table.

After the blessing, a long silence took the kitchen throughout the meal.

The telephone rang and Mrs. Tennyson excused herself from the table. She came back to the kitchen and said, "Ernie, Anna Ming from Dalat Province, Vietnam is on the phone. She says it is urgent that she speak to you."

"There is nothing urgent in my life any more I don't know anyone by that name," Ernie said. He refused to answer the phone. He was not about to put himself on the spot. He didn't know Vietnam from hell; he didn't know hell from Vietnam. He didn't know a woman by the name of Ming. He tried to imagine who the woman could be, but no image would come to his brain. He didn't even know his own name. What could he say to this woman?

Mrs. Tennyson went back to the phone and said, "Miss Ming, Mr. Tennyson says he doesn't know you. You must have confused him with someone else."

Mrs. Tennyson thought about the intelligent and charming Ernie she had once known. Now he was cold and lacked affection for all of those he had once loved. She wondered who this woman was. She had sounded desperate, but there was nothing she could do to help her.

Ernie sat at the table and looked at them. He felt as if his mind had been turned out on a platter for them to examine his weird thoughts.

Nolan broke the silence. "Ernie, let's go for a walk around the farm."

Ernie didn't say anything, but he got up and followed Nolan out the door.

The next day Mrs. Tennyson had an appointment for Ernie with Doctor McKenzie, a well-known psychiatrist in Oakdale. After an hour of examination and consultation, he called Mrs. Tennyson in and explained Ernie's condition.

Doctor McKenzie found no physical injuries to his brain or his body. He told Mrs. Tennyson that she would be wasting her time and money for the services he could give Ernie. Psychoanalysis for his illness would be expensive and take years. He explained that trauma had caused him to lose him memory, and his memory loss was likely temporary. He suggested that she introduce him to his old environment, since this had helped most of his patience with the same condition. He made her no promises for Ernie's recovery.

"Isn't there anything you can do to help my boy?" Mrs. Tennyson said with disappointment.

"I could try electric shock treatments and hypnosis, but I would suggest that you introduce him to his old environment first. After seeing and experiencing things from his past, he may gradually remember bits and pieces, put it together, and become fairly adjusted to his surroundings."

Mrs. Tennyson got up to leave and Doctor McKenzie said, "I don't want to rush into hypnosis or electric shock therapy. If he does not improve within the next three months, I will try hypnosis. We will try electric shock treatments as a last resort."

On the way home, Mrs. Tennyson thought about the options. She had heard that electric shock treatments messed up your brain. They would never do that to Ernie. If she couldn't help him, he would remain the way he was now for the rest of his life.

CHAPTER TWENTY-SIX

Anna twisted the tear stained Kleenex to fuzz. She had missed four periods, and the morning sickness lingered until noon each day. She cried and cradled her stomach with love for her baby. She wanted this baby more than anything in the world, but she was unmarried and unemployed. She wanted the life growing within her to have a father and the best life possible. How could she provide for it and give it a good life? She wrestled with her choices: abortion, adoption, or an unmarried mother. Which was the least of the three evils?

Abortion was an ugly word, a sin, and she could hardly bear the thoughts of killing the life within her. Her father would never agree for her to keep her child, and she did not want to put it up for adoption. He would pay for her to have an abortion; but abortion would bring more guilt than she could bear.

That weekend when Dong Lee returned home, Mrs. Ming told him that she was concerned about Anna's health; she had been shut up in her room and would not eat or talk to her.

Dong Lee dreaded facing his daughter, and he was tired of talking to the wind, but he had to find out what was going on. He went directly to Anna's bedroom and found the door locked. "Anna, I want to talk to you," Dong Lee said, and he knocked the third time before she answered.

Dong Lee sat down on the bed and looked at his daughter's pale face.

"What is wrong with you, Anna? Do you need to see a doctor?"

She sat up in bed and said, "Father, I am pregnant."

Dong Lee jumped up, threw his hands in the air, paced across the room, turned red with anger and shouted, "Wait until I get my hands on that damn bastard! He makes me want to chew nails! I will kill that American for bringing shame to my family." He stood with his hands propped on the door and his mind was in turmoil. He could not bear the thoughts of Anna having an illegitimate child for a married man, especially an American. He walked back to the bed and said, "I will arrange for you to have an abortion immediately. Ernie Tennyson must never know that you are carrying his bastard child."

She lowered her chin and calmly said, "Father, I will not have an abortion and take away an innocent life. My mother would turn over in her grave at the suggestion of such. I would be guilty of murder, the worst sin of all sins."

"Bearing children before marriage is also a sin," he said. "Your mother's Catholic beliefs are not to be considered at a time like this. You are not thinking clearly." He walked back across the room and turned back. "How will you provide for this baby? You do not have a husband, and you will not shame me with a bastard child."

"I will not kill my baby!"

"Face reality, my daughter! If you have this child, your life will be over. You must go to China and live with your Aunt Sean. After you have the abortion and get your head back on your shoulders, you may come back home."

She threw the cover back, jumped up from the bed, and faced him. "My head is together! I will not go to China! Why do you preach the sins you practice! You slip to many women at night! What will their husbands do if they learn that their wives are having an affair with you? What about your last fling with Lolita? Will you crawl back to her and forget that she is committing adultery?"

Dong Lee dropped his head with shame. He threw his palms up. "Holy Mother knows I have sinned, but I have made the women in my life no promises. Ernie Tennyson made promises to you that will never come to be. How could you love this beast?"

"Ernie is not a beast, and I cannot make my heart cold to the feelings of love that I have for him. Neither can I erase what happened, but I can have my baby and give it a mother that loves it."

With a wrinkled brow, he pushed his hands in his pockets and said, "Are you willing to share this American with another woman?"

"What do you mean by that question?" she said. "Ernie loves only me."

"I cannot convince you that I am right and you are wrong, but you will see clearly in time. The dirt beneath his feet on his Georgia soil means more to him than you or any other woman."

"Ernie loves me, Father."

"His declaration of love for you suited his purpose at the time. I do not intend to listen to your foolishness."

"Ernie gave me this engagement ring, Father. If he is still alive, he will come back for me and make me his wife."

Dong Lee laughed with mockery, "This American is a con artist. He never intended to marry you to begin with. That cheap ring probably came from a box of popcorn. That ring on your finger means nothing to him. Other fool women are awaiting his return."

"Ernie loves only me."

"Get your things packed immediately. You are going to China."

"I am staying right here," she said.

He slapped his temples at her reply. "I did not want to use force, but I see that you will not cooperate."

She ran to him, her head against his back, and embraced his waist as she had done when she was a child. "Please, Father. Let me handle my mistakes my own way."

He turned her about and pulled her into his arms. Flashes of his younger days stalled his thinking for minutes as he held to his sobbing daughter. Love had made him do crazy things. "You have not handled your mistakes very well so far," he said.

"Father, I love you, but I love Ernie, also. Please try to understand. I have worried so much, and I have wanted to walk away and never look upon his face again, but I cannot forget him. If I never see him again, I will have his baby to remind me of our love for each other. Somehow, I will take on my responsibility. I will be a good mother," she said with tears streaming down her cheeks.

Her Father stepped away from her and left the room. She peeped out the window and saw him pacing across the veranda. Minutes later, he came back into the house and went to his quarters.

Anna thought he had settled his anger and she was going to keep the baby. She lay back down on her bed and thought of things she must do in preparation for her little one. She must buy a baby bed, stroller, high chair, and baby clothes first of all.

When she heard the loud knocking on her door, she thought her grandmother had come to tell her dinner was ready. When she pulled the door back, she was shocked to see her father with his body guard; he had come to take her to the bus station. Bai Hoe was a tall, dark man with muscles like a water balloon about to burst, and she could not overpower him.

"You can pack your things and Bai Hoe will be waiting for you."

Less than an hour later, her father said to her, "Do you want to walk to the car on your own or do you want Bai Hoe to carry you?"

Anna gave her father an angry stare and said, "I will walk on my own to the car."

Anna sat and cried while they carried out her personal belongings.

As she was leaving, her father gave her a wad of money and a bus ticket. Bai Hoe carried her to the Dalat bus station and she was on her way to Shanghai, China, in Eastern Asia. Since she was in for an overnight ride to Shanghai, she found a seat near the back of the bus and sat down with a feeling of defeat. The world was closing in on her, covering her with a cloud of darkness that was smothering her to death. Her father still had plans for her to marry the man of his choice, but she would remain single the rest of her life before she made vows this man. She wanted to go to Georgia and find Ernie.

She took the small pillow from her bag, positioned it behind her head, and closed her eyes. She slept until the sound of traffic awoke her the next morning.

She raised her head and looked out the window. The bus neared Shanghai and the traffic was heavy near the city. Unlike Saigon, the city officials did not allow motorcycles and bicycles on the main roads and elevated expressways. They allowed motorcycles and bicycles on some roads, but they had separate lanes from the other motor vehicles.

Shanghai was made up of many beautiful cities, small towns, and townships. It was China's largest city with a population of over 18 million in the city alone. In addition, Shanghai was rated at the top for its economic growth, development, and urbanization. It was divided into provinces; divisions; villages, based on ethnic groups, and rural population; neighborhoods; and communities.

The bus moved down the streets of Shanghai, and her thoughts moved back in time. She remembered having visited her aunt and uncle when she was a child. Her Aunt Sean carried her shopping to many places, but Shanghai was her favorite. She could still feel the tight hold on her hand as they moved through the crowded streets. The art gallery and beautiful buildings had made a lasting impression on her. She also remembered visiting the beautiful parks in Shanghai.

She had been to the People's Square Park many times, because it was down town, near the shopping centers. Her Aunt Sean liked the Fuxing Park; she talked for hours about its French style gardens, bars, and cafes. Her Aunt Sean also liked to have dinner at the Fuxing Park Restaurant.

Anna had only visited the Zhongshan Park one time, because it was located in Northwestern Central Shanghai. She had gone there to see the famous monument of Chopin, a musical genius, composer, and leading Virtuoso from Warsaw, which became a part of Poland. Anna remembered the monument, because it was unusual and beautiful. Its smooth layered folds of stone looked like tall musical pipes of different lengths with a sculpture of Chopin on one side, at the top, which showed features of his long, slender, handsome face and large closed eyes draped by long folds of hair neatly parted to the side.

The bus neared the Shanghai Museum, and Anna turned in her seat to look back at the fantastic oval structure that resembled a gold dome with a gold moon on its roof. The wide entrance centered two circular levels, and another level over the entrance made up the third floor, which was covered by a flat roof, gold dome, and gold moon.

As the bus left the city, Anna thought about the islands and harbors south of Shanghai. She used to walk for miles along the warm shore to admire the sandy beach and waves.

The nearer the bus got to her Aunt's house, the colder Anna got. She reached into her bag, pulled out her sweater, and wrapped it around her body. The weather in Shanghai was different from Lat Village, where it was spring time the year round. Shanghai's summer months got very hot. In fact, her Aunt Sean always carried a fan and umbrella with her to the city, especially in July. Anna was thankful that summer had come and gone in Shanghai; however, winter was coming on, and the weather was bone chilling cold. One could not go out of the house without several layers of clothing, coat, hat, and gloves. Anna could not decide which was worse - the hot summer with no air conditioning or the cold winter with no central heating. She liked the spring time in Shanghai; the weather turned cool and they had heavy rainfall in April. The baby was due in April or May. If she got to keep her baby, she would stay in China until it was born.

Anna's Aunt Sean lived in a rural area far from Shanghai. She lived in a large house built of stone; she enjoyed all of the modern conveniences; and Hoe owned two automobiles. This was unusual, since many who lived in the city had no automobiles. If a person owned an automobile, he went through a lot of red tape in order to drive in the city. On the other hand, many people in the rural areas lived without running water and had no transportation to carry them back and forth to the city, but taxis did not charge much. The driver seldom spoke English, but most of the citizens did not understand English, either.

The bus left the main road and the pot holes on the dusty roads made her bounce in her seat. She sat with her nose pointed toward the window and took in the small mud huts with straw roofs and the bamboo huts covered with clay. Smoke curled to the sky. She hated the smell of the thick smoke. Many people had to burn grass roots, weeds, and animal dung for fuel, because there was not much wood in China. They passed rich farm land with homes built of bricks, stone, wood, and siding.

The bus finally came to familiar sites, and she recognized her Aunt Sean's white stone house. She moved to the front of the bus to pull the cord. Farm land and trees surrounded the single story house with its tile roof. She walked up the drive, climbed the steps, and knocked on the door. While she waited for someone to answer the door, she repeated her greeting to herself in Chinese. She had grown used to speaking English to the children at school, so her Chinese was rusty.

Her Aunt Sean and Uncle Hoe met her with open arms; her cousins, Mein and Tra, smiled and bowed to her with respect shown to an elderly lady. Their dark eyes twinkled when they spoke. Her uncle Hoe and his son, Tray, were slender and tall. Mein took after her mother; she was short and slender.

Her Aunt Sean moved her short, slender figure with quick little steps toward the sitting room. Her dark eyes brightened and a smile stretched her small mouth as she spoke. She reminded Anna of her mother. She wanted to hear all about the family and Anna.

Her father had already filled her Aunt Sean in on his plan, and Anna did not want to discuss the issue. She told her Aunt Sean that she was very tired and asked if she could go to her room and rest. Her Aunt Sean was kind and showed her to her room right away.

Anna looked around the neat room and was thankful that she at least had a decent place to stay. She must think of a way to save her child. Perhaps her Aunt Sean would protect her and her baby. Her Aunt Sean believed that family came first. Her home was always filled with laughter, happiness, and games. When her children married, they would live at her home or nearby. All of the family members lived near each other.

Anna slept and did not wake up until her Aunt Sean called her to breakfast the next morning. After they ate, her Aunt Sean told her that her father had made her an appointment with a gynecologist for eleven o'clock. Anna was thinking about how her father had planned everything. He had made an appointment with a doctor he knew well; but Anna did not know the doctor and did not care to listen to his advice. She dreaded going to the doctor, but she had to obey her father's wishes a few more months.

To Anna's surprise, Doctor Kim Soon was very nice. He told her and that she was more than four months pregnant; he explained that an abortion at this stage of pregnancy would put her life in danger, and he would not perform an abortion.

Anna had never been happier in her life; her father would not get his way, and he would be furious.

When they got back to her Aunt Sean's house, her father sat with her Uncle Hoe in the living room. Anna did not speak to him; she walked to her room and locked the door. Dong Lee greeted Sean with a hug and kiss; Hoe shook Dong Lee's hand, and asked them to excuse him; he had to go to a meeting.

Sean asked Dong Lee to come to the kitchen for tea. After pouring the tea, she sat down at the table with him to tell him the news. Dong Lee was very angry. He did not know Anna was four months pregnant; she had not told him how far along she was. Sean convinced him that having an abortion was a worse sin than having a child out of wed lock. She told him not to worry about the baby; she would adopt Anna's baby and raise it as her own; and no one in Vietnam would ever know, except their family, and they would never tell. Dong Lee left with a better feeling about Anna having the American's child, but he vowed to never accept the little bastard as his grandchild.

The next day, Dong Lee went back to Vietnam; Anna stayed in her room until her Aunt Sean knocked on her door and asked to come in to talk.

Sean sat down on the edge of the bed and took Anna's hand in her own. "Anna, I love you as much as my own Mein. Love for a man makes the heart throb with a pain no other knows, but you must put your mind on other things. I spoke to your father and told him I would adopt your child and raise it as my own. He seemed satisfied when he left."

"Nobody is going to adopt my baby! I am going to be my baby's mother, and I will find a way to support it. I cannot bear the thoughts of anybody else, even you, being its mother. This baby is a part of Ernie, and I love him more than life."

"Maybe we can talk to your father; maybe he will change his mind and ask you to come back home."

"He will not change. He hates Americans, especially Ernie. Father chose the man he wants me to marry, but I will die before I make vows to this man."

"The Chinese tradition of choosing a partner for the female children is still strong," she said.

"Do you believe in choosing a partner for your daughter?"

"My father chose Hoe for me," she said.

"Do you love him?"

"My father did not know Hoe and I already loved each other. We dated in secret for more than a year before my father went to his home and arranged our marriage. Had he known Hoe was secretly seeing me, he would not have chosen another for my husband. After we married, the law required that I live with Hoe in his Parents' home. I wanted privacy; I did not want to live with them at first, but I loved Hoe, and I got used to his parents' ways, which differed little from my own. His parents liked me and treated me as a daughter. I miss them now that they are both gone; but Hoe and I are still happy on our own."

"I would not mind living with Ernie in his mother's home, but I may never see him again. Luck found you betrothed to a man you already loved; but I am not so lucky, because the man I love is an American."

"I believe he will come back for you."

"He does not know where I have gone."

"Call him and tell him where you are. If he loves you, he will go to the end of the earth to see you. In the meantime, you should start reading, go to the library, take up exercises, and get interested in a hobby. A healthy mind and body brings you a healthy, happy, baby."

Anna did not want to tell her that she had called Ernie more than a dozen times, but he would not talk with her. She followed Sean to the kitchen to prepare dinner. After dinner, Anna pitched in and washed the dishes; then she went about daily chores of washing clothes, cleaning house, and ironing. She helped her Aunt Sean every day with anything that needed to be done, but she could not wait to get out on her own with her baby.

CHAPTER TWENTY-SEVEN

Two weeks before Christmas, Nolan Talked Ernie into going with him to get a Christmas tree. Ernie helped Nolan cut and load the tree, but he didn't know why he cut down a tree and hauled it to the house.

Mrs. Tennyson was proud of the tree. She tried to get Ernie excited about Christmas, but he had no idea why they were putting all of those lights on the tree. Mrs. Tennyson asked Ernie to help her decorate for Christmas; she told him this Christmas was special, because he was home to celebrate with the family. Then she told him about the meaning of Christmas and how excited he used to get when Santa left all of those toys.

Ernie finally pitched in and helped her put the tinsel, Christmas balls, and Christmas ornaments on the tree. Then she asked Ernie to help her with the poinsettias. Ernie got two poinsettias from the porch, carried them to the living room, and set them on the end tables.

Next, she showed Ernie how to decorate the door. He followed her directions and placed a beautiful wreath made from holly, berries, and red ribbons on the front door. Then she told Ernie to string lights across the edge of the porch for the finished touches of Christmas.

The next day, she went shopping for presents in Liberty Springs. She shopped for her granddaughter first; she bought her a Barbie doll, doll clothes, a tea set, and a tricycle. Then she went to Goody's Department Store and bought Tracy a navy blue suit, ear rings, and a pocket book. Next, she bought her brother, Willie, a shirt and bought his wife, Mary, a sweater.

Last of all, she went to the Home Depot and shopped for Ernie. She bought him all the things she thought he might like: a flash light, tool set, drill, a new shaving kit, and shot gun shells. While she was there, she bought Nolan a box of shot gun shells, also.

After she finished buying Christmas presents, she went grocery shopping at Walmart. She bought a turkey, milk, meal, eggs, and cranberry sauce. She stored enough vegetables in her cabinets and freezer that year to pick her choice for dinner.

That night, she wrapped all of her presents and put them under the tree. Afterwards, she sat down in her recliner and talked to Ernie about the beautiful Christmas tree. The twinkling lights and silver tinsel threw light on the presents and made them look special. She picked up each present under the tree, looked at the names and replaced them. Then she talked about the presents he got for Christmas when he was a little boy. She said the year Santa brought him a bicycle excited him more than any Christmas afterward. Ernie had no idea what she was talking about.

The day before Christmas, Mrs. Tennyson called her brother Willie and invited them to dinner. Then she planned her Christmas dinner.

The next morning, she got up at six o'clock and put on her turkey. She cooked the things that Ernie liked best for Christmas. They had to have the traditional turkey and dressing. He liked her dressing and all the other dishes she prepared: potato salad, pumpkin pie, and green bean casserole.

Tracy came in with her daughter and she ran to her grandmother for a hug, and Tracy went to talk to Ernie. He sat with a blank stare, and she broke down in tears. She had to get out of the room; she could not bear to see him in this condition.

In the meantime, Mrs. Tennyson tried to get Ernie to talk to Beth, his little niece. Beth was a beautiful child with dark hair, blue eyes, a sweet smile, and a good disposition. Ernie spoke to the child, but he said nothing more.

When Tracy came back with her arm full of presents, Beth squirmed to get down from her grandmothers lap and ran to the Christmas tree. She picked up each present and told her grandmother whose name was on the label. Then she went to Ernie and told him that she had bought him a pretty shirt. Ernie made no reply and she dashed out the door to find her mother.

Willie and Mary came in with their presents, put them under the tree and raved about Beth's beauty. Then they spoke to Ernie and socialized with Tracy a few minutes before they all went to the kitchen to put dinner on the table.

Willie carved the turkey and they all sat down to eat. Mrs. Tennyson said the blessing and added a prayer for Ernie. They all enjoyed dinner and the conversation with Tracy. Her husband worked as a hospital administrator and his job put him on the road often. She hated when he had to work on holidays.

After they finished cleaning the dishes, they all went to the living room to open presents. Nolan came in before they finished, and Mrs. Tennyson gave him his present. His face stretched with a smile when he saw the shot gun shells. He talked to Tracy a while; they had been friends since childhood. Then he took a chair next to Ernie and stayed with him all that evening. Ernie didn't know what all the fuss was about; he wanted them to go home and leave him alone with his blank mind.

Later that evening, they all left, and Ernie relaxed on the back porch. He didn't know what to think about their big celebration. He didn't know Tracy or her daughter from a sack of salt, but she seemed nice, and she had a beautiful little daughter. On the other hand, he didn't know any of the other folk either, but he had been around them for a short while.

That night, they had an early supper. Mrs. Tennyson was tired from all of the cooking, cleaning, and decorating; she went to bed early.

Tracy called often and she had promised to call her mama and let her know when she got back home. She called around ten that night, but Ernie never answered the phone. The next morning, Mrs. Tennyson got worried and called Tracy. She had forgotten that Ernie would not answer the phone.

The week after Christmas, the church always had a big dinner. Families had too much to do during Christmas to come to the church and bring food.

Mrs. Tennyson got excited about the dinner at the church. She lived for church services, prayer meetings, dinners, and socializing with her friends. She never missed a Sunday.

Mrs. Tennyson talked about the dinner at the church all that week. This was the first time she had tried to get Ernie to go to church with her, but she thought he had enough time to adjust by now. She bought Ernie a new, navy blue, gabardine suit to wear. As she pressed his suit, she thought back to the time when Ernie enjoyed going to church. She wanted him to see all of his old friends, and she prayed that he might recognize some of them.

After she got Ernie's clothes ready, she chose the prettiest dress in her closet. Then she sat before her dressing table and pushed, pulled, and adjusted the hair pen in the ball of hair on her neck. The narrow bands of gray in her dark hair glittered.

Ernie did not want to go to the social gathering at the church. He forgot his own name and his own mother, and he felt out of place.

From the looks of the crowd, his mama got the word out about the dinner. Folk attended church that Sunday who had not darted the doors in months. Ernie came to eat his mama's dumplings and fried chicken.

Ernie followed his mama down the aisle to the front pew. The choir sang Amazing Grace and he sat with a waxed face and listened. The familiar feeling that came over him made him want to sing with the choir.

After the sermon, his mama introduced him to all of the church Members, which was for his benefit; all of the members knew him well. She reminded him often that he had attended that church all of his life. She talked enough for him and several others in the crowd. She explained that his tour of duty in Vietnam in that useless, violent war impaired his ability to think, and made him lose his memory.

Ernie stood back like a dummy and listened to the church folk discuss his life as if he could not hear. He felt embarrassed and out of place. He wished God would make him whole again and give him his life back.

When the cheerful women started putting food on the table, Ernie finally got away from them. He walked over to the shade of the oaks, where the men had gathered; he did not take part in their conversation. What man among them had no name? He had forgotten all names. Worst of all, he had forgot his own name. If you don't have a name, it's the same as nothing. If you don't have any relatives, it's the same as nothing. He didn't know when he was born or anything about his childhood. He didn't know who had died that meant a right smart to him.

When the men went toward the tables, Ernie followed them. He filled his plate with the delicious dishes and went back to the shade under the trees. He would go back later for dessert. His mama had cooked a ten layer chocolate cake, and the pancake thin layers soaked in chocolate looked delicious. He sat down at the far end of the bench and enjoyed his dinner.

The church folk treated him with warmth and kindness, but warmth and kindness meant very little to a man without a memory. He wanted to go back in time and pick up the pieces of his life that went missing, but he couldn't. From what his mother told him, he was once confident and had a good self-concept. Now he had no concept of good and bad; he had no concept of right and wrong. The fear of the unknown haunted him. After he finished eating, he went to the car and waited for his mama to get tired of talking.

When they got home, Ernie sat down in the living room and stared at the wall. Mrs. Tennyson came in and took a seat on the couch across from Ernie. She saw that something was wrong with him.

"Ernie, what is bothering you?"

"I don't want to go back to that church," he said.

"Ernie, the church folk love you, and they feel proud to have you back in church."

"I don't know who I am; I don't know who you are; I don't know any of the church folk. I've got a blank mind."

"Your name is Ernie Tennyson, and you are my son. You cannot hang your head and ignore the world. Search your mind for the lost memories of the past! I don't question you much about Vietnam, but you would feel better if you talked about the things that happened to you. You seem so worried all the time; and I want to help you, but I cannot help you if you don't talk to me."

"Hell, I don't know anything to talk about," he said. He got up and went outside to walk and think. On the way out, he slammed the door with anger. He felt ashamed about losing his temper, but his mama didn't understand; he knew nothing about anything. In his mother's eyes, he was still a hero; yet, she protected him like a mother hen. He followed her rules and stayed within the limits of the laws she put down.

His loss of memory had not made him less alert. He could still reason and think things out, but he could not think about the past; he could not remember the past. There was a place in his mind full of blurred memories. He could not pull the memories out in the correct order. The unknown played havoc with his brain, and it seemed that everything had gone haywire. The two service stripes on his left sleeve represented a void in his life that had set him back and ruined him forever. Nothing excited him anymore. From what Nolan told him, he was once the life of the party and a thrill seeker. Everything he did now seemed like nonsense, except farming. The richest man in the world was nothing without his brain. He would give away all of his worldly possessions to get his memory back and live a normal life.

Mrs. Tennyson took up the task of teaching Ernie how to live again. She talked to Ernie as if he had never gone away. She cooked his meals and reminded him of the things he liked best. He didn't remember liking turnips, but he still liked them.

Every night after supper, Mrs. Tennyson pulled out the picture albums and pointed out pictures of Ernie, his friends, and his family. When she came to a picture of him, she would touch his hand and say his name.

Mrs. Tennyson also told him stories about his childhood. "As a child, you got very confused about the goose. You would look at the barn yard birds and say to me: Mama is that a goose, a goose gander, or a goose gosling?" Then she laughed and laughed.

Late every evening, Nolan came and worked with Ernie. He introduced Ernie to the game of baseball, a game Ernie once loved. He showed Ernie his old baseball, bat, and uniform. Then they played pitch.

Mrs. Copeland came in on Fridays and helped Mrs. Tennyson wash, clean, and iron. She took up a good bit of time with Ernie; she told him stories about things he and Nolan did when they were growing up; she told him about their baseball games; she told him about a camping trip they went on. Ernie seemed to listen, but he never got excited about her stories.

Pretty soon, Nolan talked Ernie into going hunting. Nolan laughed, joked, and told stories of old as he led the way across the land and through the woods. The first time Nolan took Ernie's rifle from the rack, Ernie ran from the room. Nolan urged Ernie to follow him to the woods. When Nolan fired the first shot, Ernie crouched like a gun-shy bird dog. Nolan pretended not to see him and continued to fire the gun. A squirrel tumbled from the tree and Ernie covered his head and trembled with fright.

Weeks passed before Ernie decided to try his hand with the gun. His aimed too high and his finger stalled on the trigger with the first shot. Then he went crazy and shot at everything in sight, every moving limb. Nolan grinned as if he had taught a child to say its first word. Tomorrow, they would fish.

Although everything and everybody was still foreign, Ernie paid careful attention to Mrs. Tennyson, Mrs. Copeland, and Nolan. He watched their faces, listened to their words with interest, laughed when they laughed, and asked questions. He tried to get a mental grasp on his past, but nothing came to him. However, his scanty vocabulary had improved and his life was better. He was thankful for his mama and a friend like Nolan and Mrs. Copeland. They had made his life worth living by giving him back his name and introducing him to his past. Best of all, they made a way for his future.

CHAPTER TWENTY-EIGHT

Ernie took over the farm that spring. Mr. Carver's three-year's lease was up on the land, but he came back and brought his own tractor to help Ernie with the plowing and spring planting.

Ernie had not forgotten how to farm. Farming seemed to be an inborn instinct. He still knew how to drive a tractor and handle the farm machinery; he worked like a professional farmer.

Ernie liked the farm; he got the spring fever like all farmers get when time comes to plow, plant, fertilize, and watch the green sprouts crack the earth. He used an herbicide before preparing the soil for the seeds, but the weeds and grass soon got immune to the poison, and he was left with the job of plowing and hoeing around the plants. He had little time to catch his breath even with Mr. Carver's help.

As Ernie walked across the lawn toward the barn, he watched the bees swarm around the flower garden to suck the sweet nectar from the blooms. His mama liked her flowers. She had gardens of sweet blooms all year long. The carnations bloomed in the spring; the beauty of irises, lilacs, and lilies bloomed; then sunflowers followed close behind the lilies. She gave lilies to all of her friends. He wondered if she planted all of those flowers for her pleasure or for their admiration for her green thumb. He walked on and the catalpa trees caught his eye; they had white trumpet shaped flowers, but the worms would soon devour their heart shaped leaves. Ernie saw no use for the long bean pods hanging on the tree.

He got on the tractor and drove toward the field. A thousand birds covered the open pasture and pecked the corn left from the previous year's harvest. The dogwood trees along the fence row had bloomed and spread their beauty above the wild flowers that spread their colors, yellow and purple amid the clover and violets. All of this filled the air with a sweetness not found in a perfume bottle.

Several hours later, he stopped to take a water break. He wiped the dust from his face with his shirtsleeve, and looked across the field; he was worried about getting finished with the planting by the end of the week.

When he went home for dinner, his mama told him that a girl named Anna Ming had called again; she had said that she really needed to talk to him.

Ernie looked at him mama and said, "What could I say to this girl, Mama? I don't remember my own name."

"Perhaps you should talk to her the next time she calls and see what she says. Her voice sounded urgent; you must have meant a right smart to her."

"I think it best to say nothing, since I don't remember her." Ernie said.

When the sun hid behind the trees on the fence row, the cool breeze hit his face with welcome, and he called out to the field workers to stop for the day. They helped him load the seeds and fertilizer before going home. He drove toward home and looked toward the sky for rain. Would he be a farmer the rest of his life? What good things did his future hold? If he could remember his past life, he might not be happy; but he could solve his problems and make things better for the future.

When he came in from the field every day, Cleo, the cat, greeted him with a nudge; then she walked between his legs and purred. He had grown fond of Cleo. She was a beautiful Persian cat that his mama treated special. Cleo had a hatch on the back door; she came into the house and went outside when she wanted to.

In no time, the garden came alive with blooms; green onions broke the earth and shone like white pearls on the sand. The small, green peppers looked like fat fists hiding under their leaves. Squash bugs had made hay of the squash vines, and the smaller squash had rotted. The crows had taken a liking to the cabbage, but his mother had learned how to shoot a shotgun. When the crows heard the back door slam, they flew in haste toward the branch. As soon as his mama got back into the house, the crows returned. She never hit a single crow. Her aim was always too high or too low.

He heard the pots and pans rattle, and he smelled his mama's casserole, her favorite dish to serve. She made casseroles from all of the leftover food and added her favorite spices. He swallowed a hungry lump as he waited for supper.

Ernie had taken an interest in farming. His mind was soon occupied by dirt furrows, green plants sprouting, dust flying around him, like fog in the summer heat, and trees swaying in the breeze.

At night, he read farm journals, and other books about agriculture and plant life. On days that it rained, he went to the library and checked out books to read about farming.

Ernie's crop looked good, and he started to act happier and more adjusted to his new life.

Mrs. Tennyson felt sure that he would soon snap back to normal. "I'm so happy to see you take an interest in the farm." she said. "You will soon be back to your old self."

"If I don't get my memory back, I guess I will have to take one day at a time and do the best I can with the brain that I have."

"That's a good thought," she said as she set the food on the table.

CHAPTER TWENTY-NINE

The doorbell rang at midnight, and Ernie sat upright in bed. Glancing at the clock with disgust, he said to himself, "Who in the devil could be calling at this time of the night?"

Looking through the door peeper, he saw a tall woman with dark hair hugging her shoulders like rich mink. He opened the door and gazed at her with curiosity. "Could I help you," he asked.

She threw her hair back and spoke with an unusual accent. "I'm Laquan Tennyson. I need to talk to you." She walked into his home as if she owned the place. Ernie Tennyson was more handsome than she remembered. Not only was he tall and tan; he was the sexiest man she had ever laid eyes on. His broad shoulders, tremendous muscles, and dark hair covering his chest made her want to get close to him.

Staring at her with confusion, he pushed a husky hand through his hair and waited for her to state her business. Her hesitation and the way she moved her eyes over his body made him uncomfortable.

"Did you know my father?" he asked.

"I've never met any of your family," she said. "You are the only one in this family that I know."

Mrs. Tennyson stepped in the doorway and said, "I am Ernie's mother. Are you the woman who called here every day the last two months?"

"I tried desperately to get in touch with Ernie, but I could not get his number," she said. She realized that Mrs. Tennyson was trying to size her up, and she quickly turned back to Ernie and said, "I need to talk to you in private."

When Mrs. Tennyson disappeared down the hall, Laquan ran to Ernie with an urgent embrace and said, "I thought I'd never find you." She moved her face to his. "I've missed you so much." And she kissed him smack in the mouth.

With mixed feelings of anger and confusion, he squirmed from her embrace, backed away from her and said, "What did you want to see me about, Miss?"

With a look of disappointment, she blinked her long lashes and her dark eyes pierced him with a hard stare as she spoke, "I am disappointed to hear that you do not remember me. We met in Saigon several years ago."

He tried to imagine having met her, but he didn't know Saigon from any other place in the world. He wanted this woman out of his house.

Looking down with embarrassment, he said, "I don't remember anything or anybody since the war."

"I am your wife!" she said.

His mouth dropped open with silence; he stared at her with shock. "I am your wife!" rang in his ears. Feeling as if he would choke on the scream in his throat, he took a deep breath and walked to the end of the mantle. He couldn't think of a thing to say to this stranger who had suddenly appeared in his living room and tied him down with holy matrimony. Standing with his back to her, he fiddled with the pictures on the mantle and said, "I can't be married to you! I don't know you, Miss. I have never seen you before in my life!" Turning to face her, his voice calmed. "I simply do not remember you."

She walked up to him, put her arms around his waist, and rested her head on his shoulder. "I'll make you remember me. What we had was wonderful. God, I have missed you," she said and she pressed her body closer to his.

Considering her proposal with distaste, he stepped back. "I think you should go back where you came from, Miss. You apparently do not understand that I have lost my memory, and things will never be the same with me. Whatever we had at one time will never be again."

"You will remember me soon," she said.

She was a persistent bitch, and He didn't seem to be getting through to her. "Listen, Miss, I am tired, and I have to get up early. I'm going to bed."

"Let me get my things," she said.

He pushed his palm forward and said, "I think you had better go back to Saigon, where you came from."

"I'm not going anywhere," she said, taking a seat on the couch. "I'm your wife, and I have proof of my rights! I have our marriage certificate! I have pictures too!"

"Listen, Miss," he said, feeling a little sad about her being upset, "I don't have anything against you. You're a pretty woman and seem mighty nice, but I don't know anything about you, and I am not interested."

Looking up at him with tears slowly rolling down her cheeks, she said, "I know everything about you! I know the month and day of your birthday, your favorite foods, and your favorite pastime. You like to hunt and fish better than anything, except sex." Closing her eyes, she leaned back with a sigh. "God, our relationship was wonderful. No other man can satisfy me the way you did."

"That would be kind of nice to remember, Miss Tennyson. You know what I mean?"

"Make love to me," she said, jumping up and pushing her body close to his. "You will remember." She mumbled around his ear, "Umm, umm, I want you."

Stunned by her words and sweet perfume, his brain flashed a picture of a whore, one of the whores that Nolan had fixed him up with since he got back home. He had been to bed with dozens of women since he had come back from Vietnam, but he went with them to fulfill that raging animal desire common to man. The whores Nolan fixed him up with made him remember the pleasure he got from having sex. He was familiar with that good feeling that rushed through him like the high tide, thrust violently upon the shores of heaven, and ebbed to peaceful waves floating over the sea. Like this whore, all the other women he had been to bed with had beauty, charm, sexy figures, and a desire to please. A decent woman wouldn't make vulgar suggestions as she had made. Had he been to bed with this woman? He could take this whore to bed, but he would promise her nothing. Besides, his mind was blank and promises of love to any woman were foolish.

"Miss, please excuse me a minute," Ernie said, and he rushed to his mama's door and knocked.

Mrs. Tennyson quickly answered the door with a concerned look on her face. "Who is that woman, and what does she want?"

"Mama, that woman says she is my wife!" Ernie whispered. "Can you believe I married that piece of trash?"

Mrs. Tennyson's knees weakened. She was shocked and lost for words. "She must think we are rich, and she needs a husband. Let me have my say," and she started to the living room.

"Wait, Mama, she says she's my wife and she has rights. She refused to listen to reason and says she is not leaving. We have to think of a way to make her leave."

"She's not staying here," Mrs. Tennyson said. "We will hire a lawyer and put her on the road!"

Laquan stood in the middle of the living room with wide eyes moving around the room.

Mrs. Tennyson walked up to her and said, "Miss, if you don't have a place to stay tonight, you can sleep in the guest room, but I expect you to leave tomorrow morning. The guest room is this way. She followed Mrs. Tennyson down the hall to the bedroom. Mrs. Tennyson walked to the back of the room to show her the bathroom and said, "I hope you sleep well. I am sorry you have no place to go."

This woman troubled Ernie beyond a bad thought. His life was already complicated enough. He chain smoked and worried. He didn't remember her. If he was out of his mind, he would not jump in bed with her. In fact, he felt a great dislike for her from the minute he laid eyes on her. He disliked women who caked make-up on their faces, and her face was caked with the junk.

He closed his eyes and tried to force sleep, but his brain was riddled by the unknown. He felt as if he was being pulled in two directions and his being was trying to go back together. Everything was a mystery, just as his very existence was a mystery. He was a man without a past and could not remember his own wife, whom he assumed had held a very important position in his life. His duty had clashed with his desire, and he had no intentions of being a husband to her. Whatever they had had, they didn't have any more. If he had ever had a relationship with her, he had buried her memory like all the other memories, buried and forgotten. His life now was his mama, his friends, and Tennyson Farm. He knew plenty about the furrows, green plants sprouting, a fog of dust flying around him in the summer heat, and trees swaying in the breeze. He got up, went to his liquor cabinet, and pulled out his bottle of bourbon. He drank three shots of bourbon to drown his troubles and put him to sleep.

In the meantime, Laquan tumbled with a burning desire for Ernie to make love to her. She usually got what she wanted and she was going after her desire. Pretty soon, she would have him wrapped around her little finger. She would teach him a trick or two, give him a taste of sex like he had never known before. He would soon be begging to go to bed with her.

Ernie soon fell asleep and his dream was wonderful; he could actually feel a woman lying next to him. Her body was warm and her kisses passionate. He drifted to heaven as she caressed his body. He couldn't believe her willful submission and wildness. He felt a gentle torch exploring his body; hands moved over his body and gave him chill bumps; then he heard a voice whisper close to his ear, "I want to feel you inside of me."

His eyes flew open with shock; he was not dreaming; a woman was actually in his bed. The whore was on top of him; she pulled him close and he couldn't get away from her. She set a fire in him that burned out of control, and he simmered. Anxious to take her, he pushed her beneath him. With a hot current flashing through him, he satisfied his lustful need and quickly pushed her away.

She fell limp on the pillow and rubbed his muscles with quiet murmurs that made him sick. He got up and went to the bathroom to get away from her. He paced the small room and pushed his hands through his hair with disgust. He hated himself for seducing her. He jerked the door back and said, "Miss, you need to get out of my room. We have been disrespectful to my mother."

She cupped a hand under her chin and rested her elbow on the pillow in a sexy pose that invited him back to bed. "What is wrong with you? Did you not enjoy having sex with me?"

When he made no reply, she got up and slowly walked toward him. "I want to sleep in your arms all night."

"Get out of my room!" he said and pushed her out into the hall. He slammed the door and locked it to make sure she did not return. Feeling sick about having sex with her, he sat down on the bed and cursed her for a whore. How did all of this happen so quickly? How could he have married a woman like that? He liked plain women with common sense. Laquan was a whore.

At three o'clock that morning, Ernie was still turning and tumbling. Thoughts of leaving home had come to mind several times, but he did not want to leave his mama.

He had barely closed his eyes when his mama called him to breakfast. He peeped out the window to see sunrise and lay back down to get another wink.

The smell of bacon seeped under the door, and made his mouth water for bacon, biscuits, and fried eggs. When he sat down at the table, he said, "Mama, did you forget about the new girl?"

"I called her several times, but she didn't move," Mrs. Tennyson said. "She can sleep and starve if she likes."

"I cannot put up with her," Ernie said, and he slammed the morning news down on the table.

"I can't believe that girl is moving into my house without an invitation," Mrs. Tennyson said. "She acts and looks like a prostitute; she has no morals. Did you go out with a prostitute in Vietnam when you went to fight in that terrible war?"

"I don't remember going out with a prostitute," Ernie said. "She has lost her mind."

"She probably had no mind to lose to begin with," Mrs. Tennyson said.

"I can never be a husband to that woman," Ernie said. "If you have me committed to an insane asylum, she would disappear and our problem would be solved."

Mrs. Tennyson threw her hand to her mouth, "My goodness, do you suppose she is pregnant and is trying to hook you!"

"My God, Mama, don't say things like that," Ernie said.

"Well, I know you better than anybody else, and you are not ordinarily easily led. That girl must have sweet talked you to her bed somehow."

"If she has a baby, it will be the scandal of the century. I'll have to take her and leave this town," Ernie said.

"Living with her without proof of being married to her is a scandal," Mrs. Tennyson said. "I don't believe you are married to her."

"I hope and pray that we can send her back to Saigon soon. I am going to town and I won't be home for lunch."

Near lunch time, Laquan walked into the kitchen and immediately asked where Ernie had gone.

"He left at six o'clock this morning," Mrs. Tennyson said. "He said he had to go to town to take care of some business."

Laquan walked over to the window and looked out. With a stiff posture and lifted chin, she walked back across the room, sat down at the table, and picked up the morning news.

Laquan's coat of makeup disgusted Mrs. Tennyson. In less than twenty minutes, Mrs. Tennyson had a brief history of Laquan's life. She had been born in a small village in Vietnam. Her maiden name was Chan. Her father died from yellow fever, and her mother had a heart attack and died a few years later. After her mother's death, she had moved to Saigon and got a job as a secretary for a top government official. She had several aunts and uncles living in Saigon. She claimed that her folks had money and she never had to do without anything. She had met Ernie at a club in Saigon the year before.

Trying to feel out Laquan's religious beliefs, Mrs. Tennyson said, "Are you a member of a church?"

"I am Buddhist," she said.

"Do you mean to tell me that you do not believe in God the Father, Son, and Holy Spirit?"

"Buddha is my God; I also worship my ancestors," she said. "Do you dislike people who do not believe in your God?"

"My God is also your God," Mrs. Tennyson said.

Laquan had only been there a few hours, and Mrs. Tennyson disliked her. She picked up the paper that Laquan put down and pretended to read as she spoke. "I've already poured the grits out. If you want breakfast in this house, you will have to get up at six. I don't serve breakfast at ten o'clock in the morning."

She looked at Mrs. Tennyson with disgust and said, "I don't want grits. I hate grits. I want rice and fruit."

"That is not on the menu, either," Mrs. Tennyson said.

"Do you have coffee?"

"I poured out the perked coffee, but you can make some instant if you like."

"I'll just have a glass of juice," she said.

"Fix what you please," Mrs. Tennyson, said. "I'm going to work in my flower garden when I finish reading the paper."

"Why are you being rude to me?" Laquan said, giving Mrs. Tennyson a disgusting quirk of her mouth.

"I am being rude to you, because you are not welcome here. I don't understand why you came here to begin with, and I hope you are making plans to find another place to stay." Mrs. Tennyson lowered her paper and looked at Laquan as she questioned her, "How long do you plan to stay here?"

"I plan to stay forever," Laquan said. "I am your son's wife."

"I don't believe you are Ernie's wife, and I don't believe in shacking up," Mrs. Tennyson said. "I heard you going to his room last night. You are living in sin and tempting Ernie to sin."

"Who do you think you are? You are not my mother! You can't tell me what's best for me!" she said, cutting angry eyes at Mrs. Tennyson.

"This is my house, and I can say what I please," Mrs. Tennyson said. "You should listen to reason and leave right now. Ernie went to see his lawyer. If you are smart, you will find a lawyer to defend your lies."

"You cannot make me leave," Laquan said. "I am your son's wife."

"I cannot physically remove you from that chair, but the cops can get you out of here." Mrs. Tennyson slapped the paper on the table and added, "If you stay in my house, you will live by my rules, and I will not have you being disrespectful to me. I will kick you out in the yard."

Laquan got quiet for minutes and stared at Mrs. Tennyson. Then she said, "You are a fool!"

"When you call a person a fool, you are in danger of hell according to my bible. You need to get right with the Lord."

"Do not preach your beliefs to me!" Laquan said.

"I will preach to you if I feel like preaching. I can see through your lies," Mrs. Tennyson said. "You tricked Ernie into taking you to his bed."

"How many men have you tricked in your time?" Laquan said, and she jumped up from the table and rushed out of the kitchen. Mrs. Tennyson watched her disappear behind the door to the guest room. She got up, pulled off her apron, and got her gloves before going outside.

Before leaving home, Ernie called his lawyer, Charles Nugent, to make an appointment. Mrs. Hosking, his receptionist, told Ernie that Mr. Nugent was in court and would not be back in his office until the next day. She made an appointment for Ernie at ten o'clock the next morning.

In the meantime, Laquan walked to the window and watched Mrs.Tennyson dig in her flower bed. The coast was clear for Laquan to plunder. She went to Ernie's room and found a picture album on Ernie's nightstand that had pictures, news clippings about the Vietnam War, and the deeds to the farm. She took the pictures of Ernie in his uniform, stuck them into her pocket, and closed the album. Then she searched the kitchen drawers for a pair of scissors. She replaced the soldier standing next to Ernie with pictures of herself that she had in her purse. After she glued the pictures together, she carried them with her to take to a photographer for the final picture to display. With a few finishing touches, the picture would look authentic. She was pleased with her cleaver idea.

CHAPTER THIRTY

The next morning Ernie went to see his lawyer. After he told him about Laquan and his predicament, Mr. Nugent told him there was little he could do if the woman had a marriage certificate. He warned Ernie that carrying her to court may not be a good idea. If the woman could prove she was his wife, she could have him declared insane and take everything he owned. He advised Ernie to hire a private detective to investigate the woman's history. He wrote down the name and number of a private investigator and gave it to Ernie. "Hershel Hobbs is as good as they come. If Miss Tennyson is lying about this matter, you can send her back to Saigon and your worries are over."

Ernie didn't want to go home. He drove into town and stopped by the Dingus' Bar and Grill to have a drink. He sat down at the bar and ordered a fifth of bourbon.

Nolan raised his brow and said, "Who licked the frosting off your cake?"

When he told Nolan that a painted whore woman showed up at his door, said she was his wife, and raped him, Nolan's mouth opened with shocked silence. He knew Ernie like the rough hide on his elbows; and he could not imagine Ernie having married a whore. Then he thought Ernie was joking, because women do not rape men. He accused Ernie of making up a fantasy to satisfy his needs. Ernie hit the bar with his fist and told him the woman was a damn whore; she had raped him; and he was not going to be owned by a whore.

Nolan was still not buying Ernie's story. "Did you like the way she made you feel?"

"I felt like a rooster on a hot hen house," Ernie said, "but I was not crowing for that sorry woman."

Then Nolan popped questions like a national survey and gave more advice than Dear Abby.

"Why did you invite her into your house?" Nolan said.

"I should have put my foot down and run her off, but Mama has a soft spot in her heart. She told her she could stay overnight. Once she got her foot inside my door, she grabbed me and would not let go. She tied me to a hitching post in a knot that is too tight to untangle. My lawyer says I am stuck with her unless I can prove I am not married to her. She could take everything except the handkerchief in my hip pocket. How can I prove that she is lying?"

"You have to get that woman out of your house before she accuses you of being the father to the child that she is probably already carrying."

"I have an appointment to see a private detective by the name of Hobbs," Ernie said. "Do you know anything about him?"

"Hobbs is a good man," Nolan said. "He will get to the bottom of her motive."

Ernie ate lunch in town and went back home to bury his worries with work. At sundown, he went to tell his mama not to cook supper. He drove back into town to see Nolan. If he could only remember, he could put Laquan in her place. He hated this stranger who had come into his home. She had no right to be there, and she had no right to impose on his mama. Blowing her brains out had popped in his mind several times. If he could only remember his past, he could send this crazy woman back to Saigon.

Ernie stayed at the bar and talked to Nolan until after twelve o'clock. As he drove home, he thought of Nolan's words: "She must be after your money. Tell her you have applied for a divorce. If she balks, make her wish she had never darted your door. Offer her money to leave."

When Ernie got home, he prayed that Laquan would be gone, but her car was sitting in the garage right next to his.

He took the side entrance, slipped to his bedroom, turned on the television, and fell back on the bed. Her sudden appearance in bikini pajamas interrupted his interest in the program he watched.

"I've been waiting to see you all day. You have been on my mind constantly," she said.

"Get the hell out of my room and put on some clothes! I'm not interested in you."

"What can I do to arouse your interest?" she asked.

"What can I do to make you leave?" he said. "If you want money, name your price."

"The money sounds interesting, but I want you with your money," she said.

"You are clinging to a foolish dream up there in your crazy head, woman! My past is dead and buried."

He left her standing there and went to take a shower. As he turned under the water, the curtain went back. There stood Laquan in the nude! He reached to turn off the water, and her hands stopped him. He jerked her forward and she climbed into the tub. In spite of his hate, he pulled her to him and gave her what she asked for. Minutes later, a surge of pleasure absorbed him, and he pushed her away from him.

"I want you to find a place of your own and get out of my home!"

"I will give you a divorce, but I will take everything you own."

"You are crazy!" he said. "My mother owns this farm and she handles the bank account. Get out of here and leave me alone!"

Laquan quickly made tracks to the guest room. She wanted his money, but she did not intend to settle for peanuts when she could have the whole crop.

After she had gone, he jerked the shower curtain from the rings and fisted the wall. She was a damn whore; she was a rose with nettles on the petals. He couldn't take her much longer.

The next day, Ernie went to see Hershel Hobbs, the private detective his lawyer had recommended. Hershel Hobbs was a nice man and was as sharp as new razor. Mr. Hobbs introduced himself and started his questions right away. He wrote down her name and everything she had told Ernie about where they had met and where she lived. He told Ernie that he would make some phone calls and get back with him as soon as he got some helpful information.

Hobbs saw what Ernie had told him about Laquan. She was a high class woman with a coat of heavy makeup and red lips. She was wearing short shorts and a halter top that was two sizes too small to carry its load.

Laquan asked his name and business right away. "I am Hershel Hobbs, a private detective. Ernie Tennyson hired me to find out who you really are; where you came from; and what tricks you have up your sleeve. He says that you suddenly showed up at his door and claimed he married you while he was in the military. Mr. Tennyson does not remember you; he does not remember meeting you at a bar in Saigon. Are you trying to get citizenship in the United States of America by taking advantage of Ernie Tennyson's mental condition?" he said.

She jumped up and said, "I do not know what you are talking about. I met Ernie at a night club in Saigon; we got married. I am in love with my husband; I do not have to sit here and listen to your insults."

Further questions revealed that she did not know the name of the club or the name of the justice of the peace who married them. When he asked to see the marriage license, she refused to show it to him and ordered him to get out, or she would call the cops.

The next day, the private detective called and told Ernie he had spent the day on the phone, but he had come up with an empty page. He located seven different families in Vietnam by the name of Chan and not one of them had ever heard of Laquan.

His mother said, "Try to be patient and don't worry about her. The truth will come out and things will get better soon."

How could he sit back and relax? How could he settle his past and settle down happily with his little wife?

Ernie did not believe her story about having met him at a club in Saigon. He must have been drunk when he met her, so he had no argument and no memory. She had a marriage certificate and wedding pictures. Why would this woman pose as his wife? How would she benefit from the arrangement? He felt as if a rubber hammer was pounding his brain; he felt like a trapped animal that had just been robbed of his freedom.

At the dinner table, Mrs. Tennyson raised her brow at Ernie with disgust and he gave a nod of agreement. Since Laquan moved in, they had not lived in peace and felt like strangers in their own home.

Ernie worked in the field until sundown. He dreaded going home since Laquan took over his home. She lived like a queen, and his mother waited on her. He did not know how much longer he could take her insane tricks.

When he got home, his mama had supper waiting. He sat down at the table and said, "Where is Laquan?"

"She is back there in the bedroom. She came in here after we finished eating dinner and fixed her a plate. After she ate, she went back to the bedroom. I didn't say anything to her, but I am tired of waiting on her."

"Mr. Hobbs, the private detective, told me that he had located seven families in Saigon by the name of Chan, but not one of them had ever heard of her. I think she is lying about her name."

"I think she is lying about everything," Mrs. Tennyson said. "She wants a free ride. She sleeps and eats, but she never offers to help me with the cooking, washing, and cleaning. She doesn't want her clothes washed with our things. I told her to wash her clothes by hand in the sink."

I hope and pray that Hobbs can find out what Laquan is after.

Before Mrs. Tennyson poured the tea, Laquan came in and sat down to eat, and Ernie said, "Where have you been?"

"I was reading a good book," she said.

"You should help Mama with the cooking and cleaning. She is tired of waiting on you."

"I will wash the supper dishes," She said.

"I will wash my own dishes," Mrs. Tennyson said. "Let's say the blessing." His mama did all of the cooking; She also bought groceries, cleaned the house, and washed clothes. He didn't know what he would do without her. He had offered to hire a house cleaner, but she wanted to do all things around the house. She had said that cooking and house work was woman's work.

His mother was in good health, and he thanked God for that, but she was forever taking deep breaths. That meant she was good and worn out, dead tired. She was dead tired every day, several times a day. Today, she had a hacking cough and he was worried about her.

Ernie got up from the table and said, "I enjoyed my dinner, Mama. Roast beef and potatoes are my favorite foods."

CHAPTER THIRTY-ONE

In the meantime, Anna was miserable. Her Aunt Sean was good to her and tried to keep her in a good mood. She took her shopping in Shanghai; took her on sight-seeing tours; and took her to sporting events.

They went shopping often, and shopping in Shanghai was next to a sightseeing tour. The Pudong skyline was one of the most beautiful sites in the world. To name a few of other sites, they visited the temples and museums, including the China Art Museum; Yu Garden; China Pavilion; Expo Axis; Neon Signs on Nanjing Road; and the Bund.

Yu Garden was a perfect example of Chinese architecture. Its upturned roof, long windows, wraparound porch, covered entrance, and statues on the roof made it stand out above all other buildings.

On the other hand, the Bund, located by the bank of the Huangpu River, was one of the most beautiful buildings in China. The ground section moved up to four stories with long windows spaced evenly across the front; it was topped by another section that was set back and had columns across its front. The very top section resembled the dwelling of a wealthy patron. Another building joined the Bund that was put together in different levels and had a round dome with a large clock at its summit.

In spite of her busy schedule, Anna got more restless with each passing day. Sean noticed her depressed mood and suggested they go on a tour of Guilin, located on the bank of the Li River, which flowed through the city of Guilin. Anna's father talked about his business with the merchants at Guilin. He shipped tea, pepper sauce, rice, and cinnamon, some of their main products, to other parts of China.

They left home early and went into Guilin. Anna was impressed with the beautiful city. Two rivers and four lakes with mountains in the background surrounded the city and added to its beauty. They went to Rosemary Café near the Jiefang Bridge to eat breakfast. The Cafe served Sean's favorite, Guilin Rice Noodles; Anna ordered sweet Tofu, and they had coffee to drink.

Afterward, they went to Elephant Trunk Hill on the Li River. The huge rock formation, shaped like an elephant, rested on the banks of the river. Bright green plants covered the huge stone elephant, and its trunk curved from its body and fell to the water's edge as if taking a sip from the river.

Next, they visited the Reed Flute Cave, named for the verdant reeds used to make flutes. These reeds grew in abundance outside the cave. The cave was made up of different kinds of stalactites, stone pillars, and rock formations; the colored lighting threw spectacular, colorful beauty over the formations in each section of the cave. The zigzag path, pavilions, ponds, bridges, plants and other garden structures made the cave even more interesting. They named each section of the cave. Before leaving the cave, they visited Crystal Palace; Dragon Pagoda; and Flower and Fruit Mountain.

Last, but not least, they climbed Moon Hill to discover its history. In spite of the cement path, the rock climbing adventure was tiring. They reached the site and found an arched rock formation that was shaped like a moon with a hollow center. Green plants grew beneath the arch and covered the surrounding area. If one imagined the shape of a gigantic stone tire sticking up from the earth with its lower section covered with green plants, he saw a picture of Moon Hill in his mind. They stood on the hill, took pictures, and viewed the surrounding area.

After they walked back down the rocky slope, they went to eat lunch at the West Bank Café. They sat on the veranda, where they had a view of the river and the beautiful sound of jazz music. Anna ordered Roasted Suckling Pig flavored with shallot, soy sauce and white sugar. Her aunt Sean ordered Snail served with sour peppers, shallot, ginger, and Sanhua Wine. They ordered green tea to drink.

After lunch Anna thanked Sean for dinner and told her how much she had enjoyed the tour. She hated to be rude, but her feet hurt and she was tired. She finally asked Sean if they could go home and come back another day.

Anna seldom had time to think and that was a good thing. The family enjoyed sports; Anna did not especially like sports, but she tagged along. They went to soccer games, basketball games, and football games. Shanghai had several professional soccer teams, including the Chinese Super League that Hoe liked. They also had a Basketball Association and an ice hockey team, the China Dragons. Their baseball team, the Shanghai Golden Eagles, played in the China Baseball League.

Occasionally, they went to watch her Uncle Hoe play golf, but Anna seldom attended Tra's games. He liked boat racing, horse racing, and wrestling.

Her aunt and uncle also believed in keeping physically fit. Sean finally talked Anna into going with her to the gym to exercise twice a week. Then she followed her Aunt Sean's advice and started going to the library. She needed to learn about the lands of her ancestors, and she had a feeling that her study of China would please her father. The only reason she wanted to please him was to soften him and convince him to let her keep her baby. When she was in grade school, her father helped her with her lessons, and she disliked history. Many times, he got away from her lessons and bragged about his country. He spoke of China's rivers and mountains as if they were Gods that controlled the universe.

Anna enjoyed the festivals, or family reunions, most of all. Her aunt and uncle invited their parents, cousins, aunts, and uncles to their home to enjoy the food and stories told by the older guest. They told stories about things past and what tomorrow would bring. They seldom spoke about the troubles at hand. The whole family was also very religious and prayed with Anna often, but Anna was a Catholic like her mother while her aunt and uncle practiced the traditional beliefs of her ancestors, a mixture of Buddhism, Confucianism, and Taoism.

Anna remembered that Ernie had made jokes about her father's religious beliefs, but he probably did not realize that very few Christians lived in China. She would have followed his beliefs had he given her a chance.

Her family believed that the traditions of their father must be carried on, but Anna worried very little about the traditions of her father; she worried about her future. She was carrying an American soldier's baby, and she was not married to him. According to Chinese teachings, her baby would be one year old when he came into the world. Her due date was close at hand, and she prayed that her father would let her come back home to raise her child. Her father controlled her life and she hated his beliefs. Love controlled her being; she wanted to live in America, the Land of the Free. She could think of no worldly things that meant more to her than Ernie Tennyson.

Anna walked to the window and looked out across the dusty horizon. She imagined Ernie riding through the hills like a Prince on a great white horse in a fairy tale. Her life with him had been only a fairy tale. Like magic, a figure appeared in the distance. The figure was real. As he came nearer, Anna saw a young Chinese boy leading a water buffalo to the field. Her Uncle Hoe had a garden, and he grew all the food they ate. He planted rice and vegetables every spring; and they always had plenty to eat, but they seldom ate meat. The heavy rains in the summer made the soil rich and favorable for farming. Her Uncle Hoe bragged about his rich earth. He said he was glad he did not live in the hilly mountains, where nothing was grown, except rocks. These folk raised cattle, horses, and water buffaloes. They had no rich soil for a garden.

Anna woke up early one morning with pain shooting through the lower part of her stomach. Everyone was still asleep, and she hated to disturb them. She got up, walked the floor, and held her stomach. Then she felt water running down her legs; she slowly made her way down the hall to her Aunt Sean's bedroom. She called out to her, and she came to the door in a flash. Minutes later, her Aunt Sean reached the emergency room at the hospital.

The next morning when Anna opened her eyes and looked up at Doctor Kim standing by her bed, she saw bad news written on his face.

"Miss Ming, I am sorry to have to tell you, but your baby was born dead."

Anna was too shocked to speak. She did not understand; her baby had kicked with such strength that she could not sleep. She did not believe her baby was dead. Her father had given her baby away, and she would never know what happened to it. She felt helpless. She finally got the strength to speak, "Was my baby a girl or a boy?"

"You child was a girl. She weighed seven pounds four ounces."

"Can I see her?"

"They took your baby away to spare you the pain, Miss Ming." The good doctor left her in that terrible room to stare at four walls and wish for death.

From the day the doctor said: "Your baby was born dead." Anna's laughter ceased, and she stopped living. The news shattered her dreams, and a part of her died. She was shocked and her mind was numb. She looked, but she did not see; she heard, but not words of wisdom; she ate, but she did not taste; and she reached out, but did not touch. She didn't have a headache; yet her head was bursting with painful memories. She didn't have a sick stomach; but she couldn't eat from loss of appetite. She didn't have pains in her chest; her heart had been cut out. She didn't have an ear ache; she could hear the painful ring of voices; she wasn't in pain at all; yet she hurt more than any pain she had ever suffered. She had never known there was so much ugliness to life. Her father had driven her to the brink of insanity.

She spent very little time each day without thoughts of Ernie and her baby. She needed Ernie to comfort her; she needed Ernie to help her heal. She remembered the day she found Ernie in the jungle. She felt an instant attraction to him. She remembered her excitement when she sat next to him on the steps and on the bench. She remembered the first time he kissed her; she remembered their first real date; and she remembered the times she had sneaked to see him. She did not know that he could bring her so much love and so much hate. She asked herself the same questions every day. Did he go back to his wife in America? Had they captured him and locked him away? Had they sent him out of the country? Would she ever see him again? She completely committed her body and soul to him. She granted his every wish and did everything to please him. She spilled her secrets to him. She fussed over him and cared for him when he was wounded.

She buried her mind in work around the house during the day. At night, she read or wrote in her notebook. With her pen to the pad, she wrote a poem about the last time she had seen him in Nha Trang.

"When Last I Saw Him"
When last I saw him, our love was alive.
We shared the beauty of the night.
The stars shined an impressive sight.
They twinkled and danced in the sky.
When last I saw him, the wind whistled a tune.
There was no chill from the breeze.
Sweetness filled the air with flower blooms.
When last I saw him, the moon smiled bright.
Our hearts felt happy and warm that night.
We wished on stars with all our might.

Two weeks after her baby was born, her grandmother called and told her she wanted her to come back home. She talked about how sad she had been about her grandchild being still born; but she gave Anna hope by saying she could have other children when she was married.

Anna packed her bags that night and went back to Dalat to live in her father's prison. The children in the village met her with open arms, hugs, and kisses. They asked why she had left them, and Anna told them she had to go to China to visit her Aunt Sean. They asked if she would be their teacher again, and Anna told them she would be teaching them again soon. Before going into the house, she saw Chipper moving toward her like a leopard. He jumped up and down and danced around her, and the children laughed. He had let her know that he missed her also. Then he blew her a kiss.

The children's laughter aroused her grandmother's curiosity. She came to the door and saw Anna standing among the children and she called out to Anna, "Aren't you going to come inside and see your old Grandmother?"

Anna told the children good bye, picked up her bags, and walked up the steps to greet her grandmother. "I have missed you, Granddaughter. I am happy that you are home at last. I have a fine dinner cooked just for you. Come, let's go to the kitchen and you can tell me about your visit to China."

Anna told her she did not want to talk about her terrible experience. They ate in silence, shifting glances at each other. After dinner, her grandmother told her to go to the living room and relax. She would not let Anna help with washing the dishes. Anna went to her room and unpacked her things. Then she lay down to rest; she had no worries when she was asleep. Later that evening, her grandmother knocked on her door, and Anna dreaded the lecture she was sure her grandmother had for her. Anna opened the door and her grandmother said, "Come to the living room and let's have a nice talk."

To her surprise, her Grandmother was different; she was kinder, more understanding, and loving. She gathered Anna in her arms, hugged her, and told her how sorry she was about her losing her grandchild. Anna was puzzled and could not understand the change in her grandmother, but she was happy to know that she had someone who cared.

"Your American was from a different world, a different race, and a different religion. He could not accept your way of life, especially your religion." She paused when she saw that Anna was crying. "Try to forget him. I know he left you with a broken heart, and he will never come back, but life goes on and you must be strong."

"I love him, Grandmother."

"Love gives you a natural high. Love makes your eyes glassy and numbs your senses. Love makes you crazy. When you are in love, you do not think before you speak, and your heart beats too fast. Love makes you weak in many ways. Nothing matters except the one you love, and you constantly ask yourself questions and worry about the things you have said to him, what you will say to him, and when you will see him again."

"Grandmother, you must be an expert on the subject of love."

"I have been in love once in my life. The pains of pride are much worse than the pains of a broken heart."

"I do not understand your words, Grandmother. How do you know about the pain of pride? Please tell me what hardened your heart so."

Mrs. Ming got up and carried her frail body slowly across the living room to the buffet. She picked up the bouquet of roses that she had bought that morning and began arranging them in the purple Chinese vase that she often filled with fresh flowers. As she picked up each of the long stems, she stared at the red velvet as if in a dream world.

Anna got up and walked to the end of the buffet. She watched her grandmother with shock and wonder.

"Do you know why I always keep fresh flowers in this vase?"

"Flowers are beautiful and they have a sweet smell," Anna said.

"When flowers are plucked, they are beautiful and have a sweet smell; they are fresh and young, but their life is short lived. They soon lose their beauty and sweet smell; they wilt and die, so I quickly replace the old with the new."

"I never thought of that," Anna said.

"He used to give me flowers," Mrs. Ming said.

"Who gave you flowers, Grandmother?"

"The name makes no never mind," she said.

"Grandmother, did you actually fall in love once upon a time?"

Mrs. Ming brushed the rose petal across her cheek and stared at nothing. She did not move or speak for minutes.

"I was crazy."

"You did not answer my question, Grandmother."

"Love makes you crazy," she said, and she hesitated before replying, "Yes, I loved him."

"Your words are the most shocking thing I have ever heard you speak, Grandmother. I cannot believe you kept your feelings of love for this man a secret your entire life."

"I have tucked my feelings well, Granddaughter. There is no profit to show your weakness to the world."

"Love is not a weakness, Grandmother. Love is strength; love is all that is good; love makes you a better person."

"Love is like the flowers I arrange in this vase," Mrs. Ming said, and she quickly began pushing the roses in the perfect place. "The roses will soon wilt, die, and fall to the earth to be trod upon."

"Grandmother, are you the wilted flower?"

"I pretend that I am full of life, but I replace the wilted blooms with fresh beauty when they begin to droop. I do not like to think of having been stomped into the earth."

"Who was this special man in your life, Grandmother?"

She turned and faced her granddaughter, and Anna had never seen a more humble look upon her grandmother's face. Then her face turned to steel and she spoke with anger. "This special man was an American! Need I say more?"

"Grandmother, you must be playing with my mind."

"Jokes would not burden my heart as the truth I speak, granddaughter." Tears crowded her sight and she turned back to her flowers. Anna went to her and put her arms around her. "I am sorry you loved and lost, Grandmother. Why did you hold your secret all of these years?"

"My confession does not change my life, but perhaps you will see more clearly." She laid the last rose on the buffet and never bothered to arrange it in the vase. Anna watched her move across the room. Her Grandmother seemed to have aged ten years. She made slow labored steps and slightly dragged her feet. Anna could hear her going down the hall. She wondered if she should run after her and give her comfort. Then she heard the door close. She walked to the door and listened. She could hear her grandmother crying, and she knew how she must hurt. She pushed the door to a peep and said, "Grandmother, may I come in and talk with you?"

"I have leaked my secret, so you may as well hear more. Come sit with me, dear."

Anna sat down in a chair next to her grandmother's bed. "Would you like to tell me that you know how I feel?" her grandmother said.

Anna dismissed her question and said, "Grandmother, did you love my Grandfather?"

She looked at Anna and tear bubbles filled her eyes. "I was not in love with you grandfather. I loved him, but I did not love him in the same manner as I loved the American - with a burning desire, beating heart, and no thought of tomorrow. I loved your grandfather for his attention to my needs and his never ending respect and care for me. I was his wife, the cook, the dish washer, the housemaid, the mother of his children, and most of all I was a good mother."

"Can I ask you a personal question?"

"I do not think you could get more personal than I have already been, Granddaughter. Since I have spilled the secrets that I have hidden in my heart all of my life, you may ask anything you like."

"Did you and Grandfather enjoy each other?"

"What do you mean by that question?"

"Did you enjoy sex with Grandfather?"

"The spirits have ears. I did not expect such a question."

"The spirits do not care. Tell me Grandmother."

"Your grandfather was a sex feign. He always had eyes for other women."

"I did not ask about his women. I am asking about you and your happiness."

"That is a difficult question."

"Tell me, Grandmother. Get one more secret out in the open."

"I do not wish for my secrets to fly through the village," she said and she smiled. I will tell you that your grandfather was once a great lover. Women ran after him, and I heard of his reputation before I ever met him. After he married me, he took me for granted. He knew I was here for the taking. Your grandfather was not a patient man. He never liked to play chess, because the game lasted too long. Does that answer your question?"

"You have painted a clear picture. I am sorry that you have wasted your years. I wish you could have followed the American. I wish you could feel the love that I feel for Ernie. If I never see him again, Grandmother, the time we had together will give me good memories for a life time." She looked away in deep thought. "I do not think I could live forever without seeing him again."

Her grandmother opened her arms and hugged her. "I cannot tell you that I wish for him to come back for you. On the other hand, I do not want you to live the miserable life that I have lived." She paused for words. "I thought I may be able to stop you before the crash, but I have failed."

Anna had never felt loved, really loved by her grandmother until this minute, and she felt closeness in her heart that she had never felt before. She could feel her mother in the room. She could see her smiling down on the two of them, and she felt her mother's presence in the room;

she felt as if there were a happy reunion between the three of them. Her grandmother believed the spirits listened to her secrets. What could they do? They could not tell.

Anna was shocked by her grandmother's story. Long after Anna went to bed, she thought of the loneliness her grandmother must have suffered during her life. This American had jilted her Grandmother. Now she understood why her grandmother had always been so bitter. She understood why she had always protected her from every man who had asked for her hand in marriage.

In the meantime, Lena Ming lay in bed and thought about how miserable her life had been without the man she loved. From the beginning, the war had torn her marriage apart. Now another war was taking the only family she had. Even with the war going on, Anna was luckier than she had ever been. She was born and raised in China. Her family was poor and she knew what it was to be hungry. The year the flood came, the crops went with the flood, and many starved to death. Her mother saved her family with rice she stored in large glass jars the year before the flood. Lena worked in the rice field until age fourteen, when her father betrothed her to Mr. Ming. His father gave her family a small amount of silver and a fat pig for her hand in marriage to their son. She never liked him. He ran around with hot women, and she was like a servant to him. When her oldest son came to Vietnam and got into the shipping business, she saw her chance to leave Mr. Ming behind. She left her husband and moved into the house with Dong Lee; she had lived with him since Anna was a small child. Since she came to Lat Village to live, she had an easy life. Dong Lee provided well for her, and she kept his home going. What would she do if Anna left her? She would be all alone and helpless in her old age, and she seldom saw Dong Lee.

She had learned lately that Dong Lee was exactly like his father, a weird, cold hearted man. He had no business sending Anna to China. She had not liked the American any more than Dong Lee, but he carried his punishment too far when he made his demands. Dong Lee's father seldom spoke kind, loving words to her; he never discussed anything with her as most happily married couples do. She was to do the housework, cook for his family, and satisfy his sexual needs. He never thought about her desires and needs. She had understood all along why Anna hated her father, but she had to play the role of Dong Lee's mother like she had always done; but she would never cater to Dong Lee again as long as she lived.

CHAPTER THIRTY-TWO

On Saturday after breakfast, Laquan went directly to the pool. Moving gracefully under the water, she swam across the pool and climbed out. She moved her feet to the rhythm of the song playing on her radio and danced around the pool to her lounge chair.

Mrs. Tennyson stood at the glass door and watched with shock. She could not believe her eyes. She expected the preacher to pay a visit, and Laquan was buck-naked. If the preacher saw that naked sight, he would have heart failure. She turned this way and that, and tried to think of something to get Laquan back into the house. She started to the back door, and the doorbell rang at the front door.

She opened the door and there stood Brother Hayes with a big smile and a friendly greeting, "How are you doing, Mrs. Tennyson?"

"I am doing very well, Brother Hayes. Come in," Mrs. Tennyson said, leading him in the opposite direction of the den doors.

"I smell something good cooking," Brother Hayes said. "You go ahead and finish your dinner. I can sit in the kitchen with you while you cook." He walked ahead of Mrs. Tennyson to the kitchen; she quickly pulled out a chair at the far end of the table, and said, "You can sit here, Brother Hayes. Would you like to have a cup of coffee?"

"A cup of your coffee sounds good," he said.

Mrs. Tennyson moved from the coffee pot to the window over the sink and looked out to check on the naked girl. Laquan's naked tail still sat in the same spot.

Mrs. Tennyson walked back to the cabinet, got a cup, and poured the preacher a cup of coffee. As she set it before him, she said, "Do you take cream and sugar?"

"A little sugar will do," he said. He looked toward the window and said, "The weather turned out nice today. Earlier, I thought the clouds may bring a nice shower. We need the rain."

"Since Ernie took over the farm, he has worried about the rain coming at the right time. I guess we should pray for rain at prayer meeting this week."

"That is a good thought. We will dedicate our service to prayer for rain."

Mrs. Tennyson's heart beat in her ears. She hoped with fingers crossed that the preacher did not decide to walk to the window. She said, "Well, how do you and Beverly like Georgia?"

"Georgia is great," Brother Hayes said, "Beverly and I have lived in four different states, and Georgia beats them all, except Florida. That is my home, you know. A man never gets home out of his heart. The folk in Georgia are just like home folk, though. Everyone is so friendly, just good old, common country folk."

Brother Hayes talked about his ministry, his wife, his son, his dog, and the sick folk who needed prayer.

Mrs. Tennyson still had her fingers crossed; but she really wished the preacher would leave.

"My boy, Scotty is in his last year at the University of Georgia. He's majoring in agriculture."

"I know you are proud of him," Mrs. Tennyson said, and she went to the window to take another peep.

Obviously, the preacher had noticed that Mrs. Tennyson had gone to the window a number of times. "Is there anything wrong?" he said.

"To tell you the truth, Brother Hayes, everything went wrong the day that foreigner came here to live. She claims to be Ernie's wife, but I do not believe Ernie would have married a girl of her type. That sorry woman tried to take up half of Ernie's bed the day she got here, but he put her in her own room. He says he does not remember her and does not want anything to do with her. I don't like her at all."

"Why Miss Mrs. Tennyson," the preacher said, giving her a serious look, "I have never heard you say you disliked anyone."

"Laquan Chan is a demon," Mrs. Tennyson said.

"I see," the preacher said. "I'll ask for special prayer on Sunday."

"You might need to do that praying before Sunday," Mrs. Tennyson said, and she walked to the window again.

"I know you wouldn't harm a fly," the preacher said. "Do you want to do harm to this young lady?"

"She is not a lady; and she is harming herself," Mrs. Tennyson said as she let the curtain drop.

Brother Hayes saw that changing the subject would be best. "I went to Westminster yesterday," he said. "Do you remember Brother Yarborough?"

"Yes, I remember him," Mrs. Tennyson said. "How is he doing?"

"His wife left him," the preacher said.

"I do say," Mrs. Tennyson said. "People don't take their vows seriously these days; folk don't have any morals this day and time."

Laquan sat down in her chair, put on her shades, and picked up her book. She had read more books than a famous scholar since she came to Georgia. She wanted to go back to Vietnam and have some fun. She was not accustomed to this boring country life. She was surprised when she saw that Ernie had a pool. A whining mosquito sent her hand in search for her robe. She felt all around her chair, but her robe had disappeared. She hugged her nakedness and looked around to see if anyone was watching. Ernie seldom spoke to her, so Miss Mrs. Tennyson must have taken her robe. She yelled out, "Mrs. Tennyson, bring me my robe, please."

Mrs. Tennyson had not heard her calling out.

Laquan realized that she had to go into the house without her robe. She covered her front side with her hat and walked to the glass doors.

With her backside shining, she stepped inside and turned to close the door.

That's when the preacher saw her bare ass and almost fell out of his chair.

"Where is my robe?" she said as she turned from the door.

She saw the preacher, she said, "How do you do?"

"You get some clothes on," Mrs. Tennyson said. "You have bugs in your head."

"I have darn mosquito bites all over my body," Laquan said. "What did you do with my robe?"

"If I had your robe, I'd throw it over that naked tail," Mrs. Tennyson said. "Get out of my kitchen and put on your clothes!"

"I'll do as I please," Laquan said, and she flipped her hand at Mrs. Tennyson as she walked toward her room.

"The judgment day is coming," Mrs. Tennyson said. "If you don't change your ways, you will never see the gates of heaven."

"Can you prove that your heaven exists?" Laquan called out.

"I don't need to prove anything," Mrs. Tennyson said. "I know there is a heaven."

Laquan stuck her head around the door and said, "Do you believe everything the preacher tells you?"

"You had best watch your tongue! The Lord might strike you down in your tracks," Mrs. Tennyson said.

"I guess I'd better get out of my tracks," Laquan said and ran down the hall.

"Lord, what can you say to an idiot?" Mrs. Tennyson said to Brother Hayes.

"I see what you mean," Brother Hayes said. "What a sin she is shining! I guess I had better go before she comes back."

After the preacher left, Mrs. Tennyson marched into Laquan's room unannounced.

Laquan jumped up and said, "Get out of my room!"

"This is not your room, and I have a few things to say to you," Mrs. Tennyson said, pointing her finger in Laquan's face. "You've got a touch of madness! The old devil messed up your head. If you pray about your sins, God forgives you and sets you straight. God can change your heart and take away all of that hate. God can work miracles."

"I guess you believe Moses parted the Red Sea," Laquan said and laughed.

"You best not make fun of the Lord's work! He will put you in your place when you disobey his commandments."

"When you talk fast trash, your jaws sag slightly beyond your mouth," Laquan said, cupping the side of her face in mockery.

"You should be worried about your lost soul rather than my looks," Mrs. Tennyson said. "You need to have the forces of evil prayed out of you! If you don't straighten up, I am going to put you on the road. Wait until Ernie comes home. He can handle you." Mrs. Tennyson stood and looked at Laquan for a long time. How she wished she could save her lost soul.

When Ernie came in, Mrs. Tennyson called him aside for a talk. "Ernie, tell that crazy foreign woman to wear her swim suit when she goes in swimming. The preacher came today, and she walked in here buck-naked. She did not have on a stitch of clothes, and she disgraced this household. She stays doped up on something, and I am tired of catering to her. If you ask me, she needs help."

"When I walked across the lawn this morning, I saw Laquan's robe lying on the ground near the pool, but I didn't see her. I picked the robe up and carried it to the porch," Ernie said.

"We have to get her out of this house; she is driving me crazy," Mrs. Tennyson said.

Ernie's anger boiled as he jerked the bedroom door back.

Laquan sat before the mirror and brushed her hair. She saw Ernie in the mirror and jumped up to greet him.

"Mama told me about your being disrespectful toward her; you embarrassed her in front of the preacher."

Laquan saw how angry he was, so she tried to make excuses. "I didn't mean to sound disrespectful to Mrs. Tennyson."

Ernie was coming toward her and she backed toward the other side of the room. She screamed, "Don't hit me! Get away from me!" She shook like a frightened animal.

"I want you to move out of here and go back where you came from."

"Your mother wants me to move out! She wants to break us up," Laquan said. "She tells lies on me."

"My mother doesn't tell lies," Ernie said. "You are the liar."

"She is a fool!" Laquan said.

"You are the fool!" Ernie said, and he penned her against the wall. "You must be on drugs! Something is wrong with you." Then he drew his hand back and slapped her. She threw her hands to her face and cursed him for a son-of-a-bitch. He drew his hand back and slapped her again.

Before he struck her again, Mrs. Tennyson appeared in the doorway and said, "Ernie, leave her alone. She will be punished for her sins."

"You sorry bastard!" she said. "I'll kill you!"

He slapped her again and shoved her back. "Say it again!" he said, and he wanted to knock her through the wall. "I can't take your trash any longer. I want you to get out of my house!"

Laquan looked at her bruised face, tightened her mouth, and spoke angrily through her teeth, "I will kill you for this!" Then she went straight to the kitchen and looked at Mrs. Tennyson like a devil diving for hell. "Why don't you tend to your own business?" She flipped her hand at Mrs. Tennyson as she walked back toward the guest room.

Mrs. Tennyson eased across the room and watched her through the door to see what she would do next. She wanted her to leave, but she lay down across the bed, and Mrs. Tennyson went back to the kitchen. She had not invited the new girl to church. None of the church members had heard about Ernie's new bride. She prayed that the preacher would keep quiet about what he had seen today. The quicker Ernie could get rid of that woman, the happier Mrs. Tennyson would be.

CHAPTER THIRTY-THREE

The county fair put Mrs. Tennyson in a good mood. She was excited about entering her jam and pickles for the prize, and she had her raffle ticket numbers memorized for that set of China they had for one of the prizes. She bought her tickets weeks in advance and hid them in her secret cove.

As Ernie watched his mama move around the kitchen and hum tunes, he wished he had some excitement in his life. He saw nothing to get excited about, and he never won anything in his life. If he had won anything, he wouldn't remember what he won or how he won it, but his mama was lucky. She had won the raffle the year before.

While his mama was at the county fair winning blue ribbons for her strawberry jam and pickles, he was sitting in her kitchen sipping coffee, and the woman who claimed to be his wife was cooking dinner for a change. She tried to get his attention every way she could. Laquan's sexy clothes marked her as a cheap, vulgar slut; her shorts barely covered her ass, and her halter top was two sizes too small. She had smooth tan skin and dark hair falling around a beautiful face with dark eyes that flicked fire each time she looked at him. She also had a good figure that counted with most men, but he did not give a damn about her beauty or her figure. In fact, he despised her. He could not remember her and he certainly did not believe he was married to her. The private detective he hired to check her out had found no records in South Vietnam of their marriage. He had discovered that Laquan Chan had lived in Saigon, but he could find no family members.

She set a large bowl of spaghetti on the table and came back with another bowl of meat balls bubbling with sauce. Then she put on the finishing touches with a garden salad, cheese biscuits, and ice tea to drink. He ate with a hearty appetite and told her he enjoyed his dinner. Then he got up and got a beer from the refrigerator and sat back down at the table. She put the food away, and put the dirty dishes in the sink for his mama to wash.

Then she walked up behind him and began massaging his shoulders. He pushed his chair back and tried to discourage her forward gesture, but she continued touching him, and his passion would not subside. He hated the bitch for moving into his home and taking over; he hated the bitch for being a whore; but he liked sex as much as any man with a perfectly good memory. He leaned forward on the table, picked up his beer and took a big swallow. She sat down next to him, propped her elbows on the table to keep his attention. Her vulgar flirting usually disgusted him, but his erection made him forget how much he disliked her. She must know that he hated her, and he could not understand why she kept asking for more.

"Do you have another beer?" she said.

"There is one in the refrigerator," he said. He definitely did not want to socialize with her.

As she moved her long legs across the room to the refrigerator, his eyes followed her swinging hips, but he remained calm and waited for her next move.

She wanted him to make love to her, but she did not want to push her luck. She was afraid he would turn down her offer again. She walked to the other side of the table sat down, sipped her beer, and said, "You know what I am thinking about?"

"Let me guess," he said.

She got up and walked toward his bedroom and like a horny fool he followed her.

After he satisfied his passion, he felt dirty and wanted to wash the smell of her strong perfume down the drain. He went directly to his bathroom, locked the door, and undressed to take a shower. The water spraying his face was refreshing. He scrubbed his body and turned under the water with thoughts of scrubbing her sin from his body. There was something about the way she moved with straight shoulders and swinging hips that was familiar to his memory; he couldn't remember her voice or her face.

After Ernie got a shower and dressed in clean clothes, he went out on the back porch. His mama had covered the windows across the porch with green Holland shades to keep out the evening sun. He sat down in his rocking chair and breathed in the cool evening air with hopes that Laquan Chan did not interrupt his peaceful relaxation as she often did.

He especially liked to sit on the porch after the sun set in the late spring. He liked to look at the stars and listen to the animal sounds coming from the branch. After a fresh rain, the frogs sounded all over the world.

As he sat there looking around the place, he saw a thousand things that needed repairs. Years of sun and storms had faded the wood on the house, and a paint job was past due. Most of all, the house needed a new roof. His mama never hired hands to do jobs around the house. She waited for him to do all things. He finally convinced her that he was not a good painter and was certainly not a carpenter. She had told him she would hire a man who could do both jobs, but she hated to spend her money. She pinched pennies until they lost their color. He told her she needed to live today, and stop worrying about tomorrow. She explained that she saved money to take care of her health needs when she could no longer care for herself. In spite of her tight pockets, she always had plenty of food on the table. He felt lucky to have her love and care.

After his mama returned from the county fair, he went into the house to see all the cakes she had won and all the junk she had bought. Then he told her he was going into to town to see Nolan.

When Ernie told Nolan he wanted to buy a fifth of bourbon, Nolan wrinkled his brow and said, "What in the hell is gnawing you?"

"I feel like a rubber hammer that lost its bounce. I can't take Laquan Chan much longer."

"Don't feed me that bull!" Nolan said. "You don't want Laquan to leave. Man, you could run her off if you really wanted to get rid of her. You go to bed with that woman every chance you get. If she was as ugly as the pied on a frog, I might believe you," Nolan said. Then he laughed and slapped Ernie on the back and said, "On the other hand, you don't look at the mantle while you're poking the fire."

Nolan saw that Ernie was in no mood to be joking. "I believe that woman wore you to a frazzle. Tell her to go to hell! Quit wearing deodorant. That will turn a woman off quicker than a dog licking where a gnat has been. If that don't work, rub some stinking sardine oil all over your body. When she smells that stench, she will leave your bed, and the love affair will be over. If sardine oil doesn't work, the chickens don't roost when the sun goes down."

Ernie said, "She walks around half naked in front of mama and me. She treats Mama with disrespect. I hate her for the way she sits and does nothing. Mama waits on her hand and foot. She does all of the cooking, cleaning, and washing."

When Ernie got home, he filled a glass half full of bourbon and finished it to the brim with coke and ice. Laquan met him before he got to his chair in the living room and asked if he would go on vacation with her.

"I'm not going anywhere with you!" he said. "If you have an itch to scratch, hit the road and don't come back." He sat down in his recliner, and she sat across from him on the couch.

"What can I do to make you remember me? What can I do to make you love me?"

"I don't want to remember you," Ernie said. "I'm not interested in you or anything you have to offer. I have no respect for a woman who asks men to have sex. I will never love you; I will never make a commitment to you. Why can't you get that through your thick head? My past is dead and buried." He wanted her to disappear and never show her face again.

"You need to get away for a while, and you would enjoy going with me on vacation."

"I want a divorce from you, and that is all I want."

"I will never give you a divorce!"

"I hope your life is just as miserable as you have made mine," he said, lighting a cigarette. "Get out of here and leave me alone!"

She threw the bottle of beer she was holding across the room and said, "See your lawyer!" she cursed him for a bastard as she walked down the hall."

He had lost his memory and Laquan had stacked the cards in her favor.

His mama came to the door and said, "Who was that cursing in here?"

"I will give you three guesses," Ernie said.

"I should have known the dirt was coming from Laquan's trashy mouth."

The next week, Laquan tried every trick in the book to lure him to her bed. Every day and every night Laquan Chan tempted, teased, and aroused him until he was crazy. Like the hound after the rabbit, she would not give up the chase. She lured him with vulgar gestures, X-rated performances, and he lost control of his emotions. She deserved the blue ribbon reward for first class whore and strip tease. He disliked whores, but he seduced her repeatedly.

CHAPTER THIRTY-FOUR

Ernie couldn't get away from Laquan when he was at home. If he went to the living room to watch television, she followed him. If he went to the back porch for the peace and tranquility of the night, she followed him.

After Ernie finished supper, he drove into town to see Nolan. As he neared the city, lights sprinkled the city and lit the houses with vibrant colors. In his mind's eye, he could see a family sitting around the breakfast table, talking about their troubles, their joy, and their future. He tried to remember having seen such a sight in his younger days. He looked around at the streets, buildings, and signs. Nothing he saw stirred his memory.

Cars had taken all of the parking spaces in front of the bar. Ernie drove to the parking lot, less than a block away, parked, and walked back toward the bar. Suddenly, bright car lights came toward him and he quickly moved between the parked cars to miss the on-coming car. He turned to see a red Cadillac speeding through the parking lot. Thinking the car had taken the exit, he continued walking. A loud roar of a motor sounded behind him; he quickly made a dash for the open space to his right, but the car hit him from his back-side. He could feel his body leave the ground and flip in the air. He came down on the hard cement and saw stars. He grabbed his head and pressed his temples with sights and sounds flashing in his head. His mind's eye brought the horrible war to a screen before him. He hugged his leg and cringed with pain. Afraid to move, he lay there in the jungle and listened to gun fire. All around him, he could see his buddies bleeding; hear them groaning and begging for help; he could see them dying, but he couldn't help them. He was not one who had spoken to God often, but he found himself saying, "God, help me!" He clutched the jungle grass and struggled to crawl behind a tree. Dirty faces with beady eyes peeped from beneath hard hats as they stood over him and spoke strange words. They hoisted him and let him fall with a painful jolt onto a bed of bamboo. He opened his eyes to see flies swarming around wounded soldiers, who moaned with pain. A beautiful woman came to him, lifted his head, and gave him a cool drink. He stared at the woman minutes before realizing that God had sent an angel to save him. He could hear her soft voice comforting him; he could feel her soft hands treating his wound. Anna Ming was her name, and he had to go find her. He had regained his memory, but he could not be consoled; his heart was burdened and anguish filled him forever. He remembered the war that gave no man freedom; he remembered the deaths that spared no man grief. Then an American Flag waved in the breeze, and he felt a peaceful tugging at his heart.

Piercing sounds pricked his ears, and blinking lights sprinkled his body as he struggled to stand. He had to go find the angel, Anna Ming. He tried to stand once again, but a soft, gentle hand pushed him back on a stretcher. The Americans had come to rescue him. He felt his body flying through the darkness. Where were they carrying him?

Ernie opened his eyes to see his mother standing next to his hospital bed. He reached out to her and she held him close with feelings of devotion, pity, love, and helplessness. "Mama, I got my memory back. Thank God, I remember everything."

Mrs. Tennyson hugged him and cried, "Thank the Lord."

The door slowly went back and Nolan peeped into the room before entering. Mrs. Copeland followed Nolan into the room and sat next to Mrs. Tennyson.

Ernie looked at Nolan and smiled. How could he forget this tall, skinny boy with dark hair that framed a slender face and large nose? How could he forget his large mouth with the straight, white teeth? How could he forget his deep voice and cheerful laughter? Nolan hadn't changed much in his looks nor his manner, but his overalls and plaid shirt had been replaced by khaki pants and a white shirt, and his light brown hair had thinned on top. Ernie felt ashamed that he had not remembered Nolan all of this time. Nolan had had been the brother he never had; he had been his friend; he had given him the chance to live again. How he wished he could make it all up to him, but he couldn't do a darn thing now. He grabbed Nolan in a bear hug. "God, how I've missed you," he said. "I finally got my memory back. I don't know what I would have done without you all of these months."

Stepping back, Nolan fisted his tears and said, "This is a bad time to be remembering the good times." Then he turned to his mama and said, "Ernie got his mind back, Mama."

"I never lost my mind," Ernie said, "but I sure couldn't remember anything."

"I'm mighty proud you got your memory back," Mrs. Copeland said. "I've always heard that a hard lick would bring your memory back." She turned back to Mrs. Tennyson. "Is there anything I can do?"

"The nurses check on Ernie every hour; they are wonderful," Mrs. Tennyson said. "I am going home and get some rest tonight. I can't sleep in this chair. Besides, the doctor says Ernie is going to be fine in a few more days. He busted his head open when he fell on that cement. Other than that, and the bruises all over his body, he is fine. He is lucky to be alive."

"I am sore all over," Ernie said.

"I am glad you didn't get hurt bad," Nolan said. "The law enforcement officers are still looking for the person who hit you. Have they been here to question you?"

"They have not questioned me, yet, but I can't tell them much. I know the car was a red Cadillac, but it was dark and I couldn't read the license number. Somebody wants me dead, and I can't think of anyone in Liberty Springs who dislikes me, unless Laquan wants me dead. Anna's Daddy and Grandmother hated me, and they didn't want Anna to have anything to do with me, but they are in South East Asia."

"Who is Anna?" Nolan said.

"She is a woman I fell in love with in Vietnam. She found me in the jungle after the Viet Cong almost killed me; she hid me in the rice hut, tended my wounds, and fed me until I could walk again. Her Father and Grandmother would not let her go out with me."

"What kind of car does Laquan drive?" Nolan said.

"She drives a red Cadillac, and I think she was behind the wheel, but I can't prove she was driving that car."

"The police came to the house the night of the accident, but I was leaving the house to come to the hospital. When I left home, Laquan's car was in the drive. She probably didn't answer the door when she saw who was calling."

"Was she home after Ernie left to come to town?" Nolan said.

"I go to bed early; I couldn't say one way or another, but Ernie has avoided her, especially the last two weeks; she is angry about that. There is more to her lies than we know about. I hope we can finally learn the real reason she came to Georgia."

"I have to get out of this hospital and go back to Vietnam."

"What business do you have in Vietnam?" Nolan said.

"I have to find Anna. She lives in Dalat with her grandmother and her father."

Mrs. Tennyson said, "She is the woman who called the house every week and begged to speak to you; you couldn't remember anything, so I told her you could not come to the phone. I guess she thinks you lied to her. She has not called in over a month."

"Oh my God, are you planning to bring that woman to Georgia?" Nolan said.

"If she will have me and I can sneak her away from her Father and Grandmother. I am going to bring her home with me and marry her. Her father hates Americans."

"Don't tell me you have to kidnap this woman," Nolan said.

"If her grandmother and father refuse to listen to reason, I guess I will kidnap her."

"My God, she must be a special woman," Nolan said. "If you have your head set on kidnapping her, I think I had better go with you to Vietnam."

"This is something I must do on my own," Ernie said.

"You do not need to be worrying about a woman in Vietnam at a time like this," his mama said, and her soft hand soothed him. "Besides, you still have a woman on your hands at the house. Laquan still claims to be your wife! Don't you remember Laquan?"

"Thank God, I remember her. I'm not married to Laquan Chan. I met her in Saigon at a bar in December of last year. After we went to see Bob Hope, we went to a bar. She flirted with me at a bar. After several drinks, I followed Corporal Hatcher and four other buddies of ours to Laquan's apartment. When we got there, I looked for a place to sleep, but sleep had not crossed her mind. She had a crowd of girls at the party. In fact, she had more girls there than men. Everybody had too much to drink, and she insisted that everybody drink some more.

The next morning after the party, I didn't even remember what she said her name was, but I remember her face. She begged me to take her back to America. I told her a war was going on and I had to get back to my base. Then she told me that I had married her the night before and she was going with me. I thought I would never get away from her. Corporal Hatcher left the woman he was with before I could get away from Laquan. Shortly after this incident, the Viet Cong captured me, and I lost my memory. I believe she pretended to be my wife to get citizenship in the United States."

"She would not have pulled such a caper had she not known you had lost your memory. She learned your condition and took advantage of you," Nolan said.

"Where is Laquan?" Mrs. Copeland said.

"She is still at the house," Mrs. Tennyson said. "I did not tell her about the car hitting Ernie. I knew he would not want her coming to the hospital."

"She is a strange woman," Mrs. Copeland said. "Nolan told me about the lies she told Ernie."

"I hired a private detective; he says he found several Chan families in Saigon, but he could not find any of Laquan Chan's relatives in Vietnam. He is still working on the case trying to uncover her real identity."

"You do not need to be worrying about anything or anybody," Mrs. Tennyson said. "You had a close call with death. The doctors say you are lucky to be alive. You're Aunt Mary and I prayed for you the last two days. We trusted in God, and he answered our prayers."

"I feel ashamed about my memory failing me, Mama. I caused you so much worry and trouble, but I will make everything up to you."

"Don't worry about what happened in the past?" she said and smiled. "I am thankful that you are alive. Besides, I loved you before you remembered me. Can I get anything or do anything to make you comfortable?"

"I am all right, Mama. Go home and get some rest. The doctor and nurses will take care of me."

Mrs. Tennyson hugged Ernie and told him she would say a prayer for him to recover in a hurry. As she started to the door, Ernie said, "When you get home, call Hershel Hobbs, the private detective. Tell him I have my memory back and ask him to call on Laquan tomorrow at the house."

When Mrs. Tennyson got home that evening, Laquan was sitting in the living room watching television. Mrs. Tennyson was furious about this crazy woman having taken over her home. She wanted to face Laquan with everything Ernie had told her and force her to tell the truth, but she afraid the crazy woman would kill her. She decided to let Ernie and his detective handle Laquan. She went to the kitchen to use the phone. Hershel Hobbs was happy to hear the good news and told her he would visit Laquan the next day.

Mrs. Tennyson had just hung up when Laquan came into the kitchen. She hoped Mrs. Tennyson would tell her where Ernie had gone. He had not been home for the past three days. Laquan pulled out a chair and sat down at the table, but Mrs. Tennyson was fixing a pot of coffee and said nothing to her. Laquan finally said, "Where is Ernie?"

Mrs. Tennyson turned from the sink and said, "Where Ernie goes is none of your business." Mrs. Tennyson could not bear to look at the liar. She wanted to slap her.

Laquan got up and went to her room and Mrs. Tennyson went to her bedroom to dress for bed. Ernie was to get out of the hospital the next day, and he would put that sorry woman on the road.

When she heard Laquan slam her car door, Mrs. Tennyson went to the window and watched her backing out of the drive. Then she went to the guest bedroom to find that Laquan's clothes and other personal belongings were still in the bedroom.

Mrs. Tennyson prayed that Laquan would stay gone, but she returned a few minutes later and went to her room.

The next morning, Mrs. Tennyson went to the hospital to pick up Ernie. While she was gone, Hershel Hobbs visited Laquan.

When Laquan opened the door, she said, "It is you again! What do you want?"

"I came to tell you that Ernie Tennyson has regained his memory. The only thing you told me the truth about was his having met you in Saigon. The marriage certificate is worthless. If you do not want to be arrested before sundown today, you had best be on your way before Mr. Tennyson returns home. You have lied about being his wife and used him and his mother for a free ride for almost a year now, and he intends to have you arrested and prosecuted."

"Get out!" she shouted and her eyes blazed with anger.

After Hobbs left, Laquan cursed Hobbs for a sorry bastard and made tracks back to her room.

The minute Ernie stepped inside the door, his eyes searched for Laquan. When he did not see her in the living room or kitchen, he walked to the guest bedroom and knocked on the door.

When she opened the door, her eyes brightened and she smiled as she reached for him. "Ernie, where have you been?"

"Where I have been is none of your damn business. I want you to get out of my home, and I will give you only a few minutes to get your bags packed."

"I am not going anywhere," she shouted.

"You are a sorry bitch! I got my memory back, and you are a lying dog! We met in Saigon and I was drunk out of my mind; then I lost my memory and you came here to get your citizenship." Ernie grabbed her and started hitting her as he shouted, "How did you find out I had lost my memory? Who told you where I lived. You seemed to have done your research before you got here. If you don't get out of my sight, I will kill you."

Nolan came in and heard Ernie yelling and Laquan screaming before he got to the living room. Nolan ran to the bedroom and Ernie was hitting Laquan in the face with his fist; he threatened to kill her. Nolan pulled him away from Laquan and Mrs. Tennyson came into the room. She told Ernie to call the sheriff and have her put in jail.

Ernie shouted at her, "If you don't move out of here immediately, you will be arrested before the day is done." Ernie grabbed Laquan again and called her a liar with his fist ready to hit her again. Nolan stepped up and pulled Ernie back, but he fisted Nolan, while he cursed Laquan for a sorry bitch. Laquan ran across the room toward the phone, but Ernie grabbed her by her hair and pulled her back. "You are the hit and run driver! You threatened to kill me the day I slapped you for walking around naked and showing disrespect for Mama; I should have know that you suffered from a psychotic disorder. Why did you want to kill me? My mother would never give you a dime."

"I didn't try to kill you! I do not know what you are talking about!"

"You are a lying bitch," Ernie said, and Nolan pulled him out of the room before he hit her again.

After Ernie and Nolan left, Laquan quickly locked the door and rushed to the closet to get her suitcases. She had no time to think about where she would go or what she would do; Ernie was going to kill her. If he didn't kill her, he would carry her to court, and she did not want a trial. She waited until Mrs. Tennyson and Ernie were eating supper to slip out the side door. She drove into Liberty Springs and got a room at Days Inn. She made a few telephone calls, and made arrangements for her flight and shipment of the car back to Saigon.

The next morning, Laquan left Liberty Springs behind and drove toward Jacksonville, Florida, where she was instructed to leave her Cadillac for shipment back to Saigon. She got a flight out of Jacksonville and was on her way to Saigon in South Vietnam.

When Mrs. Tennyson got up the next morning, she called out to Ernie with happiness, "Laquan moved out. All of her clothes are gone."

Ernie went to his bedroom and started packing his suitcase to go to Vietnam.

His mother came into his bedroom, sat down on the edge of his bed, and said, "Ernie, I know you want to see this girl, but I think you should make some phone calls before you go to Vietnam."

"You are probably right Mama. Neither her father nor her grandmother was fond of me. They have done everything in their power to keep her from seeing me. I will call and see if they will let her talk to me. At least, she will know that I am alive and maybe she will try to get in touch with me."

Ernie was disappointed when Dong Lee answered the phone. "Mr. Ming, this is Ernie Tennyson. I would like to speak to Anna, please."

"Haven't you caused enough trouble?" Dong Lee said. "I do not like what you have done to my Anna. Only a fool would propose marriage when he is already taken with a wife, and a man who denies his wife is a weasel of a man. Why did you play my Anna for a fool?"

"How did you know about this other woman who claims to be my wife?"

"I hired a detective to inquire about your disappearance. My Anna did not eat or sleep for weeks after you stopped calling her."

"I do not know the woman who claims to be my wife. I am not married to that woman. I promise to marry Anna as soon as I can get to Saigon."

"You cannot prove that this woman you live with is not your wife." Dong Lee said.

"I damn sure can prove that she is not my wife. I lost my memory for seven months, but my head is clear now."

"Your promises are weak and easily spoken. I do not believe you had intentions to marry Anna in the first place."

"The stranger who claimed to be my wife went back to Saigon, where she came from."

"There will always be other women and broken promises," Dong Lee said. "I once promised marriage to get invited to a party that I longed to enjoy with another woman."

"That was a dirty trick," Ernie said.

"I am afraid you have many dirty tricks up your sleeve, Mr. Tennyson," Dong lee said.

"I don't have any tricks up my sleeve. I intend to come back to Saigon and bring Anna Back to America with me."

"You will do so over my dead body," Dong Lee said and he slammed the phone down.

The sun faded and the sun set on another miserable day. He went into town and drank several beers while he talked to Nolan. When he got home, he went to the kitchen and put on a fresh pot of coffee and drank three cups to sober his mind. After a quick shower, he lay in bed, chain smoked, and worried.

On Sunday, after church Ernie went to visit his daddy's grave. His daddy had been a devout Christian, who went to church every time the doors opened. Ernie went to church to hear the choir sing. Many of the graves still looked dangerous to put a foot, and the green moss still grew in wads like green frogs hopping about the cracked cement slabs. He got down on his knees and said, "Daddy I finished my tour with the Army. I miss you not being there in your rocker every night, talking about old times, reading the good book, and putting good words in my head that never stayed long enough to stick to my thick head. I plan to remodel the old house like you talked about. Mama is doing fine and Tracy is married with a baby girl." He stood up, took a good breath, looked at the grave several minutes before walking back to the church. His daddy was no longer around to tell him what he should do to solve his problems, but he felt better after having talked to him.

CHAPTER THIRTY-FIVE

Ernie called the Ming residence every day that week to no avail. On Saturday, he got up early and dialed the Ming residence once again. He held to the phone and listened to it ring ten times before Dong Lee answered. When he asked to speak to Anna, Dong Lee recognized his voice and called him by name. In a hateful tone, he told Ernie that Anna disappeared the day bombs fell on the city of Dalat. She went to town to do some shopping that day and never returned. The spirits told him the bandits killed his daughter; but Anna's blood was on his hands, since he brought bad omens to his family. Then he shouted so loudly that Ernie held the phone away from his ear. "If you come back to Dalat, I will kill you."

"I have been in my homeland more than eight months. Why do you blame me for the devil's work?"

"I have nothing more to say to you," he said, and he slammed the phone down in Ernie's face.

Ernie did not trust Dong Lee. He was sure Anna was alive; her father had locked her away some place to keep her from getting in touch with him. If he went to Vietnam, he would waste his time and money; he would never find her.

In the meantime, he called Corporal Hatcher to find out if he made it home alive. The phone rang three times before the lady answered. He told her who was calling and asked to speak to Harold Hatcher. Hatcher came to the phone right away and Ernie said, "God, man, I am glad to hear your voice."

"Where in the hell have you been?" Hatcher said. "I called your home a dozen times, and the lady who answered the phone told me you could not come to the phone."

"I was in no condition to speak to anyone," Ernie said, "The Viet Cong captured me and put me in a prison for almost two months. Then they kept me in the hospital for six weeks before they shipped me home. When I finally got home, my mama carried me to a psychiatrist and he gave the same diagnosis as the military doctors, but I could not tell her, because I did not know I had been diagnosed with post traumatic stress; I lost my memory of all things and people. Then I got hit by an automobile and the shock brought my memory back."

"Man, I am so sorry about your being captured and the accident. We searched for you the day the bombs fell; we went down every street and alley we could get through. I was afraid you got killed. Hobbit got killed that day. Thank God you are alive."

"I am sorry to hear that Hobbit got killed; he was strange, but everybody liked him."

"Slater and Purvis both got injured from shrapnel. Four of us stuck together after we lost you. Fish helped me pull them to a shelter. After several hours in the ruined city of Danang, we found a pay phone that still worked and called the base; paramedics picked us up less than an hour later. I have never been more scared in my life. I didn't think we would make it out of the city alive."

"We need to thank our lucky stars," Ernie said. "I think I will recover now that I got my memory back. Do you remember the girl you went out with in Saigon?"

"I have her number around here some place, but I was not planning on calling her."

"I don't want you to go out on a date with her, but the girl I was with that night was named Laquan, and she was her friend. Laquan caused me more trouble than cows in the corn patch. She came to my home in the spring and announced that she was my wife."

"Run that by me again," Hatcher said. "Did you say she claimed she was your wife?"

"Hell yes, she told me I married her in Saigon, and she had a fake marriage certificate."

"She told you that you married her that night you went out with her in Saigon. Do you remember her telling you that?"

"Yes, I remember, but she was lying then; and she is lying now. When I got home from the hospital, I put her ass on the road, but I want to know her motive for telling that big lie in the first place. I want to take her to court and make her serve time."

"I cannot believe anybody would be that low down," Hatcher said. "I will call her friend."

"Ask her friend where Laquan Chan is living now and pretend that your friend, Ernie, is interested in asking her out for a date. Find out everything you can about the bitch."

"What about Anna?"

"I called her home and her father told me she was dead. I don't believe that bastard, either, but I don't know what to do."

"Call the Bureau of Records in Vietnam. If she is dead, they should have a record of her death."

"I thought about that, but Dong Lee is rich and powerful. If he does not want me to find her, he probably had the records fixed."

"What about her friends?"

"She had a friend at one of the restaurants we went to, but I don't remember her name or the name of the restaurant."

"I am engaged now to a girl from my hometown," Hatcher said. "We are getting married in June. Man, I want you to come to my wedding."

"I will do that," Ernie said. "I will sleep better tonight knowing that you are still alive."

"I will call Laquan friend and call you back," Hatcher said.

"Thanks, old buddy."

Ernie told his mother that he had come up with another blank page, but he wanted to go to Vietnam and search until he found Anna.

Once again she convinced him that a telephone call would save him time and money, since Anna's father did not want him to see her. She added that he had probably locked her away some place to keep her from getting in touch with him. Then she placed her hand on his shoulder and told him that God tested a person's faith sometimes by presenting situations that seemed unbearable, but God had a plan for him, and everything was going to be alright.

Ernie told her that God had not told him about his plan, yet; and he did not see the Promised Land in his future.

She told him that he was not to question God's work, and he would find another woman who loved him as much or more than Anna Ming. She added that he must have faith and know that God would provide what was best for him.

Ernie knew in his heart that he would never love another woman as much as he loved Anna. Her disappearance had turned his hopes to despair. She was special; she was his reason for living. There was no need to argue with his mother. She was as stubborn as Dong Lee when it came to her beliefs.

The next evening, Corporal Harold Hatcher called and told Ernie that Seta Ching was Laquan's friend, and she still lived in the apartment in Saigon, but Laquan had been gone almost a year. Seta heard recently that Laquan was back; she lived in an apartment on the beach in Saigon."

Ernie thanked Hatcher and told him to keep in touch. He fell back in his chair and thought about the beach house Dong Lee owned in Saigon. Anna told him she went there every summer to spend her vacation. He wondered if Anna was in Saigon.

The next evening after Ernie got down from the tractor, walked to the house and got his gun to hunt for squirrels. As he walked through the branch frogs croaked, mosquitoes whined, crickets chirped, and all of the squirrels hid in their nest. He sat down on a huge rock near the creek bank and threw acorns in the water. He could see Anna's face in the stream. He worried about what he would do if he went back to Vietnam and found that she was dead. When he came up to no solution to his problem, he got up and walked wearily back toward home.

CHAPTER THIRTY-SIX

It was early May, and Ernie worked hard in the field every day. He got down from the tractor and walked home to eat lunch. As his Mother set dinner on the table, the doorbell rang. Ernie thought the caller was Nolan, since he often came by to eat dinner with them. When he opened the door, he was surprised to see two tall, well dressed strangers. They flipped badges toward him with the Letters "FBI" in bold print.

"Are you Ernie Tennyson?" one of the agents said.

"Yes, I am Ernie. What can I do for you?"

"My name is Mark Mackey, and this is my partner, John Kite. We would like to ask you a few questions."

Anna was the first thing that popped into Ernie's mind. They had found her body. Ernie invited them in and asked them to sit in the living room. "What happened? What is this all about?"

"Are you acquainted with a man by the name of Dong Lee Ming from South Vietnam?"

"Yes, I know Mr. Ming. I have just returned from a tour of duty in South Vietnam. I dated Mr. Ming's daughter, Anna Ming. Why do you ask?"

"Mr. Ming was found murdered in his beach house yesterday evening. He died from a .45 caliber bullet to the heart."

"My God, do you think I killed him?"

"We have to check out all persons who had dealings with Mr. Ming, and phone records indicate that you have called the Ming residence on many occasions the past month."

"I talked to Mr. Ming on the phone last Friday, but I had called to speak to his daughter. He told me his daughter was missing and he thought she had been killed by the recent bomb that hit Dalat."

The officers looked at each other and John said, "There has been no bombing of Dalat that I know about."

"Can you tell me if Anna Ming is alive and where she is living?" Ernie said.

"We talked to Anna Ming and her grandmother yesterday at Mr. Dong Lee's residence in Dalat. We went there immediately after the murder. The daughter, Anna Ming, said she had recently returned from China. She had been living with one of her aunts for several months."

"That dirty dog," Ernie said before he thought of what he was saying.

"Who is the dirty dog?" John asked.

"I was thinking out loud," Ernie said. "Neither Dong Lee nor Mrs. Ming liked me. Dong Lee hated Americans, and he would not allow his daughter to go out with me or have anything to do with me. He had chosen the man he wanted Anna to marry. Anna and I had secret meeting places."

"Was one of your secret meeting places at Mr. Ming's beach house in Saigon?"

"No, we never went to the beach house together. Anna mentioned that she went there only once a year to spend her vacation."

"When was the last time you saw Anna Ming?"

"I saw her last year during the month of June in Nha Trang, where I was stationed. My tour of duty ended the last of August; but the Viet Cong captured me and took me to a prison camp in the North."

"I am sorry to hear about your ordeal with the Viet Cong," Mr. Mackey said. "We need to have a look at your firearms."

Ernie got up and came back with his rifle and a .38 caliber pistol. The agents looked at the guns and handed them back to him. Then they asked his whereabouts the evening Dong Lee was murdered.

Ernie told them that he was either at home, in the field working, or in town at the bar with his friend, Nolan.

When the agents left, they seemed satisfied with his answers; but they told him they may have additional questions as the investigation progressed.

Ernie rushed back to the kitchen to tell his mama what had happened, but she had been standing in the hall listening to every word said.

"I am not laughing or shouting with joy about Dong Lee's death, but I am happy that Anna is alive and well. I am going to call her grandmother and see what she says."

"You should have told them about Laquan Chan and asked them to run a criminal record on her. That girl wanted citizenship. When she married you, she got a free ticket to come over here and live with you."

"After they find who killed Dong Lee, I will tell the law officials everything. I intend to get to the bottom of her lies, but I didn't want to tell those agents that I had lost my memory. Anytime something happens to a man's mind, the law officials immediately think that person is guilty of a crime. I didn't want to be arrested and thrown into jail."

Ernie didn't finish eating. He went straight to the phone and called the Ming residence, but no one answered the phone. He waited ten minutes and called back, but he still got no answer. He continued to call every hour until he went to bed. The next morning, he called again, but he still got no answer.

His mama came in and told him that Anna had things to do after her father got murdered; she had to make funeral arrangements, see about the guest and dinner, and take care of her grandmother.

Ernie had not thought of that, so he did not call again that day, but he did tell his mama that Lena Ming was as mean as a rattle snake, and she was able to care for herself.

His mama could not believe what he had said, and she told him he should respect his elders.

That is when he told his mama a mouth full about Lena Ming. He started from the first time she saw him and wouldn't let him use the phone.

Afterwards, he mama said she must be related to Laquan, and Ernie laughed.

In the meantime, Mrs. Ming and Anna had learned of Dong Lee Ming's death. Anna and her grandmother cried a while; then, Mrs. Ming called Sean. She and her family could not come until late the next evening. Anna went outside to find the children. She told them what had happened, and they all tried to give her a hug at the same time. She asked them to go around the village and tell the neighbors. Then she went back into the house to clean the kitchen and straighten the house. Dong Lee's friends and their neighbors would be there soon. The neighbors came right away; they came back every night to visit, eat, and play games.

Since Mrs. Ming delayed the cremation ceremony until his daughter, Sean, and her family arrived, Monks fulfilled their duty by coming to the house the next day to chant from Abhidharma. As they did so, they held to a ribbon that streamed from the casket. Afterward, Mrs. Ming gave them food.

Later that evening, Anna's Aunt Sean and her family arrived. After a brief time of grieving, the family performed the bathing ceremony. Each of them poured water over Dong Lee's hand. Afterward, the attendants placed Dong Lee's body in the coffin.

Anna followed her grandmother's instructions and placed an eight by ten photograph of her father on a table next to his coffin. Then she suspended colored lights around his coffin. The coffin was soon surrounded with wreaths of beautiful flowers, candles, and sticks of incense.

Since Dong Lee died before one could whisper words that would encourage him to think about Buddha and be blessed with good things after his reincarnation; Anna did as Lena Ming told her and wrote "Nibbana" on a piece of paper. Mrs. Ming took the note and placed it into Dong Lee mouth.

On the third day, they prepared for the crematorium. The monks chanted a service at home before they moved the coffin down the steps. They covered the steps with leaves to have a different route to carry Dong Lee's body from his home to the funeral car, which carried his body to the crematorium grounds.

Her father's burial rites were elaborate like all other Buddhist funeral rites. One of Dong Lee's friends carried a white banner on a long pole and led the funeral procession; he was followed by several elderly men who carried flowers in silver bowls. Eight Monks chanted portions of the Abhidharma as they walked ahead of the coffin and held a Bhusa Yhong ribbon that ran from Dong Lee's body into their hands. This union put Dong Lee in contact with the holy sutras.

Once at the Crematory grounds, the monks sat facing the coffin on which rested the Pangsukula robes. People came forward with gifts and placed them on the casket.

Then a Monk performed all of the funeral rites. First, he preached Dong Lee's sermon. He reminded those who attended that all deaths are universal. Then he stood before Dong Lee's body and chanted to the surtras to benefit the deceased, since the monk expected his rebirth on earth, in heaven of Indra, or as a spirit. Afterward, the Monk offered food in Dong Lee Ming's name in order to receive benefits and joy until the end of time.

After the chanting, people came forward and placed the coffin on a structure that looked like a furnace made of bricks. People came up to the casket and threw burning candles, incense, and fragrant wood under the casket. The fire quickly cremated Dong Lee's body. Anna and Mrs. Ming would come back and collect the ashes later and place them in an urn.

Before everyone parted, Mrs. Ming gave out pamphlets that set forth the Buddhist teachings and an explanation of the burial ceremony.

Back in Georgia, Ernie got an early start. He went to the kitchen, poured a cup of coffee, and went to the phone to call Anna. When he asked to speak to Anna Ming, a sweet voice fell on his ear.

"This is Anna Ming. May I ask who is calling?"

"Anna, this is Ernie Tennyson."

"Ernie!" she screamed. "Is this really you?"

"This is really me, Ernie Tennyson," he said, and he felt as if the angels from heaven flew down and surrounded him. Her soft voice was heaven to his ears, and he wanted to jump up and shout with happiness.

"I cannot believe I am hearing your voice," she said "I have called your home in Georgia many times, and the lady who answered the phone told me that you were not home. After calling a number of times, she told me that you did not know me and did not wish to speak with me. Where have you been? Why did you not get in touch with me?"

"The Viet Cong captured me and carried me to a prison in North Vietnam. I tried many times recently to find you, but your father told me you had disappeared; then he told me he believed the bandits killed you the day the bomb fell on Dalat. He also told me that your death was my fault."

"I cannot believe the lies my father told to keep us apart. I am alive and well, but my father was murdered," she said. "My grandmother and I are still mourning his death."

"Who killed your father?" Ernie asked. He did not want her to know the agents had visited him until he could tell her face to face.

"The law officials are investigating the case. They told us that they have several suspects in mind. The murderer shot my father with a .45 caliber pistol. His maid found him in his bedroom at the beach house in Saigon."

"I am sorry for your loss," he said.

"Where are you? When will I see you?"

"I am in Georgia, but I am coming to Dalat. I will call you when I get to Saigon and you can meet me in Dalat at the hotel. I will explain everything when I get there."

"I cannot wait to see you," she said. "I thank God that you are alive. I love you."

"I love you, too," Ernie said.

When she heard the click of the receiver, she stood in a daze. She could not believe Ernie had called her after all of this time. She ran to her grandmother and shouted, "Ernie is still alive. He is coming to Dalat to see me."

"Where was Mr. Tennyson when you needed him?"

"The Viet Cong captured him and took him to a prison of war camp in North Vietnam."

"I am sorry about his bad luck," her grandmother said, but I do not want him to take you away from me. You are all I have left in this world."

"Grandmother, you have your daughter Sean and you have two other grandchildren. You also still have grandfather. Have you ever thought of going back to live with him."

"Heck, do you think I want that old goat back in my bed?"

Anna wanted to laugh at her remark, but she remained serious. "Grandfather is a nice man. He still asks about you."

"I do not wish to talk about your grandfather. I want to know what you plan to do."

"We will talk about my plans when Ernie gets here. Right now, I have to prepare for his visit. Do we have vegetables and meat that we can prepare for dinner this weekend? I expect him on Friday or Saturday."

"He can eat rice," her grandmother said.

"I will go into town and buy groceries, Grandmother. I want him to have a special dinner to welcome him to our home. He never felt welcome here before."

"Buy what you please, and do as you please. Forget about your old grandmother. She can care for herself in her old age."

"Grandmother, you are not being fair. Think of what you told me about the wilted flower. Do you want me to be a wilted flower?"

"That reminds me," her grandmother said. "I need to put fresh flowers in the vase. We cannot have a visitor without fresh flowers."

Anna went to her and hugged her. "Grandmother, I love you and I will never forget all that you have done for my sake."

Anna was too excited to sit still; she danced around her room with happiness and thought of their wedding day. She could hear the wedding march; she could feel his hand in hers; she could see the wedding ring as he slipped it on her finger to seal their vows as man and wife. Then doubt crowded her mind and she paced back and forth across the room. She had not seen him in almost a year. Did he still feel the same about her? Had he been with other women? She tossed and turned for hours before she fell asleep.

The next morning, she went to the kitchen and was surprised to see that her grandmother had written a menu for dinner. She turned to Anna and said, "When he gets here, I will cook dinner. Right now, we need to eat breakfast. I fixed eggs and toast for breakfast. Won't you sit down and eat with me."

Her grandmother had softened quite a bit since she had been in China. She had called and told her she missed her and she wanted her to come home many weeks before her father was murdered, but Anna did not want to be around her father. He had been a selfish man and she hated his control over her life. She had been a prisoner to his wishes. She did not wish for him to die, and was saddened by his death, but she deserved the freedom she enjoyed since his death.

CHAPTER THIRTY-SEVEN

The Saigon air terminal was a huge building with glass panels across the front centered with double doors. As Ernie stepped on the paving stones, he found himself counting like a kid. He came to his senses and looked around at the people walking around him.

He took a cab from the airport into Saigon and told the driver to take him to a hotel that served good food. Ernie sat in the back seat and looked out the window as the cab driver drove toward Saigon. The fishing boats docked at the banks of the Saigon River looked peaceful on the still water. The city even looked happy and alive. Motor scooters and bicycles still rode with the traffic on the main streets.

After passing the central market and the railroad station, the cab driver took a right turn. He pointed to famous sites, including the Theater of Fine Arts and the Notre-Dame Cathedral.

When the driver reached the Continental Palace hotel, he pulled into the drive before the double doors and said, "Sir, this hotel serves the best food in Saigon."

Ernie paid his fare, grabbed his bags, and thanked him. Ernie wanted to eat and get a good night's sleep before spending time with Anna. After he registered and unpacked his suitcase, he called the Ming residence and told Anna to meet him the next morning at eight o'clock at the Villa Nine Restaurant in Dalat. They had a nice hotel next door to the restaurant that Anna and Ernie had stayed at before.

After talking to Anna, he went to the hotel and ate dinner. Then he took a bath, and went to bed. He slept until six the next morning. After breakfast, he packed his bags and walked to Kong's Car Rental, where he rented an old Dodge van with plenty of room for luggage. He assumed that Anna would have a bundle packed to take with her to America. Then he went to the exchange bureau to change his dollars to dongs. He counted his dong dollars and figured the cost for each day in Vietnam. A budget meal cost three dollars, and a mid rage hotel cost around thirty-five dollars plus a ten percent coverage charge. He must find a job if he stayed more than two weeks. He mashed the accelerator on the Dodge and sped toward the city. At Mac Bai border checkpoint, the immigration police thoroughly checked his credentials, passport, and run down Dodge van.

When he turned off the main road into the Dalat Palace Hotel parking lot, he saw her waiting in a fairly new, red Cadillac. He got out and walked toward her car.

When she saw him, her heart beat like a herd of stampeding horses. She jumped out of her car and ran to meet him. Her face glowed with happiness, and her eyes bubbled with tears. He held her close for minutes before turning her face to his and looking into her eyes. Then he kissed her, and the pleasure set a fire in him that begged to be quenched.

"I've missed you," he whispered. "You are still beautiful."

"God, I have missed you, too. I have been out of my mind. I thought you jilted me; I did not think you would come back for me."

Their lips met again and he mumbled between kisses. "I want you, baby. I love you." She wilted to his embrace. He kissed her and kissed her again without thoughts of the people going in and out of the hotel.

She finally stepped back, and he told her to pop the trunk. He set her luggage out and went to the rented car to get his. When he came back, she said, "You can carry that old run-down car back where you got it."

"Are you making fun of my car?"

"I have a new Cadillac that we can use to go anywhere you wish to go."

"Thank you, sweet heart. I will take my old run-down car back tomorrow morning."

After he registered and they settled in their room, she sat down on the bed and he sat next to her.

"Where have you been? What happened to you all the months that I did not hear from you?"

"I have been in Georgia.

"The last year of my life is a long story, and I don't know where or how to begin telling you."

"Begin with the day you left me at the beach in Nha Trang," she said.

"I told you I was captured by Viet Cong or bandits that day. At first, I thought the Viet Cong had captured me; then I realized they were bandits. They carried me to a filthy prison, beat me, put me in solitary confinement, and gave me only bread to eat and water to drink."

She touched his face and kissed him. "I am so sorry. How long did the brutal pigs keep you in prison?"

"I stayed there during the month of August and part of September. They would have kept me there forever, but Americans broke into the prison and set all of the prisoners free. Then I stayed in a hospital in Columbus, Georgia for six weeks."

"Why didn't you call me or try to get in touch with me?"

Suddenly, he blurted, "Have you ever heard of a man losing his memory?"

She laughed, thinking he was telling a cute joke. "Am I that easy to forget?"

"The doctors diagnosed my condition as Post Traumatic Stress or something like that. Anyhow, I didn't remember anything that happened before the war, during the war, or after the war for over a year. My life was a total blank; I didn't remember my own mother or my closest friend."

She knew he must be serious and wondered what was wrong with him. She questioned his sanity. She felt fear run up her spine and hit her brain, and she felt faint. She had fallen in love with this man. Now she was afraid of him. Was he one of those psychotic lunatics who went about telling women weird stories? Would he do something weird and crazy? Suppose he planned to murder her! She wanted to jump up and run, but she was too afraid to move.

"The government shipped me back to the military hospital at Fort Benning Army Base in Columbus, Georgia. I stayed there until they contacted my Uncle Willie. He took me back home to Georgia, and I have been there ever since. My mother and my best friend, Nolan, took up time with me in hopes of my recovery. In April, some fool tried to kill me. I had parked in the parking lot down town and was walking toward the bar. The hit-and-run driver came at me two different times. I dodged the hit the first time; the car turned around and came at me from the back side. I didn't have time to get out of its path. I flipped in the air and fell on hard cement parking lot. The cops have not found the hit-and-run driver, yet. To make a long story short, the jolt to my brain brought my memory back. I have been trying to get in touch with you since the day I got home from the hospital."

Seeing his dismay, and sensing the dread in his voice, she was no longer afraid. "What a terrible and unusual thing to happen. How terrified you must be," she said.

"At first, I did not feel anything, because I didn't remember anything. I tried to feel something, put some meaning to my life, but I felt nothing."

"Do not worry," she said, touching his hand. "It is not so bad, and I am sure everything will be all right. Who would want to kill you?"

He was silent for some time before he mentioned her father. "I know your father wanted me dead. He told me a bomb fell on Dalat and you disappeared; he also told me your blood was on my hands, because I caused your death."

The feel of her hand covering his and her consideration of his mood filled him with love.

"I am so sorry," she said. "My father is dead, bless his soul," and she made the sign of the cross, "but I will never forgive him for his cold and brutal heart. He had no feeling for me or anyone else. He would have done anything to keep us apart."

"I didn't tell you this when I talked to you on the phone; but the FBI came to my house and told me your father had been murdered. They questioned me as to where I was at the time and asked to see my guns. I have not been out of my home town since I got back home. They said they might want to talk to me again as the investigation progressed. I answered their questions truthfully and they seemed satisfied when they left."

"I know you had nothing to do with my father's murder. He had many enemies. I do not know who they are, but my father was not a very likeable man. He wanted money and power; he loved no one. I do not believe he loved my mother, either."

"Did he buy the new Cadillac for you?"

The week before he was killed, he came driving up in the new Cadillac. He did not give the car to me, but it is mine now."

"What happened in your life the past year?" he said.

She did not want to tell him; she must tell him. "I discovered that I was pregnant right after I left Nha Trang."

"Oh, baby, I am so sorry I was not there for you." He wanted to make up for all the hurt he had caused her, but what could he say now? "Your pain was my fault. I will make this horrible experience up to you somehow. Why didn't you tell me when I was running my mouth about my problems?"

"I did not want to tell you. Talking about this is very painful." His eyes had told her more than his words. He seemed to be such a sensitive, gentle man.

"God, you must have hated me. Your pregnancy was my fault."

"I did not hate you; I did not understand why you had not contacted me. I could talk to no one. I did not want to tell grandmother, and I certainly did not want to tell Father; but time tells on one who gets fat in her belly, and is too sick to eat. I had morning sickness so bad that I would throw up after drinking water. Not only was I sick, I was too depressed to live. In fact, I wanted to die. I had to hide my pregnancy for four months. My Grandmother was concerned about my health. When my father questioned me, I confessed to him that I was pregnant. He had a duck fit and sent me to China to have an abortion, but I was too far along for the doctors to perform an abortion. I was very happy and was going to keep the baby, but Father said I must put it up for adoption. Aunt Sean finally calmed Father by telling him she would adopt my baby and raise it as her own."

"Where is our baby? What happened to our baby?" he said.

"I carried the baby full term. The doctor told me my baby was still born. They never let me see it. I imagine our little girl was beautiful. I will always believe that our little girl is in someone's home in another country, but I will never know. My father was a vicious man."

He held her and they both cried a long time. Afterward, he felt closer to her than before and he gently pulled her to him and said, "You are the best thing that ever happened to me."

"I could say the same," she said. "You are the man who made me a woman." She smiled and her eyes shined with happiness.

"You make me feel like every bit the man I always wanted to be," he said. "Now that I've found you again, I will never let you go. I want to spend the rest of my life with you."

Before kissing her again, he pulled a black velvet box from his pocket. Her eyes widened with surprise as he opened the box.

"I love you, Anna Ming," he said. "Will you marry me?"

"Yes! Yes!" she said with her head in the clouds. "I thought you would never ask." Her face beamed with happiness.

He placed the ring on her finger and she held her hand out and marveled at its beauty. "Please, kiss me again and hold me forever. I do not need diamonds when I have you."

"What happened to your black onyx engagement ring?" he said.

"I have it here around my neck," she said. "When I was pregnant, my feet and hands swelled, and I could not get the ring on my finger. I put my ring on this chain and wore it around my neck. When you did not return for me, I continued to wear it around my neck, because I thought we were no longer engaged and I would never see you again."

"We are together again at last, and you are going to America with me. I will fight anyone who tries to stop you."

She said, "It seems that many years have passed since we first met here in this same hotel room."

"I want you," he said. "Don't you want me?"

"That is not a good question?"

"Come here," he said. His lips found hers and the world turned carrying them on a soft cloud to heaven. Minutes later he was in bed with her. She was a golden tan from head to toe and as beautiful as a butterfly fresh lit on a sweet smelling rose. He pulled her under his arm and the smell of her perfume was delightful. He brushed his lips teasingly and then he kissed her with a hungry desire that sent a chill through her.

At last, she did not feel ashamed as she lay beside him naked; she did not feel ashamed when she allowed him to move his hands all over her body. She could feel his erection next to her nakedness and she melted to his body. He was completely devoted to her, and she was crazy with the lofty feeling that flooded her. He liked her mumbling with pleasure; her passion he craved; his passion she satisfied. She felt loved and happier than she had since she had last slept with him.

"Um, I can't get enough of you." He kissed her breast and went down her body with kisses, and she was reminded of the first time he made love to her.

"I am only a tease the second time around," she said and fell on his chest.

"I will rape hell out of you," he said. "How would you like to be raped?"

"I would love for you to rape me!" she said. She became weak with the warmth of his kiss, and they made love the next hour.

Forgetting all things, she surrendered to his desire; and his need for her made her blood run hot. She needed him desperately. A good feeling rippled through her and made her happier than she had been since the last time in Nha Trang.

"My love for you will never die." She cuddled closer to him and closed her eyes.

The next morning, she called her grandmother and told her they would be there for dinner. Then they went to the Le Café La Poste Restaurant in the hotel, where they had met in secret many times before. Anna's friend still worked there and she was very happy that she had finally found Ernie and they got back together.

That evening, Anna followed Ernie to Kong's Car Rental Chain in Dalat to return the rented car. Ernie paid his rental fee and they got on the road. As they drove toward Lat village, Anna told him she could not wait to break the news of their engagement to her Grandmother Ming. Then she told him that her grandmother had changed for the better, and he would not believe the change in her. She added that her grandmother was sad about the baby being born dead, and had changed her attitude somewhat about American men.

Ernie told Anna that he would believe she had changed when he saw that she had changed.

CHAPTER THIRTY-EIGHT

Anna's face sparkled with happiness as she held her hand out to her grandmother. "Look at my engagement ring, Grandmother. Isn't my ring beautiful?"

"What is this? You are engaged to this man who deserted you?" she said with her eyes on Ernie. "Mr. Tennyson, Anna did not hear from you for many moons; now you suddenly appear and sweet talk her again. Why should she believe you after all of this time of absence? You want to kiss and make all things good between us. The pain you caused is not easily forgotten. I do not trust you, and Anna's injury is more than skin deep. Since you went away, Anna has constantly wrung her hands with worry about what had happened to you. She feared that the Viet Cong killed you. If you had you been concerned about Anna, you would have called or tried to get in touch with her." Then she looked at Anna and said, "Is your precious diamond an offering of peace, or does the ring mean that you will soon marry Mr. Tennyson?" She gave Ernie a side glance that said she still did not like him.

"Grandmother, Ernie and I are getting married."

"Anna is the only person I have left in the world. How can you come in and take her away from me?"

"Please, Grandmother, try to be happy for me. I need your blessings for our marriage and a happy future."

Ernie went to grandmother put his arms around her and hugged her. "I am sorry for the pain that I have caused you and Anna. I meant no harm. You know something, Grandmother; I have grown fond of you. I respect you as much as I respect the Queen of England."

"I do not know the Queen of England," she said, and she dismissed his sweet words with her own sweetness, "This engagement calls for a celebration, I suppose. I have dinner waiting. We must have rice wine and drink to the occasion." Then she looked directly at Ernie and said, "I suppose you are moving in with us."

"I have to go back to Georgia. I have a small farm to tend and the crop just started growing."

"I am going back to America with Ernie," Anna said.

"We plan to stay here with you a few weeks," Ernie said. "Anna is concerned with the investigation of Dong Lee's murder."

Mrs. Ming said, "I think they will soon solve Dong Lee's Murder."

"Have you heard news that you have not told me?" Anna said.

"I have heard nothing the past week. The agents are taking their sweet time in making an arrest. However, I think they are on the right trail," Mrs. Ming said. "Anna, take our guest to the dining room and set the table with the fine China. I will join you shortly."

Mrs. Ming walked down the hall to Dong Lee's quarters. She parted the beads and entered his office. Her mind flashed back to the day she answered her door and faced the tall woman with dark hair, dark skin, dark eyes, and very red lips who had visited Dong Lee on numerous occasions. In fact, she had visited Dong Lee the week Ernie Tennyson went missing, and Lena had slipped quietly down the hall to Dong Lee's quarters and stood next to the tropical plant to watch them through the beads hanging in the doorway.

Mrs. Ming could not believe her ears. Her son paid that woman to lure Ernie Tennyson to her bed when he was in Saigon. Then Dong Lee hired a private detective to find Tennyson. When he learned that Tennyson had lost his memory, he offered that woman fifty thousand dollars to go to Tennyson's home in Georgia and tell him she was his wife and they got married in Saigon. Dong Lee gave the woman a fake marriage certificate to use as proof of their marriage. Then Dong Lee told the woman that she must live with Tennyson at least two years to get full payment of the money. Worst of all, Lena Ming learned that her son had hired that woman to write Tennyson a letter, when he was station in Nha Trang, Vietnam; and he had instructed her to sign Lena Ming's name to the letter.

Mrs. Ming was shocked by what she had heard. She saw where she had been wrong to agree with Dong Lee, and she felt sorry for Anna and Ernie Tennyson. On the other hand, she had said many things to Anna about Tennyson that she could not take back. If she told Tennyson that she did not write the letter, he would wonder how she knew he got a letter. She was curious as to what the letter said, but she would never know.

Then that same woman with the dark hair, dark skin, dark eyes, and very red lips came back to visit Dong Lee recently; only a few days before Ernie Tennyson called and asked to speak to Anna.

Mrs. Tennyson knew exactly what was going on, and she did not approve of her son's dirty tricks. Once again, she had spied on Dong Lee and the woman.

Dong Lee invited the woman to have a seat in his quarters, and his large brown eyes moved from the woman's face to her feet. As he poured drinks, he bragged about how beautiful she looked and how much he had missed her. Then he settled in the chair behind his desk and began questions about her progress with Ernie Tennyson.

The woman told Dong Lee that she was lucky to still be alive, because Tennyson and his mother had constantly tried to force her to leave their home; and Ernie Tennyson was about to cause serious trouble that neither of them could easily sweep under the rug. She explained that she had run Tennyson over with her car as he had instructed, but the accident back-fired. After the accident, Tennyson regained his memory and came after her; he beat her, and threatened to kill her if she did not leave his home at once. His private detective had been following her and had questioned her for the second time the day she left. She told Dong Lee that the authorities would have arrested her had she not escaped during the night after Tennyson came home from the hospital.

Then the woman got up from her chair and told Dong Lee that their business deal was over; and she had no intentions of going back to Georgia.

Dong Lee turned red with anger, hit his fist on his desk, and argued with the woman as he pointed his finger in her face. He told her that he was not going to pay her another dime of the fifty thousand dollars, because she had not held to her end of the bargain. Then he shouted that he was taking his red Cadillac back, and he would see her the next day to collect his property.

Then the woman threatened to tell his daughter, Anna, all of his dirty little secrets if he did not pay her the money he had promised her.

That's when Dong lee jumped up from his chair and threatened to kill the woman if she did not get out of his sight that minute.

Mrs. Ming moved behind the large tropical plant in the hall when she saw the woman coming from Dong Lee's quarters. She watched the woman stomp down the hall toward the front door. When Mrs. Ming got to the front door, the red Cadillac disappeared in the dust.

Mrs. Ming said to herself, "My, what a nice car."

After Lena Ming discovered the truth about her son, she decided that he was a cold, ruthless, man and unfit to be called a Father. He had punished his daughter for falling in love with an American, and he had committed a crime to keep this American away from her. Dong Lee's had betrayed his daughter, and the Gods did not forgive such sins. This was the day that Lena Ming changed her mind about the American; this was the day she decided that she must do something to stop Dong Lee's insane acts.

The next day after Dong Lee left for work, Lena Ming called the local authorities and reported the tall woman with the dark hair, dark skin, and very red lips. She did not know her name, but she had given the law officers a good description and told them that the woman was involved in criminal activity with her son, Dong Lee Ming. She had also told them that the woman was wanted for a hit and run in Liberty Springs, Georgia, and had tried to kill Ernie Tennyson, an American, who had recently been sent home from military duty in South Vietnam. She had added that she did not want the woman back in her home; she wanted her behind bars.

Anna called out from the kitchen, "Grandmother, I have everything on the table. The food is getting cold."

"I am coming," Mrs. Ming said. "I was in Dong Lee's office looking over a few things." She sat down at the table and Ernie thought he saw a smile on the old lady's face as she spoke, "Let's have dinner, children. I think I will enjoy my dinner tonight. In fact, a load has been lifted from my old heart."

Anna looked at Ernie and smiled as she passed the food. Ernie noticed right away that Anna had placed that same two pronged fork and large spoon next to his plate. A large spoon and a small fork suited his hand better than the sticks they were eating with, but he wished he had a good fork and spoon from his mama's cabinet drawer.

That night before Lena Ming went to bed, she thought about her miserable life. She did not want Anna to live as she had to live. She did not want Anna to know that her father had betrayed her. She hoped that Ernie Tennyson never told Anna about the tall woman with the dark hair, dark skin, dark eyes, and very red lips that came to his home and claimed to be his wife. They would arrest this woman in a few days, since they would find all the evidence they needed. Ernie Tennyson was a smart man, and he would put two and two together. He would realize that her son, Dong Lee Ming, was at the root of all the evil. Dong Lee Ming had caused all of his problems as well as Anna's suffering. The ironical thing about Dong Lee's betrayal was that he had made Ernie Tennyson regain his memory when he had intended for the hit and run to kill him.

After Lena Ming dressed for bed, she lay on her pillow and tried to remember a poem her mother often read to the children. Lena could only recall the first two lines, but those lines had been engraved in her memory and suited the purpose well.

Dust has already covered the shameful sins he sowed.

Let them not be rustled to reveal things men don't know.

The next morning, Ernie left Anna sleeping peacefully and went to find the morning paper and a cup of coffee. He stepped outside and found the paper on the porch. In the kitchen, he found a can of Brazilian ground, and made a pot of coffee. After his coffee brewed, he poured a cup and sat down at the table. When he unfolded the Dalat Morning News, his eyes grew to the bold headlines: "Laquan Chan arrested and charged with the murder of Dong Lee Ming, a prominent shipping magistrate from Lat Village." An anonymous tip led the FBI to the arrest. Ernie immediately thought his mother had called the FBI, but he still couldn't put the pieces of the puzzle together. How did Laquan know Dong Lee Ming? Why did she murder him?

Suddenly, he felt a hand on his shoulder. Mrs. Ming got a cup of coffee, walked around the table, and sat across from him. She told him that the authorities had already called her the day before and told her about Laquan Chan's arrest, but she did not want to tell Anna. She had not known the woman's name until the law enforcement called; but she had seen her when she visited Dong Lee on several occasions, and she had spied on them to learn the dirty truth. She paused minutes as if in deep thought.

Then she told Ernie everything about Laquan Chan and the deal Dong Lee had made with Laquan: the money he had paid Laquan to pose as his wife; Laquan's having hit him with the red Cadillac, which Dong Lee had owned; and the letter Laquan had written to Ernie with Mrs. Ming's forged signature. Last, but not least, she told him that she was the anonymous caller who had reported Laquan long before Dong Lee was killed; she believed Laquan thought Dong Lee had called the authorities and killed him, because they had been following Laquan since the day she returned to Saigon and visited Dong Lee here at her home. That is the day she had reported Laquan's criminal activity with her son.

After she told Ernie the terrible news, she told him she had one last request: she did not want Anna to know about her father's betrayal. She explained that Anna only needed to know that her father was having an affair with the woman. If Anna learned that her father was the evil monster behind all of her misery, she would live the rest of her life with a heart filled with hatred for her father. She added that hatred would gnaw away her insides.

Ernie had never been more shocked in his life; but he was happy to know that Laquan Chan was behind bars for murdering Dong Lee. Most of all, he was happy that Laquan would pay for making his own life miserable and trying to kill him. He would never let Laquan get near Anna; but he was not sure that he could keep the terrible secret about her father and Laquan Chan the rest of their married lives. Now was not the time to tell her the bad news; he wanted to share some happy times with her for a change.

CHAPTER THIRTY-NINE

Anna was excited and happy; she was sad and more frightened than she had ever been in her life. She loved Ernie more than all things, but she would miss her family. She did not know the strange land of America or its customs. Her clan was very different from Americans. She looked around the room that she had lived in since she was a small child. She wanted to take the room and everything in it with her, but she must leave all of these things behind and carry memories of her past the rest of her days. She walked across the room and stood before the life size portrait of her beautiful mother. As she touched her face, she spoke to her as she had done so many times in the past when she felt a need for her advice.

"Mother, I am going to America. You know all about him. I have told you about the American that I fell in love with. Mother, he will make me so happy. You see, I am nothing good without him."

With her words, her mother seemed to smile at her, and Anna knew she was making the right decision to leave her country and her family behind. Anna smeared her tears across her hand and went to the old trunk to look at the things that her mother had left her. She held the gifts dear to her heart and did not want to part with them. As she touched each piece of jewelry, she came to the gold locket that her mother used to wear. She picked up the heart shaped locket and opened it to remember the little girl with the dark silk hair fringing her happy face. She had been very happy as a child. This was before the war tore her family apart and took her mother. She remembered the good times when she had followed her mother around the market, the shops, the boutiques, and the art galleries; she remembered sitting next to her in the chapel; she remembered the vacations they had taken to China to see her grandparents; she remembered the expensive gifts her mother had bought for her. She could not leave the jewelry box behind. She picked it up and placed it in the large wooden box that she had packed with the rest of her belongings. Then she chose two of her favorite photo albums to take along. She closed the trunk on the memories there and walked to the bed. As she ran her hand over the hand-made quilt that her grandmother had made for her, she thought of the hours she must have spent making the quilt. She could not leave the quilt behind. She must fold it carefully and pack it between the fragile things in the box.

The next morning at breakfast, Anna's Grandmother suggested that she sell Anna's Cadillac and send her the money to buy a new car. Anna thought that was a very good idea. Then she told Anna that she would send her money for a wedding dress and promised to come to the wedding. Anna smiled, hugged her grandmother, and thanked her for everything she had done for her. Anna never dreamed that she would agree for her to marry Ernie in the first place; now she had said she would attend their wedding, and Anna was shocked; yet, she was pleased that her grandmother had changed for the better.

After breakfast, Ernie loaded the car with their luggage, and the large trunk packed with things Anna could not part with. The trunk was packed, and the back seat crammed to the ceiling with her things.

Anna's Grandmother went with Ernie and Anna to the Tan Su Nut International Airport near Saigon to drive Anna's car back home. She talked from the time they left Lat Village until they arrived at the airport. She did not know what she would do without Anna; she would have no one to go into town for her if she got sick; she would have no one to help her with the housework and cooking; she would have no one to talk with, and she would be lonely.

Anna suggested that she go to China and stay with Sean. She had two lovely children, and they would do everything they could to make her happy. Her grandmother told her she would try to make it on her own, unless she became disabled.

When they got to the airport, Ernie went to the terminal to get a cart to carry their luggage and trunk. When he got back to the car, Mrs. Tennyson was holding Anna, crying, and catching her breath between words.

Ernie got their bags from the trunk and back seat, loaded them on the cart, and went to hugged Mrs. Tennyson. She was crying too hard to speak. She finally got back into the car and rolled her window down to wish them a safe trip. She sat there in the car and watched them until they entered the doors of the terminal.

Ernie and Anna got settled for their long flight to Georgia. They read, took naps, ate, drank, and talked about their future. Ernie had picked up a house plan book at the airport. He showed Anna every house plan he liked, and she told him to pick the plan that suited him. Then she added that she would be happy in a two room shack as long as she was with him. He kissed her and kept flipping the pages. She finally fell asleep and he awoke her when the flight attendant announced that the plane was landing at the Atlanta Airport.

They arrived in Atlanta at eleven A.M., and Ernie rented a 1968 Impala Chevrolet for their trip to Liberty Springs in South Georgia.

On the way home, Ernie told her about the United States: cities, mountain ranges, regions, climate, businesses, foods, and observed holidays. Anna sat quietly and listened with interest as Ernie bragged about his country.

"We have fifty states and the city of Washington, D.C., the nation's capital, home of our president, and the place where senators and representatives meet to conduct government business. Our country is made up of ten thousand cities, towns, and villages; and three mountain ranges - the Appalachians, which extend from Canada to the state of Alabama; the Rockies, which extend from Alaska to New Mexico; the Sierra Nevada Range, and Cascade Range, which includes California with sites such as Lake Tahoe, Yosemite National Park, and the Great Lakes. Then we have regions with states in each region - New England; Mid Atlantic; South; Midwest; Texas; Great Plains; Rocky Mountains; Southwest; California; Alaska; and Hawaii."

"I will never remember all that you are saying; but I like what I have seen so far."

"If you don't remember anything else, remember that Georgia is located in the South Region with its sister states: Alabama, Arkansas, Kentucky, Louisiana, Mississippi, North Carolina, South Carolina, Tennessee, Virginia, West Virginia, and Florida. Texas is the biggest state in the United States; it is like a separate country."

"I will remember that Georgia is where we will live; I will remember that it is in the South."

"You will dislike the climate in Georgia, since you are used to spring-like weather the year round. Most of the regions have a temperate climate, except Alaska, where it stays cold as a frog's nose all the time. The temperature in the South varies from hot and humid in the summer; mild temperatures in the fall; and freezing temperatures in the winter."

"I can take the heat," she said and laughed.

"You can take the heat under an air conditioner," he said. "You will see when you feel. The hot humid weather in the south takes some getting used to."

"I want to hear about the food and grocery shopping."

"We have supermarkets instead of markets in the United States; of course, we do have some markets in the larger cities, but our markets are not usually out in the open like they are in your country. Then we have chain stores, factory outlet stores, warehouse club stores, and shopping centers that sell clothes, movies, music, books, art, and about anything else you want. The United States is the cultural center of the world.

"You have not told me about the kinds of food you have in America," she said.

"At different restaurants, you can order Mexican food, Chinese food, Italian food, Middle Eastern and Greek foods, and Vegetarian food. The truck stops cater to truck drivers and serve breakfast and sandwiches mostly. Last, but not least, we have those good old fast food restaurants: McDonald's, Burger King, KFC, Taco Bell, Dairy Queen, and Sub Way to name a few; they have more business than all of the other restaurants put together. Barbecue is an American specialty at most fast foods restaurants and bigger restaurants. You have a choice of barbecue sandwiches, barbecue chicken, burgers, pizza, tacos, and good old French fries. As far as drinks are concerned, you know I like red tea with sugar; but most American go for soft drinks - Cokes, Pepsi, Sprite, Doctor Pepper, and Ginger Ale. I take that back; most folk go for beer, wine, and liquor."

You are only kidding," she said.

"I am not kidding. I would like to have a cold beer right now."

"I will drive if you would like to have a beer," she said.

"I can wait," he said and paused. "I think our country has your beat in technology. How did you let China get ahead of you? China is king in technology and the United States is running her a good race. We have cell phones, computers with an internet, machines to fax messages, television, cable news channels, and I cannot count the number of newspapers and magazines published daily in our country."

"Sounds as if you have a fabulous country," she said.

"I hope you like Georgia, at least," he said. "I want to keep you here a long time."

She laughed and said, "I want to stay in Georgia as long as my husband lives in Georgia."

As they neared Macon, Georgia, Ernie asked Anna what she would like for dinner. She asked about a Chinese restaurant, and Ernie watched the signs. Ernie followed the signs to the Hong Kong Restaurant on Pionono Avenue. The restaurant was clean and neatly arranged with small wooden tables and ladder back chairs. Red linen covered the tables. The waitress came right away with glasses of water. She gave them a menu and told them they also had the buffet. Ernie ordered broiled shrimp with a baked potato and salad; Anna had the buffet. She got a taste of all of the Chinese dishes; she was sure Mrs. Tennyson was not used to cooking foreign dishes, and she must learn to like southern style dishes.

After they left Macon, Ernie started on his lessons again. He told her that he had failed to mention that the United States observed more holidays that any country in the world. Anna thought he was joking, since he had made jokes about their TET celebration. After he started naming off the holidays, she saw that he was not joking.

"We have a holiday every time you turn around," he said. "Martin Luther King Day; Chinese New Year; Super Bowl Sunday; Valentine's Day; Presidents Day; Washington's Birthday; St. Patrick's Day; Easter; Passover; Memorial Day; Independence Day; Labor Day; Columbus Day; Halloween; Veterans Day; Thanksgiving Day; Kwanzaa; and New Year's Eve."

"Gosh, I cannot believe you celebrate so many days of your year."

"I don't celebrate all of those days; I celebrate only the days we have big dinners."

"You are not fair to those celebrated," she said.

"I don't have time to celebrate much," he said, and pointed to a sign. "We are only fifty miles from Liberty Springs."

Anna turned her head to the window and took notice of the trees, farmland, houses, and signs. The entire state was made of bricks, rich hardwood, and mansions. She saw only a few run-down shacks. Even the farm animals had private green pastures to graze and barns to protect them from the cold winter common to the south.

America was different, very different. She saw no huts or villages; she saw no jungle paths; she saw no rice paddies, banana trees, pineapple trees, or palms. She did see plenty of pine trees. She saw no young boys with bare brown chests carrying baskets of produce on their shoulders. She saw no buffaloes plowing the fields or elephants tramping the trails of tall grasses. There were no monkeys. She thought about Chipper and wondered if he survived the destruction.

When Ernie got to Liberty Springs, he suggested they go to the Southern Star for a sandwich or a salad before going home.

Anna liked the quiet southern atmosphere. The waitress was friendly and the restaurant was very clean. She ordered a garden salad topped with baked chicken and her first glass of red, sweet tea. Ernie ordered a hamburger and fries with sweet tea to drink. Anna remarked that she had never eaten a hamburger. When the waiter brought their order, Ernie cut a small piece of his hamburger for her to taste. She was surprised; the hamburger was delicious.

Ernie told her she could forget about the strange dishes her country served, because Americans did not eat bats, rats, turtles, or snakes.

She laughed and said, "I will learn to like what you like, because I love you."

Ernie's mother was the perfect mother-in-law. She opened her arms to Anna and welcomed her to her home. Anna called her Mom right away. She was easy to talk with and Anna could see why Ernie was so close to her.

In spite of the difference in America and Vietnam, Anna was happy. The sun shined on America. The rains seldom turned to floods, and the place seemed perfect. She would not miss the monsoons and the rolling streams of water under foot that China experienced during the summer.

The farms were hilly plains and flat lands covered with crops that were planted and harvested by machines. The produce was hauled, processed, and stacked in large grocery stores for consumers to choose from.

Anna had arrived just in time for the ripe corn and tomatoes. Taking the shucks and silks from corn was a new experience for Anna, but she did not mind. The first time she tasted Mrs. Tennyson's creamed corn and fried chicken, she forgot about her usual daily helping of rice. She soon learned to like the taste of red, sweet tea, which was a treat for Ernie.

Anna and Ernie had their own private bedroom with a nice, modern bathroom at one end of the house. They were perfectly happy, and Mrs. Tennyson had already introduced her to every member of the church and most of the people in the small town.

CHAPTER FORTY

Anna had plenty of help with her wedding plans. Mrs. Tennyson had volunteers to do all of the things needed for a wedding. Anna did not plan for the traditional Vietnamese wedding; she planned the traditional American wedding. She had contacted her Aunt Sean; and her family planned to attend the wedding. They were all taking a part.

Ernie had called Harold Hatcher and asked him if he would sing at his wedding. Hatcher was bubbling over with happiness and told him that singing at his wedding would give him great pleasure. Before hanging up, Ernie promised to go to Hatcher's wedding that was also coming up in June, but he added that he could do anything Hatcher asked, but he couldn't sing.

The first day of June was a beautiful day for a wedding. Anna Ming was nervous, but she was happy. She had spent sleepless nights planning the perfect wedding. The church was decorated to perfection. A huge gold bucket of pink roses centered the table before the altar. The pews were decorated with pink carnations and streamed with satin ribbons. Green ivy clung to tall candle arbors on each side of the podium; green ivy and tiny lights surrounded the stained glass portrait of Christ and made him shimmer with spirit.

Long tables flowed with white lace and were accented by pink carnations and green ivy. A five-tier wedding cake centered the long table that was covered with a white lace table cloth. Crystal punch bowls sparkled with red punch, which were surrounded by crystal dishes filled with nuts, mints, candies, chips and sandwiches. A three-tier chocolate groom's cake sat on a smaller table at the end of the room.

Ernie complained about his tight collar and pulled on his tuxedo.

"You look sharp, Mr. Tennyson," Nolan said, straightening his tie and standing tall. "I haven't worn a choker like this since Daddy's funeral, but being the Best Man is worth the misery."

Ernie punched him in the gut and said, "Let's go. I don't want to be late for my own wedding."

"By the time a man gets all that experience it takes to handle a woman, she has him committed," Nolan said. "I'm not getting married until I'm thirty-five years old."

"You'll probably be thirty-five before you find a woman who will have you," Ernie said.

Anna's cousin, Tra, and two friends from the church were the ushers; they escorted the guest into the church and lit the candles.

Brother Carver, followed by Ernie, Uncle Willie, and Nolan came in and stood before the altar.

The little flower girl was Ernie's niece, Beth. She wore a beautiful pink lace dress and carried a basket to match. She dropped white pedals from her basket, took her place in front of the altar, and looked up at her Uncle Ernie with a big smile and he smiled back.

She had taken to Ernie the minute they met back in December, but he had very little to say to her then. Tracy had told him that Beth talked about her Uncle Ernie since their visit at Christmas. Now he loved his little niece the way an uncle should.

Lena Ming, Anna Grandmother, played a mother's part and sent Anna enough money to buy the most beautiful wedding dress any bride had ever owned. Lena Ming walked with poise on her grandson's arm. She was dressed in a fine purple linen suit trimmed in black silk cord; she had a purple orchid pinned to her collar. She took her seat on the bride's side of the church and kept her eyes on the pulpit. She was not happy about Anna marrying an American, but she had accepted him as her son-in-law and would provide for their needs as long as she lived.

Anna's Aunt Sean beamed with pride as she walked down the aisle in her dark rose taffeta dress. She carried a cluster of white orchids, because Anna had insisted. Being the maid of honor was the only way she would ever walk down the aisle again. If anything happened to Hoe, she would live alone the rest of her life.

Ernie's sister, Tracy; Anna's cousin, Mein; and two of Anna's friends were brides' maids. They were dressed in beautiful pink taffeta dresses; they carried a bouquet of pink roses surrounded by lace and pink ribbons.

With the wedding party in place, the pianist pounded the keys, and the song, "Here Comes the Bride." echoed to the ceiling. Everyone turned to see Anna on Uncle Hoe's arm. Ernie felt proud of her; she was the most beautiful woman in the world. The white lace, long sleeves gown with its low cut bodice was covered with tiny white pearls.

After her Uncle Hoe gave her hand to Ernie, he took his place beside Sean and Mrs. Ming. They smiled at each other as her Uncle Hoe took his time getting to his seat.

Mrs. Tennyson's friend, Peggy Sanders, played the piano and Ernie's friend, Harold Hatcher sang, "I Can't Help Falling in Love with you," by Elvis Presley. Then, he sang, "From this Moment on," by Shania Twain. The audience as well as Anna was amazed at Hatcher's voice, and Ernie beamed with pride.

Before the last song ended, Mrs. Tennyson had tears streaming and a Kleenex wiping.

The preacher said, "Ladies and gentlemen, we have gathered to witness this man and this woman being joined in holy matrimony."

Silence fell over the congregation as the bride and groom vowed to love, honor, and obey.

Then, the preacher searched the faces of the audience and said, "If there be a man who is opposed to this man and this woman being united in holy matrimony, let him speak now or forever hold his tongue." He looked at the bride and groom as he spoke, "I now pronounce you man and wife. Ernie, you may kiss your bride."

At the wedding reception, Ernie met Hatcher's bride to be. She was a beautiful blond, and Ernie liked her right away. He told her a few stories about Hatcher that made her laugh.

After the wedding reception, they went to Panama City, Florida for their honeymoon. They had reservations at the Panama City Resort on the beach, and Anna admitted that Panama City beach was almost as beautiful as the beaches in Nha Trang.

Ernie swept her off her feet and carried her to the bedroom. Inside the door, he stood her on her feet, and said, "This gown drives me crazy." He pushed the straps down over her shoulders and tugged at the silk until the gown fell around her feet. That night was better than all the other times he had made love to her, because she was Mrs. Ernie Tennyson.

One week later, Anna and Ernie got back home. Ernie pulled into the drive, and a 1968, dark blue Pontiac took Ernie's space. Ernie pulled over on the lawn, parked, and went to the trunk to get their luggage. Anna walked by his side with a happy face.

When they walked into the living room, Anna was shocked to see her Aunt Sean and her grandmother. She greeted them with a hug and went to give Mrs. Tennyson a hug before demanding an explanation. She found Mrs. Tennyson in the kitchen, and she followed Anna back to the living room.

Right away, Mrs. Tennyson offered them dinner, but they had stopped at the Southern Star in Liberty Springs to eat lunch. Anna walked over to the couch and sat next to Ernie. Her Grandmother and Aunt Sean carried on a conversation as if nothing were out of the ordinary, but Anna was sure they had not made a trip from China to Liberty Springs to simply pass the time of day.

Anna finally interrupted their conversation and asked if anything had happened that she should know about.

Her grandmother and Aunt Sean spoke at the same time, "We wanted," then her grandmother let Sean take the floor.

"Anna, I have a surprise for you and Ernie." She got up from the couch and said, "Come with me."

Ernie got up and followed Anna and her Aunt Sean down the hall. When she reached their bedroom, she carefully pushed the door back and said, "I found your baby and there she is, the most beautiful baby girl I have ever laid my eyes on, except my own Mein."

Anna's legs almost folded and Ernie held her until the shock soaked into her brain. Then she ran across the room and looked down in the new crib at her beautiful baby. Ernie rushed over to her side and they stood there marveling at the sight that they still did not believe. Anna reached over into the crib and took her baby into her arms. She held her close to her chest and tears streamed from her face. She looked up at Ernie and smiled through her tears and saw that he, too, was crying.

After Sean left the room, Anna and Ernie sat down on the bed with their daughter lying between them. They talked to her, laughed, and cried, as they noted every detail of their baby girl. She had Ernie's dark curly hair and blue eyes. To them, she was the most beautiful baby in the world. Her face, hands, feet, everything about her was perfect. Ernie thought the baby favored Anna and this made her happy for him to say so. Anna had never been happier in her entire life; she was Ernie Tennyson's wife and she had her baby.

An hour later, Ernie and Anna were still in the bedroom talking to their baby. When she began to fret, Anna got up to find Mrs. Tennyson. She would know what she wanted.

Mrs. Tennyson smiled and showed her the bottles she had already fixed for her grandbaby. She told her to warm the bottle and test it on her arm before feeding her. Anna did exactly as Mrs. Tennyson instructed; the baby clamped down on the nipple with an urgency that made Anna laugh. Her little one was hungry. She drank every drop of her milk and went to sleep. Anna carried her back to her crib and touched her all over before covering her with the baby blanket. She turned to go back to the living room and saw Ernie standing in the door watching her. He pulled her into his arms, held her close and said, "Thank you for giving me a daughter."

Overcome with emotions, she fell on his shoulder and cried; he comforted her, and she finally got calm. Then they went back to the living room to hear how Sean had found their baby. Anna never dreamed that she would ever see her baby; she knew she was not dead; a mother knows.

Before they got seated, Mrs. Tennyson asked if anybody wanted a cup of coffee and a slice of cake or pie. She had a chocolate cake and a strawberry pie. They all took her up on her offer and gathered around the long mahogany table in the dining room to enjoy their dessert and coffee.

While they ate dessert and drank coffee, Sean explained how she got their baby back. She had known all along that the baby was not dead, but she did not know who Dong Lee had authorized to adopt the baby.

First of all, Sean had gone to visit Doctor Kim; he told her that Dong Lee had signed papers for the baby to be adopted. In the meantime, they had placed the child with an adoption agency in Shanghai. The adoption agency would not release information about the baby after they discovered that its mother had not signed the adoption papers. Since the baby had been born, she had been under the care of attendants at the Children's Home in Shanghai.

Sean explained that she had to go through a lot of red tape before the adoption agency would even talk to her. After they learned that she was the baby's aunt, they listened more carefully. She told the agency the entire story: Dong Lee Ming, her own father, had forced his daughter to go to China to have an abortion; he took the child without its mother's permission; he paid the doctor to tell lies and keep quiet about the baby's whereabouts.

After she told the adoption agency the facts, they contacted Anna Ming's residence. Mrs. Ming told them that Anna was not home, but she was Anna Ming's grandmother. When the adoption agency stated their purpose for calling, Mrs. Ming told them that her granddaughter wanted her baby, and she would hire a lawyer if they did not turn the baby over to its Aunt Sean.

The day after their wedding Sean returned to China, and the adoption agency called to tell her she could come and get the baby.

Mrs. Ming had asked to come with her to Georgia; she wanted to help with the baby and celebrate their happiness. They had taken a flight from Saigon and had spent the last two nights with Mrs. Tennyson. They had a flight scheduled for that afternoon at six and would be leaving soon.

Anna and Ernie got up and walked around the table to hug Sean and thank her again. Then they asked who had bought the baby bed, and Mrs. Ming told them she had bought the baby bed after they got to Liberty Springs; and they would also find a stroller and high chair in Mrs. Tennyson's room. She had put them there until they were needed. She wanted them to have more room in their bedroom for the baby's bed.

After they finished their coffee and dessert, Sean and Mrs. Ming carried their bags to the rental car; they came back to see the baby, and to say their good bye. Anna promised to visit them after Ernie finished with the harvest in December.

After they left, Ernie asked Anna to sit on the porch with him. Anna got the baby out of its bed and followed Ernie to the porch. She rocked and talked to the baby between answering Ernie's questions.

"What are we going to name our Baby?"

"She does not have to be named right away," Anna said.

"Yes, she has to have a name right now."

They threw names back and forth, and Ernie said, "What was your mother's name?"

"She was named Lin Lan."

Ernie didn't say anything for several minutes. He was thinking that no one around these parts would know how to pronounce Lin Lan. They had to come up with something better.

"My mother's name is Cassie," Ernie said. "Why don't we name her Casey Lynn?"

"That sounds unique," she said and smiled, "but I think we should spell her name with a "K" instead of a "C"."

"That suits me." He got up, walked over to where Anna sat, and looked down at his little daughter as he tickled her cheek and called her name, "Kasey Lynn, my sweet little Kasey Lynn."

He sat back down in his rocker and talked about the house he wanted to build. He asked about things Anna wanted in the house, and told her he had already called a carpenter; he had an appointment with him the next day and was to carry him a house plan to get an estimate on the house.

She looked from him to their sweet Kasey Lynn and said, "I am the happiest mother and wife in the world."

"I am the lucky dog that finally got you," he said, and they both laughed.